WALTZING JIMMY JACKBOY

A NOVEL

WALTZING JIMMY JACKBOY

A NOVEL

JENNIFER DINN KORMAN

Library of Congress Cataloging-in-Publication Data.
Waltzing Jimmy Jackboy
Robbers Nest Press
ISBN (Trade pbk.)
978-0-9841-2070-3
Library of Congress Control Number: 20099310401

Interior book design: Sonya Unrein
Cover by Davis Branding & Marketing

Robbers Nest Press
Denver, Colorado

ROBBERSNESTPRESS.COM

WALTZINGJIMMYJACKBOY.COM

For Scott,
And for Maddie, Sam, and Charlie

Who makes winds his messengers; his ministers a flaming fire.
Who lay the foundation of the earth, that it should not be moved for ever.

—*Psalms 104:4-5*

Prologue

MONSOON SEASON

\∩/

Gray was not a plush color for velvet. Donna would have chosen blood red, coal black, or spruce green for the small bag. But not gray, the color of the ashes inside, the color of the New York sky in the tiny window that framed the mortician's face. He dangled the velvet bag from its gold sash, pinched between his fingers, attached to a wrist that disappeared into a black suit, the color the bag should have been. He moved the tiny bag of ashes closer to her. *Don't be surprised how little there will be for you.* It had taken her three months to summon the courage to retrieve it. Now she was supposed to take it.

She stuffed the bag in the pocket of her down vest as soon as she walked out into the slanted light. She didn't remember crossing Broadway or Columbus, didn't remember treading the familiar cobblestones that led to the entrance to Central Park until she felt the naked trees, which gave her shelter from the city. She followed the pedestrian path north, her feet taking her where she needed to go. As she rounded the bend at 77th she saw Greg. He was standing by their favorite park bench, hands deep in his pockets, shoulders hunched, stubbornly with no hat for his bald head even though the steam was curling up from the Boathouse Pond and his breath hung in the air each time he exhaled.

She'd spent twenty thousand dollars of her inheritance from her parents' estate to buy a brass plaque for their park bench, memorializing her stillborn baby. Because Greg had insisted they not name him, the plaque had only the sketch of an angel holding a baby. Today, she planned to spread the ashes under their bench.

She came up to Greg and her shoulder brushed his arm as she

held up the velvet bag. They stood in the spot where he'd asked her to marry him eleven years earlier, when the web of branches above had been full of buds. On that spring day, he'd handed her the Tiffany-blue bag, so similar to the bag of ashes in her hand now, but heavier.

As she opened the sash to pour the ashes to the ground, Greg held out his hand to stop her. "I want a divorce."

She stepped away to see his face. She could see her own long black hair, and her heart-shaped face in his sunglasses. She searched for his eyes beneath her reflection. "What?"

He cleared his throat and repeated himself, this time speaking slowly. "It's a sign. We're not meant to be together."

She stroked the gray velvet bag in her hand. "Who is she?"

He shrugged, hands burrowing deeper in his pockets as if to guard the secret to his words. "Don't let the ashes blow into the water."

She pulled the sash tight and put the bag back into her pocket. The words she spoke next surprised her. They were practical, curious, even. She saw them hang in the crystal fog of her breath, an edge of anger tracing them against the gray sky. "Why didn't you tell me before I turned down the sabbatical in Perth? Now I'll have to take Mount Isa."

"You'd go to Australia without me?"

A gust of wind sent crinkled brown leaves afloat in the pond.

The Australian sky is the bluest of blue, a reflection of the waters of Lake Moondarra, of the Indirri Waterhole, of Lawn Hill Gorge, and the waters at the edge of the earth. But during the dry winter months, when desiccating winds sweep the desert, in the hour between the day and the night's dark, and the hour between the night's dark and the clear light of day, the Australian sky is the color of the Galah. During the rippling heat of the summer monsoon season, when the dawn breaks, cresting over the rolling thunderheads, the sky is the Galah. When the lightning laces together the clouds and stabs its needles down into the brooding head rocks of Kata Tjuta, when gray bluffs melt into gray clouds behind a haze of rain turned pink as the sun pierces the veil, the world becomes the color of the Galah.

The musky monsoon smell is in the air, and the Galah hangs upside down on a branch of the gum tree where she was hatched fifty monsoons ago. She is watching the sky turn from blue to pink to gray, a white tuft of cloud like the tuft on her head, outlining her black feet. She feels the warmth of the sun shifting from her magenta belly down to her chest and then, away, as the sky turns gray, the color of her back. She feels the pull of the earth on the topside of her wings, a relief from the usual pull on her delicate underfeathers. She feels life rush into her pink head.

It is the moment of in between, both day and night, the moon and the sun force pulling evenly on each wing, when the ancient energy of the First Day comes to her on the wind. She flutters her wings and flits to a near branch, head to the sky, feet towards the ground, and watches as the wind blows the tumbleweed as far as she can see. The tumbleweed *bounces, momentarily flying like a bird, then crashes into prickly wattle, dense with yellow flowers, puffballs like the down on a Galah chick.*

The south wind lifts the desert grasses, rustles the spinifex and nuzzles the earth as it whispers over the bush. The grasses dance the story of a boy born in the old way under her tree, twelve monsoons past. They dance his birth, the making of his manhood, his mating, his children, and his death. The grasses dance the cockatoo woman, come from afar to bear his wife.

The grasses bend to the Galah, yellow tips gently handing her the boy, handing her the children of his seed to be forever linked with the hatchlings of her eggs. The wind dies as the ancient energy retreats, having unloaded its charge. The grasses stand upright and still, their moonlit tips dot the land.

The Galah calls the parrot song to her flock before she sleeps. She has the Queensland sunset, the wind, and the boy's future in her song. The notes fly up and down the octaves, tracing the history of the colors of the sunless sky.

Jimmy Jackboy crouched naked by the huge fire on the night Hector and the Uncles seized him for his initiation, his nose full of the scent of blood, ochre, bushgrass, and wet feathers being dried by the flames. There was no moon to warm him. He concentrated on the pulses of his heartbeat to keep from panic. *One, two, one, two, didgeridoo, one, two.* After a while he realized he was not counting heartbeats but was counting the claquing of the Dreaming sticks.

When the sun finally rose, Uncles stopped the heartbeats, and fingers dipped in hot man-blood began to trace him, starting at his penis, up his belly, chest, into his tangled hair. For hours the men sang and he sat, two cousins across from him, drinking the song, the blood, the earth.

The moon rose twice and no food. After a while he no longer cared. He was ready to die, for he'd seen twelve monsoons. He lingered in the pains like a dip in the billabong during the Wet, and then let the music's pulses pick up the pains and float them out through his bumhole into the earth. There was an empty space in his belly for the words that filled him like yucca and damper.

When they finally carried him back to camp, stiff as a gum branch, Jimmy could not move his legs, not twitch a shoulder. Mum was wailing. She held food to his mouth, tears streaming down her face. He was sure he was dead, but why would she feed the dead? Would he need food to make it to the Warambool?

She whispered in his ear, her tears clinging to his hair, "It is time for you to leave. Do not miss me or Yuendumu. You must Behold Galah Land." He waited for Mum to call him *Jimmy Jackboy,* but she did not.

The sun was barely in the sky when he set out on walkabout to become an initiated man, heel-toe, behind Hector. He'd wanted to tell Mum a proper *g'day*, but the words echoed in his head, finishing their journey before they reached his lips. He walked as Mum had taught him. *Concentrate on feet when you feel out of sorts, Jimmy Jackboy. They'll ground you, ha ha*. Heel-toe. That was what he knew. Heel-toe.

Part One

THE ISA

\ᴨ/

Four months after her husband had asked for the divorce, Donna drove east from the Mount Isa airport on the Barkly Highway, a well-paved two-lane road. Spindly acacias with yellow puffball flowers—*Lonely Planet* called it *wattle*, Australia's unofficial national tree—rolled past the front window of her Queensland government-issued black Land Rover, glowing in the late afternoon sun. Land that had seemed barren from her airplane window sprouted tufts of scrub, reminiscent of a teenager's first beard. As she reached town, two smokestacks popped up like jack-in-the-boxes. Smoke undulated from the larger one, a Chinese dragon swaying day-glo orange in the wind, welcoming her to her new home.

In tourist brochures, she'd seen the maps of routes to Isa—paved roads marked in red, dirt roads in blue—from Tennant Creek in the Northern Territory, Karumba on the North Coast, Rockhampton and Townsville on the east. Mount Isa was known as the *Crossroads of the Outback*. People passed through the Isa. Like an overgrown airport, the city was in many people's minds a non-place, a way to get somewhere else.

After she'd accepted the Medical Chief post at the Base Hospital, she'd met more than one Australian. They all had the same reaction. *Mount Isa? Are you in mining?* She would shake her head, and their eyes would widen. *Why on earth would you go there?* She'd answer with a laugh and a toss of her jet black hair, *Why, escaping, of course. I'm wanted by the law.*

With only minor jerking she slowed onto a wider two-lane road, lined with mature elms, evergreens, and fruit trees. Behind square green lawns, aluminum-sided houses stood like tin soldiers, perfectly aligned. Chain fences created a grid, marking off each house's territory. The area was like the working-class neighborhoods she'd seen along the highway from Ohio to Michigan when she'd visited residency programs, not what she'd expected from a desert town. She downshifted to second—surprisingly, she was already getting comfortable with left-handed gear shifting—as she glanced at the map of town that had been left for her with her car and house keys at the information station at the airport. Her route and her Queensland Health house, 51 Gracie, were highlighted in yellow.

She passed through the residential neighborhood into the center of town where, at a quick glance, she saw signs for Kmart, McDonald's, and Pizza Hut—not exactly the charming small-town shops and diners she'd hoped for. After one stoplight, she was back in a residential section. Donna saluted the meticulous lawns, the lush flowers, the immaculate small homes cradled in the desert.

After two jet-lag amplified scares with wrong-side-of-the-road driving, she pulled onto Gracie Street. As she inched along looking for her address, she almost ran over the birds congregating like rubberneckers at an accident scene on the side of the road. Galah parrots. She'd seen them along with the stuffed kangaroos and wombats, frozen in mid-motion in the Australia diorama at the Museum of Natural History. How ridiculously beautiful they were, dusty rose and gray, her wedding colors. Their pale pink crowns were the exact shade of the bow on her bridesmaid dresses. She shifted into neutral, threw on the emergency brake and looked over her passenger seat to have a better look. Rubberneckers were exactly what they were. One of them had been hit by a car, clearly dead, and the others were nudging it, as if trying to get it to fly.

She thought of her honeymoon in Nepal, when she and Greg had walked hand in hand up the Swayambhunath Stupa at sunrise, surrounded by tiny birds chirping and the monkeys chattering, begging for food. At the top of the stairs was a monkey who clutched her dead baby. Surrounded by the pink glow of all that holiness, she dragged the limp body around like a rag doll, an offering to the Buddha.

Donna reached into her pocket to finger the gray velvet bag she'd carried for the last few months, warm from her body heat. She was over the original shock of losing Greg. After losing her parents and the baby, the grief felt familiar, almost homey. She'd known what to do with it, what music to listen to, how many cigarettes to smoke while looking up at the water towers of the buildings near theirs, and how the sadness would lessen with time.

Carefully avoiding the Galahs, she negotiated the clutch and continued to search for her house. She needn't have looked at house numbers. The houses were identical, but hers stood out, a patch of brown grass sandwiched between two lush lawns. The previous doctor had clearly never watered, and Donna vowed to be a better citizen.

She parked in the gravel driveway and walked up the crumbling concrete stairs, digging for the house key in her pocket. As she turned the key in the lock, the ground beneath her shook. Earthquake? She imagined being trapped under concrete and pea-green aluminum siding with no one to report her missing. She would be swallowed up in this strange earth, miles from anyone she'd ever known. She grabbed onto the doorknob with both hands. It seared her palm with the heat it had collected from the day's sun, but she would not let go.

The flock rose with the south wind. The Wet had come and gone. It was autumn, time again to move. They flew as one, he her left wing, she, his right. The pair glided on the wind's back, stretching their wings. She watched below her as the sands turned from tan to orange to red to brown, reflecting the path of the sun. Green tops of gum trees invited her to land in their shady branches, but she stayed with her flock.

The first square of bright green grass came as a shock to her eyes, and the flock rode a current up to the sky as if to escape it. She had been born to the muted colors of the desert, the deep greens of the gum leaves, the cool greens of the acacia leaves. Now that she was getting old, eyes tired, she did not like the lush bright grasses that surrounded the pale humans. She liked only colors that could be muted, muted like a Galah's scream as a kite tore into it with its talons.

The flock glided tight-winged back toward the earth, undulating like grasses in the wind, about to swoop up again towards the sky, when her mate was thrown against the wind by the monster belching black smoke. He landed on his wing.

The Galah swooped to his side, followed by the others. A sparse clump of spinifex grew beside the road, and they tried to drag the body with them, into the relative safety of the prickly grass. Her mate was too heavy. She tried prodding him, brought him a grasshopper, carried a drop of water to his beak from the underside of a stray leaf. But he would not swallow. With her hooked beak she pulled out two of her own pink feathers to cover his eyes against the setting sun.

She supposed that he could be dead. She had lost chicks before, when she and her mate were younger and had not known all the secrets of hiding a nest, of using the prickly wattle and spinifex as an outer nest layer, instead of looking at it as something that would make her bleed, little pricks between her underfeathers, each time she would squeeze into her nest. Before she and he had learned to withstand the pain of their own defenses, they had lost chicks to willy wagtails, to goannas, even to snakes.

As her flock waited on the wires above, the Galah paced back and forth beside her mate's motionless body, her actions mimicked by the few chicks that still flew with her. She would wait. Wait until the sky turned the colors of the Galah, then to black. She would wait until his spirit flew to the dark side of the moon, eternal yet unseen, before she would abandon his body.

Up ahead the orange smoke curled like an adder, leaving its trail in the sky instead of in the earth. Jimmy Jackboy was one of the best trackers in Yuendumu and could find a snake from the faintest displacement of sand. He wasn't as familiar with smoke, though it was used often by the old folks to communicate with the Ancestors, but he could take a good guess at what the wind would do that night. Probably would be a cold sleep.

He watched the smoke from the corner of his eye as he weighed scrub branches in his arm. He needed a few more. Heel-toe, heel-toe, heel-toe, big toe, small toe, middleman—he walked as Mum had taught him as he searched for good burning gum. He used to spend hours walking in the bush with Mum, matching his feet to hers while Da pumped and hung out at the servo. She would notice after a while and rest her hand flat on his back. When she'd remove it, the warmth would be there for hours, as if she'd left a handprint in the warm mud of his back, the way the ranchers on the stations brand their cattle. Sometimes she'd press a little harder and he would stumble. *Do you feel how easily you can alter your balance, Jimmy? How the world is a different place when you are walking toe-heel, instead of heel-toe?*

On walkabout he'd thought of Mum in a way he hadn't for the last year or so. Noticed things she'd like and things she wouldn't. Imagined her wrapping him in her brown arms and pulling tight, so that all he could smell was yucca smoke and her sweetness as she kissed his forehead, right between the eyes. She hadn't hugged him like that in ages. She'd been separating from him without him realizing, before the formal separation of his initiation. Bugger.

Three moons before he was seized, he found his first hair between his legs. He plucked it out as he lay in bed, holding it between thumb and finger toward the morning sun. Thick and dark, the color of his lashes, not of his blond head. Now after two moons on walkabout there were more, behind his penis and under his arms. Mum and Uncles must have known he was becoming a man. Jimmy should have guessed that Uncles wouldn't wait for school holiday to seize him. They weren't concerned if he missed school.

Hector said that becoming an initiated Aboriginal man would make Jimmy Jackboy stronger and would give him a life without fear, which was more important than a quarter at school, especially since he was already ahead of his mob in maths and reading. Initiation would help him do whatever he wanted with his life. Well, he already knew that he wanted to be a doctor.

First, he wanted to Behold his Land as a man, to have what Da couldn't. Bad luck on Da, stolen by the whites at age nine, before he'd had a chance to be initiated, like so many aunties and uncles. Too bad Da had died last year. Jimmy had long imagined going on walkabout with him. Now it would be only Da's pointing-finger bone that would get to Behold his Galah Land.

Though he missed Da and of course Mum, the walk with Uncle Hector had been a good one, even if it was long. Since that first day, Hector and he had walked to the Stuart Highway, then hitched the Stuart and Sandover through to Amaroo and walked since then. Jimmy's mates had gone back to class two moons ago—the Fire Ant boys had stayed south of the Tanami for their initiation. But he was Galah and had much further to go.

Arms full of scrub, he headed back to their camp. Heel-toe, heel-toe. Jimmy concentrated on the vibrations traveling up through his soles each time he planted his foot in the warm sand, imagining the vibrations of the Ancestors' footprints marking the Land forever. The vibrations ran up his legs through his bum and then over his back and into his belly. His eye caught some white smoke way up high, above the curling smoke adder. It was an airplane slowly sinking in the sky. Would probably be landing on the other side of town. Someday, when he was a doctor, he'd fly in one. Maybe be a Flying Doc and visit Yuendumu.

Across camp, Hector sat on his rolled-up swag, his wide back facing Jimmy. Jimmy left his branches in the firepit and crept, heel-toe, light as a fire ant on the earth, over to Hector. Gray curly hairs poked out from under the back of Hector's hat. His huge shoulders rose up and down as he blew his didg. Uncle said they couldn't follow the Galah path exactly. Tomorrow they needed to make a detour to Mount Isa and meet Gus, a Galah Pintupi man. Gus was a friend of the stationmaster who ran the Galah Land. Hector figured that Gus could get them permission to cross onto the station so Jimmy could finish his initiation. In the old days, they would have just traded Dreaming sticks with the local tribes who ran that land, and those tribesmen would have helped with the initiation. Instead, they were forced to deal with the modern world and gates and permits. Jimmy hoped it would take a few days before they got permission, so he'd have time to look around town.

"Hah," Jimmy blew into Hector's ear and got elbowed in the gut as Hector jumped.

Hector propped his didgeridoo against a stump. His nose bounced like a black ball as he sniffed the air. "You're a good hunter, boy. It's lucky I'm no roo. You'd a had me for tea."

Jimmy sucked in his breath, holding his sore belly. "You're deafer than a ghost gum. Maybe it's all that hair around your ears. I was making heaps of noise."

Hector motioned past the gum branches Jimmy had collected. "Should be goannas with tails longer than your arms down by that rock. He always has goannas."

Jimmy had hoped for some bush turkey, but goannas would do. "You get them or me?"

"I'm working here."

Jimmy looked at the didg. "Call that work? Get you in trouble with the white man, hah."

"Don't see their sorry bums frying out here in the bush. Go on. I'll make Mister Fire."

Jimmy retreated, spear in hand, happy to stay busy. He wished he could've brought his Australian Rules and Rugby League cards on walkabout to entertain himself—he collected footy cards with his mates—but Uncles had given him no time to prepare. One moment he'd been sleeping, and the next he was dead to Mum, off on walkabout. Only sport on walkabout was tracking animals and collecting fossils and rocks to weigh down his pockets. He scrambled down the hot sand by the rock Hector had pointed to and screwed his eyes shut so hard that he saw lines of the ghost gum tree in purple on the inside of his eyelids. He watched the little squiggles that were moving upwards in the dark as he stepped lightly, tapping on the ground with the end of the spear. This ground was tricky, so close to the mine. Felt hollow even when it wasn't, like its legs were a bit shaky. Hector said it was because the shovels had dug the Old People out of the earth.

Jimmy plunged his spear into the sand three times—usually he hit it on the first try—before he felt the tip sink deep into reptile flesh. Goannas were where they were supposed to be, where Ancestors had put them. He thanked Ancestors out of habit and plucked Mister Goanna from under the ground like Bugs Bunny did with carrots on the telly in the community center. The goanna's spotted body twisted on Jimmy's spear, its forked tongue reacting to the change in temperature.

Jimmy lay the speared goanna on the hard sand and hit it over the head with the flat end of his bush knife. Its sharp claws stopped slicing the air. He pierced the tough skin and stabbed its brain, then spun his spear above him and marveled at the fat goanna, blood dripping down the tip of his spear.

He set off to look for water when three goannas were swinging from his belt next to his dented tinbilly. Hector wanted him to find a waterhole without using fire. He wished Hector would let him burn the spinifex to find water. Would have been much faster to see where the spinifex didn't burn, dig down a meter, and free the water.

Heel-toe. Jimmy listened for birds. Usually a bird would tip him off that water was nearby. He'd learned early never to ignore birdcalls, because Ancestors' spirits used birds as messengers. A birdcall was instruction from the spirits. A body just needed to understand the message.

Partly shaded by a boulder, the waterhole was no wider than the length of his arm. He bent down and stuck his finger in to watch the ripples disturb the peaceful glass, then took his billy off his belt and drew out enough water for No Worries Tea. Lucky Hector had packed them a bush tea kit and a lighter. They'd gone through the damper early on their walkabout, but Jimmy had found some money—he guessed from Mum—in his pocket, so he planned to buy more in the Isa for the walk home. Jimmy loved No Worries Tea, especially when Auntie Tess made the damper with a bit of honey ant. He knew the instructions on the tea tin by heart. *One teaspoon of tea per person and one for the billy. Add gum leaves for flavor. Windmill the billy to settle the tea leaves.*

The smell of Hector's fire led him back to camp. Jimmy sat on his heels across from the big man as Hector sliced the goannas down the middle with his knife. Hector had lines in his face, cut deep like the billabongs in the Dry. His gray beard was spotted with goanna blood. Hector'd been around. "City's quite nice, huh, Hector?"

"Naw." Hector handed Jimmy the flayed goannas. "Would rather spend me life with me Land."

Jimmy stuck the lizards on the spit, bum to head, bum to head. "I'm going to live there someday. Be a Flying Doc. Fly out to help the Yapa."

Hector stirred the embers, yellow, orange, black. "Learn your strength first."

Jimmy knew already. He was too slow to make it as an AFL winger. But he was sharp as a blade of spinifex, sharpest of his mates.

Jimmy woke as Hector pushed him over onto his right side. He liked to sleep on his back, his eyes beneath his eyelids watching Ancestors in the sky as he slept. He rolled onto his back again and was met by Hector's solid palm. "Aw."

Hector held his hand firm. "Heard a black crow calling. Don't want a bad spirit to crawl in your mouth while you sleep."

Jimmy rolled back onto his side, now wide awake, aware of a pebble under his swag. He got up to remove it and threw it across their dead fire into the blackness. As he settled back down between the thick layers of tarp, Hector's breathing rocked the ground. He could tell by the sky it was after midnight. He watched the four stars of Yaraandoo rise in the sky, the place of the first coming of death to the world. He never had trouble finding it. The Mooyi, the white cockatoos, pointed to the white gum tree from the east. How they glittered in the sky as they flew after their favorite branch, forever trying to reach their roost. Yaraandoo had planted roots near the Warambool, which his teacher had called the Milky Way. She'd called Yaraandoo the Southern Cross. Someday, after he traveled this world, he would travel past Yaraandoo, past the Meamei, the seven sisters, to travel along the Warambool, to live with his Ancestors.

He imagined his body growing gently paler, whiter than white folks, as he floated up to the sky. He was itchy and restless on his right side. He rolled and poked Hector. "Can't sleep. Tell me the story of Yaraandoo." He stared at Hector's closed eyes, head resting on his rolled up swag. Like many of the elders, Hector didn't need blankets to keep him warm. Jimmy willed him to wake.

Hector's eyes opened wide. "Quit looking at me. I'm not talking about dying now."

"Teach me something else." How could Hector resist? Initiation was about filling Jimmy's brain with Yapa knowledge, to make sure he learned the Warlpiri ways before he became too Australian. Jimmy felt Hector's chuckle through the ground.

"Jimmy Jackboy, go to sleep."

"Sleep will not come."

Jimmy had given up hope of rousing him when Hector spoke. "Your mum waited on you a long time."

"Yeah?"

"Finally a child called to your da while we were out hunting. He put it inside your mum. But five moons later, she began to bleed. The child's spirit moved on to another mother."

Jimmy rolled toward Hector. "Child made a bad decision. Mum's a good mum."

"Her belly did not fit him well."

"But that's not me," Jimmy wiggled his toes deep inside his swag.

"Your da waited years for the child to come back—didn't hear the other children calling because he didn't understand—not his fault of course. Too many years stolen away with the Kardiya. So your mum decided to attract a spirit child without him."

"Me?"

"You born with a tooth?"

Jimmy ran his tongue over his straight white teeth.

"You are a spirit child and you will marry a spirit child."

"Who is she?" Jimmy rested his cheek on his palm and watched Hector's face, illuminated in the moonshine. Hector was missing two teeth on the left side of his mouth. Made his upper lip look swollen and it barely moved as he spoke.

"Wife will be born this year. Her mum is coming from across the Ocean."

"She's not Yapa?"

Hector's upper lip twitched. "Your mum used her earth magnet to attract your spirit."

Birds had magnets in their brains to help them migrate. Jimmy had magnets in his cells that turned him toward his Land. The spilling of his blood on his Land during his initiation would strengthen those magnets. He reached down and grabbed his penis and a shiver went up his spine. He reminded himself that after he was cut, he'd live a life without fear. It would be worth it.

Jimmy kept a firm grip on his penis and Hector continued. "Then your mum went to a waterhole where women had seen spirit children playing on the branches of the coolabah trees. Jumping into the water."

"Like we boys do."

"She sat there for two days. When she came home she got crook all over her digging stick, so we knew. At first your da threw a wobbly but then he and the elders visited the waterhole. The Galah had visited there during Jukurrpa. That is why you are a Galah boy, like your da, me, and Grandpa rather than a Fire Ant boy of your mum's moiety."

Jimmy stared at the face in the moon, just past full round, easily illuminating the night sky. Hector continued quietly, "You were a hard birth. Thought we had made a mistake not to send your mum to hospital in the Alice. Your da cried. Back to the old ways, he'd said. He'd missed so much, he wanted your birth to be traditional. But you did not want to come out. Then Auntie Tess took your mum to lean against a ghost gum, your Minggah tree. She called to you about the kin who were waiting to meet you. You stayed put. She called to you the kangaroo berries hanging ripe like boomer balls. That did not work. She called to you the Galahs chatting under pink and gray clouds. For Galahs you came. Galah boy in every bone."

Hector rested his large hand on Jimmy's chest. "Tess held the pink Jimmy baby over the fire. She smoked you in the spinifex to bring you into the world of the living. You turned good and brown, color of tea. She breathed into your nostrils your sacred names, your plant, animal, and earth responsibilities. Last real Warlpiri birthing done in Yuendumu."

Mum had never told him about his birth, only that he was a spirit child. Jimmy imagined Mum's hands holding him as a baby. He knew her hands like his own. It was impossible to believe those fingers would never again trace rivers up his spine now that he was going to be an initiated man.

He woke at dawn to the call of the kookaburra, his protector. Kookaburra would eat the poison adders, keep the ground safe. Jimmy half-expected that the kookaburra had eaten the smoke from the sky, but it was still there, laying sky tracks. He played with his stiffie as he watched the smoke. Would his initiation make his penis feel different? What would it be like in the mornings without that extra flap of skin? More sensitive to the sheet skimming over it?

Jimmy willed his stiffie to wilt like the flowers in the Dry. He smelled the burnt spinifex of a fire and hopped over on the cold ground to where Hector was preparing maku for brekky. He watched Hector's huge wrinkled hands slice the ghost gum roots they'd gathered. Hector tapped hard on the root with the butt of his knife, and out slid a pinky-white grub. He cut the grubs in half longways so Jimmy could see their yellow insides, then stuck them on the coals. Not as good as Cocoa-Bombs, but they'd do. He reached for one that was ready. Sweet and crunchy.

Once, he'd found witchetty grubs hidden in the roots of a snappy gum. Auntie Tess roasted them and then they ate them all. No one could poo for days and Tess got mad. Said that grubs from a snappy gum were always constipating and he should have learned better by now.

After brekky Hector rolled his didg, spear, and digging stick into his swag, and Jimmy did the same with his gear. Hector dusted off his hat, which hardly ever left his head. The hatband was cockeyed, and the hole in the brim had been widening each day of their walkabout. Jimmy hated wearing hats and had left without one. They started to walk as the sun climbed shoulder-height into the sky.

Each time Hector's foot hit the ground, a cloud of dust rose up to his calves. Pat, pat, pat, reminding Jimmy of when Mum beat the rugs outside the tin walls of their home. Jimmy's cloud did not rise past his ankles. Jimmy studied his feet and thought they looked bigger than when he'd left Yuendumu. Soon they would be man's feet with long cracks that marked the paths he'd taken. He imagined the dust as he walked, layer upon layer of burnt oranges and reds on his soles, etching a map so his feet could find their way home.

\n/

When the vibrations woke Donna, she'd been dreaming that she was standing with her boy beside a dusty red road lined with yellow wattle. But fear replaced the warmth of his company as she opened her eyes to the dancing coins on her Queensland Health dresser. Her Queensland clock read six AM. Was it an aftershock or a new tremor? She contemplated taking shelter in the doorway, then thought better of it. Her new house was a tin can. Weren't most earthquake victims crushed by heavy things? The one tree in her backyard was on the other side of the house. It couldn't hurt her.

As her bed settled, she closed her eyes again and there was the boy, curly dark hair blowing in a light wind, translucent skin framed by the yellow wattle behind him. She guessed he was either the soul of her baby or an angel sent by her deceased mother. He'd shown up ever more persistently in her dreams these last few months, so often that she missed him on the nights he made no cameo appearance. One night he'd be a patient, another, a friend, another, a random pedestrian on the streets of New York. So the angel boy had followed her to Australia.

Despite Donna's scientific mind and her training as a doctor, she believed in angels. Watching her dying patients find comfort in their communications with the air had strengthened her belief, though she admitted it to few colleagues. In her final hours, Donna's own mother had said *My angel is here* and then had settled into her last hour of labored breathing. When Donna was a child, her Catholic mother had spoken often of angels. When the dog would suddenly jump up, Mother would say, *Oh the angels woke him*, or when Donna would stare off in space Mother

34

would ask *Which angel do you see?* Donna had always pictured the fat-cheeked, winged angels from the Raphael poster that hung in her mother's study.

Her father's religion had been science. But he too had spoken to her of God's accountants, the angels of his Jewish God. His angels sat behind the curtain of heaven with a giant ledger, the book of life between them. They debited bad deeds and credited the good. Donna always tried to keep track of what the angels might be writing next to her name in the ledger.

Now, in her Australian bed, the dream boy disappeared. She was decidedly awake, but why get up? It was Sunday and there would be no *New York Times* crossword delivered to her door. Missing the city noises that would drift from 84th Street to her apartment, she imagined the smell of the brownstone, the crumbling exposed brick, yesterday's coffee cups in the sink. Her Australian house—two bedrooms, a bath, toilet room, kitchen, and living room—was not much larger than her apartment. Here it took thirty-five steps to walk from one end of the house to the other. In New York it had taken thirty-one, too small a space to share with a husband. They'd shrunk their souls from each other so as not to collide.

She pulled the Queensland Government cotton blanket up to her chin, tracing the blanket's embroidered *Q* with her index finger. Most of her current possessions had *Queensland Government* or *Queensland Health* emblazoned on them. The night before, she'd opened cupboards to find plenty of Queensland Health pots, pans, plates, glasses, and utensils. Unmarked by the government had been a stack of napkins and two rolls of toilet paper. The fridge held a six-pack of Fourex, Canadian maple syrup, cumin, and a gift basket of fruit and cheese that had been her dinner.

Realizing she would never fall back to sleep, Donna made her way to the shower in the pre-dawn gloom. She stripped off her Benny's Burritos T-shirt and threw it on the floor—one of the benefits of living alone. She stretched her back as she bent over the tub, twisting the tap for warm water. As the water spurted, she heard a plop and felt something large and wet hit her shoulder. She turned her head and her ear was an inch away from a fuzzy black-and-brown, hand-sized spider. She shrieked, making eye contact with two rows of eyes. Legs like pipe cleaners reared up in the air, giving Donna a perfect view of its half-inch long fangs. She jerked her shoulder forward, throwing it off before its fangs could dig into her skin. Shivers coursed through her nude body as she brushed her shoulder as if trying to brush away its footprints.

She turned round and round, like a child spinning to make herself dizzy. Where was it? How could she misplace a tarantula in a freezer-size bathroom? Her father would have loved to trap this spider. She remembered her child self, crouched with a magnifying glass over the wood spiders she and her father caught hiding in the shaggy brown rug of their apartment. Had she ever seen all eight eyes? Had she known that a spider would feel like a cotton swab brushing her shoulder? Or that it would actually have weight? What a specimen this would have been. Better a dead specimen. Could you kill a sparrow-sized spider with a Birkenstock?

Five steps from the door to the sink and two across before you'd hit the tub. Where in the hell could a spider that big hide? She shook the towel, rattled the slightly moldy shower curtain—she'd have to buy a new one right away—could it have slipped out under the door? Made its way toward the bedroom?

Hyperventilating, she clutched the sink and looked into her almond eyes in the mirror. A wave on the top of her long black hair moved. She remembered the time she had mice in her apartment and would catch shadows of movement from the corner of her eye. Her hair seemed to move again. She inched her nose closer to the mirror. The spider was clinging to her hair with its barbed feet.

Shrieks and shrieks later, she managed to knock it into the

bathtub. She turned the water to scalding, and directed the stream directly onto the hairy creature. He was battered into the holes of the drain, far too large to go down. She grabbed her toothbrush holder and tried to push him into the holes. A leg came off and stuck to the purple plastic. She mashed him like grinding drugs with a mortar and pestle.

Satisfied she'd pulverized him, she wrapped herself in a thoroughly-shaken towel and turned off the water. Then she pulled a Queensland Health face towel from the linen shelf in the hall and with it removed the body from the drain.

But before she was out of the bathroom, the spider in the towel began to move. Donna felt its feet pushing against her hand through the cloth, as if it were stretching after a night's slumber. She ran to the front door, fumbled with the lock, and bounded down the steps into the yard. The dried grass sliced her bare soles as she ran with both hands extended in front of her. She felt her bath towel loosen from her chest. With her left hand she clutched at air, while her right hand flung the face towel and its contents toward the neighbor's yard. For a moment she stood there empty-handed, aware of the bath towel making a semi-circle at her feet, her arms stretched in front of her, her body exposed to a sudden gust of wind, wondering whether the Queensland Government would notice a missing face towel or the neighbors would notice a naked newcomer.

The vibrations traveled from the earth, up the trunk of the ghost gum and startled the Galah into the sky. She followed her flock onto the lines that hung taut, far away from any kestrel eagles or kites, here where the humans lived. The Galah and the human were kin, though the People had mostly forgotten.

As the earth stopped shaking, she dozed in the early morning sun, wing-to-wing with the rest of her flock, missing the feel of her mate beside her. A noise awoke her. A human reached out to the sunrise, and a spider flew from her hands. The Galah knew the human from the story danced by the spinifex, when the ancient energy of the First Day had come to her on the wind.

As mother spider turned to wriggle away through the bright grass, the Galah swooped down and speared her with a sharp curved beak. This was a spider that could eat a bird if she trapped it. Today, the spider would be eaten by a bird. The Galah pinched off each leg to eat separately, savoring the four legs of the male winds: north, south, west, and east. Then the legs of the female seasons: hatching, copulating, dying. The mothering leg was missing.

The ancient energy had reminded her of the cycle of life. Despite her age, the Galah would lay one last clutch. She rustled her wings, spider heavy in her belly, thankful that she could both fly among the spirits and travel among the People. Oh how silly the emu had been to trade its wings for size and speed. She dozed off again, thinking of the emu who never again would travel like sunlight on the water.

\n/

Donna spent the rest of Sunday looking for hidden spiders and organizing her few possessions—including the gray velvet bag of ashes now resting on her dresser next to a photo of her parents. The house's empty white walls and sparse furnishings gave her a feeling of space, compared to her New York apartment, which had been filled with keepsakes, photos, and art from her travels. She tried to hook up the computer, her link to her best friend, Kate, and the rest of her New York gang. But she'd forgotten to pack a converter. Since all stores, including the grocers, were closed on Sundays, she resigned herself to a quiet, jet-lagged day.

Monday morning, she left a half-hour early for the three-minute drive to work, nervous energy propelling her. Donna stood in the parking lot and surveyed her new workplace: a four-story white hospital building that looked to have been built in the last quarter century, the sign for the ER clearly posted just to the left of the sliding doors of the main entrance. Donna entered the ER, the screen door slamming loudly behind her. An Aboriginal nurse, surely one of the largest women that Donna had ever seen, turned as she took the pulse of a patient. Her badge read *Sister Esther.* She pointed to a clipboard and pen sitting on an orange plastic chair. "Sit down and fill it out. Doctor's busy now, but he'll get to you."

Donna couldn't help but sit down. The pen dangled from the clipboard in her lap, clanking against the chair leg. "Sister Esther?"

Hands on hips, the woman spun to look at her faster than Donna thought a woman her size could move. But she wasn't fat. She was tall with broad shoulders, a barrel-chest, lanky arms, and a gut that was squeezed into white pants a size too small. Her torso seemed to sit forward on her pelvis. By the shape of her body, Donna thought she looked transgender, but a closer look at her face revealed soft, beautiful features.

"I'm Dr. Cooper. The new doc." Donna knew enough not to introduce herself as the Medical Chief. Her guess was that in a transient place like Mount Isa, position mattered less than longevity. "I neglected to ask exactly where to show up on my first day of work."

Esther smiled wide. Straight white teeth matched her nurse's whites. "Huh. We've never had a sheila in this position." She walked over to Donna as if to get a good look at a strange new creature. "But we mob'll take anyone who'll come out."

She stuck out her hand and clasped Donna's hard. "You'll be better than the last jackeroo we had." Esther's arms were hairy down to her knuckles and her hand made Donna think of a small dark rabbit.

"Come on in. I'll show you around." She kept Donna's hand. "By the way, we go by first names here."

"Doctor Donna then."

Esther squeezed her hand. "Welcome, Donna." She turned and yelled to a twenty-something redheaded nurse that Donna hadn't noticed. "Nan, take over." She turned back to Donna. "I'm Head Sister. I teach these youngsters responsibility."

Donna waved hello to Nan with her free hand, the other settled in Esther's broad palm. Esther led her up to the third floor for a tour of the ICU and then to the second floor medical ward, announcing as they entered rooms, "Hey, you mob, here's our new doc."

Donna was heartened by the surroundings. It was a first world hospital, full of all the latest equipment. Yes, the windows opened, letting in the Outback dust, but she'd have all the tools she'd need to help her patients, other than a hospital full of specialists. They stopped at the second floor nurses' station—Esther called it the *sisters'* station—to grab a handful of Easter candy. *Sister* must have been a leftover term from when nuns staffed the Base Hospital.

Esther showed Donna how to use the computer system to look up patient information and lab reports, and how to write electronic notes. Isa was far ahead of her New York hospital in its use of technology. When Esther was called away by a nurse, Donna couldn't help but Google *spiders Queensland Australia*. She shuddered as she read the University of Brisbane web site.

Esther peeked over her shoulder. "Spiders?"

"I think I had a funnel-web on my head yesterday."

Esther put her hot hand over Donna's on the mouse and scrolled it down through the photos to another large spider. "Probably a wolf. Funnel-web'll kill you. They don't like to be disturbed."

Donna stopped the mouse and pointed to the screen. "This is the spider. A face too hard to forget."

Esther stepped back and looked her up and down, finally shaking her head. "Did you get your man to kill the bugger?"

Donna clicked to close the site. "Came here alone."

"Pretty doc like you, no hubby?"

Donna hoped her voice was steady. "Divorce was final ten days ago. Shall we continue the tour?"

Esther took her elbow and led her into the stairwell. "Me man left me years ago. Went on walkabout, then sent a note he was staying up in the Daintree. I was off me face for a long time. Now I've got two men that put him to shame."

Donna smiled, "Two, huh?"

Esther's full lips and cheeks looked like they'd been created with collagen injections or a side-effect of steroids. Her nose was wide and round, the only nose that wouldn't be lost in those cheeks. "One's me favo, but when he's not around got another.

Won't take you long to find a man in Isa."

"I don't know."

"Mobs of men. You got your choice." Esther's cheeks seemed to lift up her smile by its ends. "Need to pick a good one." As they walked out onto the first floor, Esther held the door. "Aye, lucky Sheila. Even a wolf spider bite would've hurt. Not toxic, though."

Donna mulled over the words *lucky sheila* as they headed to the Admin office. Friends in New York looked at her life in the last fifteen years and saw it as full of bad luck. Losing her parents, infertility, losing the baby, divorce. But she couldn't help feeling grateful for who she was, for the life she'd been given. Greg, who could always identify potential doom, had accused her of being a perennial optimist. It was true. Her few bad reviews in her medical career came from her dogged insistence that there was still something to do to save a dying person, her refusal to succumb to the odds when they were not on her side.

Esther stopped short in the hallway. "Let's check in on Nan first. Then I'll take you for your papers and badge."

They turned back and when they entered the ER, a young man—more an overgrown boy, Donna thought—looked up. He'd been whistling *Waltzing Matilda*, leaning over an Aboriginal man on a gurney. Nan stood close, her arm brushing his, cheeks flushed under her freckles.

The young man smiled, revealing slightly crooked teeth. "Who've we got here, me gorgeous Esther?" Laugh lines, surprisingly deep, framed his mouth like parentheses, and Donna automatically added a few years to the twenty-three she'd first guessed. She pondered what lines were etched in her face that this young man would notice.

Esther stalked over to the gurney and, using her hips, forced herself between Nan and the young doc. "Your new boss. That's what."

He waved Donna over and held out his hand. "Doctor Andy.

Patient won't make it, I think." His bright smile looked like a permanent fixture, despite the words he was delivering. "Just arrived on the plane from Mornington."

Donna gave him her hand without meeting his eyes, focusing instead on the patient's oily skin. She pulled back an eyelid to see yellow sclera. The man's liver and kidneys had shut down. She wrinkled her nose at the sour toxic discharge erupting through his pores.

"Do you need help?" She looked up at Andy and he shook his head. Two light brown curls bounced on his smooth forehead. Donna took a step back. Too many cooks, as they say. Donna watched as Nan busied herself with the IV while Esther inventoried the supply tray.

Donna shifted her weight from one foot to the other, having to restrain herself from jumping in and taking over. Andy was working at half the speed she could have. She looked over the patient, jutting jaw, prominent brow, thick black hair that like Esther's had started growing low down on a huge forehead. The patient was running from death, but death was catching up quickly. She watched Andy's cracked hands—nails jagged but clean—gliding over the man's rough brown skin, and willed Andy to hurry in his examination, though haste would make no difference at this point. With this patient, she could temper her optimism.

Esther broke the silence. "Doctor Donna's already survived an encounter with a funnel-web."

Andy looked up briefly. "Really? Ever hear of Slim Newton?" Andy started whistling a tune. "Song's called *Redback on the Toilet Seat*. Come over to my place and I'll play it for you."

Donna noticed Nan's frown and moved to the other side of the patient, across from the whistling Andy. She picked up the patient's wrist and took his pulse. The banter of the ER was familiar and she relaxed into it. "What is it with the earthquakes?"

Andy's whistle stopped abruptly. "Earthquakes?"

Donna looked at him, then Nan, then Esther. "Didn't you feel one? This morning around six. Last night too."

"Round six?" Nan asked, biting her lip.

Before anyone could say anything else, Donna slapped her forehead with her palm. "Mining town. Chalk it up to jet lag. How long will they be blasting?"

"Twice a day at shift change until the hole's empty. 'Til the end of Isa," Esther answered.

Donna couldn't believe there was that much material to pull out of the ground. "Even Sundays?"

Nan spoke in her sing-song voice. "No such thing as a Sunday for miners. Day one through eight."

Half-listening, Donna moved to the bottom of the gurney, next to the patient's swollen feet. His toes were splayed wide, probably never having been molded by shoes for his fifty-some years. The pale soles were full of cracks, like tributaries that spilled the dirt of his travels over hills of calluses. From heel to toe the journey of his life had been marked. Donna remembered the hardened feet she'd glimpsed when she and Greg had volunteered in a mountain clinic in Nepal. In order to not offend, patients had always been careful to hide the soles of their feet under a cloth or rag. Donna thought how mortified this man would be if he were Nepali, pointing his feet toward the doctor.

A toe flinched as though castigating her for thinking poorly of him for his manners. She was halfway between Nepal and the ER, unconsciously drinking in the hospital sounds and smells: lye soap, whirring oxygen tanks, familiar as the creaks of her old apartment. It was then that Andy called the code. She'd heard the desperate sucking, the last intake of this world's air, but she hadn't wanted to acknowledge last breaths, not in the first hours of her new job.

After two attempts at resuscitation, Esther wiped her hands on her tight pants. "Stop." Andy obeyed. Esther grabbed the patient's chart and thrust it to Donna's chest. She towered above

Donna's slender frame, and looked over Donna's shoulder as she compliantly opened the chart. Esther pointed to his vitals. "No chance."

Donna was stunned. "He was only thirty-two."

"Should have died at home." Esther took back the chart. "I'll get the papers."

Andy stood still beside the man, no longer touching him. Without his smile Andy's face was that of a boy's, framed by big ears and tousled hair.

Donna walked over to him and put her hand on his shoulder. "It's going to happen."

He shrugged her off. "Bloody hell, mate," Andy muttered, then stalked out the front door of the ER, Nan following like a puppy at his heels.

Used to the reactions of young doctors, Donna focused on the patient. She moved the dead man's arms to a resting position by his side, then peered into his frozen yellow eyes, eyes that had opened wide as he sucked in his last breaths of air. But now she couldn't glimpse even a hint of his soul. She repeated his name, Michael Robson, over and over in her head. She liked men named Michael. She added it to her list of the dead. Every patient she'd lost over the years was on the list. Her baby was on the list, as was every failed in vitro treatment—she numbered them IVF 1-4. Also on the list were her father, who died at fifty-seven, and then her mother, who died at sixty-four. Donna also included Greg, her failed marriage its own form of death.

It was a list of failures, but it was also a catalogue of memories, the only way she could honor them all. She'd started it during her second year of residency, when she was still losing sleep over the patients who would die on her watch. Now, whenever she felt anxious, she would roll through the names, somewhere between one and five times through, and she'd feel grateful for her life, despite her failures.

Michael Robson. As she signed the death certificate, a young

Aboriginal woman rushed to the dead man's bedside.

"You gotta save him or I'm stone dead," she wailed to no one in particular.

"No one left to save," Esther grunted. "Grogged himself to death. Diabetic fair dinkum."

The girl squeezed the dead man's hand. "Bad magic."

Donna watched Esther wrap her arms around the girl. She stroked the girl's hair saying, "What can you do? Bad magic."

"Well then I'll go drown in the billabong." The girl looked pleadingly at Esther.

"Billabong's dry," Esther countered.

On her way into town from the airport, Donna had crossed the dry creek bed on the outskirts of Isa proper. *Lonely Planet* said it was full during the two or three monsoon weeks in the summer—except for once a decade, when it would run for two months. Monsoon had come and gone three months prior, and now, in April, the Aboriginals drank and camped there.

The girl plopped down in an orange chair in defeat. "His kin'll kill me anyway. Think I cursed him."

Esther scooped the girl up. "Come with me."

Donna watched them recede into the hospital hallway, Esther's pants betraying her yellow flowered underwear.

Donna was alone with the dead Michael Robson. She readjusted his arms. "Now you look more comfy. I need a cup of coffee."

"I'll take you."

Donna jumped. She turned and saw Andy poking his head through the ER screen door. He said, "Let's get bikkies and a cuppa. We'll cut through the car park."

At the canteen, Donna fumbled with the Aussie money she'd exchanged before leaving New York and paid for her coffee—Andy would not let her pay for his. She clutched her Styrofoam cup as she sat down at one of the plastic tables, watching the cream lighten the coffee to brown in a whirlpool as she stirred, blowing away the coffee steam. It seemed ridiculous to drink hot coffee in the heat. The canteen was not privileged to the air conditioning of the hospital. Its sole source of air circulation was a rickety ceiling fan. Andy paced back and forth in front of the sweets selection, his thighs flexing under his jeans. Her high school boyfriend had had an ass like his, full enough so that the Levi's creased where the thigh met the glutes. He turned to her. "Any requests, Doc?"

She shook her head.

"Please, me straw." She turned to see an Aboriginal boy at her side. He was pointing under the table to her feet. She looked at his wiry blond hair, roots dark like the New York skater boys who bleached their spiky hair. His chocolate skin shone two shades lighter than his round dark eyes.

He was a negative image of the angel boy from her dreams, brown where he should be pale, blond wiry hair where he should be dark and curly. Yet she knew he was the same boy, with same the certainty that people *knew* things in dreams.

He pointed again. "Me straw," he repeated louder.

She bent down and retrieved the clear straw from under her feet. As she did, she was met by his wiggling toes, planted on the white-flecked linoleum, next to her clogs. Donna tried to imagine those feet walking through the desert, scampering over shale and cracked clay, sliding down sand dunes, eventually turning into the feet of Michael Robson, but she couldn't make a connection.

She took her time releasing the straw into his tightening grip so she could memorize his face. There were the early signs of puberty, his mustache thickening towards the center of his upper lip with only a trace of fuzz at the corner of his mouth, wisps of sideburns—dark, not blond like his hair. He looked her in the eye. "Ta."

"No problem." She was captivated by his broad forehead. His gigantic head looked like a boulder about to fall off a cliff. His body was stocky and his legs spindly. Everything about him looked out of balance. Yet as soon as he held the straw, he swaggered gracefully toward the door, taking time to spin a saltshaker on the table without dropping his pat of Nutella nor his Coke.

When he turned at the door, she caught his eye again. "What's your name?"

He smiled at her, as if daring her to come with him. "Where do you come from?"

"The States. New York."

He leaned against the door. "Thought so."

"And you?"

He turned around, waved, and as he left the light seemed to dim, as though the boy were radiating his own personal sunshine. Angels. *They are formed of fire and encompassed by light.*

Andy threw three packs of cookies and a Caramello Koala on the table. "Couldn't decide." As he pulled his chair up beside Donna, the table wobbled and spilled her coffee. "Whoops. Table's got a bad leg."

"Got a napkin?"

He laughed and with a flourish leaned back on one leg of his chair and reached behind him to the next table. "Nappies are for baby's bottom." He handed her a stack. "These are serviettes." He bent over, jamming some napkins under the bad leg.

"Too fancy," she muttered.

Andy wiped a bead of sweat off his forehead. "You'll get used to it. The Isa grows on you pretty quick. She's a hard town, but a good town."

The screen door slammed and Esther walked in, her shoulder-length hair now pulled back into a neat bun. Andy waved her over. "Plenty of bikkies to share." Esther sat down without buying a drink and ripped open a package of Arnott's. The three sat in silence, Donna folding her serviette into a tiny football, Andy staring out the screen door, and Esther breaking her cookies into tiny pieces before popping them into her mouth. Andy finally stood up, blowing on his tea, though it looked to Donna as if it had already cooled. "Got to get back to work. I'm leaving for Doomadgee clinic this evo."

Donna flicked her paper football. "A rotation? From here?"

Andy stood above her. "Isa's the base for the residents. Have to do two months in the bush. I owe Queensland for paying me schooling."

"Isn't this the bush?"

"Not if you've seen Doomadgee," he said as he turned away.

Donna supposed it would be part of her job to see Doomadgee. That must have been what the job description had meant by *some travel to outlying clinics*. She'd neglected to ask the headhunters about some of the job's details, so focused had she been on getting out of New York. Donna turned to Esther. "Have you been there?"

"One of me men's up there. Jocko, me favo." Her cheeks became large globes as she smiled. "We best get you a badge and papers."

Donna stood up as Esther did, pulled the squeaky canteen door shut behind them, then watched Andy's back disappear into the ER across the car park, as Andy had called it. She shielded her eyes against the glare of the sun on the asphalt and followed in Esther's shadow, making a note to never leave the house without sunglasses and to buy a wide-brimmed hat and sunscreen—even though with her olive skin she'd never used it before—as soon as she could get to Kmart. She wasn't going to take the chance of age spots, much less skin cancer.

She stopped in mid-stride. The Aboriginal boy was kicking an empty Victoria Bitter can in the wake of a large man as he traced S-curves along the edge of the lot. The boy raised his arms above his head, then brought them down abruptly like a bird. Maybe those are his angel wings, thought Donna as she crushed her cup. She cursed as a few leftover drops made three large coffee blotches on her khaki skirt. When she lifted her eyes, the two males were gone. She tossed her coffee cup into a trash can, hurrying to catch up with Esther, who'd bent down to feed her last cookies to a Galah. Donna watched as the bird hopped into Esther's palm—her hand was so large she could have wrapped her fingers all the way around its fat torso. Esther's other hand fed the parrot the cookie as she cooed at it.

Donna slowly crouched beside her and whispered, "Lots of parrots out here."

Esther looked over at Donna, black eyes like those of the Galah, and jerked her arm up, sending the parrot into flight. "Lonely in this town until you know folk. Want to go for a VB after work?"

"Sure. You know I like your hair pulled back like that."

Esther patted her bun. "Fair dinkum? Wish I had hair like yours. Your hair makes you look like a black cockatoo. When you throw your hair back and nod."

The Galah paced back and forth in the lifeless meadow, her sharp toes gripping the tar as if to rip away the suffocating blackness. It was then that the woman came to her. The Galah stepped carefully onto the woman's outstretched hand, grasping the dry food with her hooked beak. She examined the creases etched into the woman's open palm. The lines traced the flight of the Galah over the earth. The ancient energy had sent a Galah woman to share the burden.

The Galah looked into the woman's clear eyes, and replayed the dance of the spinifex. She showed her the spirit child waiting to be born from the womb of the black cockatoo woman. She showed the spirit child's marriage to the Galah boy.

When the Galah finished, she flew up over the blackness. Below, she could see the boy fighting the tar as he dragged behind Uncle. He looked like a baby emu forced to follow its mother. He was a Galah boy, not an emu. A chick about to fly the nest—in the grass dance she had seen that black hair between arm and torso, and that black hair nestled underneath his penis like a snake hiding behind warm rocks. As soon as he had his feathers he would fly away.

Jimmy and Hector tucked their swags under the arches of the coolabah roots in the bone-dry billabong. Hector made Jimmy put on the clean shirt he'd saved at the bottom of his swag, and after weeks of being free to the air, Jimmy's back itched from the cotton. Gus, the friend of the stationmaster, was an orderly at the Mount Isa Base Hospital, so they asked around for directions until an old Yapa hanging out by his campfire told them the way to go. Old man said a bloke could find grog by the Isa Hotel. Hector nodded and Jimmy's stomach sank. Yuendumu was a dry town, since the grog was killing blokes left and right. He tried not to think about grog as they followed the billabong into town.

They rounded a bend and houses seemed to rise up suddenly out of the desert like his house did in Yuendumu, only there were so many more of them here, right next to each other in straight lines. He'd seen the footprint of a town on their walkabout, the cement foundations marking where the houses once stood, and even an old tin street sign that pointed to the movie theater and the general store. He'd walked row after row of those concrete squares, feeling the earth scarred from the closed mine. Spinifex had poked up wildly between the cracks in the concrete. The bush was reclaiming the land, and he could imagine the ground had sighed in relief when the weight of those homes had been carted away. But the Isa was so much bigger. A tiny piece of Isa could fit into that abandoned mining town.

"How many houses you reckon are here?" Jimmy asked Hector as they walked past well-trimmed yards with dogs penned between fences. In Yuendumu the dogs ran free like animals should, in and out of houses, over the canvases, leaving doggie foot prints on the paintings that the women sold to Sydney art galleries.

"Too many to count, fair dinkum."

"Like ants?"

"Not that many," Hector laughed. "Bloody lot of them. Maybe like the leaves on one ghost gum."

It was the hospital lawn that was the most beautiful thing to Jimmy. The grass was a shade of green he'd never seen in Yuendumu, not even in the paint pots at the Yuendumu Community Center.

They walked through the hospital's sliding glass doors. He'd seen automatic doors many times on the telly, but had never been through them himself. They opened more slowly than he expected, so that a bloke would have to slow to a walk if he'd been running or else he'd bump his head on the glass. In action films, the blokes never had to slow.

They stopped at the info desk and a pale old woman looked up Gus's name. "You sure you don't know his last name?" The woman leaned forward with arched eyebrows and sagging eyelids.

Hector shook his head. "Sorry."

She took a deep breath and then shrugged. "Well, let's try another way."

Ten minutes later she put her gnarled knuckles to her cheeks. "I can't find any Gus who works here." She gave a tired smile and added quietly. "Do you want to ask over at Aboriginal Affairs?"

Hector couldn't hide his disappointment, but he smiled pleasantly at the woman and took Jimmy's shoulder. "Can I borrow a phone book?"

A few minutes later they were headed down Miles Street. Jimmy looked up at Hector, who'd been silent since he'd thanked the old lady. "Are we going to try Aboriginal Affairs?"

Hector snorted and lengthened his stride. "Useless. Going to the Barrington Downs office meself."

They stopped in front of a two-story office building, and Hector led the way in. He checked the directory. "Come on then, boy."

They walked into a door labeled "102." A girl who was about twenty sat at a desk with a black phone and papers strewn about. She was blowing bubbles with her gum, her feet propped sideways on another chair, her skirt scrunched between her legs. Quickly she sat up, "Got the right place?"

Hector cleared his throat. "Is this the office for Barrington Downs Station?"

She nodded vigorously, popping her gum.

"We need permission to cross into the station."

The girl looked at Hector, then at Jimmy. "Why?"

Hector sucked in his puffy lip where his teeth were missing. "Religious and cultural reasons. You know we blacks have ties to our Land."

The girl stared at him with vacant eyes, her mouth still working. "Is this about a native title claim?"

Hector shook his head and stayed calm. Jimmy clenched a fist. Were the whites worried only about losing money? Hector said quietly, "We just want to visit a site, bow our heads and pray, like you do in church."

That's a lie, Jimmy thought and almost let a smile escape despite his anger. He'd never seen a Yapa lie to another Yapa—only to a white person.

After a minute of silence, she said, "Never dealt with that before. Don't know what to do."

Hector sighed and Jimmy shifted from one foot to the other. He wanted to tell her to use her brain, but he held back. Hector spoke softly. "Is there someone we could call? Stationmaster?"

Her smile brightened. "Sure. There's a new bloke on. Big company's just bought us, you know? Fired the old stationmaster, poor bugger. Only spoke to the new bloke once. He faxes and e-mails."

Jimmy didn't know what a fax was, but had seen the e-mail on the computer at the community center. She scribbled a number on a piece of paper and pushed it over to Hector. "Gavin Childs is your man."

"Could you call for us, please?"

Jimmy blushed. They didn't have a phone, of course, and were completely at this woman's mercy. But she smiled an easy smile and popped a bubble. "No worries."

They stood in front of her desk as she waited on the phone, first for one person, then another. Jimmy surveyed her office for something of interest. The poster on the wall showed a sunset faded by the greenish tube lights above them. Without a window, it was more of a hole than an office. Finally she smiled and mouthed, "His secretary."

Jimmy listened to her describe their *pilgrimage*. So she'd understood the basics. She chewed her gum vigorously and repeated herself. By the third time, her smile had dimmed. She finished off the conversation in a small voice, staring at the fake sunset. "You're sure then?"

She put the phone down hard. "I'm sorry." She took out her gum and threw it in the wastebasket that stood overflowing beside her desk. "They say they don't have procedures in place yet for visitors. Maybe in six months or so." She absently shuffled papers on her desk. "Fair dinkum, I'm sorry."

This time it was Hector who assured her, "No worries." Jimmy followed him out of the office, relieved to feel the sun again as they exited the building. They stopped at the corner, and Hector took off his hat and ruffled through his gray-and-black hair. They leaned against the building and watched the cars take turns at the stop sign. Finally Hector spoke. "Wait for me at wijipirtili. Eat tea at the tuck shop. I'm off to Isa Hotel." Hector pointed at him with his long finger, "Don't bum a dollar off the white man. I know your mum's got you set up."

Worrying about Hector and the grog available to him at the Isa Hotel, Jimmy made his way back to the vast greenness outside the hospital, and instead of going to buy tea, sat down in the grass fingering the coins in his pocket. He watched an ant crawl all the way up a blade of grass, stop at the tip as if to Behold his country, then walk down again. If you were traveling, you greeted the ant spirits first since they were the keepers of the Land. Hector and he had forgotten. Jimmy whispered, *Thank you, ant, for allowing us on your Land.*

The ant waved an antenna at him and Jimmy felt better. He watched the ant repeat its quest on four more blades. His gaze wandered from the ant to the whitefellas and blackfellas walking in and out of the hospital, sisters in their whites pushing patients in chairs or helping them to walk.

After the sun had moved higher in the sky, though it was not yet midday, he wandered into the tiny hospital tuck shop, a house that was plopped in the car park, away from the main building. A lady with frizzy yellow hair and skin like bleached desert bones stood behind the counter. He looked longingly at the packs of Nutella as his stomach grumbled. He wished Mum were calling him in for morning tea right then.

"You'll break me heart looking like that."

Jimmy smiled at her. "Mum says the same thing."

"Let me guess. Like the rest of your mob you're waiting for the dole this Thursday before you eat again?"

Jimmy felt the red rise on his cheeks. "Me mob's in Yuendumu. Mum works. We're not on the dole." He turned to leave the store.

She called after him. "Hey. Have some Nutella on me. Coke too. Just show me that pretty smile again." She waved him back. "No worries."

Jimmy wasn't about to pass up free Coke and chocolate. He stood on the cool floor, carefully peeling back the paper from the corner of the package and flashing his teeth at the bleached woman who was examining his smile. Soon he got tired of being watched and pretended to follow a fly around the place. He sat down and contemplated the ceiling fans twirling round and round like lazy eagles gliding on the wind. After he was under them for a few minutes, he could feel the little hairs on his arms stand up. He waved at the bleached woman and walked out into the hot sun and watched the hairs relax. One more time he opened the screen door, to feel his hairs rise.

"Forget something?" The woman smiled.

"Naw. Doing a science experiment."

"Seeing if you can let all the hot air in and me cool air out?"

Jimmy let his smile work its magic. He sipped his Coke and read the labels on the biscuit packages, looking up when the door slammed. A woman with silver-green skin the color of spinifex and hair the color of moonless night walked in with a tall whitefella, bought coffee, and sat down at a table. Jimmy was startled to hear the white man call her doc. So startled that he flicked his straw and it flew under her table. He'd never seen a woman doc before, at least, not a white woman. Of course Yapa had medicine women, as powerful as any medicine man. But in all the years of going to the whitefella's clinics, never once had a woman been anything but a sister.

He asked the woman for his straw. She reminded him of a black cockatoo, her head bobbing back and forth and a faraway look in her eyes. She was probably a bird woman and didn't know it, a cousin of his. The hairs on his skin were rising again, and he was anxious to get back to the sun to look out for Hector.

Eventually Hector returned, weaving back and forth like a snake escaping a wombat.

Jimmy barely looked up as Hector's shadow fell over him. "You pissed?"

"Bugger. Bloody whitefellas saying that the station can't have visitors. What we gonna do? Wait for six months and then have them turn us down again? Bloody Gus."

Jimmy was less concerned with permission to go on the Land, and more concerned with Hector's slurring. "Let's get back to the billabong."

"Don't they know I'm no ignorant Yapa? They don't want to let me on my Land. *My* Land, you hear that? Bloody procedures. *He's* the bloody visitor."

No way any whites were going to give them permission with Hector looking like that. There was nothing more to do about it today. Jimmy pulled Hector away from the hospital entrance. "You need a sleep."

Hector was mumbling something about native title claims. "Just might find me a solicitor to file one."

Jimmy followed Hector's meandering path out of the car park, and they weren't headed in the direction of the billabong. Jimmy lifted his hands above his head and made flapping motions. If only he could fly away. Fly to his Dreaming and be done with it. Well, Hector could get stuffed.

Jimmy turned around quietly and walked away. He looked over his shoulder at Hector's weaving backside. Uncle hadn't noticed him gone. He followed the sun down a road that seemed to lead to the center of town. He might as well have a good peek at the Isa while he was here.

He wandered down the road, counting more cars than passed through Yuendumu in half a year. They were emptying out down the road into a large flat area. Jimmy followed them and saw the sign. Kmart. He'd seen Kmart ads on the telly. He stood by a post and watched big fat whitefellas, skinny whitefellas, Yapa in all shades, all clutching plastic bags on their way out.

As he walked into the Kmart, he felt the cold dry air rushing out. It was like plunging into the billabong during the Wet, not like in the hospital tuck shop where his hairs had slowly risen. He fingered the ten two-dollar coins in his pocket. They'd probably only be in Isa a day or two more so he figured he'd splurge on a Violet Crumble, anxious to feel the honeycomb melt in his mouth, taste the chocolate on the tip of his tongue.

He tore open the purple wrapper as he walked back out into the sun. As he ate tiny nibbles, he meandered through a neighborhood of pretty houses and green lawns. A bus drove by, and he was tempted to find the bus station and head back to Yuendumu. Leave Hector stinking of grog and make it home in two days. Or better, go off to Cairns, see the coast and the reef that he studied in school. Carefully, he folded the empty candy bar wrapper as a souvenir of Isa and put it in his pocket. He couldn't go back to Yuendumu as the only one of his mates who didn't finish his initiation.

His last morsel of Violet Crumble had long ago melted on his tongue when he came upon his kin. Legs stiff, beak open, dead for a day or two by the looks of the worms in the open belly. Black flies didn't waste any time. They were probably already on their fifth generation, hah! But it wouldn't do to leave a relation there like that.

Jimmy fished out the flint knife from his pocket and pricked his thumb the way the adults did. He bent down and rubbed a drop of blood into the bird's open beak. Then he took his finger and smeared a drop behind each of his own ears. Two pink feathers lay on the bird's face, and he stuck those into the blood, hidden underneath his hair. Next he plucked out some gray from the wings, white from the crest, and light pink from the underwings and stuffed them in his pocket next to his knife. Then he picked up the bird, worms and all, and carried him through the streets filled with houses until he found an empty lot. He laid the body on the dirt and found some pebbles to pour over him.

Jimmy had a sharp pain in his belly. Too much chocolate and not enough food. He knew all about the food pyramid. A faded copy was on the wall in his schoolroom. Time to go back to the billabong.

The Galah felt the pull of the earth. Red parrot blood, red crystal between her eyes pulled her south to mate, to nurture, to feed, to dream; north to build nests, to fly tricks on the wind. She flew over her land, heeding the call, the pull. Every cell in her body knew the pattern of her seasons, which meadow they would fly to and when. The flock flew as one bird responding to the magnetic pull. Pull. Feel. Know.

The red crystal was her map, through her feathers and blood she pulsed with the earth, she knew exactly her position above the round planet. Heeding the crystal, she flew without question to her mate's body. The maggots had come. Black fly eggs were hatching and larvae feasting. They would help turn him into the pink sands and gray dust through which she would fly for another monsoon. Then she too would lie with the maggots, or become one with the kestrel eagle as she died in its belly. Or she would be fed in pieces to the horned owl chick.

She was ready to rejoin her flock when a shadow approached. The maggots froze. Yellow crown atop the brown body. The Galah boy. She watched as he sank to his knees like the bracken fern did at night, shrinking in on itself to preserve the day's heat. Then he lifted feathers to the sun, to the sky, as if to show her. Pink feathers plucked from her mate's chest and head, and gray feathers from his back. Feathers upon feathers, he put on the feathers, as his own feathers were beginning to grow. He had bound her to him, readied himself for flight to their land, though she doubted that he knew what he had done. Brown boy with Galah feathers, together we will fly.

It was time for evening tea when Jimmy arrived at the billabong. Their swags were tucked under the coolabah roots as he'd left them, with no sign of Hector. Jimmy checked around for Hector's footprints, but there were only those from the morning. He took out his billy and stood there, trying to decide whether or not to make a fire when a woman beckoned him to join her. "Let me feed you. Me boys all grown now, don't let me put food in their bellies."

"Ta." Jimmy smiled as she spread some vegemite on a bun and handed it to him. He licked the bread and let the salty spread linger on his tongue before taking a huge bite. His stomach thanked him for finally feeding it some real food that day. Hector would have to stay away from the grog and Jimmy would have to stay away from the chocolate. Everybody had their poisons in the city.

The woman sat and stared at him as he ate. She looked older than Mum but younger than Tess. She pointed to his billy. "Use me fire to make some tea?"

He stretched his arm out with the tin but she didn't reach for it. "Looks like you're old enough to do it yourself."

Jimmy had been cooking billy tea since he was a joey. "Mum likes to do it, that's all."

"I'm not your mum."

Jimmy made tea for the two of them and they drank in silence. He wondered where she was from but didn't ask. She wasn't kin. He thanked the woman when he was done, unrolled his swag under the coolabah and stared into the face of the dying sun until it burnt his eyes. When he shut them tight, the pink-yellow ball seared into his vision. He imagined his kin in Yuendumu watching the same sun sink over the Yigandani.

As the last traces of light disappeared into the sky, the starseeds began to twinkle. They'd been dropped by the Galah Ancestor as he ate during the Jukurrpa. Jimmy had watched parrots for hours and knew the messy creatures dropped half of what they ate. Seeded the Land like his Ancestors seeded the sky. His Galah Ancestor was a jokester who liked to play, play, play, when he should be hunting for food. Ancestor's wise mum realized he needed supervision, so his punishment was to forever have to fly in flocks, never alone.

Like Ant-Yapa, Galah-Yapa were not meant to be alone. He'd never before been separated from his kin. He thought of the Galahs who rested in the hospital car park, hanging upside down on the wires, and wished he could be one of them. What he'd do now to be with a flock of mates.

Black sky, smile moon. Shadows danced from the coolabah leaves in the wind. After ten falling starseeds, he stood up to stretch and rested back on his heels, no toes, no center foot, leaning back as far as he could without falling. He imagined he was leaning against his mother's warm body. She'd taught him to rest his own heart on the back of his body when he was sad. Heels, heels, no toes.

Bloody native title. Full foot. Heel-toe. Heel-toe. Heel-toe. Out to the field beyond the billabong where he could feel the air cool, away from the fires of the Yapa. Here he could see Yaraandoo shining brightest in the sky.

He walked the pattern of Yaraandoo. This time of year, he was high in the night sky. Right foot forward, left back, right foot side, left foot side, a little square. He could see why the whitefellas called it the Southern Cross. Right, left, right, left, rocking his body. Neck craned to the sky, he became Yowie, the spirit of death, flying to the giant gum tree in the sky with the first Yapa to die. He stretched his arms out further, like an eagle's wide wings, and rocked. Right foot front, left foot back, right foot side, left foot side. Jimmy kept his arms still and wide and felt the rise and fall of his body as his feet met the earth. As if his mother were rocking him, rocking him, cradled in her arms, rocking forward and side.

His hips swayed like tall grasses in the breeze as he looked above and traced the crystal droppings of mulla mulla seeds that trailed from Yowie's tree, shimmering under the left branch. He shivered as he focused on Yowie's black shadow that followed him as he soared.

Jimmy's arms grew heavy. They needed to rise. He began to turn slowly around—could feel the wind on his arms when he twirled, under his arms, air pushing them higher, pushing him up in the air.

He twirled faster, like the fans in the tuck shop, the wind grew and he flew. Round and round and round, cool wind whispered in his ears. He flopped onto the cool grass and laughed as he watched the stars spin above him. They spun as he had, the winds whipping them. He was still flying among them, could not anchor to the ground, had no support. Yet he could not fly home. He tried to sit up and slopped down, the spinning stars throwing him back. He forced himself up, to feel his feet push on the ground. It felt hollow. He was thrown right and left as he walked further from the billabong. Did he look as Hector had when he was poisoned, the snake outrunning the wombat? Heel-toe, right, heel-toe, left.

He wiped his nose on his shirt, the one he'd kept clean for town, then ripped it off. He didn't want to be in Isa anyway. Stupid grog. Stupid permission. Stupid whitefellas. He threw the shirt into the darkness. It billowed up and then snagged on a termite mound, as tall as Jimmy Jackboy.

Give me back me shirt. He kicked at the mound even as he knew he'd be punished for harming the creatures inside. He kicked again. With each kick he found sounds escaping from deep inside his belly and he did not know what they meant. Only that the kick made him want to scream, and the scream made him want to kick.

The red brown tower toppled over with a satisfying thud, broken clean in half, rusty dust floating up into the moonlight. Termites poured out like Coke from a broken bottle. The ground darkened around him.

He was taken in by the movement of the termites, shadows in the night. He bent down and watched them circle as they decided how to rebuild their home. They were picking up pieces of dust sand to pile back on the base. Jimmy wanted to help but couldn't, so he flopped down on his belly to watch the termites swarm.

Absently he drew lines in the dirt with his finger, then began to paint first his face, then his body with the red dust as the men had done the night before he left. Each line was important. Each curve an Ancestor, each circle a waterhole, each squiggle the dried salt soak. Waterhole, Yapa, rocks.

Jimmy covered his skin with the dirt, imagining Uncles' thick fingers on his chest. He painted his story, the path to the pile of starseeds his Ancestor Galah had dropped while eating. He felt the rough sands cling to the hairs on his arms. He would make it to that starseed pile on the Barrington Downs Station, and he would not leave before he sang that song, before he Beheld his country.

He took the Galah feathers out of his pocket and stuck them onto his chest using dirt moistened with spit. His body covered with dust, he rolled over and over, away from the termites. He watched Yaraandoo flicker as he fell asleep.

The feathers took him home. He flew, flew, flapping gray wings, pink head turned toward Yuendumu. He landed on the branch of the ghost gum outside Mum's window. Mum looked up from washing dishes and frowned. "Jimmy, you should not visit me."

He saw a wrinkle on her forehead he'd never seen before. He missed her down to the core of his belly. He shivered in the tree. "I am alone."

She paused and lifted her hands from the water, soap bubbles clinging to them as she wiped them on her faded pink shirt. "You can hunt. You can take care of yourself."

Jimmy willed her to understand. "Hector has the poison. Me initiation."

Mum tapped her fingers on the edge of the sink and closed her eyes. He waited in the tree, spying Yaraandoo through the branches. Her eyes opened suddenly and she nodded. "Have patience. You will be initiated. I will talk to Tess."

When he woke, it was dark and there was a throbbing in the initiation scar on his ankle, the scar he earned on the day his uncles had seized him.

The Galah flew along the path of the sun, the fireball on her back like the koala carrying its babe. The red metals of the desert called to the crystal between her eyes. Where the shells of the ocean animals could still be found and the earth crust was only a gentle cover between her and the mother, the soils begged her to come down and bathe in the womb of the earth.

Her shadow fell further away, crossing a lone gum, dead for so many years, practically turned to stone below her. The gum's crooked branch beckoned her to rest, echoed by the shadow beside it.

She flew on until the ripples of sand became bigger, so that sand waves became waves of stone, leftover waves from the ocean, from the earth clapping its wings together. Green dots covered the tops of the ripples. Trees and grasses reached up to the setting sun and pulled moisture from the air. The air was visible around her in the heat. It floated off her wings like the ripples of sand.

Finally she saw the stone pillar, carved from the ocean floor by the tides. She had been here during the Wet, when rainbows of light connected the heavens and the pillar. Now, in the Dry, the reds and the oranges were blown by the wind into browns and tans. The pillar became a shadow in the distance, growing shorter as the night came closer.

Wings aching she rested on a tree the moment the sun ball dropped behind the mountains to the west. She was close to the Center and felt Uluru pulling her south. The woman stood at the window looking past the tree to the east and the Galah studied her. Hands dropped in water, moving around as fish in the stream, she did not have a yellow crown on her head like the boy, but she had the same black lashes.

The woman smiled at the Galah. Spoke to her softly. The Galah could tell by her gentle voice that the woman was a good mother to the boy. Like the wallaby who kept her young always on her belly.

The Galah rested her head under her wing. She would fly back to the bright greens of town as soon as the first feathers of the sun graced the earth.

Early in the morning, Jimmy clutched two packs of Nutella as he walked toward the grassy spot by the hospital entrance. Not knowing where else to go, it had become his routine to pick up Nutella from the frizzy-haired lady each morning after the daily fruitless trip to the Barrington Downs Station office. Hector figured if they were persistent, the stationmaster would finally give them permission to cross onto the Land. But the day before, after almost a moon of visits, the bubblegum girl asked Jimmy and Hector to please not return to her office on Miles Street. Permission was not going to be given, and she found the whole mess too depressing.

After having been dismissed, Jimmy and Hector marched over to Aboriginal Affairs, and as Hector had suspected, its staff was sympathetic, but useless. The Yapa in the office wanted to start a native title claim. But by the time the claim would go through the court system, Jimmy would be way past initiation age. Hector repeated that all they wanted was a quick visit to the Galah seedpile so Jimmy could get on with his life. The woman in the office told them to check back the next week.

Jimmy dipped into the Nutella, feeling the spikes of grass prick his back. Last night Hector had gone over to the Isa Hotel to get pissed and hadn't come back to the billabong. Hector'd been over to the hotel every afternoon since they'd got to town, getting blotto early enough to sleep off the VB before their daily visit to the Barrington office. Mum had said to have patience, but this was ridiculous. When he met Hector back at the billabong that night—if Hector weren't already passed out—he would tell Hector that they should Behold his Land without permission.

Maybe years ago they'd have shot Yapa for trespassing, but not now. Not since Mabo.

He watched the cockatoo doctor with the voice from the telly get into a Land Rover with some jillaroo. Jimmy wondered what it would be like to have a Land Rover. He would take his cousins for rides. Visit all their Dreaming sites in one day. Maybe go fossiking up at Devil's Marbles.

He emptied his pockets onto the grass. Despite the frizzy-haired woman's generosity, he was almost out of money—only three two-dollar coins jingled in his pocket, with a random twenty cent piece or two. He missed his footy cards, but he'd managed to find some new treasures. Next to his coins he laid his Galah feathers and the bleached white bone that had been his father's pointing finger, which needed to be buried at the seedpile so his father could finally fly up to Yaraandoo. He laid out the fossils he'd collected on his way to the Isa. Australia was chockers with good fossiking sites because of the great oceans that had once covered the Center, forcing the Old People to move to the coasts. His favo was a limestone fossil with a leaf-like animal. He'd found it early on walkabout where the red-and-black striped rocks still looked like home. He also had a piece of fossil bone that they'd chipped out of the limestone with Jimmy's knife, not even twenty sleeps before they'd arrived in the Isa. He'd cut his toe on the sharp white lace that had stuck out from the rocks. Hector said it was the bone of a bird bigger than old man emu, who lived after the oceans left the Center. Next to the old bird bone he laid the half beetle he found in Beetle Creek.

"Hey, boy."

Jimmy looked up to see a stubby dark man who had become Hector's mate waving at him. In his other hand was a box of poison. Jimmy pretended he didn't know the man, who shouted again, "Uncle's out back of the Isa Hotel. Passed out. Go get him."

Jimmy found Uncle in an alley. He stood at Hector's bare feet, his shadow covering the length of the still body. Soon Jimmy'd be as tall as his shadow. He thought Hector'd wake up as he blocked out the sun, yelling, *Jimmy Jackboy, don't steal me warmth*, but Hector didn't move. His hands were beside his body, palms up to the sun, but his left foot was turned in at the ankle funny. Jimmy moved over to Hector's side, kicked away an empty cardboard box and crouched by his head, lifting the brim of the hat that was still firmly in place. "Hector, wake up." Hector didn't flinch, not even a snore. Jimmy put his hand in front of Uncle's nose and felt his moist breath.

He yelled, "Hector!"

Jimmy wanted tea. He wanted Hector to get up so he could tell him *Let's sneak onto Galah Land without permission*. He heard the clinking of plates inside the Isa Hotel and smelled chips frying. He sat back on his bum to wait for Hector to sleep off the grog. Black flies circled a garbage can, popping up and down, trying to find a more comfortable place to land than the steel lid baked by the sun. Jimmy laughed as he thought about little burnt fly feet. He walked up and down the length of the alley, forty-four heel-toes, following a big crack in the cement. It was like the rivers when they flowed, branching off into little fingers that led nowhere. Then he explored the width of the alley. Feet pushed heel-toe three times fast from one side to the other, the last toe going up the wall. He ran back and forth, each time slapping up higher on the crumbly white walls with the momentum. He imagined he was the water climbing up the sides of the river and wondered how the water could do that all day without getting tired.

Breathing hard, Jimmy listened to the grumbles in his belly. He gathered some pebbles from where the alley met the sidewalk and started practicing his aim at the garbage can. He liked the way they clinked before bouncing off and quietly thudding against the cement. *Clink, Clink, Clink.*

He looked back at Uncle and tiptoed over to his side. He took his big toe and poked Uncle's shoulder. He did that over and over for a few minutes, watching the way the shoulder rocked back into Jimmy's toe, marveling at his toe's power. He rocked him as he sang a lizard song, *Goanna, good onya, bake all day in the sun, hey, hey.* He didn't want to spend all day baking in the sun in the alley, and Hector shouldn't either.

Jimmy strained as he crouched down and threw his whole body weight into Hector to get him to roll first onto his belly and then again onto his back, while using one hand to protect Hector's head. When Hector lay in the sliver of shade of the building, Jimmy rearranged Hector's arms and legs to what looked like a comfortable position. Bored, he took out his fossils, feathers and bones, lined them up next to the white cement wall and examined them. Each time he got up to stretch his legs, his shadow fell longer and longer in the alley. Seemed like Hector was taking an awful long time to wake from the grog.

Soon there was no more clinking of dishes inside, only the sound of the money clinking in the pokies. "Bad luck, eh?" A sweaty white man in a dirty apron had come round the back door and was stuffing a bag of trash into the can in the alley. The man pointed at Uncle. "Looks like you may be here for a while."

Jimmy followed the man's gaze. "How long is a bloke usually passed out?"

The man wiped his bald head with a hanky that came out of one of the apron pockets. "Been known to need a whole night to sleep it off meself."

"Already been most of a day."

"How 'bout some chips while you wait?"

A minute later the man brought him out a red basket of greasy fish and chips and a Coke, one of the best meals Jimmy had ever eaten. He sat next to his fossils, his back against the wall, and felt the warm grease coat the insides of his mouth as the batter melted on his tongue. The salt and vinegar chips made his lips pucker. He held some fish under Hector's nose. He offered out of habit—sharing was part of being Yapa. The Coke fizz made Jimmy sneeze as he opened the can, and he accidentally slopped some over onto Hector's chest. Brown fizz tipped the white hairs that poked out of Uncle's v-neck. Jimmy watched the Coke stain spread on the white cotton like the sunshine spread in the sky. Hector was missing a good meal.

When the lights came on around town and the warmth of the sun began to fade, Jimmy ripped open the cardboard box that he'd kicked away earlier and covered Hector. He crawled to the end of the alley and watched the shop windows light up, moths and other insects whorling around like tornadoes underneath the lights. He watched the sky darken until it was black as the bitumen. The only stars that could be seen over the bright streetlights were Yaraandoo. He dodged the shadows that people cast as they walked past the alley and into the hotel for tea. He listened to the clinking plates, the pokies, a lady laughing, a car's brakes. When finally there were no more shadows of people under the lights, only the slight whir of the lights themselves and the flutter of moth wings, he crawled back down the alley. The moon did not follow him, and it felt as if the air were heavy, stale, trapped by the tightness of the walls, their mass emptier than the black of the night. How long had it been since he'd slept between walls? Already he missed the open air of the billabong, the wind off the desert. He lay next to Uncle and focused on the few stars he could finally make out. They were broken pieces of a constellation, a slice of the sky like the highways the whitefellas had carved through the desert. There was no sense of horizon to give him his bearings, only the dark canyon that Uncle had chosen for their bed.

A dog howled not far away, and he thought he heard the

scuttling of rats. Rats were feral beasts, some of the only animals Jimmy feared because they were fearless. Desert rats were bigger than the dingo pup his cousin had found wandering half-starved. Did city rats grow as big? Hector would know but he couldn't ask him. How big would that pup be now? Big enough to catch a rat? He heard a scratching near the garbage can and inched closer to Hector. He could still smell grog as Hector exhaled his wet breath onto the back of Jimmy's neck.

Behind the grog, Jimmy smelled Yuendumu. He smelled the yucca smoke that would wake him each morning as Auntie Tess cooked brekky. He would look out the window of their tin shelter and squint to see orange stripes of sun on the rocks by Wombat Hill. The stripes would become wider and wider until he couldn't stand it anymore and he'd open his eyes fully. When the stripes hit the waterhole, he knew it was okay to make noise, maybe tap on the tin walls to wake his cousins.

When he got out of bed, Mum or Tess would be standing over a fire in the pit, stirring syrupy tea, baking the damper. The smoke would fill the house with a haze that made everyone feel close. Mum made her fire with a yucca leaf since only good spirits could find their way through yucca smoke.

Yucca smoke hung in his hair all day. How he missed Mum's sweet black billy tea. He missed Tortoise Rock, with the head peeking out like Jimmy's to start the day. During creation time his Ancestor had created Tortoise Rock for his son, molding every crevice and bump like clay. Jimmy was lucky that Ancestor had taken the time to make such a wonderful place to climb. Once he'd lost a boomerang at the top. It was one that Tess had said would fetch a lot of money from the tourist shops. As he ran panicked between each sharp outcropping to find it, he'd found a pool of water, still standing in the mid-winter months. At first he thought it was full of tar, but as he looked closer, the tar began to separate itself into little squirming tadpoles. What had become of all those frogs?

Jimmy woke to the clinking of the dishes in the Isa Hotel, not to Mum's yucca smoke. "Good dreams, Hector?" He rolled over and poked the unmoving man. Shouldn't he be begging Jimmy for a cuppa like he did every morning after the grog? He yelled in Hector's ear. "Bloody wake up already."

Jimmy stood up and folded away the cardboard. He'd never heard of a man passed out so long. Maybe Hector needed a doctor. At home Mum would probably have called one of the elders from the clan to fix Hector, to drain the poisons from him. Should he walk to Aboriginal Affairs and ask for help? Should he take Hector to hospital?

As he pondered his options, he saw the white man coming around the corner with a bag of trash. Jimmy waved. "Me uncle's crook. Think he needs a doc."

The man crouched by Hector's side and took hold of his wrist. "Heart's still beating," he said, looking down into Hector's face.

Jimmy would have noticed if Hector were dead. But he didn't want to be smart with the man. "Uncle should've woken up by now, don't you think?"

The man stood and put his hands on his hips. "I'll call medics."

Jimmy watched the man go round the back of the hotel. He left Hector's side and walked to the end of the alley. People were hurrying along Miles Street as usual, everyone with a place to go.

"Hey." The man motioned him back down the alley. He stood with his back against the plaster wall, a basket of fish and chips held out to Jimmy. As Jimmy approached, the man sat down onto his bum as if his knees hurt. He patted the ground next to him for Jimmy to sit, and pushed the basket over. Jimmy offered him a piece of fish, but the man shook his head.

Jimmy let the grease warm his belly. "What you think they'll do to him in hospital?"

"May I?" The man took a chip. "Maybe some smelling salts. But I'm no doc."

Jimmy doubted smelling salts would work if the smell of fish 'n chips didn't. His belly jumped from either the greasy chips or from worry. As he finished his chips, he felt a shadow over him. An ambulance was blocking the sun from the end of the alley. He'd never seen a real one before the Isa. Now he liked to watch for them outside the hospital. Two men in white shorts and shirts were getting out, their tiny shadows leading the way. Well, Uncle'd have a ride to hospital in an ambulance and not even get to enjoy it.

The tall man whispered something to the shorter man. Then after a few listens with a stethoscope and a peek under Hector's eyelids with a flashlight, the two men hoisted Hector onto a stretcher and carried him down the alley. Jimmy followed the chips man down to the end of the alley and gave a short nod to Hector as the medics closed the door behind him.

The tall medic started round to the front of the ambulance then came back to where Jimmy stood with the chips man. "Ever ride in an ambulance before?"

"No, sir."

The medic unhinged the ambulance doors again and took Jimmy's arm. "Well then this is your lucky day. Put on a belt."

As the man secured the ambulance door behind him, Jimmy looked over at Hector's huge brown body on the white stretcher. He fingered his father's smooth bone in his pocket and clutched it in his fist. He held it tight, held Da's hand as the ambulance swung around the corner.

\\∩/

It was the mine's rumble, shaking the glasses in her plywood cabinets at six at night and six in the morning, which made it so hard for Donna to sleep in the Isa. Anticipating the morning's blast, she felt the hollow beneath her. She was sure her house lay above a giant cavern, and she worried that the infrastructure would not hold. One stick of dynamite placed a foot off, and boom. The clock flipped to 5:46. She'd slept less than three hours. After four weeks in the Isa, her circadian rhythms still beat to the time of New York.

It was spring in New York—Kate had e-mailed that the cherry blossoms at the reservoir had sprung open overnight. Kate had jogged baby Stella and four-year-old Ryan around the dirt path, and they'd come home with fistfuls of the pinkish-white petals. Donna shook away the thought that if all had gone as it should have, *she* would have been jogging her son alongside Kate's double stroller to the pace of the familiar conversation.

In Mount Isa it was obvious that winter was approaching only by the shortening of the days. It was thirty-six degrees Celsius in the daytime, then down to nine degrees at night. Nothing moved during the day except for the shimmering air. Mirages hovered a foot off the ground like poisonous vapor, and the sun felt too close. It was a place to burn sin away.

There was no point in staying in bed to watch the coins dancing next to the gray velvet bag and her parents' photo on the bureau. Donna swung her legs out of bed and pulled on her T-shirt and running shorts. She was stretching her Achilles tendon when the blast brought on her usual morning stomach flip-flops.

Donna rounded Gracie Street, turned onto Marie and with

a last look at the pink smoke waving her off like a starting flag, she headed out the Barkly Highway—more of a road than what Donna considered a highway—which stretched a hundred and eighteen kilometers from the Isa to Cloncurry with nothing between. The Barkly forged on through Julia Creek along the Flinders River, and finally to Townsville on the coast.

The sun was turning the spinifex into fingers pricked with blood. All Donna could hear was the thud, thud, thud of her Nikes slapping the road until a kookaburra laughed at her from a barbed-wire fence. She sang a childhood song: *Kookaburra sits on the old gum tree, merry, merry king of the bushes, he. Laugh, kookaburra, laugh, kookaburra, gay your life must be.* She would describe the laugh as eerie, not gay.

She heard a crunch alongside her and peered through the wattle. Was something following her? She'd never checked to see if it was safe to run alone, but she hadn't wanted to hear that it wasn't. The kookaburra cackled again, and she had to restrain herself from bolting back to the Isa. Damn it, her plan was to run sixteen kilometers before work today, and she wasn't going to let a kookaburra stop her.

Last weekend, she'd driven out the Barkly in search of a destination point for her run, but had found nothing. The terrain was like patterned wallpaper, ever repeating. After driving back and forth on the empty highway, she went to Kmart to buy fluorescent pink spray-paint to mark off kilometers on the side of the road.

With relief, Donna reached the eighth pink marker that she'd spray-painted on the side of the cracking asphalt. She turned back toward the smokestacks, feeling strong. Her pace quickened now that she was no longer running into a vast horizon of nothingness. Three pink marks later, with only five kilometers to go, she registered her vibrating beeper, the vibrations matching almost perfectly the shocks running from the highway up through her knees and to her lower back. Thud, thud, buzz.

Emergency. Andy. The page had been sent fifteen minutes earlier, from the Doomadgee clinic, but had just come through to the pager. Donna must have been running out of range. She kept her pace and put the pager back, got the cell phone out of her fanny-pack, while remembering that she should call it a waist-pack since she'd come to understand (after miscommunication with a patient) that the Aussie word for vagina was *fanny.*

She dialed Doomadgee, trying to remember what Andy looked like. Since their first meeting, he'd called daily, asking basic medical questions, making sure that his diagnosis and treatment plans were right. She was impressed with his diligence and composure. It couldn't be easy to be in training and have to consult an attending physician via telephone. She guessed he was lonely in the bush, since after a serious consult he would always turn the conversation personal at the end and would not let her off the line.

"What's up?" She puffed into the phone.

"Twenty-nine-year-old woman. Hemothorax. Left lung collapsed, and I'm afraid for the right." Andy's voice was barely a whisper. Donna stopped in mid-stride and kicked a stone across the road. "Do you have a chest tube in?"

"I've never done one. I don't know how."

Donna felt her breath catch. She shouldn't have run outside the range of the pager, should have found someone to cover her. "They send you out to Doomadgee without emergency medicine training?"

"There's a waiting room full of family."

"Did you call the Flying Docs?"

"They'll be here in three hours."

"I'll teach you to do a tube over the phone." Donna looked around. She was surrounded by the smooth bark of the wattle, dappled red in the morning sun. The first time she'd seen a chest tube put in, she'd run from the ER and thrown up in the hall. "Don't let the family see you unsure of yourself. Hook up a speakerphone next to the patient."

"We don't have one out here." Donna felt her phone slip in her sweaty palm. She wanted to run, to escape. "Give me to your nurse and I'll give her instructions to pass on to you. Get the patient on a morphine-versed drip and take a Valium if you need one."

Donna walked down the side of the road kicking stones and imagined the small clinic. The waiting room filled by parents, husband, friends, and the young woman, a small Esther, lying on the examining table, her chest filling with blood. Did she have children? Were the children playing between the ankles of the grown-ups, oblivious that in the next room the pressure was building in their mother's chest and would soon collapse the other lung and implode the heart? Or were they still in their beds, about to wake to a world without a mother?

The nurse got on the phone. "Alice here. Patient is medicated." But Alice didn't say whether she and the doctor were.

Donna looked out over the rocks and shrubs, pictured her own fingers feeling for the third rib, numbing the skin and muscles with an eight-gauge needle. She talked the nurse through the incision, precise in her instructions. "Go over the fourth rib, erring on the side of cutting into four. If you get too close to the third, you nick an artery and the patient bleeds out." She'd made that mistake once when she was practicing the procedure on a cute three-legged beagle.

Donna heard her own words being echoed imperfectly by the nurse to Andy. "That is not what I said. Say it exactly, Alice." Feeling a presence, Donna looked over her shoulder. Only vast bush. Maybe she felt the kite—or was it a crow—wheeling high overhead? She quickened her stride toward town. She heard Andy asking the nurse to hold the skin taut.

The dicey part was using your index finger to pry open a hole between the muscle and ribs without piercing anything vital, then immediately threading the tube through the hole under your finger. The venal blood should rush out like a chocolate fountain and the patient should soon breathe more easily. Crude, but highly effective.

Donna stared at the road as Andy bore through the woman's chest with his gloved finger. She tried to imagine Andy's hands, willed them to precision. The road was beginning to hold the heat of the morning sun that soon would meet her in shimmering waves. She looked down at her legs, covered in a thin coat of red dust. She tried to brush them off as she walked, but the dust abraded her skin. "Be ready with the tube," she reminded, and heard Alice repeat her words.

"Where is it?" growled Andy. "Alice, that's you."

"Bugger," echoed in Donna's ears as she heard the phone clatter.

"Alice?" Donna yelled. She heard someone rummaging around and once Andy cursed, "Bloody tube."

Was that *bloody* as in *blood* or as in an Australian swear word? Donna eyed the sky hoping to see the airplane of the Flying Doctors cruising overhead on its way to Doomadgee. But the sky was clear, turning blue with only a few high clouds that would soon be burned off by the sun. The crow wheeled closer.

She swiped at a branch of a gum that overhung the road, stripping off a handful of silver-green leaves. She raised her arm, ready to fling leaves far into the scrub and stopped, her hand held high, as she caught the eye of a big red standing by a ghost gum less than twenty feet from the road. Her first kangaroo sighting. Its coat was the same color as the red dirt stuck to her body, and his belly was the color of bleached rocks.

She brought her arm down slowly and let the leaves float to the ground by her side. Her other hand clutched the phone closer to her ear. "Aha, here 'tis," she heard from a far-off Alice. Donna let the sweat drip down the tip of her nose without catching it. She stood as a statue, the silence magnified by the singing grasshoppers.

Alice returned to the phone. "I don't think we have any arterial bleeds."

Only then did Donna feel the pain in her lower back caused by holding herself at attention. As Andy sewed the tube to the patient's side, Donna and the kangaroo looked at each other. The air shimmered between them and knife-blades of spinifex waved slightly in the wind. The roo's nose twitched. Donna breathed in the dry warm dust and the hint of fresh grasses. The patient had been lucky.

She was about to hang up when she heard Andy grunt, "We're losing her, damn it."

Donna closed her eyes. A successful outcome would have been too much to hope for. They'd either been too late, or Andy had nicked an artery without realizing it. It would be hard to do a chest tube perfectly your first time.

Donna imagined the young mother dying on the exam table. Dead from what accident? In the car maybe, walking out of it relieved that she hadn't broken an arm or leg, not realizing she was slowly dying until thirty minutes later when she couldn't catch her breath and the chest pains became unbearable?

Minutes later the dreaded words came in Andy's cracking voice. "Bad luck." The line went dead. Donna knew how it went from there. Like a movie playing on the back of her eyelids, she saw Andy talking to the family. The devastation in the husband's eyes, surrounded by children whining for *Mommy*.

Her worst patient loss on her list of the dead was Judy Allen, a young mother who hemorrhaged while in labor. As the newborn's first cries rang out, Judy had taken her last breaths. A thousand times she'd imagined Judy's three-year-old child wondering why a baby had come home from the hospital but Mommy hadn't. That three-year-old would be a teenager now, probably with no memory of his mother.

Here, Donna wasn't worried about liability. Unlike in the U.S., there'd be no lawyers to reconstruct the events of the morning in an attempt to lay blame. And there was no one in the hospital to nail her for running outside of pager range. Doctor Archie, the *locums* hospital administrator, wouldn't pay attention to such details. His was a temporary position as well, and he was busy exploring the bush most days, never physically in the hospital.

It had been years since she'd lost a patient under the age of fifty, and in four weeks in Australia, she'd lost two. Death was all around her, following her. The Galah, the spider. Dead trees. Dead land. An inauspicious start to a new life.

She opened her eyes as the crow cawed above and flew off. The kangaroo hadn't moved. She called the Doomadgee clinic to ask the last question. "What was her name?"

She added *Jill, no last name*, to her mental list, right after Michael Robson. As she zipped the phone into her pack, the roo flicked an ear. The red's forearms dangled useless against its chest, but its tail was tensed like a third leg. She'd watched kangaroo videos on her computer in New York as she prepared for Australia. She remembered the males boxing with their hind legs in their quest to win the right to mate, jumping three feet in the air to try to open up the bellies of their opponent with their sharp black hind claws, grunting and screeching. She made a fleeting wish that this roo would rip open her belly, rid her of the pain, the guilt, the list of names, but she quickly took it back. With Donna's vicious optimism came a will to live that she could never squelch.

She turned a quarter-turn, keeping the roo in her peripheral vision and, finding the smokestacks, stepped forward on the road and began to run. A moment later the roo took off in giant jumps, parallel to the road. Donna's dusty legs moved, but she didn't see or feel the road. Instead, she ran to the names, each syllable of the dead beating out against the pavement. Beating them out to forget and grinding them in to remember. Her lungs burst to catch air and her thigh muscles tightened as she watched the animal outdistance her, fading into the bright light, its graceful leaps creating a path over the pointed spines of the spinifex. The roo barely touched the tips of the grass, undulating above it like a bird in flight.

She was still kilometers from the pea green house when she stopped to watch puffs of dust floating along the ground, glinting in the sun in the roo's wake like fairy dust. She ran off the road into the bush and dragged her open palm through the dusty air, grabbing at the lingering dust and rubbing it over her body as she stumbled over the uneven ground.

That evening, Donna stared out past the comatose Aboriginal man, over the flat roofs of the nurses' quarters and into the bush beyond, where the setting sun was turning the grass to pale orange. She jumped as Esther elbowed her.

"What ya dreaming up, doc?"

Before she could answer, Doctor Archie poked his head in the room. "Hey Donna, I've been looking for you. Flying Docs can't take you to Doomadgee tomorrow. You'll have to drive. Is this your first drive out of town?"

Donna nodded.

Archie sprung into the visitor's chair, legs sprawling outward so Esther had to step over his legs to fix the patient's bed. "Make sure both petrol tanks are full. You can go for hours without seeing a shack once you leave town. Always keep water in the boot and never leave your car. You leave it, you die of exposure and dehydration in one day. People break down, get off the road and figure *I'll just see what's on the other side of that hill*, but every hill's the same in the never-never. No landmarks, sun's overhead. You'll never find your way back. At least the metal on the car will glint if we send out a search plane."

Donna looked to Esther for help, but Esther's back was toward Archie as he gesticulated, "If you get stuck behind a road train, wait until he puts on his indicator, then haul your bum as fast as you can to overtake him. Trust him and watch carefully because he won't give you a second chance."

Donna had no idea what he was talking about. "Maybe I..."

Archie popped out of the chair like he'd been bitten by a wolf spider. "Good luck." And he was gone.

Esther rolled the patient over to change his bed sheet and smiled at Donna. "That's some hot air the bush doesn't need." Maybe she noted Donna's distress, because Esther's smile faded. "Clinic's not too far. Only six hours in the Dry. Can't drive in the Wet." Esther smoothed the sheet by the patient's feet, even though it was already smooth.

Donna dreaded the thought of driving alone into the bush. "You call six hours a short drive?" Donna flipped through the patient's charts. Alcohol-induced coma, admitted by a resident at noon. Condition stable.

As they exited the patient's room together, Esther took Donna's arm. "I'll come with you."

Donna shook her head. "I'll be fine. The American doc doesn't need an escort."

"Tomorrow's me day off anyway, so it's only Friday I've got to take. Besides, remember I mentioned me man, Jocko?"

"So I am a ride for a booty call?" Donna pinched Esther's arm.

Esther swiveled her huge hips and strutted away, saying, "Aren't you off to that squash date? You should get some too."

"Eight-thirty tomorrow morning in the car park. Don't be late." As she made her way down the stairs, she thought back to a few nights ago at the Isa Hotel. Nan had joined Donna and Esther for beers. Donna had told the women about the baby and Greg in detail, Nan told them about the abusive boyfriend she'd escaped in Perth, and Esther shared rollicking stories about Jocko and his prowess in bed. Each gave a personal nugget in return for friendship.

In the States, she never would have been hanging out with the nurses. But here in the Isa, there was no hierarchy to worry about, no reputations to guard. In the Isa, it was easy to make friends. They all were *passing through*—even those who'd been there for ten years or more. Unafraid of goodbyes and eager to say hello.

Donna checked her watch—it was already five-thirty so she'd be five minutes late—applied her lipstick in the rearview mirror, and drove carefully to the squash club. She'd met Nick, handsome in a fifty-something way, at Sunday's round robin and he'd asked her for a game that night. He was one of Isa's top players, so Donna knew he hadn't asked her for the challenge of playing her. She'd been an A player at Princeton, but now after years of only sporadic games, she could call herself at best a low B.

Donna had had no problem getting dates in college and med school. She looked like her Italian mother and had been told more than once that she looked like a famous Bollywood actress. But it had been many years since she'd been *dating*. She'd had two flings after Greg moved out, one with an old boyfriend so it was completely non-threatening, and the other a one-nighter with a ski instructor when she went to Hunter Mountain for a weekend. Donna had sensed that the instructor—she couldn't think of his name—slept with his female clients as a perk of the job, and she'd hustled out of his bed.

Esther and Nan had teased her that it was a disgrace that she'd been in the Isa for a month and hadn't gotten laid. Mount Isa was like a ski town—full of men from all over the world and lacking women because of the mine. It was the right place to come as a newly-divorced single woman if you were interested in meeting men. Donna wouldn't mind some sex, but she was determined to take it slowly.

Nick was waiting for her in front of their court. He greeted her with a peck on the cheek before Donna ran to the locker room to change. Nick had the ball warmed up for them when they entered the court, passing the test as a gentleman.

Donna and Nick volleyed in silence. She breathed in the scent of the new rubber ball, felt the familiar sweep of her arm and the swish of the loaner racquet, heard the satisfying sharp twang of the ball hitting the wall. During their games, conversation flowed with the rhythm of competition. They played until the next pair forced them off the court.

At dinner they drank Australian wine and fell into easy conversation about careers, their lives, their hopes for the future. Nick worked in finance for the mine and traveled half the year. He'd been married, had two kids already graduated from university and living in Brisbane. When the waiter asked them to settle their check, they realized they were the last ones in the restaurant. Nick took her hand and led her out to his car. As he opened her door he blocked the way, and kissed her. Donna felt her hips push forward against his body. He stepped away and she slid in to the passenger seat, mentally running through her options, Esther's words in the back of her head. She was tempted to invite him home, but she had to get up early the next morning for Doomadgee. No, she'd hold back. He'd ask her out again. She had him drive her back to her car at the squash club.

As she got into her Land Rover, Donna imagined Esther's scolding that would come in the morning. Nick called to her from his open window, "I'll call when I get back from Brisbane. I look forward to seeing you again."

Esther met her at the hospital early the next morning. Donna eyed her own full duffle bag in the trunk as Esther threw a practically-empty plastic bag in the back seat, along with two gallons of water. "So Archie was right about the water?"

"Shouldn't go out bush without it." Esther strapped on her seatbelt and stared forward as if willing the car to move.

Donna crawled into the driver's seat and started the car. "Need to stop at Riversleigh to buy a map. Hope they're open."

"They're not open and I know the way." Esther sat with a straight spine, the curly black hair piled on top of her head almost brushing the car ceiling. "Get on the Barkly toward Tennant Creek."

Donna was reluctant to leave town without a map, but Esther looked so sturdy and reliable. With a sigh, she steered the car out Main to the corner of Jasmine. A sign pointing west read *The Alice 1194 Kilometers*. The other direction read *Townsville 886 Kilometers*. Nothing worth noting in between.

One minute the windshield was full of aluminum siding and the next it was full of wattle. Esther turned to her. "So?"

Donna watched the speedometer climb over one-hundred. "I like him. No sex."

The Land Rover sped along the smooth bitumen and Esther hummed without comment. They'd been driving for forty-five minutes of the six-hour drive when suddenly Esther sat forward. "Road train."

"What?

"Pull over!" Esther pointed frantically at the shoulder. "On the gravel and roll up your window!"

Donna did as she was told and moments later the truck came barreling past them pulling three trailers filled with triple tiers of sheep, driving straight down the center. Sheep piss spattered the windshield.

Esther was fingering the silver choker that was almost buried in a flap of skin around her neck. Donna pulled back onto the road. "Now I know what Archie was talking about." She'd just reached one hundred again when she passed a dead cow with four legs up in the air.

"Usually, you'd see a cloud of black flies round something that big. Fresh kill. Trucker shoulda stopped to eat it!" Esther said.

"Why is there a cow out here?"

"Road crosses a station. Cows got to be able to wander far to find food."

The next kill looked like a line that crossed the lane but turned out to be a long green snake, freshly flattened. Donna approached a dead roo with three kites perched on top. *Whap.*

The front of the car shook and Esther yelled, "What'd you do that for?"

"What happened?" But by the sight of black feathers floating up over the hood, she knew the answer. She'd never thought to slow or swerve. Birds always moved out of the way before the car hit. "Did I kill it?"

Esther looked at her as she'd looked at the stupid cow. "Them. Lucky for that kangaroo bar or you'd have a dent in the bonnet."

"Why didn't they fly out of the way?" Donna thought of the beautiful hawks she'd just killed. Her hands shook on the wheel.

Esther looked straight ahead, her hands relaxed in her lap. "Kites ate too much. Too heavy to fly."

Donna sighed and focused on the wattle, on the never-ending expanse of scrub on either side of the road, until Esther pointed to a wooden sign ahead. Donna slowed. Esther rolled up her window as they turned onto the packed dirt road and cleared her throat. "Can you close your window, Doc?"

"I hate air conditioning. Don't you?"

"Hate the dust more."

Donna glanced around the car's interior. After only a minute on the packed dirt, a fine layer of red silt covered everything. She rolled the window up and pressed the air conditioning. As they threw up clouds of dust that turned the clear sky cloudy in her rearview mirror, Donna was relieved there would be no more roadtrains.

"Couple hours we'll reach Gregory Downs," Esther said.

Donna couldn't believe she was taking a dirt road into nothingness, but she trusted Esther. "Would have to be named Gregory, huh?"

Donna sped along the dirt. She'd absolutely hated Greg when he first asked for a divorce. But Kate had helped her see that the stress of their careers and Donna's single-minded focus on getting pregnant for so many years had taken its toll. Like so many infertile couples, Donna had lost sight of everything but the pursuit of baby-making, so by the end, there was nothing left of their marriage. She'd refused to travel in case it was an opportune time to try in vitro. She hadn't wanted to go to exotic locales because the anti-malarial drug would set her back three months. She and Greg had lost passion, or maybe there had *never* been enough passion to carry them through.

Donna married Greg before she understood what she needed from a partner. Thirty would not have been young for most people, but it was for doctors. Years of schooling and training seemed to artificially strand them in young adulthood, so that they matured years after their non-medical peers. When they were twenty-six, Donna marveled at Kate's self-assurance and her financial independence as an investment banker, while Donna, still but an intern, was stuck in the role of student.

"Greg was my best friend. Probably never should have become my lover."

"That's why you need a husband and a lover."

They passed Thorntonia, which had only a few tin shacks, not even a pump to refill the gas tanks, then again were surrounded by rocks and wattle. "Just wish he'd left me for someone more exotic than his secretary, world traveler and freethinker that he is."

Esther reached over and put her strong hand on Donna's thigh. "We surround ourselves with the people we need."

Donna prided herself on her diagnostic skills, but she'd missed the signs with Greg. The demise of her marriage was like the common cold, perhaps not preventable, but absolutely foreseeable. How often he'd spoken of his secretary's inexhaustible *joie de vivre*?

Surprisingly, Donna was more angry at the secretary than at Greg. How could the young woman look herself in the mirror each morning, knowing about Donna's desire for a pregnancy, and then the death of the baby? She slowed as termite mounds formed a New York City skyline. Humans were not the first to reach for the stars with their homes. A few high wisps of clouds trailed above the mounds.

She realized they'd driven through a forest of spindly trees once the land lacked anything over knee-height. When the red dirt was dotted with only a few clumps of spinifex for as far as she could see, Donna asked, "Do you really believe that you can have more than one man in your life?"

"And a man can have more than one woman. Works if there is balance."

Donna shook her head. "Hard to imagine going from one man's bed to another. And I'm not willing to share again."

Esther tapped her window. "You will be, dead cert."

Donna wondered what it would be like to sleep with Nick. With his travels, he could have women all over the world. Should that matter to her if she didn't love him? Maybe not as long as she made him use a condom. Unprotected sex was one thing she'd miss about marriage. Yet she doubted that Greg had used a condom with his secretary. One couldn't protect against everything. Death and disease were always lurking in wait.

They stopped to pee and Esther squatted on the side of the road. After checking the car for damage from the kite—Donna almost gagged as she saw the little pieces of meat frying on the front grill—Donna looked around for a place that was more discreet, then figured *what the hell* and squatted a few feet off.

Esther dozed and Donna watched the never-ending sameness, fiddled with the CD player and sang along to keep awake. After passing through The Gregory, as Esther called it, the road ended and they headed west on another unpaved road. Donna was deep into the rhythm of travel, marking the increasing size of the gum trees, when Esther opened her eyes. "Slow down. Here's the road to Doomadgee."

The road to Doomadgee was a dirt path that led into the scrub. Donna stopped the car and looked at Esther. "Sure?"

"Shortcut. Hold on." Esther got out of the car and fiddled with the passenger wheel and then the driver side wheel.

Donna leaned out her window and called, "Anything wrong?"

Esther shouted, "You'll need four-wheel drive."

When Esther slid back into her seat, hands red from the dirt, Donna asked, "Isn't this car always a four-wheel drive car?"

Esther clicked into her seatbelt. "Didn't Archie show you how to operate it?"

Donna shook her head.

"You did fill both petrol tanks before we left, didn't you?"

Donna nodded. Luckily when she'd said *Fill it up, please*, the gas station attendant asked if she meant both tanks.

Ten minutes later they bumped up to a beautiful square house with a wrap-around porch, full of Aboriginal women lolling about on elegantly crafted iron chairs and tables, some with a smoke, others watching the air shimmer above the hot sand.

"Old homestead used as the art center," Esther said as they got out of the car.

After the air conditioning, the hot dry air hit Donna hard. She checked the key chain thermometer Greg had given her as a Christmas stocking stuffer. 41 Celsius, 106 Fahrenheit. Doomadgee was close to the Northcoast—Donna longed to keep driving, to see the end of the land.

"G'day." A thin old woman with shiny white hair came over and gave Esther a hug. She wore a threadbare T-shirt and no bra, and nodded at Donna.

Esther said, "Meet Doctor Donna. Medicine woman from the Isa. She's out to see Doomadgee. Give her a tour?"

The woman smiled a huge toothless smile and clasped Donna's hand. Unlike with a handshake, she didn't let go. "Me name's Pearl. Come see Witchetty Grub Dreaming, me Dreaming. But you'll buy Honey Ant."

This was the third-world travel Donna was used to, the cab driver stopping *for a moment* at a shop *on the way* to her destination, then the craftswomen pushing their wares. She'd taken tea with rug salesmen in Istanbul, negotiated over thankas in tiny shops filled with kerosene smoke in Nepal, had been practically taken hostage in Laos until she bought a ceramic Buddha that cracked in half before she got it home. All those possessions sat in storage now in New York, holding her memories of far-off cultures and adventures. She was surprised Esther had led her into such a trap, but the traveler in Donna was too interested to be angry.

Pearl led them into the homestead. Ignoring the stares of the other women, Donna followed Esther up the four wide steps. Donna felt dizzy, her eyes unable to focus as she was met on all sides and the floor by color, dots, and squiggles. The room looked like one huge graffiti mural, not an inch of space where one's eyes could rest without being bombarded by movement or color. Even the faded wallpaper was a sea of blue daisies. It was a departure from the blank slate of random rocks and scrub trees they'd just traveled through.

Five women were hunched over their canvases, spines curved, with paint brushes sticking out of old coffee cans. A can of brown had spilled and the stain oozed over the corner of a canvas, but no one seemed to notice. Empty packages of Tim Tams and Arnott's biscuits littered the ground. Black flies buzzed and a dog wandered around, looking for a spot to lie down. It sniffed a spot, circled a few times and, ignored, curled up right in the middle of an old woman's canvas. The smell was of acrylics and dirt, tea, and meat cooking somewhere. A child darted in, bent down to whisper in a woman's ear, then darted out the back door. Donna craned to see where the child was going. It seemed like the building was alone. But it was possible that the mesa behind it hid an entire town.

Above, a ceiling fan clunked. Donna's eyes went to the pressed tin squares etched with flowers that covered the ceiling. There was not a stick of furniture in the room. No easels, no benches. Just color.

She stepped gingerly between the canvases as Pearl led her to an earthy-hued painting. They stood above it. "Beautiful colors," Donna said. It was made of dots, circles, broken lines.

Pearl pointed to the bottom and moved to the top as she spoke. "This is me story and this is me Land. Wintertime now so we paint winter colors. Come summer the colors will change."

Donna looked at the canvas in silence. What else was she supposed to say?

Pearl pointed at some inverted *u* shapes. "These are the women. The shape is what is left in the sand when they stand up. Next to them are their digging sticks and pitti bowls. You can find the witchetty grubs everywhere you see these digging sticks."

"What's this?" Donna pointed at seven concentric half-circles, each nestled into the next.

"Ah. The healer. You find the power of woman."

Donna had been looking for a more tangible answer. "Another symbol for women?"

"The seven sisters, the Pleiades." Pearl pointed to three circles. "Waterholes. Need to know where to find water."

Donna nodded and stood there a moment to show respect. Pearl didn't seem concerned whether Donna liked the painting. She took Donna's arm and turned her toward a neighbor's canvas, pointing at some broken lines. "Goanna's tracks" she gestured at a ring of circles. "Smooth boulders left after he made a meal of wild onions during the Dreaming."

Esther inserted, "Good wild onions still grow there."

Then Pearl led Donna around the room. The painting Donna liked best was the Rainbow Serpent, who traveled through the earth leaving waterholes whereever he lifted his head. The painting had rich brown lines tracing his path, with blue circles placed like ornaments on a Christmas tree. A line of blue ran up the center of it. "And that?" Donna pointed.

"Lawn Hill Gorge," Pearl replied. Lawn Hill was south of Doomadgee and northwest of Isa. It was too bad they hadn't had time to see it, but Donna planned to visit on her next trip to the Doomadgee clinic. She'd read about this oasis in the desert, formed when an ancient meteorite collided with the earth.

The maps Greg and she had studied on their treks in Nepal and southeast Asia flashed through her mind. She'd loved the hours they'd sat shoulder-to-shoulder, plotting journeys, making sense of a foreign land's history through its hills, valleys, lakes, and rivers. She'd loved that the maps turned wandering into a journey, linking remote villages to each other, giving her direction as she and Greg marched through the dense March fog of the Himalayas, some days not seeing farther than the pack in front of them. She laid her palm on the Rainbow Serpent painting and felt as if the ground were more solid beneath her. "It is a topographical map, right? These are real places in all these paintings."

Pearl let out a loud peal of laughter. "We aren't painting dots willy-nilly. We sell our maps in Sydney and Kardiya take them home to their country but don't even know how to use them. Pay good money for our maps."

Esther squeezed Donna's shoulder. "We Behold our Land from the sky. That's how we paint it."

Donna wanted to buy the Rainbow Serpent painting with its distinct reference to a major Queensland landmark. She imagined being able to explain the painting to a guest as it hung in her apartment next to photos of Lawn Hill Gorge. "How much for the Rainbow Serpent?" Donna asked, her hand still on the painting.

Pearl shook her head. "You'll buy the Honey Ant." Pearl pulled her toward a painting in browns, blacks, and whites. There were no pretty blues to rest her eyes upon. Would Pearl not make money if Donna bought Rainbow Serpent? Why had she shown it to her? "But I'd prefer…"

"Honey Ant." Pearl put her palm on the back of Donna's head and pushed it so she'd to look down over the painting. She held it there so that Donna could not look up and Donna marveled at the old woman's strength. Donna felt her neck tense in response and was surprised at that moment to feel the fingers of Pearl's other hand slowly massaging her neck, so that she'd no choice but to relax as she stretched her neural spine. As she looked down at the Honey Ant Dreaming, her eyes became heavy in their sockets, her lids drooped, and the dots began to shimmer beneath her.

The land was opening up below her, dots were clumps of spinifex, the waterhole gleamed amid the scrub, brown, not blue, with its muddy bottom. At that moment she lost her body, became a bird that flew above, could see the land as she flew from one end to another. Below her, spinifex rippled like waves, yet she could see that every piece of it was static, had its own personality, unlike the ever-changing waters of the ocean. She saw the women digging with their digging sticks, standing in chest-deep holes where Donna could see dirt years layered one atop the other, like a seven-layer cake. The women dumped ants into their dilly bags. Ants swarmed at the women's feet trying to guard their larders.

Pearl stopped massaging, took her hand from Donna's head, and Donna was back in her body. She'd floated out of her body once before—in the hospital when she'd lost the baby. She'd hovered over the hospital bed, watching her body in the throes of labor, pitying herself below. When she'd told Greg about it, he'd said, *Morphine high.*

"How did you do that?" Donna looked around the colorful room, which she saw was not the opposite of the barren land— it *was* the land.

Pearl's skinny, wrinkled hand grasped Donna's. "Yapa magic. Like it?"

"I'd like it again."

"Esther'll teach you some magic." Pearl bent her tiny body in half and retrieved the honey ant canvas. She pressed it into Donna's hand. "Two-hundred-fifty for the Doctor."

When they were back in the car, Donna watched Esther buckle her seat belt. Her fingers—hairy down to the last knuckle—were as graceful as sea anemones rippling in the gentle ocean current of a reef. Even in the hospital chaos, Esther seemed to let the tides of panic flow over her so that every move of her hands and large body was purposeful, calculated to flow with her surroundings. Donna started to turn on the engine and then stopped. "Pearl made me fly over the Dreaming painting. She said you could do that too."

Esther's sea anemone hands smoothed her pants, then she folded one over the other in her lap. Her body faced straight ahead, did not turn towards Donna. "Pearl is a wise woman of high initiation. She has strong magic." Esther pointed to the right, still looking out the front window. "Go that way. Clinic's at the very end of the road."

Donna took her hands off the wheel, made them mirror Esther's, and followed Esther's gaze to the women on the porch of the homestead. "Tell me about the magic."

"Our medicine. Taps into the spirit energy."

Even though she did not look at Esther, Donna could feel her, knew exactly how far apart their shoulders were from the other. Was that spirit energy? "What can you do?"

Esther chuckled, "I Dreamt you, that first day in the car park."

As Donna started the ignition, put the clutch into gear and followed the road to the right, she thought of her own vivid dreams and the angel boy. She turned to look at Esther's profile. Her nose was almost hidden by her high round cheeks. "But I was already beside you."

Esther's cheek rose a tad with her smile, hiding her round nose even further. "I *learned* you from the Galah."

Donna drove slower than twenty KPH, and sure enough, behind the homestead, the road opened up around a mesa into town. "Well, that makes sense," Donna snorted. They passed three houses, a general store, and a one-pump Esso which looked like it was right out of Mayberry. "Can you help the American woman understand?"

"You are making fun. But I knew. You will be my friend and Queensland will always be your home, even if you do not live here."

Donna thought about how peaceful she'd felt as she floated over the painting. Her body held tensions she never knew existed, so losing her body had given her a carefree lightness she'd never felt before. "What did it feel like to know me?"

"Pictures popped into me head like on the telly."

ESP. Donna's mother had had a well-honed sixth sense. Before the days of Caller ID she could always tell who'd be on the phone before she picked up. She'd announce it proudly then pick up the receiver, leaving Donna and her father shaking their heads in amazement. Donna reached over and put her own hand on top of Esther's. It looked so small in comparison. "I hope we will always be friends."

They passed ten more houses and Esther pointed to a gray-sided trailer. "Alice's. That's where we'll stay the night."

Donna hadn't thought of making sleeping arrangements. She'd figured there was a room for her to sleep in at the clinic. But that must be where Andy lived. "Not at Jocko's?"

"He doesn't have a place here. Shacks up with his kin. There's the clinic."

Ahead, at the very end of town was a small white-sided house. Donna pulled into the clinic driveway. Tucking her long dark hair behind her ears, she followed Esther through the flimsy screen door of the clinic, and Donna let her eyes adjust from the sun's glare. There was a toilet and sink off to the side of the dingy waiting room. The door to the toilet seemed to be falling off its hinges. Five of the same orange Queensland Health bucket chairs they had in the Isa were lined up against the waiting room's faded green walls. She imagined the family of *Jill, no last name* who had died from the hemothorax, sitting in those uncomfortable chairs. There were no magazines or soothing posters to have distracted them. Only pieces of paper tacked randomly to the wall with push pins, urging patients to *Wash Up Before You Eat*, and reminding them that *Condoms Save Lives*. On a wall filled with dried pieces of old masking tape, there was a 1950s eye chart, faded to washed-out watercolors.

Donna excused herself and ducked into the toilet. She looked in the tarnished mirror. Her hands were red from the dirt of the road, and her face and hair were caked with dust. She splashed her face with water, then relished the feel of rough paper towel on her skin.

When she opened the door, both Andy and Esther turned to look at her. She was suddenly self-conscious that the toilet was still making gurgling sounds from the flush. She reminded herself that as medical people, they all knew that everyone had to pee.

"Welcome to Doomadgee." Andy stood with his hands deep in his pockets—just like Greg had used to stand—rocking back and forth in his round-toed Aussie boots. "Come with me and I'll show you the clinic."

She and Esther followed Andy three steps down the hall that led to the exam room, crowded with an x-ray machine, blood pressure cuff, blood-draw trays, and a microscope. Across from the exam room was Andy's office. The office was stuffed with a desk, chair, and an x-ray window. That was it for the clinic.

Andy pointed up a back staircase. "Me bedroom's upstairs, but it's too much of a mess to show you." He looked pointedly at Donna as he added, "Maybe you can come up later to see it after I give it a tidy."

Donna imagined the room strewn with beer bottles, dirty blue jeans, and boxer shorts like the boys' dorms at Princeton. "That's okay."

"So what's Donna's schedule?" asked Esther with her hands on her hips and her eye on the door.

Andy led them back into the exam room, picked up a list of patient names, and handed it to Donna. "Clinic starts at nine tomorrow. Didn't know when you'd make it here today." Andy put his hand out to take the schedule back. "I can take you on a bush tour this afternoon, though Doctor Donna doesn't look dressed for it."

Donna felt their eyes travel from her sandals, up her sundress, to her face. She'd dressed for the clinic, not having anticipated hiking or anything else. Esther waved. "I'm not on duty here. See you tomorrow when we leave." She called over her shoulder, "Bring the doc back to Alice's, eh?"

Donna watched the door slam. "Maybe we should go over chest tubes."

Andy's face was smooth, no smile, no frown. "We can do that. Let me get the supplies." He pulled a cart from the corner and laid out the few instruments needed: blades, tubes, sutures. He stood back. "I'm listening."

Donna approached the exam table, which was missing a body to practice on. What was there to show? Anyone could read about putting in a chest tube, but you had to *do* it, make it part of the memory of your fingers. She laid her hands on the cold instrument tray. It was too late for *Jill, no last name.* "Let's go for a walk. Can we go easy? I didn't bring other shoes."

Andy nodded without smiling. "Easy it is." He grabbed his wide-brimmed leather hat from the coat rack and led Donna out the door to his Queensland Health Land Rover.

She was sorry she'd brought up the chest tube without a plan on how to instruct him. She wanted to help the young doc, not make him feel guilty. She tucked her skirt around her legs as she slid into the car—which was an older version of hers—and after Andy closed his door, she cleared her throat. "I never apologized for being out of pager range when you had that hemothorax."

He rubbed the scruff on the back of his neck. "I poked an artery. Wasn't too late to save her."

Donna noted how badly he needed a haircut. "It happens to everyone."

He put his hand on her knee and gave it a squeeze before starting the engine. "I almost quit. Thought maybe I picked the wrong profession."

She was taken aback by the gesture, his hand on her bare skin, but she reminded herself that this was the Outback, its working relationships as casual as can be. "What stopped you?"

He shifted into gear. "Dead girl's family. Aussies don't expect some daddy's always there to save our bums. You go out bush, you take care of yourself."

Americans were the opposite. Donna had seen Americans hiking Anapurna and ignoring rock slide warnings, assuming their cell phones and an American passport could save them in any emergency. She looked behind the car, the dust cloud obscuring any view of Doomadgee. "We can leave the clinic unmanned this afternoon?"

He looked at her as they bumped along. "Like I said, Aboriginals don't expect us to be there for them. Never asked for us to be here." He opened his mouth, then shut it as if struggling for words. After a moment he said, "They expect miracles from white medicine, it's true. Family was surprised that I couldn't save her. But they weren't angry. Pitied me maybe, for thinking I could in the first place."

She watched Andy's hand maneuver the stick shift. Competent. Made for the bush. His cephalic vein popped and she imagined it carrying the blood back to his heart. "How long have you been stationed in Isa?"

"It's me second year, but I grew up in Isa."

Donna must have looked surprised, because Andy laughed. "I know, no one really lives in Isa. Went to Brisbane for med school, but came home to pay off me loans."

"Will you stay?"

Andy adjusted the brim of his hat. "Will go to the coast soon.

Townsville if I get the post." He thought for a moment then added, "Me joeys aren't going to be born in the Center. They're going to surf on Bondi or be divers in the Whitsundays."

"Living your lost dreams?"

"If you don't dream it, it'll never be. Ask Esther."

They rode in silence for a time, bumping along until they came upon a round waterhole. Andy pointed. "Old quarry. There's a mine we can go into a bit further down if you don't mind dark and bats. It's all about hole-hopping out here."

"I'll pass on the bats, thanks." They looked at the waterhole from the car, the same brown she'd seen as she flew over her Honey Ant painting, gentle ripples glinting in the sunlight. "Looks inviting," Donna said. She relaxed into the seat, starting to recognize the energy of the land. She remembered entering Jerusalem for the first time, stunned by how the limestone city glowed, its holiness apparent to the naked eye.

"Then I have a surprise for you."

They bumped back along the dirt road, Donna noticing for the first time the large trees with exposed roots that grew along the dirt track. "What are those?"

"Coolabahs. They like water."

"You seem to know your way around."

"I'm a bushie, too right." Andy shifted the car hard and Donna jerked back. They climbed over a huge stone. Andy concentrated on the road. "Me mum and dad divorced when I was eight. Many years back me dad went feral. Married an Abo. Has a bunch of wives, older, younger. It was pretty confusing to me as a teenager. But me stepmum taught me more about the Land than I'd ever learned from Australia Scouts and such."

"Your mom is in Isa then?" His mother probably wasn't much older than Donna.

"Mackay now." Andy brought the car to a screeching halt next to a rock cliff. "Brilliant. Here's where we'll picnic."

Donna followed Andy and his backpack out of the car and

down a path that rounded the cliff. To the side of the path were spider webs as big as her front windshield, each individual thread as thick as yarn, hanging one after another between the Coolabah branches, and each sporting a hand-sized spider. She shuddered and crept closer to the cliff wall. Boulders littered the path, and Donna's smooth-soled sandals slid around. How ridiculous she must look in her dress. She should be wearing khaki shorts, a long-sleeved button-down, a wide-brimmed hat, and hiking boots, like Andy. Donna winced as she twisted her ankle on the rocks and Andy reached his hand behind. "Keep hold of me. You look pretty but those aren't shoes for bushwhacking."

She almost missed the compliment as she shot back, "I didn't know we'd be hiking today. Thought I'd be seeing patients." She took his hand and felt his grip tighten around hers.

"In the future you should wear socks to prevent snake bites."

She started to pull away. "Maybe…"

Andy clasped her hand tighter as Pearl had at the art center. "We're making so much noise we'd scare anything off."

Heart pounding and on the lookout for spiderwebs and snakes, Donna followed Andy through some prickly wattle, yellow petals brushing her hair, then around the side of a rusty red rock wall. They followed the wall around, Andy's head craned upward. The smooth rock was cool and Donna balanced against it as she tread.

Andy removed his hat with his free hand and pointed with it to some red lines in a crevice of the rock. It was as though he were afraid that if he released her hand she would run back to the car. And she might have. "Those carvings are the Goanna Ancestor tracks." He replaced his hat over his matted waves, reached over and picked a yellow petal out of her hair, then craned his neck up at the wall. She took a moment to study his profile, pretending to follow his gaze. The self-assured set of his jaw was his most striking feature.

She was again aware of her hand held tightly by his and she

studied the rock painting. "I saw some art like that today at the center."

"Artists are related. Separated by thirty thousand years."

Donna saw the petal that had been in her hair float down from his hand. She took a deep breath and smelled the earth of thirty thousand years ago, an earth twenty-five thousand years older than the Old Testament. Earth that had existed without her and would continue long after she was dead. She could hardly imagine her ancestors of a hundred years ago, much less a tradition passed down over three hundred *centuries*.

They circled the large rocks, Donna thankful for their shade. She felt her underarms and thighs sticky with sweat. The sweat cut through the dust on her face, beading at the tip of her nose in dirty drops. A few paces ahead, Andy dropped her hand and left the rocks. He followed a lightly-tread path through the acacias. The dirt clumped at Donna's feet, tripping her every few paces, until it became mud. She wished for Andy's hand again, but didn't ask. At once Donna saw the glint of sunlight on water. A red granite wall lined the far side of the lake, casting half into shade. Acacias and coolabahs with their twisting long roots dotted its sides. This water was muddy green, but welcoming. Andy stood to the side of the path, sweeping his arm as if to pull back a curtain. It was the Rainbow Serpent's magic kiss upon the land. "Beautiful," she exhaled.

He put his hand on the small of her back, leading her forward. The parrots called above, *chi chi,* and insects hummed. Donna longed to slide into the water and feel the dirt and sand wash away from her body. She turned to see Andy peeling off his shirt, his nipples erect in the breeze off the lake. He tossed it onto a branch and watched her as he unlaced his hiking boots, yanked off his socks, and unzipped his shorts. She caught her breath as he stood in his boxers. Yes, it was as she'd thought that first day in the canteen. His body was the body of her high school boyfriend—a swimmer's broad shoulders and runners' lean torso.

She wished he were a patient to examine, to give her a reason to touch his body, feel the energy stored beneath his skin.

"Race you," he laughed.

Donna hadn't worn a bra under her gauzy pink sun dress. She didn't need to because her breasts were so small. They were still pert for her forty-one years, her only consolation for never breast-feeding. But how could she go in with only panties? The last time she'd skinny-dipped with colleagues was in Nepal, where the sheer primitiveness of society meant that they shared a hole in the ground to defecate and bathed with each other in sarongs when they found a river.

She decided she'd rather have a wet dress for the day than go naked in front of another doctor. She hung her sandals on a tree and ran in like a kid bounding toward the ocean, dragging her hands through the water, her skirt billowing out around her until she was waist deep. Then she dove, the water filling the space where she'd been. This must be how it would feel to wade through Monet's water lilies, to swim in a painting, through the blue circles on the Rainbow Serpent's canvas.

Donna swept her arm to gather the water, felt its weight in her hands. She pushed off the muddy bottom, wondering if the mud had been touched by strange animals a millennia ago, and glided backward under the sky, one shade lighter than the blues of the painting she held in her mind. As she floated, she peered through her toes. Ripples made v's from her body to the center of the lake.

The coolabah roots reached deep into the lake and the leaves hung over the banks, providing spots of dappled shade. Donna moved in and out of the dapples, feeling the shifts of heat on her body from sun to shade, blotches of skin hot and others cool, ever shifting down her body. She would have no descendents, be no one's ancestor thirty thousand years hence. But she will have been baptized in the pure waters of Queensland, the gift of the Rainbow Serpent.

Her head bumped against a stick. The leaves shimmered above her in the light breeze, and a Galah called, *chi chi*. Again she bumped the stick. She flipped over, wanting to pick it up and throw it into the center of the lake so she could see the shock of its impact spread outward to the shore where her footprints baked in the mud. Her arm was outstretched, fingers splayed wide to grab the stick, when she realized that two tiny hooded eyes peered at her above a pointed bumpy jaw as long as her forearm. Brown hide shimmered as it cut through the water, slowly circling her. *The Rainbow Serpent? That thing looking at me is a crocodile.*

She turned quickly and started paddling, the water syrup under her, pulling her in, down, into its thick brownness. She would drown, and she was leaving no one, no Greg, no baby. The dapples held her back. Would it hurt when the jaws closed around her leg? Death, death. Salty tears mingled with the fresh lake as she finally felt the muddy bottom under her feet. Her hands tore at the mud, trying to pull her to shore. She clawed away from the dead baby, the dead marriage, the crocodile.

"Donna." She felt warm hands on her back, pulling at her shoulders, lifting her up as her arms still tried to propel her forward, grasping the mud that oozed under her fingernails and between her toes. A voice was yelling in her ear, between strands of her mud-tangled hair. "Donna, I've got you."

"Crocodile," Donna gasped.

He pulled her down in his lap, held her down like the struggling child in a tantrum, forced his mouth to her ear, and she struggled to get away. His chest pressed her back, arms wrapped around her. Strong hands clamped down on her arms. "A freshie," he whispered forcefully.

Her body went limp. "Everything's dangerous. Everyone dies." Donna sobbed. "It's hell here."

Donna felt Andy's body shake with laughter. Andy twisted their bodies toward the lake. "Look at your lazy crocodile. He was curious. See that pointy snout? It can't eat more than min-nows, small fish."

His mouth was close to her ear. It felt good to be held. She looked down at muscled forearms, felt his razor-stubble against her jaw, felt the lump in his boxers below her. She'd wished for a reason to touch him.

"The salties are in the mangroves by the coast. Usually there are signs. *Beware of man-eating crocodiles*. We're safer here in the Center. Only poison snakes and spiders. A few scorpions maybe."

She couldn't muster a laugh but sat there, saved, in his lap. She tasted the metals of the mine, nickel, copper, silver lining her tongue, the lead coursing through her veins. *This is what it means to taste fear.*

Andy slowly unclasped his arms and with his hands on her hips, pushed her out of his lap and on to her feet. He took her hand. "Let's rinse off this mud then have a snack?"

Donna looked at Andy's muddied boxers and then at her own mud-caked body. Her expensive lace panties were showing through the dress.

He should have kissed me. Who cared if he was a colleague fifteen years younger. Angry, she let him lead her down to the water's edge, his grip tightening as they waded back into the water. Donna stopped when the water was waist level, motioning Andy to go ahead. If she went in again, something might happen between them. Her fear was stronger than her desire. She watched the gray mud slowly unglue from her thighs and arms, floating gently into the water, tiny flecks dissipating into the murky green. After eyeing the lake for nearby crocodiles, she bent her knees, ducked down so the water could close over her head. When she came up, Andy was eyeing her. She willed him to come to her, but he swam in circles, never fully taking his eyes off her.

They sat on a blanket under the coolabahs—something unfin-ished besides the fruit and cheese—waiting for their clothes to dry. Donna leaned back on her hands, watching the waterhole for signs of her crocodile. She took long sips from her jug of water, feeling it slosh in her waterlogged belly. She'd have to take antibiotics that night.

Andy twirled the stem of an apple, snapped it off, then tossed the smooth green globe to Donna. "Most folks in Brisbane wouldn't dream of going bush. And you're an American girl. Why'd you come out here alone?"

Donna watched the shadows on the water mark the path of the breeze. The Granny Smith was tart and crisp. "I had a baby boy and a marriage. Lost both."

Andy cut the coon cheese, as he called it, with his pocket knife and handed a piece to Donna. "Boy's with his pop?"

"Born dead." Donna had held her son for a half-hour, his red hands over the tiny flannel blanket the hospital volunteers had stitched for stillborns. She hadn't unwrapped him from the blue-and-yellow flowers to check his ten toes, for fear of seeing his spindly legs flop out, rubbery and flaccid instead of kicking and balling themselves up against the world. Now she wondered what his toes had looked like.

After twelve hours of labor, she'd held the swaddled body until the nurse unfolded Donna's hands from the blanket, saying *It's time, Donna*. Donna had wondered when someone would take him away. She'd so wanted to sleep. She'd only anticipated the happy endings of labor, sweating women with howling babies lying on their bellies as the umbilical cord was cut. She hadn't prepared herself to be afraid to kiss him because he was dead, the lack of life his most evident feature, more prominent than his upturned chin, his elf nose, black hair. She watched the nurse leave the room with the bundle, shoulders rounded over as she peeked at his face.

The next time Donna held him was in the gray velvet bag that weighed practically nothing. The same day Greg said it was over. Now it was just Donna and the bag and a picture of an oak leaf, red and gold, floating in a puddle of water, raindrops beaded along its delicate veins the nurses had put on her door so that anyone entering would know she was delivering a dead baby.

Andy watched her with clear blue eyes. "Can't fix everything, even if you're a doc."

Donna took a bite of cheese. She felt a shadow over her shoulder, and a parrot dove towards them. Donna leaned in toward Andy. He ducked too and they clunked heads. She held her hand to her temple. "I told you Australia is a dangerous place."

Andy hopped up onto his feet to shoo the bird away. "Feral country. Pest wants me apple." He waved his hands at the bird, who did not show signs of leaving.

"I'd take Galahs over pigeons any day. How great if we had flocks of parrots cruising around New York." Donna wondered at their numbers, at their aerial tricks, at their surprising beauty in the midst of such a harsh environment. It was as though the birds had seen how plain the landscape was and said, *I'll be pink and brighten up the place.*

Andy threw his apple core at the Galah, wiped his hands on his boxers and looked up at the sky. "Sun's going to be down soon. Happens quick out here. We best get back."

Andy dropped Donna at her car, giving her directions to Alice's house. It wasn't hard, since you could see everyone's trailer from the clinic's steps. She tried to hide her disappointment that he hadn't invited her to dinner.

She reminded herself that she should be thinking about her job as the attending physician, not about a potential romance with a young resident. She should have slept with Nick and gotten sex off her mind.

She spent the night at Alice's and in the morning woke to a rhythmic vibration that was much more pleasant than the blast from the mine. At first she thought it was the gentle rocking of the trailer accompanied by grunts and squeals that had woken her periodically through the night. Esther had clearly found Jocko. But soon she realized that the low vibration came from outside the window. She wrapped the blanket around her and looked outside. A didgeridoo. Low notes jumped around an unfamiliar scale, reminding Donna of a bagpipe, of a requiem, of *Ave Maria*.

As Esther had taught her, Donna shook out her shoes for spiders. She closed the trailer door behind her and approached the man who was blowing the didgeridoo. Rugged, with bulging biceps, he looked at least sixty. His long straight nose made a triangle, exactly opposite of Esther's big bulb. He didn't stop playing when Donna, wrapped in her blanket, sat on the ground next to him, her back sharing the smooth white trunk of the ghost gum standing guard between the trailer and the open bush. A long didgeridoo painted with circles and dots was propped between his knees, its end resting in the dirt. Clouds of dust were being stirred by the air blowing through the didgeridoo, so that it looked as if he were taking a toke on an extremely long bong. For a moment he lifted up the instrument like Artie Shaw on the clarinet, then closed his eyes and brought the end back down to earth.

Donna watched the pinking sky where the full moon still hung next to a morning star. The man's cheeks puffed in and out. Otherwise not a muscle of his expression changed. At one point the music was the trumpeting of elephants, next it was apes calling through the jungle. Then it was the twang of a rubber-band. Next, it was speaking. Donna strained her ear, wondering if she could ever decipher its language.

She shivered in the morning cold and the reality of the day ahead came to her. Clinic with Andy. Why had she told him about the baby? It was a story for women. It belonged to Nan and Esther in Australia, and Kate in New York. It belonged to mothers and daughters. She'd wished during those years struggling with infertility that her mother had been alive to tell her stories.

Her mother had miscarriages, before and after Donna was born. Donna's parents, both only children, hadn't intended to perpetuate that circumstance. But Donna never asked for details. There was a grave in their family plot—*Baby Girl Meyer, June 5, 1959*—in the crowded cemetery in Queens where tombstones stood shoulder-to-shoulder, mirroring the skyscrapers across the river. Had Baby Girl Meyer been stillborn in late term as Donna's boy had? Or had she lived for a few days?

As the didgeridoo resonated, she pressed her cheek against the smooth tree trunk, swallowing her regret. Esther poked her head out the window. "Jocko. Donna. Brekky's on."

Jocko continued to buzz and pulse, but Donna rose to go in and noticed the bead of sweat on Jocko's forehead, despite the coolness of the morning. The music stopped and Donna heard the cackling of the kookaburra who sat on the tin roof above them. Jocko smiled at her.

There was an indentation around his lips from the pressure of the mouth hole. "Morning now. Bird didn't like me calling ahead of him."

"Your music is beautiful."

"Didgeridoo, he works wonders. Cleaned you out."

Donna smiled, "I needed cleaning?"

Jocko stood up. He was taller than Esther, almost lanky compared to most of her Aboriginal patients. "Your face looks much better now." With that he opened the door to the trailer and they went in. Donna didn't know what else to say, so she let Esther's whistling and humming carry them through brekky.

Donna, Andy, and Alice, the Doomadgee nurse, spent an uneventful day in the clinic. Every so often Donna would look up and find Andy staring at her, or she would catch herself staring at him. She'd look down quickly and say something medical. She couldn't help but think of Nan fawning over Andy on Donna's first day of work.

By three, they'd finished with their last patient and Donna was anxious to pick up Esther at Alice's so they could navigate the rougher terrain between Doomadgee and Gregory Downs before dark. She said goodbye to Andy and the nurse, slamming her car door behind her.

Andy made a motion for her to roll down her window. She obliged and he leaned in. "How do you feel about going Waltzing Matilda?"

"Waltzing?" She hadn't waltzed since her wedding.

"Camping in swags. You know, Matilda's who you sleep with? You sleep with your swag?"

Her hand felt sweaty on the wheel.

"Camel races are in Boulia next weekend. Shouldn't miss them. Wanna meet me? Flying Docs are bringing me down as an extra hand, but it's only a three-hour drive for you."

As they drove south to Isa, Esther reached out her arm and patted Donna's thigh. "Jocko cleaned out your belly so you can have another baby." A mob of wallabies shot out from under a gum and Esther pointed at them. "Look to the left."

Donna watched them bouncing in a line. Like the Galahs, they were a reminder of how far away she was from New York. "Who said I wanted another baby?"

Esther's full lips were pulled tight, no smile creases setting off her globe cheeks. "Yapa magic."

"Hah."

Now Esther's cheeks made two round balls. "You will have a baby here. You need to let go of your son because a child is waiting to jump into your womb." Esther shifted her hips in the passenger seat. "Women are dangerous if they don't get their sex. Pent up energies make the world sick."

The setting sun shone on the wattle, turning the yellow flowers into bursts of orange. "I'm not having another baby. Anyway, it sounded like you healed the world last night."

"Why didn't you do it by the waterhole?"

Donna shot a sideways glance at the woman. "What did Andy tell you?"

"Never forget I learned you from a Galah."

Donna thought about the ubiquitous pink-and-gray parrots. Hadn't wizards in every fantasy novel she'd ever read used birds as spies? Whether or not she actually spoke to birds, Esther's ESP was remarkable. Donna kept her hands firmly on the wheel. "I should have turned around when he was holding me. I messed up the signals. Out of practice, I guess. Plus, I'm fifteen years older than Andy. My body isn't quite that of a twenty-five-year- old."

Esther laughed. "Yapa always take the younger men. They love us. How do you think they learn good tricks? It's every-body's responsibility to make sure all women—even we old women—are satisfied."

Donna looked over at Esther, who was sitting comfortably de-spite the bumpy road. She was probably a few years older than Donna. "Shocking."

Esther insisted, "An older lover and a younger one too. That's the balance I spoke of. It isn't Yapa ruining the planet."

"He invited me to Boulia."

Esther snorted, "Andy or Nick or both. Don't waste any more time."

Coolabah trees. Great coolabah trees. Green teardrop leaves rustle and weave nets overhead. Coolabah roots dangle from branches, winding circles, ribbons of brown around their trunks, searching for water. Like Galah beaks poking for stag beetles in the sand, the roots reach down into the powdery earth to find moisture.

The Galah lands on a gnarled branch of a coolabah tree. Strong branch, an old branch, knotted with roots. Like the roots, tendrils of sun and shadows wind their way through the branches and the leaves. Through the branch she feels the water that the coolabah drinks. How the Galah loves the coolabah tree. She rustles her wings.

Little pools of water between the coolabah roots. When the sky is quiet, when it has shifted from the magenta of the Galah head, traveled down the light pink neck and become the feathered gray body of the Galah, yes, when the sky has melted from the color of water to that of the Galah, she will hop down into a pool and from every inch of herself she will wash the desert sands, the tiny grains she has collected as she flew through the dusty haze, little grains that rub beneath the fine layers of her gray underwings. She will glide down to the pool, dipping once then twice her wings, then her head, then her tailfeathers into the pool. She will take long cool sips through the night, arching her neck gently into the pool, to savor the coolness of the nighttime water as it envelops her beak tip, then the beak neck, then her whole beak.

But first, the black cockatoo woman. Why can she not see the spirit child hanging from the gnarled branches, laughing and jumping into the clear water, creating ripples among the long roots, making boats of the downed leaves? The Galah dives down to the woman, drives her into the man. Grab the child, it is the season. But the human does not. The Galah flies back to her branch. She has done her best. The spirit child will have to wait for the Galah woman to do her magic.

Now the sky is almost gray. She can see each individual piece of dust in the air, pink crystals turning to sand. She is about to hop down to begin her bath, but instead she is distracted by the kangaroo near a neighboring tree that has just perked up its ears. He stands, balancing on his strong hind legs, his tail, like a root of the coolabah tree anchoring him to the ground. Ears twitch, momentarily clearing the haze around him. The Galah sniffs for a dingo. No scent. She waits and watches the last cloud of pink disappear from the newborn gray sky and over a neighboring bluff, and still the kangaroo stands. Only when the Galah sees the first star reflected in the pool does the kangaroo unfold its muscles as it makes its way to drink from the star water. And then with the kangaroo, the Galah flutters down to the edge of the small pool, dipping in her wing, watching ripples reach the pool's fine boundaries.

Heel-toe, heel-toe. Soles pressed earth flat. Jimmy bent his knees, walking lower to the earth. Each foot long, like the kangaroo, pushing into sand then flying with the wind over grasses, floating, hardly touching the ground. Heel-toe, heel-toe, so fast he could hardly feel the push before he felt flight. Push-release, push-release, kangaroo feet, push-release.

He didn't stop until he was out in the bush, away from the town, the white poisons, white people. Lungs aching from flight, he flopped down in the dust, feeling his naked back mold the earth. Blue sky. Hot salty tears trickled down his temples and into his hair.

He could not stay in hospital with Uncle, all those people poking and prodding him. There had been such a panicked flurry around Hector when they took him out of the ambulance. Big Yapa woman had taken Jimmy by the shoulders and put him in an orange chair. Said, "Don't move. I'm Galah kin. I will help you." Jimmy didn't want help. He was a hunter. Could sneak out quietly as all the doctors were yelling *Coma, intubation, vitals.* Jimmy knew what a coma was. Well, there wasn't time for Dreaming now. Jimmy wanted to get to his seedpile, bury Da's bone, Behold his country, and get home before winter holiday. He wanted to lie in his bed and look through the musty footy cards he'd hidden in the old tinbilly tea box. He wanted Tess's damper for brekky.

He bent his knees to his chest and held the bottoms of his feet. He could still feel the vibrations in the sole where his feet had met the land on his run. He should have stopped at the billabong to collect his swag and billy pot. No matter. He'd wrap himself in the tall grasses when it got cold at night. He patted his pocket. His knife was there next to the bone and the other rocks. In the other pocket were granola bars he'd taken from the big glass bowl at the sisters' station at hospital. He'd taken enough to last him for a week, he figured.

He let his body relax like a dead man's, feeling the earth support him, and cupped his hands around his wet eyes so all he could see was sky. He pretended it was the sky above Yuendumu. But he missed the sounds of his aunties and cousins yelling in the background. The sky here was so deep blue he could drown in it. The thought scared him and he hopped back onto his feet and started to walk. He looked over his shoulder to see if he could see the smokestacks in the distance, rising like middle fingers from the earth to say *get stuffed*, but they'd already been erased from his horizon. Good riddance. Especially the angry pipe that brought up the gray gases from the center of the earth. Bloody Hector and his bloody deep sleep. Jimmy was gonna bloody well finish his Dreaming himself.

He wondered how he could initiate himself, cut himself like that. He'd have to hold his penis in one hand and cut round with the other. How would he keep cutting as he felt the blood drip? Sure, he could sing the songs, but the cutting? He felt his knife sharp in his pocket. He'd just have to sharpen it again when he got to his Land and figure it out then.

He looked to his side and thought he saw fresh kangaroo track. He got up and followed it. It headed southeast, the general direction he was going. Every ten paces he would bend over and feel the air above the prints. The roo was close. Jimmy could recognize the footprints of everyone in his mob of almost three hundred, could guess within an hour when they'd been made. Hector had taught him how. Uncle was a famous tracker and an excellent jackeroo. Helped the police every once in a while when they needed to know when a car had passed through town. He could say if it had been going fast and how many people were in it. Hector's da had been a man of high initiation. He could go hunting out bush and never get cold. Had trained himself so that if he rolled over on the campfire by accident, he wouldn't burn. Jimmy had good blood. Galah blood, Fire Ant blood.

As he moved along the track, Jimmy collected berries and nuts to eat with his granola. He sang *Turtle, turtle poke your head, find some water or you'll end up dead.* Silver glinted off to his side. He abandoned the track and followed to investigate. Maybe it would be a squatter's home of tin, with a cushion chair that he could sleep in that night.

He was disappointed to find only the mud guard of a car. As he turned back to his tracks, he heard a squawk and a splash. A splash? He followed the sound past the rusty metal. The dust became gray granite. A few steps further Jimmy stopped short and drew in his breath as the granite opened into a perfectly round hole in the ground. An old quarry, what luck. Probably left over from an old mine. He'd have to be careful not to fall into any hidden holes in the wounded ground.

How far away he was from Yuendumu. No one would have any idea where to look for him if he dropped into a mineshaft filled with bats and snakes. He followed the smooth gray stone edges around the quarry hole. On the western side he could see a rock ledge that was easy to climb down. Maybe two meters or so, and then there was a beach of small pebbles that sidled right up to the water.

He scrambled down the rocks, his toes finding easy holds in the shale and quartz. He walked gingerly over to the water. His turtle song must have brought him there. Jukurrpa became Yuti, Dreaming became reality. That was how the world worked.

He didn't bend down on his hands and knees, scooping up water as the white man might. How easily a boy could be ambushed, thrown off balance and into the green water to drown. Instead, he lay down to drink, his belly flattened on the warm orange dust. He curled his fists under his chest and his toes under his feet, so if he had to rise quickly, he'd have the power of his arms and legs.

As his lips parted to take in the cool water, he saw his reflection in the ripples. His yellow hair had gotten long, and his cheeks red, even on his dark skin. The setting sun drew stripes of light on his face, like the ochre the Uncles would paint on his face for a Dreaming dance. And on the hairs of his shoulders, the dust settled like a shirt, each short light hair with its own covering.

He loosened a fist to flick a pebble into the center of his reflection. He became one of the ripples in the water. But as the ripples hit the shore, he reappeared. "This is Jimmy Jackboy?"

His mum had been right; he looked different. One morning he'd come to brekky and Mum had held the cook pan in midair. "You went to sleep a boy and woke up a man, fair dinkum." She'd slapped the damper down on his plate and said no more that morning. Every so often after that day he'd catch her staring. That morning was only months before the Uncles had seized him. Yes, he should have known initiation was coming.

The water was still; his reflection had come back to normal. He could throw stones, but in the end he was who he was and wasn't who he wasn't. He hadn't always been a Jackboy, hadn't even been one for very long. But when Da had been killed, they changed all their names, since they'd been too close to Da's. He hadn't said their old names in a year—didn't want Da's spirit to hear it and think he was calling him to stick around.

Jimmy Jackboy had a nice ring to it. Hoped he could keep that name for a while. His white teacher had been frustrated when he first changed it, but Auntie Tess had gone in to explain. Then Mrs. Westbrook had done what so many grownups do—gone overboard to be accepting. Called on him even more than before, just to say his new name. Still, she was a good teacher. Had let him start long division before the others.

He felt Da's smooth finger bone in his pocket. Da's spirit should already be up in the Warambool instead of causing mischief around Yuendumu. Maybe once the bone was buried on Galah Land, his spirit would fly up to the Warambool where it belonged. Mum said part of the problem was that they didn't ever avenge his death. But whom do you go after? Road train had run him right over, his swag too close to the side of the road. Didn't seem right. Why would Da camp right on the road? He'd been smarter than that.

Jimmy thought Da's spirit hadn't flown because Da hadn't had enough time to prepare to die, his childhood stolen away with the whitefellas. Jimmy was lucky. His generation could learn the ways, and still go to the white world.

Jimmy watched his reflection in the pool change as the sky changed above him. Soon it was dark and he could see his eyes shining like the stars reflected in the pool. The moon rose, turning the spinifex on the side of the waterhole into silver blue spears, and now it was the moon in the pool and only a shadow of Jimmy Jackboy. "I am still here, though." He ran his hands all over his body.

A Galah cried, *chi chi*, overhead. His kin was near. Jimmy finally moved away from the pool and sat with his back against the wall of the quarry to watch the animals come to drink. There was the roo he'd tracked, a rock wallaroo actually. She stood with her ears cocked to the side, the joey's branch-like feet sticking out of her pouch. Was he nursing or had he just stayed in the same position after jumping in, maybe falling asleep immediately as Jimmy's little cousins sometimes did while playing. One minute they'd all be searching for kangaroo berries, and the next, his cousins would be lying in the dirt dreaming away.

Jimmy thought about trying to kill the wallaroo for dinner, but didn't feel like making a fire. Sure the meat would last for a day or two without cooking. Kangaroo meat formed its own gooey coating that would protect it from the flies. But the roo was company now. He'd find another one to kill tomorrow or he'd manage on maku and goanna. Jimmy shrank back into the rock wall that still held some of the sun's warmth.

The night breeze began to blow and the moon danced in the water, and then Jimmy's kin came to take their baths in the pool, preening feathers, laughing, joking. They did somersaults, then dipped wings into the water, keeping him entertained until the moon was straight above and Jimmy fell asleep.

S nappy gum roots burrow deep inside the layers of rusty cliffs. Shale flakes off and becomes dust as it hits the rock below. The gum grows out into the void, breaking into the still air between the canyon walls, not another tree in sight. Its silver-green oval leaves shimmer in the sun, the only thing other than dust that blows in the western wind. The Galah's wing brushes the flaky shale, and pebbles start a landslide that grows and grows down the canyon wall. Once at the gorge, she had sent a cliff down in a clean break with just a wing tip. Lizards scurried from underneath rocks falling from the sky.

Farther down the canyon, boulders big as hills, smooth and round from the days of water, pile atop each other. A wing tip cannot loose them. If they roll, they will crunch Galah and lizard and tree alike. But between canyon walls and round boulders, still the only tree, that snappy gum.

The Galah does not know why the tree would choose to grow there, to send its roots deeper in, strengthening its hold. Why it would choose to be alone? Better to spread its seeds on the wind and loosen its roots, crash down into splinters among the rocks, until the wind and time turned it into thousands of grains of sand. She understood sand, its many grains rippling together in the winds to make a dune. She understood spinifex, each tip, each blade, part of the waves of the wind, a fluid motion, making a meadow. She understood the bird in its flock, making a cloud in the sky.

Maybe the boy as he flies on the wind will find the gum. Maybe he will rest in its meager shade. He turns. He will not. The snappy gum *will be the gum, without a boy to twirl fallen leaves below it. It will give shade only to the ungrateful rocks.*

    Maybe she will come back to keep the snappy gum company. The spinifex and the sand do not need her. But now she and her flock fly between canyon walls etched by sunrises that her kind never knew. They rise on the wind then fall, following the banks of an ancient lake as it lapped the sands millennia ago.

\\∩/

It was with Kate's e-mailed encouragement—*Remember I'm envi-ous. How delicious to try a new partner. Shit, the baby's throwing up*—and Esther's admonitions in mind—*Don't you waste any more time*—that Donna drove to Boulia the following Saturday morn-ing, gray velvet bag tucked safely into her glove compartment for company. Nick had another week in Brisbane, so Donna would have to see what would happen with Andy. How long it had been since she was interested in a man, much less two men at the same time? And they couldn't be more different. One older, one younger. Balance. All week she'd halfheartedly tended her patients—the sixty-six-year-old woman with failing kidneys, the Aboriginal man who lay in a coma—anticipating the moment she could leave the Isa for Boulia.

The drive was four hours, instead of the three Andy and every-one else whom she'd asked had predicted. Clearly she didn't drive as fast as the Aussies. She slowed the Rover as green-and-yellow budgies flew alongside her car, flocks of a hundred or more un-dulating up and down with the breeze. She sang along to Esther's tapes; they helped her stay awake on the straightaway highway.

The Cowboy Junkies melted into Slim Dusty, Keith Urban, and Split Enz as clumps of wattle turned into a forest of yellow-flowered bushes, then thinned out again to where lonely ghost gums marked empty land. She saw kestrel eagles on the roadkills. When they flew up to avoid her car, their wing span covered her entire lane.

The giant budgie-colored *Welcome to Boulia* sign rose out of the emptiness to greet her. According to Esther, Boulia was nothing more than twenty faded, yellowish green-sided houses, abruptly plopped down in the desert like houses on an abandoned Monopoly game. Boulia stood three (or four) hours from the Isa and twenty hours from the Alice if you could get through the Plenty Highway without getting stuck. Esther said Boulia would have been good for a just a petrol stop or a beer were it not for the annual camel races. The pub owner had the idea to build the track in the scrubland behind the town, where not even the roos tried to graze. He'd bought a few mean camels from the army, and convinced local ranchers and retired army men from the Sixteenth Camel Division to participate. Within two years, it was a Queensland must-see.

Donna followed the neon orange *Parking* signs to a field, and was happy to see spots reserved for medics. Hundreds of trucks and cars were parked every which way, turning the field into an unofficial campground: doors open, green-and-white striped awnings erected over card tables, beer cans crushed into the ground.

She stretched her legs and got out of the car. This time, she was dressed appropriately. Andy had called to say it got cool at night, to wear jeans, and now they felt sweaty against her legs. She was thankful for her long-sleeved shirt as protection against the sun. Everyone was dressed the same, despite the heat. Protection was clearly more important than comfort. She followed the signs to the medical tent.

She stood at the open flap and let her eyes adjust. There was Andy, bending over a man's calf. A Flying Doc who had a stethoscope draped around his shoulders lounged in a canvas chair, hat over his face. As Andy looked up, the patient removed his hat and nodded. Andy cleared his throat. "Doctor Donna, we've had our first broken fibula of the weekend."

"Anything I can do?"

"Why don't you go out and have yourself a look-see? Bet on a race or two." He pointed at the sleeping man. "Mick is on in two hours. Then I'll take you to our camp across the field by the billabong. Little secret that most of these blokes in the car park don't know about." He spoke to the patient, "Don't you go telling the doctor's secrets."

The cowboy lifted his hat in hand. "Ya have me word."

Donna hesitated and looked over the x-ray taken on the mobile machine. It was a clean, simple, non-displaced fracture. Nothing to it. A med student could take care of it. She put the x-ray down and looked out the tent flap. She hadn't expected to be on her own, but why not? With a wave, she left the shade of the medical tent and wandered toward the grandstands. There were lines at the betting booths and Donna fell into one. She picked up a race card from the ground. There were nine more races that day, and Donna chose her camels by their names. Lookin' Lucky was a gimmee with all the Aussie talk of good luck and bad luck. She bet on Curly Sue and Fairy Flyer. Jessie had long odds—but she'd had a good friend from college named Jessica. She put a dollar on each.

Pocketing her tickets, she headed over to the track. Jockeys dressed in outlandish costumes—a banana in striped pajamas, an Arabian knight—were cajoling their mounts toward the starting blocks. One camel, whose jockey sported a rainbow wig, folded its knees down the way Greg folded his maps one square at a time, then refused to budge. Donna stood against the track rail. Finally the camels were in the starting gate and with a bang they were off. She became carried away by the excitement of the crowd, found herself cheering for Lookin' Lucky, screaming as he almost made it to the finish, then stopped abruptly. Other camels spit and balked, ran backwards and laid down, forcing their jockeys to jump off quickly. Curly Sue, in the second heat, refused to move out of the starting gate. It was like a drunken clown act. But on the third race, the animals cooperated and it looked to Donna like a vision from the Middle East, camels swaying back and forth as they kicked up the dust, jockey whips flailing, wigs, robes, ribbons flying in the wind. She sucked in her breath and closed her eyes, smelling for the exotic spices of Arab lands, but instead smelled camel dung, grass, and beer.

As she opened her eyes, she lost her balance and stumbled off the low rail. An older Aboriginal man standing next to her put his warm hand on her back to steady her. "Ta," she thanked him and he smiled a bright white smile. The warmth lingered where the man's hand had been and suddenly she craved beer. Not from a bottle, but from the cheap plastic glasses filled with piss-colored brew from vendors who were generous with the froth.

She pushed her way through the crowd of mostly men to the beer line. It looked like many had come off the stations in their tight Wrangler jeans, bandanas, and big belt buckles, Horizon and Holiday cigarettes dangling from their lips. Whites and Aboriginals mingled freely here, unlike in the Isa. She slid a toothless vendor her two-dollar coin and her hands were doused in beer as he passed her a plastic cup. She moved aside and sipped the bitter froth, aware of and not caring about her budding white mustache. Much of the froth spilled and was immediately absorbed into the dry ground as she dodged three kids holding their cones of cotton candy aloft—the sign on the machine called it *fairy floss*—which stained their teeth blue as it melted in their mouths. They eyed the rickety carnival rides that would be turned on after the races, a spinning wheel like an oversized rusted bicycle wheel, the topsy-turvy cars, and the Zipper. Too bad there was no Ferris wheel from which to view the town.

As she found her place on the track rail, she stopped and looked at the men, their hats pulled low, pumping their fists. The crease in the butt of the Aboriginal man's Wranglers was almost as nice as the crease in Andy's. He had three boys standing next to him, wide-brimmed hats in a row like descending rungs on a ladder, the youngest of whom was about ten.

As though he had eyes in the back of his head, the man scooted over to let Donna back in as she approached, never taking his eyes from the camels. She glanced at the boys. Their smiles were wide. The oldest chewed on a blade of spinifex and was laughing. Donna would love to have had her son standing at the rail, and instead of watching the camels, she'd have watched the wonder and delight in his eyes. Then she would have looked over his head and seen Greg's knowing smile.

"Jessie will win." The man pointed at her race card and then to the far side of the track where #12 had broken from the pack.

Donna jumped up and down, her beer spilling over her hand and trickling down to her elbow, while the other hand clutched the tin rail of the track, yelling "Jessie!" Jessie rounded the track minutes ahead of the pack. She turned to the man. "That was a twenty dollar race."

"Fair dinkum? Good onya."

As she was cheering on Fairy Flyer, she felt strong hands circle her waist. She stumbled off the rail and into Andy, allowing her body to linger there. She was certain his intentions for the night were similar to her own. He looked at her race card. "Making money?"

"Twenty dollars."

"Great. Tea's on you. Let's go to camp before we go to the fete. Yeah?"

The Aboriginal man gave her a wink as she left.

Andy took the wheel of her Land Rover and drove them past the race track, then along the edge of a field filled with orange dirt and the barest dressing of grass. In the States, Donna would have been worried they might get stuck in some unseen soft bog, but in the Outback, the ground was as hard as cement. There hadn't been any rain since December, hardly a wispy cloud in the huge sky since the day Donna had come to Queensland. Andy stopped the car at the edge of the field. "Look at that view. Have you ever seen such a big sky, such an expanse of land? No horizon. Anything is possible."

Beyond the field was a grove of eucalyptus trees and a few coolabahs, full and inviting from a distance, but spindly with flaking bark up close. Once they were at the trees, Donna saw the billabong. They passed other campers and parked next to a blue pickup.

"Mick's buddy, Clive, picked us up at the landing strip. There's another doc too, Simon." Andy pointed to a man lazing in a canvas chair that matched the one Mick had been in.

"A whole gang," she thought.

As Donna opened the car door, Simon jumped up. He came around to greet her, pumping her hand. "Just in time for tea."

"When is it not time for tea with you Aussies? Morning tea, afternoon tea, dinner."

"We take our tea seriously in Oz." Simon handed her a blue-and-white ceramic teacup as he put the kettle on the Jackaroo stove set up behind their truck. Donna picked up the tea tin—No Worries Tea. While the tea boiled, Simon took out a generous slice of brie from his eskie.

"I could get used to camping Aussie style," Donna said as she took stock of the two other Jackaroo stoves that sat by the truck, a gas-powered floor lamp, fold-up chairs, pots, pans, five jugs of water, the eskie full of steak, potatoes, avocado, apples, cheese, and biscuits. Esther had sent Donna with wine and whiskey, in addition to Donna's own stash of gourmet food. Donna thought Esther was crazy when they shopped together at Woolies and Esther piled things in Donna's basket. But now Donna was happy to be able to contribute.

"That's Clive." Simon pointed to a man who was setting up hammocks between three large eucalypts.

"Do we sleep in those?" Andy had promised to bring something for her to sleep in, but Donna wondered if she'd fall out of a hammock.

Simon was settling the tea leaves by swinging the teapot. "I like hammocks because the snakes can't get you up there."

Andy interrupted. "Don't scare Doctor Donna." He turned to her. "I brought us two swags. Best way to sleep out bush." He pointed to the army-green bedrolls leaning against some trees fifteen feet away. They were made out of tarp, with padding and a cotton sheet built in.

Simon said, "Just wad up a jacket for a pillow and you've got yourself an Outback bed. They're warm. Don't need to wear more than a skivvy."

Donna wondered about spiders. No tent walls to keep them out of your hair. "So when you camp, you bring everything but the kitchen sink and a tent."

Andy waved at the sky. "Not even enough dew here to get you wet in the morn. Great sleep, looking up at the stars."

Donna thought she'd probably have the sheet over her head all night. She'd rather keep the spiders and snakes out than let the starlight in.

Andy opened a folding chair and motioned Donna to have a seat. Donna sat back, munching on cheese and tea sandwiches, watching Andy pour gasoline from a tin through a funnel into her gas tanks. "Want you to be refueled for the way home. Don't want you getting stuck on account of me."

It was early evening, and with the loss of the sun, the desert cooled. Everyone added another layer of clothing. Two bottles of Shiraz later, Donna was enjoying a quiet buzz and the four kicked clods of dirt across the field for the evening entertainment. Donna looked sideways at Andy in his Aussie wide-brimmed hat with a gray feather in the rim. She fingered her Mets baseball cap. Would she look ridiculous in an Aussie hat?

After passing the empty track, they joined the throng. She felt the warming air and tied her fleece jacket around her hips. Clive and Simon had wandered away and Andy took her hand as they wound their way through the crowd to the medical tent. "I promised Mick I'd spell him for a half hour so he could get tea. Why don't you go watch the music?" He squeezed her hand.

"Save me a dance. I've been looking forward to one all day."

"I'll be near the grandstand." She sat in the first row and watched the band picking on guitars and banjos. People circled in a wild dance, women pressing themselves against men, stopping in the middle of the crowd to make out, oblivious to anyone who might be watching. That would be her and Andy out there, the two of them loosened by the wine, by the fact that they were surrounded by strangers, nobody to know them. She would dance with abandon, not caring if she looked drunk or sloppy or if they kissed in front of all these people. It would be like her early days in New York, dirty-dancing with strangers late nights at the Tunnel or Studio 54 after a few lines of cocaine or a joint shared with girlfriends.

Her view of the dancers became blocked by a white hat and large body. It was the Aboriginal man from the railing. "May I have this dance?"

This wasn't the dance she was waiting for, yet there was no reason to say no. The man whirled her around under the bright stadium lights in his wild version of Texas two-step. She couldn't find his beat and kept stepping on his toes, but he didn't seem to mind. Once she had to hop over a cowboy who'd passed out at their feet, and they moved around to find free ground. Donna watched the sky spin as the last hint of blue disappeared into inky blackness, the twinkling pink and green party lights strung on the bleachers blurring into streaks. She smelled sweat and beer, along with sporadic whiffs of vomit. Speakers pounded above her head. The Shiraz and the music made her head feel fuzzy. Donna tightened her grip on the man's shoulder and she looked down at their feet. Round-toed R.H. Williams boots and bare feet surrounded her, each in its own cloud of dust sparkling under the bright stadium lights.

The band slowed and he still gripped her tight. "What's your name?"

"Donna."

"Peter." He pulled her toward him and she saw teeth, white teeth, as he planted his mouth on hers and kissed as if he were responding to her pent-up need. She surprised herself by kissing back. The kiss didn't stop, became a breath, as though he were playing her the way Jocko played the didgeridoo. She vibrated like the instrument, felt his air sweep in and then out of her body, and still his mouth pressed. She knew she could have sex with him, a sixty-something Aboriginal man, even though it was Andy she'd been waiting for.

The lack of control she was feeling, the fullness, the willingness to give herself to this stranger—this Black stranger. She stepped back but he held her tight.

"Donna, I've been expecting you."

She'd an inkling of the magic she'd felt when she'd been to the waterhole with Andy and as she'd flown over her Honey Ant painting. Too bizarre. She pushed his chest, but he caught her by the arm. "Name the baby Jessie. The Honey Ant will be her kin."

Honey Ant. Pearl. The camel's name was Jessie. She wrenched her arm free and ran. Esther, too, had said she would have a baby. What could these Aboriginal people know about her? These interactions with strangers weren't random; was she being sought out? She ran around dancers and through the crowd until she felt herself being swept away. She didn't care where the crowd took her as long as she could choose whom she was with, so *they* couldn't choose her.

She was being pushed towards a huge orange carnival tent with pictures of white and Aboriginal boxers painted on the canvas. She could just make out the handmade signs on the outside, advertising *Fred Brophy's Famous Boxing Troupe—Fourth Generation Showman!—The Boys from the Bush are Back—Challenging all Comers.*

At the tent's flap, people were handing tickets to a woman with very few teeth and stringy gray hair. Donna fumbled for money, but the woman waved her in. She was near the front row and looked around for exits; the place was a fire hazard. The tent's air felt close, full of sweat and dust brought up in puffs by their shifting feet, but at least inside, Donna could be anonymous. All eyes were on the ring. As she peeked from behind a cowboy's broad shoulders, Donna saw a rope, which made a circle in the dirt. The crowd pressed forward against her, but Brophy's men went around and shoved people back. She closed her eyes, then opened them to Brophy's booming voice, "Welcome all comers! Any blood, I stop the fight. Men can't go outside the rope. All hits must be waist and above. Otherwise, anything goes."

The first contestants were two roosters—she hadn't known cockfighting was legal in Australia. The animals fluttered their wings and clawed at each other. The crowd encouraged the birds, and if she weren't so horrified, Donna would have deemed the fight graceful. The black bird suddenly collapsed; she could see its heavy breathing as it lay on its side, the owners swiftly recovering the champion.

Immediately after the cocks left the ring, the first human fight began. The challenger was a cowboy from a nearby station. His fresh buzz cut stood proud above a scarred forehead. He hardly landed a punch. And true to his word, Brophy stopped the match when the local cowboy got a bloody nose. As the buzz-cut cowboy spit and swore, Brophy unlaced his gloves and passed them to the next contender. An assistant sprinkled a layer of sawdust on the dirt. Donna looked through the crowd. No sign of Peter. Yet that kiss….

The next match began, and a tear rolled down Donna's cheek as she watched a drunken Aboriginal man try to fight. He looked the same age as Peter, but was probably no more than forty. Barefoot, stomach hanging over shorts that fell down to show the crack of his behind, he yelled as he swung wildly. She brushed tears away and laughed with the crowd at the next act, tag teams made up of a big man and a small man. The crowd went ballistic as the small amateur pummeled the pro big man, inflicting no damage but pleasing the crowd nonetheless. Brophy called a draw and awarded each of them one hundred dollars.

Donna watched the successive matches, each contender using the same sweaty gloves and bloody water bottle. Blood was spattered around the floor, pooling in dark patches in the sawdust, the smell of sweat overwhelming. Brophy's goons continually pushed the crowd back as it surged forward, calling for more blood. She wanted to leave, but she couldn't tear her eyes away. Barbaric and gratifying. And so male. As blood poured from a contender's face, she licked her lips, still tasting Peter no matter how many times she wiped her mouth. The blood around her was not the same blood of the ER. This was the blood of men competing for a woman.

The next match featured a young Aboriginal man as the contender. He looked as if he might win, until he suddenly went down as something flew into the crowd, over their heads.

Donna reached into her hair where she'd felt something drop, then rubbed wet and sticky fluid between her thumb and forefinger. Blood had an unmistakable viscosity. As she rubbed the blood, Brophy's tent was no more, and once again she was flying above her body. As she flew, she could see circular clumps of spinifex under clouds pregnant with monsoon rains. The air smelled metallic, and the wind kicked up dust so that she had to shield her eyes. Black flies were buzzing in excitement. There in front of her was the boy from the ring, behind a scraggly wattle bush, humping a girl, her eyes shining bright.

Donna came back to her body, to the sawdust and sweat. She looked around wildly, trying to figure out where the magic that made her fly had come from. The spinifex had been replaced by the circles of cowboy hats crouched down around her. "Got 'em," someone yelled from behind her, and Brophy himself made his way through the crowd. Young boys reached out to finger Brophy's starched shirt as he passed.

She saw the boy in her mind, the desperate fucking, and could think of nothing but getting out of the tent. In the cool night air, she saw Andy standing not fifty feet away in front of the medical tent. She took a deep breath, but he saw her before she was completely composed. "Ventured into Brophy's? That's a rough place."

She wanted to tell him about Australia and the magic of no horizons. The Aboriginals were making her soul separate from her body and fly. They were telling her future. They were...oh, Andy looked so beautiful, skin so smooth under the festival lights. So young, like the boy who'd just fought, who'd been with the girl in the spinifex. "That poor boy. Teeth knocked out."

"Broph pays them good. You'll see the boy in the Isa on Monday visiting Dr. Irving. He splints them back in."

Donna wiped her bloody fingers on her jeans. "Can't believe it's legal."

"Only in Queensland. What's on your cheek?" He cupped her chin and turned her towards him. The lights were dim, and she reached up as he did to brush it away. Their fingers met on her cheek. "Blood."

So close was his earnest, confident jaw, his full lips. He procured a bandana from his pocket and wiped her cheek. "Good luck that is. Stepmum says blood carries supernatural powers."

"It made me...transported me. My body was there in Brophy's but I was like a bird. Yes, I think I was a bird." She expected him to laugh, call her drunk, but instead he leaned down and kissed her.

They were standing there kissing under the privacy of his hat, his hand groping under her shirt, lightly pinching her breasts, her hips grinding into his erection, when the familiar strains of *Waltzing Matilda* began to waft over the crowd. Whooping had been replaced by genuine singing. A thousand gruff, off-key voices sang along to Australia's anthem of the Outback. Andy pulled his hand out from under her shirt with a groan, taking his hat from his head. "Come."

Oh! There once was a swagman camped in a billabong. The stationheads, white and Aboriginal, were swaying with their arms around each other. Following Andy's lead, Donna put an arm around Andy and one around a cowboy whom she'd never meet again. It felt like the homecoming game in her senior year at Princeton, on a crisp fall day when she and the friends she'd accumulated over four years, stood up, drunk as skunks, to sing *Old Nassau.* She'd felt such promise then, as the song had welled up inside her and around her gang of friends.

Donna's eyes teared. Was it the memory? Was it that life had already turned out to be full of more choices, sacrifices, and disappointments than she could ever have imagined during her college years? Yet she wouldn't have it any other way—except maybe for her ending with Greg. Or was it that hanging in the air, under a sky with no horizon, was a song of misfortune and suicide, and these people around her, fighters that they were, had chosen it for their own? She knew what it meant to jump into a billabong, and she could imagine the swagman's ghost among the coolabahs.

Andy squeezed her waist and then whispered, "Dance with me." He took her in his arms loosely, not to hold her captive, as Peter had. She thought of Peter's kiss and then Andy's, how Andy's was the familiar kiss of desire. Peter's had been homey, like they'd known each other forever. *I've been expecting you.* Should she try to find him to ask what he meant?

Andy's warm breath smelled of a relationship in its earliest bloom. How Greg had smelled when he'd taken her to see Tom Waits at the Blue Note on one of their early dates. *Waltzing Matilda, Waltzing Matilda. You'll go Waltzing Matilda with me.*

She leaned her cheek on Andy's shoulder. Not wanting to speak, but needing to. It was as if she needed to confide her infidelity. "Some Aboriginal man acted like he knew me and told me to name a daughter Jessie."

Andy's breath was moist on her neck. "I like that name. Would name a girl that meself."

"Why would he say it?"

"He's an alkie, fair dinkum."

As the song ended, she clung to Andy, but the whole lot of Aussies grunted and moaned their way onto the ground, most on their backs and looking up at the night sky. Donna felt the earth cool on her back as she and Andy lay down. He pointed to the shooting stars that crossed the sky behind the orange, green, purple, and red streaks of fireworks. She felt Andy's strong hand in hers, the pebbles that traced the contours of her back, the hairs on her arm brushing the leg of another random cowboy.

"Let's go." Andy pulled at her suddenly. "We can watch the finale from the field."

He lifted her to her feet and they hopped between arms and legs splayed on the dirt, past the crowd, past the bandstand and the track, and into the field between camp and the celebration. They were halfway across the field when the booms of the finale rang overhead. He pulled her down and rolled on top of her, elbows propping up his upper body. "I can't wait." He took off his hat and tucked it under her head and then his lips met hers. The last boom of the finale died off and the band played in the distance. She heard the whoops of the cowboys. As Andy kissed her neck, she looked up at the night sky, the stars twinkling through the dissipating smoke of the fireworks. She expected him to work quickly, a furtive fuck, like she and Greg had had once in Central Park. But no, he worked as if they were alone in the bedroom. Andy kissed her until she let her muscles relax and he whispered, "Ah, much better." Only then did he unbutton her shirt, slowly, not fumbling at all, and pulled down her camisole. He reached for something in his pocket—was it a pocket knife?—and held it above their heads. She felt him flinch and then he began to trace the circles of her breasts with his finger—wet, rough, sandy— and he traced paths down towards her belly. Every so often he'd pause and it took her some time before she understood he was gathering dirt from beneath her on his finger. Donna was being painted. Concentric half-circles.

She closed her eyes to the sky, breathed him in and concentrated on the painting. It was a story map. She moved her arm to caress him, maybe unbutton his shirt, but he stopped her and brought her arms to her side. His index finger on her lips silenced her. She licked his finger, tasted dirt, metals, warmth, and blood. There was a cut on his finger—had he cut it deliberately with the knife? He reached under her head, into his hat, and pulled out a feather. Then he ran it up and down along the lines he'd painted.

He unsnapped her jeans and gently pulled them off, then continued his painting down her legs, between her thighs, and...yes, he was painting her insides. She banished a quick thought of HIV. As a doctor, blood had come to be so dangerous to her. It had been so long since anyone had taken such time with her. Sex with Greg had been pleasant but perfunctory, timed along with ovulation.

Too late for a condom. Life was a risk. Australia knew no horizon, no end to possibility. Peter had predicted a child, absurd as it might seem. *Name the child Jessie.* Her hips arched upward against him. Andy moved to the rhythm of the music wafting over the field and pulsing through the earth. She felt the earth's hot magma shifting below her, vibrations—not like those of mine blasting—more like long sighs. When Donna and Andy finally sat up, the parched earth absorbed the wetness spilling from her.

Shadowy figures were heading toward them, but passing them, giving them wide berth. People were drifting back to the billabong for the night. Andy held her hand as they walked back to camp. Once there, he laid their swags together, overlapping their covers so they became one bed. "No better canopy than the night sky of the southern hemisphere."

She kicked off her boots and, following his lead, stripped off her jeans and jacket and climbed between the soft sheet lining the tarp. He rolled over and whispered, "You'll be warmest naked.

Trust me." She shimmied the rest of her clothes off and Andy pulled her close.

The Southern Cross was high in the sky, reminding her of her mother's crucifix that, with her mother's pearls, was locked in Donna's New York safe deposit box. She pictured Jesus hanging above her on the stars. At the time of Christ, the Southern Cross had been visible from Jerusalem. Had Mary understood the warning as she watched the Crux rise in the night sky?

Mary, more than Jesus, was for whom Donna had felt love as a child, before she'd taken her father's lead and allowed science to replace religion. Before she'd let religion go, Donna and her mother would hide in her parents' walk-in closet, kneeling between the silk dresses and wool suits, reciting Hail Marys, Our Fathers, and David's Psalms. They had an unspoken understanding that Donna shouldn't mention the prayers to her father. Donna didn't have her own rosary for the Hail Marys, so her mother would give her a strand of pearls as a substitute. And after her mother died, Donna wore those pearls all the time, until the day she left for Australia.

The Southern Cross was so clear out here, away from the town's light. Donna thought the Australian sky could be her church, more than her mother's St. Patrick's ever had been. Donna had gone to St. Patrick's after she'd lost the baby, but she'd felt like a foreigner and left after a few minutes. That had been her final visit.

Andy pointed at some of the constellations. "Can you tell the real cross from the false one?"

"How?"

"The false one's part of Carina and Vela. The real one is in the bright part of the Milky Way. See the Jewel Box?"

Sapphire, ruby, and topaz stars glittered under the left beam. Donna hadn't realized that some stars had distinct colors.

"See that jet-black hole in the Milky Way at its base? That's the Coal Sack, the most famous dark nebula in the galaxy. Look for the two pointers. They point to the bottom star from the east," Andy pointed.

She removed the swag cover, let her chest point to the stars in the moonlight. She could see faint traces of red over her belly, seven concentric half-circles. "Why did you do this?" Andy's finger joined hers as she traced them.

He landed his finger in her belly button. "Increases magnetic connection. You, with the moon, the South Pole, with me."

The stars blinked on and off above them. How many of those stars were already dead, yet the earth still received their light, generated millions of years ago? "Is there proof that would stand up in a science journal?"

His finger dug further into a circle that bordered her belly button. "Every cell in our body is magnetized. You learn in med school how the body responds on a magnetic level—increased blood coagulation during the day but drops at night, responding to the change in the earth's electromagnetic field."

Of course Donna knew patients were sensitive to the rhythm of the earth. Heart attacks happened at four AM, strokes at noon.

"The veins of metals in the earth are like our veins, what you've heard called songlines. I paint the lines with magnetized cells and you can tune into the earth's pulses. We're more in tune with each other."

Donna let the words drift over her as she concentrated on his fingers. He continued, "That's one of the things I like about you, Donna. What happened to you at Brophy's."

"I'm so much older than you." She let her fingers run up and down his flank, feeling the spot where each muscle connected to the bone. She stopped at the spot where she would make the incision for a chest tube, and he flinched. "Back in the Isa, at work, well ... " She moved her hands down toward his glutes.

He moved so that his nose almost touched hers. "I'll be back in Isa in a few weeks and I'd like company. It's between us."

"I can be company." She looked over his shoulder at the Crux.

"But it seems like there are no secrets out here. Everyone knows my business."

Andy laughed, "You're wrong. This land is made from secrets."

Naked all night, she didn't feel the cold. Donna squinted her eyes and looked over at the sleeping Aussie, his budding crow's feet smooth in his sleep, his face illuminated by the stars and the flicker of the dying bonfire. A twenty-six-year-old Aussie—she'd finally asked his age—looked older than a twenty-six-year-old American, yet he was a boy. She could smell alcohol as he exhaled, mixed with the dust in the heavy night air. She stuck her hand under his balled-up jacket and felt the weight of his head on her hand. He shifted in his sleep, turning in such a way that his hot cheek pinned her wrist.

Donna didn't sleep. Instead, she followed the upright of the Cross down the sky and imagined following it to the South Pole as it had guided so many explorers. Stars, like angels, were messengers.

She thought of the Aboriginal boy who'd been the angel in her dreams, that yellow-haired, chocolate-skinned angel—where was he now? And Peter, whose lips she could still taste under the kisses of Andy's, had delivered a message. If it hadn't been for all the coincidences, she would have thought Peter was just a drunk, as Andy suggested.

Donna thought she'd given up the desire for a child. But tonight she imagined the sperm inside her colliding with an egg. With her free hand she traced the circles of dirt painted on her stomach. She brought her thumb to her forehead, her chest, her right shoulder and left, mirroring the Cross above, tracing the magnetic lines buried deep within the body of her childhood.

Seven days after his night at the waterhole, Jimmy came to the second barbed wire fence. He imagined many a kangaroo jumping right into its twisted points without ever seeing the barrier. Who would expect a fence out there in the middle of the Land? The roos would die for sure, blood spurting from holes in their chests.

Two days earlier, he'd climbed the rusty barbed wire of the first fence and, anxious to get to the seedpile, hadn't been careful as he jumped down and so sliced his thigh. Despite the pain, he searched for mangol bark for the wound for several hours. If his wound had been a scorpion sting or fire ant bite, the cure would have been right there. The Land always provided a cure next to the curse. But what was the natural balance for a biting fence?

He'd broken off the skin of the mangol tree and pushed the bark onto his wound, the blood acting like glue, then shoved more bark into his pockets, walking as he sang what Hector had taught him. He knew the Land even though he'd never been there before. His feet sighed in relief every time they touched, heel-toe, heel-toe to this Galah Land. The Land pulsed through his feet and into his blood, helping the mangol heal his gash. Da's finger bone weighed heavy in his pocket. It wanted out.

The fence standing before him now was tall and rusty. He looked down at his thigh, hot to the touch, and knew he couldn't risk another fence bite, and besides, he couldn't climb it. Hoping for a gate, he followed the fence around for a day and night and another day without sleeping, often times dragging his hand along the rusty wire, collecting the rust and painting his body with the iron. The fence was well-mended. Were they afraid of cattle rustlers? It couldn't be there just to keep the blackfellas out. Jimmy kicked a rock in front of him as he traveled, feeling every cell of his body turn toward his path, yet always there was the fence, pushing him off the track like a false scent. The bone grew agitated as he veered off-course. *Da, I bloody know where I'm going*, he yelled to the blue sky.

On the evening of the second day with the fence, a Galah settled onto the fence wire just ahead of him and began to scold. As the sun was setting to turn the whole sky pink, Jimmy sat down and listened to her. He hated her, was jealous that he was not her, yet loved her all the same for keeping him company. If only he were like his kin with real wings, he could listen to magnets embedded in his cells, fly over the barrier, and Behold his Land.

He lay down next to the fence and the Galah, Da's bone making his thigh throb harder. Should he throw the bone over the fence? Would that be as close as his father would get? But he desperately wanted to walk on his Land, feel the earth that was part of him, and celebrate his Ancestors in the place where they gave birth to his energy. Only then could he cut himself properly and add his penis blood to his Land. He buried his face in the dust.

He woke in the night to see Yaraandoo above him, the Galah gone, but a gray feather on the ground. He added it to the contents of his pockets and massaged the foot scar from the night he'd been seized.

Mum sat by him. "Half day's walk west, wait on the Boulia road for the black cockatoo woman. We have dreamt her. She will help you Behold your Land. Auntie Tess will find a medicine man to wake Hector. Don't leave Isa until the Kardachi man comes. You will finish initiation." Jimmy sighed as Mum examined the fresh cut on his thigh with her long fingers. "That's a bad one, Jimmy. You let the cockatoo medicine woman take care of it. Stay close to her."

Jimmy woke to the *chi chi* of the Galah as it headed in the direction of the Boulia road. Da's bone was weightless in his pocket. Inhaling the smell of yucca, he got up and ate his last granola bar for brekky, then followed the bird in search of the cockatoo medicine woman. Well, galahs and cockatoos often traveled together in mixed flocks. He could travel with her. No worries.

All night, she stood on the fence, at times climbing up, beak then four toes, and at times climbing down, four toes and then beak. Her body wanted her to be at the waterhole, or searching for berries in the cool night. But she could not leave. What was she to do with the wires beneath her? Her beak was sharp, would crack the hardest macadamia nut, but still she could not snap the wire for him.

Agitated she plucked out a tail feather and let it fall to the ground. Give him a wing. But she looked at the body, open on the ground, offering itself without hesitation to the winds, and she knew he would never be able to catch an updraft over the wires.

She looked out over his Land with her sharp eyes. It was her destiny danced by the spinifex, to bring him here. She could feel the seed power that created him, created her. Her third eye, that magnet of her forehead, pulled her there, so that it almost lifted her up off the fence and beyond to the pile of rock eggs. She had seen them as she flew, and now she could barely resist their pull. Ah, but for the boy. Her magnet sense burned with his. Yet it was not enough. He could not visit in a dream. He had to go to it with his legs.

When the moon was overhead, a white cockatoo alighted beside her, the mother's messenger. Together they watched over the sleeping boy, pacing the wires.

With the first feather of dawn stretching over the sky, the cockatoo flew north, and the Galah, west. There was nothing to do but fly on the wind.

He saw the Land Rover when it was still far away, trailed by its cloud of dust on the horizon. He stepped to the edge of the road, but wasn't stupid enough to stand in it. She flew right by, but then the Rover's red lights gleamed through her tail-cloud.

He jogged to where her car was pulled over, almost a kilometer ahead. The cut on his thigh burned each time his foot hit bitumen. She stood on the side of the road next to the car. "I know you," she said.

Without answering, he climbed up into the passenger seat. She looked surprised, but what had she expected? If you stop for a bloke out here, he's gonna demand a ride. She crossed in front of the car and got in. "I'm Donna Cooper."

She was prettier than he'd remembered from the hospital tuck shop. Her legs tensed against the brake pedal, disappearing into her skirt. She waited with her hands on the wheel, so he told her, "Jimmy Jackboy." He looked ahead, wishing for the car to pull forward, willing this new chapter of his life to begin. The tug of his Land was a burden now that he'd failed.

"Heading back to the Isa?" she asked as she pulled back onto the road.

"Ta."

"Seat belt, please," she said in her American accent, and he obeyed, buckling with sweaty palms. He snuck a look at her profile. Her dark lashes blinked against the sun, and then she pulled her sunglasses down from her forehead, just like a cockatoo would close its lid. Her red lips were tight. She wasn't as white as most whitefellas, more of a greenish-brown. Not skin from the land of the dead, but definitely from the living.

She eyed him and he turned his head to the road. Didn't want her to see him examining her. Jimmy watched the wattle fly by and thought how much easier it was to cover distance in a car.

They drove a while before she spoke again. "What are you doing out here alone? Are you lost?"

"No such thing as a lost Yapa. Haven't you heard?" Jimmy liked her laugh, was glad she got his joke. Jimmy was all for jokes, all for people and things who made and understood them. Like the grass outside the hospital that looked so inviting but was full of tiny prickly spears. That grass had a sense of humor, like the whoopee cushion his teacher, Mrs. Westbrook, had brought back to Yuendumu from holiday in Brisbane.

The doctor sat up straight as a roo and kept her eye on the road, gripping the steering wheel. Da had driven with one hand, lounging back into the seat, his free hand out the window feeling the air rush by, looking at the land, never at the road. She glanced at his thigh. "You were limping."

"Cut me leg. No worries, nothing broken." He needed to stay close to her, but he would not let her—or any woman now—act as a mother in his life. He was becoming a man, and he would act like one, initiated or not.

"I'm a doctor. Want me to have a look at it?"

"I know."

She had a smile that wanted to peek out often, but tried to hide. "What do you know?"

"You're a medicine woman." His voice wavered as he said it. *Stay close to her*, Mum had said. As he'd sat on the warm bitumen waiting for her, he realized the medicine woman would help him in more ways than one, just as the stories of the Dreaming meant many things at the same time. The doctor would heal his wound, help him get to his Land, but more important, from her he could begin to learn the ways to become a doctor.

The doctor spoke again. "Didn't I see you in town with your dad?"

Jimmy sighed. "Me uncle's in hospital. Doing some Dreaming."

They passed a mob of wallaroos resting under some ghost gums. He was sure the doctor hadn't seen them lolling in the shade. Jimmy longed to get out and relax with them, his back against the smooth white bark of the trees, no worries. "Maybe he's awake now."

"How'd you hurt your leg?"

If only the fence hadn't been high as the sky. "Tried to get over a fence. Rusty dingo bit me."

The doctor's fingers felt for his thigh. He jumped as her finger touched his wound. "Sorry. You'll need a tetanus shot. How about we stop at the hospital when we get to town and I look at it? Then we'll visit your uncle."

Jimmy watched the budgies racing the car. They were not happy that Jimmy was traveling faster than them. He'd let her give him a shot. "I was thinking I'd be a doctor someday. A Flying Doc."

"Australia can use more good docs," she paused. "Shouldn't you be in school if you're going to be a doctor?"

He looked at her sideways. "It's Easter holiday." Sort of a lie, but it wasn't her business whether he was in school. White folks were always worrying. As if the blackfellas didn't know a thing. As if blackfellas were all a bunch of bludgers.

"Thought that was over a few weeks ago."

He'd been taught since he was a baby that you can't fool a medicine woman, but he wouldn't explain himself. He kept his gaze forward to match hers.

After a minute she smiled. "So for Easter holiday you decided to come out to the bush and climb fences?"

Jimmy laid his head back on the leather seat. Good joke. "If a whitefella forgets to put in a gate, you gotta climb a fence."

"Some people call that trespassing."

Jimmy smiled. "It's me Land. Gave them a chance to give me permission."

"Your family's there?"

"Yeah." Clearly Doctor Donna had no idea what he was talking about. Smart, but she'd need a lot of education if she were going to help him. He let his cheek rest against the window. "Uncle better be Dreaming up some permission."

They traveled in silence past an old tin squatter's shack, past an emu with her four chicks feeding in the short grass by the side of the road, past big reds hopping through orange dust at the horizon before she spoke again. "What do you smell like? I smell something sweet."

Jimmy lifted his forearm to his nose and took a whiff. "That's Mum's yucca. Can I change the radio?" Jimmy liked country music. She nodded and he pushed the radio dial, searching for Mob Radio.

They were silent for a while again when she whispered, "Is there anything I need to know? A message maybe?"

Did she know they'd Dreamt her up? Well, he wasn't going to be the one to tell her and anyway, he had no idea why the elders had Dreamt her. An American doc. Funny, that.

She pointed out the smokestacks when they rose on the horizon. Twenty minutes later they pulled into the hospital car park. She locked the car and motioned him to follow. "Who's your uncle?"

"Hector Aintree."

"I know him." She bobbed her head like a cockatoo. "Come with me first."

\∩/

Donna held Jimmy's brown calf and studied his thigh. His skin was smooth, though its hairs were starting to grow. Just on the verge of manhood. What a handsome man he'd be, tall, with his muscles beautifully defined. She let her hand linger on his ankle longer than necessary, just to feel the pulse of his posterior tibial artery, which was like the pulse of Andy's heart against her chest as he'd laid on her in the swag early that morning.

Here was her angel, maybe the soul of her son, and she was noticing the cut of his muscles, his blood pulsing. For shame. But she hadn't showered or slept, and all she could smell was Jimmy's yucca and sex. Jimmy sat on the exam table, lit up by the fluorescent hospital lights. She shined her overhead lamp on the cut. His skin glowed. She searched for lidocaine in the supply cart. "I'll numb your leg before I stitch."

He shook his head.

She thought he'd change his mind after the first suture, but they went in easily and he never flinched. "The needle doesn't bother you?"

He swung his good leg. "It's a trick we learn for our initiation."

She concentrated on making a neat line with the sutures and he bent over her, watching the needle thread the skin. His breath was so close it moistened her ear. Messy scars were a pet peeve of hers —usually easily avoided—but she was having a hard time concentrating. "When was your initiation?"

He tensed. "Haven't finished it yet. Told you I need to get to me Land."

"Tell me about it." She used the doctor's trick of asking open-ended questions. It was usually the best means of gathering information, though it hadn't been working as well with the Aboriginals. Whites, Americans, and Aussies would go on and on with their problems, making her crazy but giving her ample information for a diagnosis. The Aboriginals kept things private.

"Teach me how to sew," he countered.

"I forgot. You want to be a doctor." She pointed to both sides of the cut. "To make it neat, you make tiny stitches. No rushing. Practice at home on something thicker than cloth. Tag board is good." She covered the sutures with tape, then filled the tetanus syringe. He gave her his arm and she shook her head. "It's your bum. Want me to get a man to give it to you?" She remembered the embarrassment of hitting puberty and her own pediatrician being unaware of her need for modesty. She was extra careful with teens. He laughed and dropped his shorts—no underwear of course, and again he didn't flinch as she emptied the syringe into his fleshy behind.

She thought she'd fallen asleep at the wheel when she first saw him by the road, his arm extended in a wave. Thought that after her sleepless night with Andy, she'd dreamt the angel boy. But when she'd pulled over, she saw him jogging up in the rearview mirror. As though she'd summoned him the night before, in her swag, thinking of him and looking at the Crux. Furtively, she'd checked the glove compartment and felt the gray velvet bag, as though somehow the ashes and the angel boy were linked.

Australia was turning into a land of coincidences, not to mention out-of-body experiences. In her scientific training, coincidence was not correlation, yet multiple coincidences were statistically meaningful. Since one of the basic tenets of science was that there were no miracles, she would have to try to explain her brushes with the spider and crocodile, why this boy kept popping up, why certain Aboriginals seemed to be finding her. *Name the child, Jessie. Honey Ant will be her kin.*

Donna disposed of the needle as Jimmy pulled his pants up.

It was time for a visit to Hector Aintree. Hector had shown no signs of improvement in the week-and-a-half he'd been in the hospital, but there might have been changes when she was in Boulia. As they walked upstairs to the medical ward, Jimmy holding his leg stiff beside her and pulling up on the rails, she prayed that in her absence, Hector had awoken. She was no neurosurgeon, but knew that if he didn't improve soon, there'd be very little hope. Forcing a smile, she swung open the heavy door to the second floor. "Promise me you won't be climbing over any more rusty fences."

He shrugged, "Can't promise."

"Can't you bring wire cutters?" She could see by his smile that he got her joke.

As they entered Hector's room Jimmy yelled, "Hector, you awake yet?"

As Donna feared, there was no response. She checked the charts as Jimmy loudly repeated, "Hector." She sat down at the end of the bed, her hand resting atop the sheet-covered, motionless leg. "Jimmy, has anyone explained coma to you?"

He ran his finger along the wall, tracing a crack in the paint. "I know about coma. Mum is sure he'll wake. He's taking his time."

Donna played with her clipboard, afraid to look the boy in the eye. "Jimmy, we need to get in touch with your mum. Your uncle can't take care of you."

"Mum's sending someone for us." Jimmy had Andy's confidence, the confidence of a young man who hasn't seen heartbreak.

"Good. Can I talk to her?"

Jimmy squeezed Hector's toes, one by one.

Donna stood up and rested her hands on his shoulders. He was less than a head smaller than she. "Jimmy, I need to talk to her. We need more information on Hector."

He shrugged her off and she stepped back.

"Sorry. It would be a help."

Esther came in with a pile of fresh sheets and stopped. She flung the sheets on the visitor's chair, and, hands on hips, pointed at Jimmy. "Thought I told you not to get out of the chair. Gone walkabout, eh?"

"You've met?" Donna asked.

"Briefly." Esther glared at the boy.

He gave a small wave and turned to leave. "Call the Yuendumu Community Center. Mum doesn't have a phone."

Esther maneuvered her large frame so that she blocked the doorway. "I am Galah, too. You can't run away again. Where are you staying while Uncle's in hospital?"

"Camp in the billabong with the Yapa."

"How about food? Do you need money?"

He shook his blond head, letting the spiky hair fall in front of his eyes. "Been out there for weeks. Camp's all set up. Want to get back before sundown."

Donna mouthed to Esther, "Is it safe?"

Esther nodded slightly. "You come see me every day, do you hear? Or I'll let your mum know."

That reminded Donna. "When I call, who should I ask for at the community center?"

"Gloreen or Tess," he said as he squeezed between Esther and the door.

Donna and Esther stared at each other, Hector's room was noticeably darker without the boy.

"Excuse me." Donna hurried past Esther and ran out into the hall. She was not going to lose her angel now that he'd waltzed into her life, seemingly dropped from the sky into the middle of nowhere for her to pick up. "Jimmy, wait," she called.

She stopped closer to him than she'd intended, so that only a few inches separated her nose from the top of his yellow head. His hair smelled of the bush, of fresh breezes and dust. "You said you wanted to become a doctor. Meet me here tomorrow at eight and I'll show you what you can do for your uncle."

He backed away, smiling. "You have me word." He took off, surprisingly fast for a boy with new stitches, darting into the elevator a moment before the doors closed.

She wouldn't be able to relax until he showed himself the next morning. Without going back to talk to Esther, she hurried to her office and called *Information* to get the number for the Yuendumu Community Center. After fifteen minutes of staring at the crazy designs of her screen saver and endless ringing of the phone at the other end, a man answered.

Donna turned her eyes away from the screen and looked out bush. "Hello, this is Donna Cooper, a doctor at the Mount Isa Base Hospital."

The voice laughed. "So you got our Hector in hospital, do you?"

How had they known? "Yes, did someone from the hospital already call you?" The charts didn't indicate that anyone had been in touch with family. The man laughed again. "Someone'll be out to fetch him soon."

"Who is this I'm speaking to?"

"Daniel's me name. Cousin."

Donna was relieved to have a contact, finally. "Can I ask you questions about family history? And do you know Jimmy Jackboy?"

"Of course." There was a commotion in the background and he yelled something at someone. "If you hold you can talk to Jimmy's mum."

After some fumbling of the receiver on the other end a woman's low voice spoke. "G'day. This is Gloreen."

Donna was surprised how serene Gloreen sounded. Not the panicked mother of a missing child who was stranded in a far-off town with his uncle in a coma. When presented with the current situation, Gloreen thanked Donna for picking up Jimmy on the road from Boulia and gave permission for him to continue camping in the billabong. Donna tried one more tack. "Shouldn't he be in school? We can arrange to put him on a bus back to Yuendumu."

Gloreen answered quickly. "No. Next quarter starts in two weeks. If Hector is still in hospital, we can send Jimmy to school in Isa. Someone will come for them."

Donna looked out the window at the blue sky. This woman existed on the far end of that horizon. "Who?"

Like her son, Gloreen didn't answer questions she wasn't interested in hearing. "Here's Daniel."

After a lengthy conversation about Hector's history, Donna hung up the phone. If Hector didn't improve by the end of the week, she'd get a social worker involved to watch over Jimmy.

But something felt odd, as it had felt yesterday with Peter. As if Donna weren't choosing to befriend Jimmy, although of course she had—he'd come to her in a dream—but instead as if these people were placing themselves in her path. As if Hector had fallen into a coma in order to become her patient. Boys don't just appear in the middle of nowhere and ask for a ride. Why wasn't his mother concerned that he'd run off to the bush? Had someone dropped him there in wait for her? She shook her head. Sleep deprivation could make your mind work in funny ways, could impair rational thinking, could make you paranoid. This wasn't a *Twilight Zone* episode. This was real life.

The sunset was turning the smoke from the mine neon orange when she left the hospital. She followed it home, where a flock of Galahs—there looked to be more than a hundred—gathered on the telephone wires. The parrots chattered, performed circus tricks, twirled around the wires, their gray wings flapping. Under their noisy *chi chi*s, she pulled the velvet bag from the glove compartment and her duffle from the back of the car. Then she took them into her bedroom, carefully placing the velvet bag back on the dresser.

As the hot day cooled, Donna sat on her front stoop with a glass of Shiraz and surveyed the neighborhood. On whole, the residents of Isa were a practical people. The men spent their days in the mine, emerging in an orange stream at the end of the shift, then stripping off their day-glo jumpsuits for their wives to wash and hang on the line. The jumpsuit was the official flag of the Isa, waving in the backyards between the white sheets.

The houses were impeccably maintained, but looked like they could barely withstand a strong wind. They were made to be removed when the mine shut down, as all mines eventually do. Each newly discovered deposit was met with a collective sigh of relief; it meant five or ten more years that Isa would survive amid the bougainvillea.

On even-numbered days, she'd sit on the three steps that served as the house's front porch and watch the even neighbors across the street go to battle with their hoses, embarrassed about her own front lawn. But today was an odd-numbered day. She set her glass down on the crumbling concrete and unwound the hose. Her neighbors to the right and left were outside as well, wielding their hoses like sabers against the natural desert that was fighting to reclaim their lawns. Donna's was slowly coming back to life. There was no point in watering during the heat of the day, since the water evaporated before it hit the ground. She'd hoped to water her mango tree enough to coax some fruit, but Doctor Archie seemed to think it was the variety with sour fruit. Who would plant a sour mango tree?

As she watered, she watched her neighbor out of her peripheral vision, coveting his dangling oranges, which were just an arm's length away from the chain fence. She'd complimented him on how wonderful they looked, but he hadn't given her any. He'd nod, but never offered encouragement for conversation. He was probably tired of watching the docs rotate through and not keep up the lawn.

When she was finished watering, she went inside and e-mailed Kate—*I had sex... Esther and Nan coming over for dinner soon. Wish it were you, too*—then undressed for a shower. When she turned on the shower, the spigot came loose. Shit. She'd have to clean the tub and take a bath after Esther and Nan brought dinner. She pulled her sweats over her dirty body—she could still see traces of Andy's bloody dirt lines on her belly—and listened to her stomach growl. She was looking forward to a Big Mac. She hadn't eaten fast food since college, but given the options in the Isa, McDonald's was now a takeout staple.

Donna wanted to sleep, but what newly-divorced, forty-one-year-old woman could have a night of animal sex with a twenty-six-year-old and not hash out the wonderful, gory details with a girlfriend the next day? She tried not to feel guilty about spilling the beans.

She wished just Esther were coming, but the red-headed Aussie Nan had been on shift with Esther and overheard their conversation. Donna thought back to her first day when she'd watched Nan chase Andy out of the ER. Nan had probably been sleeping with him as well. Donna would have to be careful what she shared.

When the nurses arrived, they all sat on Donna's tiny couch with their burgers and fries. She meant to talk only about Andy, but somehow sex with him seemed to be inexplicably linked to the story of Peter, to the blood hitting her face at Brophy's, and to picking up Jimmy on the Boulia road. "Isn't it odd? More than a coincidence?" Donna asked, wiping the mustard from her cheek with a serviette.

Nan looked into her fries. "I think kissing the old man sounds gross."

Esther's nose seemed to disappear into her burger, but her eyes held Donna's. "Told you about the baby." She closed her eyes either choosing her next words or enjoying her burger.

As Esther was about to speak, Nan interrupted. "More sex details. Enough about that mumbo jumbo."

Esther shook a fry at Nan. "For all those years you whites built cities, learned to farm, and learned to control the land, we were busy cultivating spiritual powers. She's having a baby."

Nan leaned back into the couch, spreading her arms as if she owned it. "Donna told you. Years of in vitro. Why are you getting her hopes up?"

Esther's black eyes flashed under her prominent brow. "Australia is different. Our earth has been tended, energized for thousands of years," she pretended to spit, "until Captain Cook."

"Excuse me." Donna stood up between the two women, holding her burger high like a flag. "I'm still here. Can we not discuss my fertility?" She looked at Nan's clear skin, unlined forehead, a woman who still had so many fertile years ahead of her. "I'll approach all of this with a rational mind."

Nan crossed her arms over a perky and ample chest. "Just one question, Miss Rational Mind. Did you practice safe sex? Who had the condom?"

Donna blushed. She'd tried not to think about her lack of caution. Had she been driven to have unprotected sex by Peter's prediction? Or had it been lust? They were all health care professionals, had seen the ravages of AIDS. Unsafe sex was inexcusable. She had to assume Andy was disease-free—he surely would have tested himself periodically as she'd recently learned was the norm for modern singles. She looked down at Nan's face, cheeks full from baby fat, not puffy like Esther's nor lined like her own. "You don't have any idea what it feels like not to be able to have a baby." At Nan's shifting eyes she added, "Is it so bad that I still want one?"

Donna heard her desire bounce off the empty walls. She hadn't admitted it since the day Greg had left, but even without him, she still wanted a baby. Esther slurped her soda loudly. Nan set the rest of her burger on a serviette and rose from the couch, her hardened, sarcastic look turning into one of pity, which annoyed Donna more. Nan hugged Donna. "I'm sorry." Donna hugged back reluctantly. As Nan pulled away, she laughed. "You need a bath, if you don't mind me saying."

"Tried. Shower's broken."

Esther put her fries down and put out her hand. "Got a screw driver?"

Donna followed them into the bathroom. They worked on the shower head, arguing about the best way to fix it. As Donna watched, her hand slid down to her belly. What if she *were* pregnant? What would a little girl—Peter had said *her dreaming*—born from the Australian soil be like? Would she be tough and competent like Esther and Nan? Soft down outside, but prickly and wild inside like the yellow wattle? She thought of the spider that had dropped from the same shower head. Her daughter would not fear Outback creatures; she would be one of them, born of sex in the bush.

Nan stood with the shower head and a tiny washer in each hand as she waited for Esther to tighten a screw. "Every sister's been trying to shag that boy for months, including me. Never thought you'd be the one to win the Andy lotto."

"Has he slept with a bunch of them?" Donna twirled her ponytail and watched her own face in the mirror.

"I don't know of any for certain," Nan looked down as she handed Esther the washer. "Though I did hear he had a gal in Townsville he's going to marry at Christmas."

Donna let go of her hair. Touché. As long as Andy didn't have a string of women in the Isa, she'd ignore that bit of information. Townsville was far away and she was not looking for a twenty-six-year-old husband. "Are you shocked that the old hag got the man?"

Nan smiled her beautiful smile. "Nah, Doctor Donna, you know that's not what I meant."

Of course that's what you meant, thought Donna, but she smiled back.

"Think you're an item?"

"No. Still want to see Nick."

Esther tightened the last washer and chimed in. "Good onya.

And I hate to say I told you. Get a little sex and it reminds you that you need more."

Nan kicked at Esther's shoe with her own. "Slut."

Esther shook her head. "It's like me and Jocko. I go up or he comes down two weekends a month. What happens in the other time, doesn't matter."

The shower was fixed. Esther excused herself for a *dunny break*, and Donna walked Nan to the door.

When Esther came back to where Donna was cleaning up the bags from dinner she asked, "Nan gone?"

Donna nodded and Esther held the velvet bag high. Donna grabbed the bag from Esther's hand. "How'd you find it?"

Esther smoothed her nurse's whites and walked to the door. "Empty the bag if you want to be pregnant. Baby's spirit needs to rest. Thanks for tea."

Donna watched the screen door slam behind her friend's back, as she stood silent in her living room, holding the trash in one hand and her baby's ashes in the other.

Part Two

WALTZING JIMMY JACKBOY

\\∩/

Donna was in Hector's room on Monday, waiting to see if Jimmy would show. After checking the feeding tube and squeezing Hector's hand, she said a loud *Good morning* to the comatose man.

Jimmy waltzed in at exactly eight and jumped up on the foot of Hector's bed. "Quit Dreaming, Uncle. I don't think it took the Ancestors this long." Jimmy laughed and pinched Hector's foot. "Stubborn old man." Jimmy looked up at Donna. "What will you teach me?"

"Not even a g'day first?" She took a long look at her angel. As he aged, his nose would be a bulb like Esther's, not straight and lean like Jocko's. One day he'd have scarred skin with big pores and bushy eyebrows—they were already particularly full. Would his eyebrows hide those curved black lashes, or his deep eyes that looked like they were ringed with eyeliner?

Donna showed him how to move Hector's limbs to try to prevent bed sores, how to massage his appendages, how to check that his IV was dripping appropriately. Jimmy pointed to the machines. Their green and blue lights blinked with Hector's breathing, measuring heartbeat, oxygen levels, and brain function. "I want to read them. And I want to take blood pressure."

She flipped the machines on *sound* so Jimmy could hear the patterns as well as see them. "Anything else?"

"I'd like to give him a needle." Such confidence emanated from the way he stood, weight forward on the balls of his feet as if ready to jump.

"Injections are lesson ten. Let's start with blood pressure."

A half hour later Donna was expected in clinic. "Have to go

downstairs. I'll be back in the afternoon to go over the EKGs. "

"I'll go with you."

"Other patients expect privacy." They walked out of the room side by side. His shoulder was almost the height of hers.

"I can do the blood pressures."

She shook her head. "Only for your uncle."

Jimmy shadowed her as she entered the ER, where there was a clinic room off to one side. Orange chairs were full of patients. Nan presented her with charts as soon as Donna came in. "Feral day. Thirty patients scheduled."

"What? This is a hospital, not a doctor's office." Donna hurried into the exam room where an older Aboriginal woman with a facial rash sat on the exam table, and a middle-aged man sat in the orange chair. A black fly bumped against the exam room window as it tried to escape. Donna didn't blame it. She wasn't so happy herself to be cooped up in this room for the next six hours. "Do you mind if I keep the door open a crack?"

The patient, Mildred Nichols, had been sent from the Cloncurry clinic for a lupus evaluation. Donna launched into doctor mode, asking the usual questions. *How long had she had the rash? What has she done for it?*

The patient answered and Donna wrote orders for labs. When she looked up from her papers, she noticed a face peeking through the crack of the door. "Jimmy. This is private."

His blond hair led as he peeked his whole head in. "How else am I gonna learn to be a doctor?"

She moved to push him out. "You'll go to med school like everyone else."

Mildred interrupted. "He can come in."

"Really?"

The woman nodded. "Fair dinkum."

Donna pointed to an open chair. "Have a seat," and she turned back to Mildred to do a physical examine of her arms, legs, and torso.

"Doc, her eyes are dull. I think you'd better check them." Jimmy's voice rang confidently from his chair.

"Thank you, Jimmy." Eye problems were often a side effect of lupus. But if you treated the eye before identifying the underlying condition, all you were doing is masking a symptom. Donna needed to listen to her lungs. "Uh, ma'am, I have to lift your shirt. Would you like the men to leave?" Mildred gave a half-shake of her head. Neither Jimmy nor the patient's friend moved. As Donna had expected, Mildred wore no bra and had no qualm about exposing her breasts. Donna took a quick peek at Jimmy. Unlike an American teenager, he didn't seem to notice the woman's breasts any more than he would her arm or leg. Donna thought back to a photograph of an Aboriginal woman preparing for a festival. In the image, the woman was drawing ochre circles over her breasts and down her belly. Her chest was the community canvas for the celebration.

Jimmy whispered, "Hey doc, the eyes."

Donna had thirty patients to see, most of whom would probably not talk to her, and she had a teenager at her side giving medical advice. *Be careful what you wish for.* She'd wanted to spend time with her angel, but hadn't wanted another doctor in the room. "Where did you learn your medicine, Jimmy?"

"From Auntie Tess. Eyes like that? Use mangol." He sat expectantly, awaiting Donna's examination of the eyes. Donna obliged and thought she saw the first signs of glaucoma. When she announced her finding, Jimmy nodded, "Mangol root."

Donna ended the exam by agreeing with the lupus diagnosis, adjusting the steroid dosages, and writing orders for Mildred's doctor in Cloncurry to watch blood pressure in the future. She explained to them—though it seemed that only Jimmy were listening—that with the steroid adjustment, she hoped Mildred's eyes would improve. As Mildred left the room, Jimmy whispered to Donna, "You sure? No mangol?"

Donna squinted. Yes, his smile was still as bright with her eyes half shut. "No mangol," she muttered, and ushered in the next patient. What was mangol, anyway?

Throughout her shift, patients continued to allow Jimmy to stay in the room, and Donna introduced him as an *intern-to-be*, even going so far as to hand him her stethoscope to hold between chest exams. The smell of each patient lingered, blending with the smells of the next, the mélange whirling around each time they opened the exam room door for the next patient. It reminded her of the clinic halls in Khadbari, where she had to step over sleeping Nepalese who'd walked days for three minutes with the Western doctor. Yet when Jimmy came close to deliver her stethoscope or to get a better look, she smelled only warm breezes.

Jimmy was at Hector's room at eight in the morning for the next two days. On Thursday, they stood outside Hector's door after the morning checkup, Jimmy having read all the vitals. "Can I do clinic again? Can I go on rounds? I'm tired of following Esther. All she does is change bedpans."

"Esther has an important job." Donna was privately happy he wanted to be with her, had been a bit jealous of how much time he'd been spending with Esther. She pondered her options. She wouldn't hold another clinic until Monday and didn't think it appropriate to bring Jimmy into the ICU. Yet his tenacity was wearing her down. She wanted to see only smiles on his brown face, did not want to send him back to her friend. "Remember, medicine is private stuff. People don't want a strange boy knowing their secrets."

"Yapa don't care about these secrets." Jimmy tapped his toe impatiently.

She looked at her watch. It was an hour early to start ICU rounds, but what the hell? This was the Isa and rules here were meant to be broken. She turned down the hall. "Only if the patient is conscious and can agree." She eyed the boy, who easily kept up her pace. If he'd been her dog, she would have named him Shadow. Or Bulldog.

"When we see the next patient, can I take the blood pressure?"

She introduced Jimmy to the rest of her patients and each one would smile, even those from whom she'd heard nothing but complaints. She let Jimmy wear the stethoscope. She'd put out her hand and say, *Stethoscope, please,* and he'd hand it to her saying, *Stethoscope, Doctor.* Most patients let him listen to their lungs.

Jimmy in tow, Donna checked the chart of Bernice Edwards, an Aboriginal woman in her fifties. Bernice's labs had come back with bad news. Donna sat down next to her bed, and since Bernice was hard of hearing, Donna shouted, "Your kidneys are filters for your blood. The labs tell me that your kidneys are no longer working. Wastes are building up."

Donna paused to look for a sign that the woman understood her. Bernice continued to stare at the wall. Donna glanced at the wall to see if there were a spider or something else absorbing Bernice's attention. Donna shouted louder, "We'll have to send you to Townsville for dialysis." Jimmy was staring at her intensely. She began to fiddle with the chart and lost her train of thought. It was as if she had stage fright, as if he were a renowned nephrologist and was judging her analysis. She began chewing on her pen, something she never did while giving a patient bad news. That kind of behavior could make them think the doctor was unsure of the diagnosis. Bernice sat there without a grunt or nod. The woman was like a stone, other than her constant fiddling with her super-sized pack of Holiday 50s and its warning *Smoking is Addictive* on her moveable night stand.

Donna yelled again, "Do you understand?"

Bernice studied the wall. Exasperated, Donna rolled her eyes at Jimmy but was immediately sorry. She didn't want him to think she disrespected the old woman. She put her hand on the woman's shoulder and said, "I'll come back in a bit. We'll try again."

Jimmy popped out of his chair like a pinball and came over to Bernice's side. "Let me." He nodded a hello to Bernice.

Donna's *That's okay* was interrupted by Jimmy yelling at Bernice. "Doctor Donna says your kidneys like didgeridoo." He mimed a long tube with his hands, careful not to hit Bernice's IV "Didg cleans out your dirty blood."

Jimmy held his hands as if he were holding a didg to his mouth, then began to shake them as if music were flowing through. As she watched Jimmy play his imaginary instrument, she had a vision of her mother in her hospice bed, refusing any last blood transfusions. Her mother had believed the soul was anchored to the body through the blood, and she hadn't wanted to be tied to her cancerous body any longer.

Jocko, like Jimmy, had said the didg cleaned people out. And Esther had explained how Yapa magic worked on the spirit, not the actual body. She imagined Jimmy's didgeridoo cleansing the soul anchored to Bernice's blood. She thought about her baby's ashes. When blood burned, did any of it turn to ash? Jimmy stopped the pantomime and Donna reached out as if to grasp a piece of wisdom that eluded her.

"Whitefellas have big machine." Jimmy then motioned a big square box. "Whitefella machine clean out your kidneys." He mimed didgeridoo again.

Donna looked at Bernice and yelled, "Understand?"

"Yeah," she grumbled, looking at Jimmy and not at Donna. "Me kidneys are crook."

Donna turned to Jimmy. "How did you know about the big machine?"

"I listened to you. Dialysis."

"You listen well."

"In Warlpiri, *to listen* means *to be.*" Jimmy admonished, and held up the stethoscope. "Time for blood pressure?"

She held her hand out for the stethoscope. He would be a good doctor. He would intuit the bodily systems better than she ever had. "I'll do this one." She leaned over Bernice, and for a moment her mother's body was prone beneath her on the bed.

Donna called Gloreen on the following Monday, after a morning clinic of Jimmy diagnosing her patients. He sat on the corner of her desk looking out at the bush as Donna spoke to his mother at the Yuendumu Community Center. Gloreen said they would send someone for him during Rodeo—which Gloreen pronounced *Ro-DAY-oh*. Three months away. Donna's heartbeat quickened at the thought of him remaining in Isa for three whole months. Though if Hector didn't wake before that, Jimmy would go home without a functioning uncle.

After Gloreen, Mrs. Westbrook, Jimmy's teacher in Yuendumu, got on the phone to speak to Jimmy. Donna tried to picture the tiny town, Gloreen ambling over from the community center to the school, and Mrs. Westbrook leaving her class in order to take a phone call. Donna had heard a number of *Yes, missus* and *No, missus* as Jimmy nodded. He hung up the phone. "So let's find me a new school."

"Do you want me to call back so you can speak to your mum?"

"No worries."

Donna followed Jimmy's gaze out the window. His long black eyelashes hid his eyes. "Does that mean yes or no?"

"No."

"Why?"

He turned his dark eyes on Donna. "I'm being initiated, Doctor. Can't become a man if I still need Mum."

Three months until Rodeo sounded like an awfully long time to wait so he could finish his initiation. Why couldn't the Kardachi man hurry? The thought of three whole moons passing was almost more than Jimmy could bear. But what choice did he have? He needed Hector or another Galah man to initiate him.

After speaking to Mrs. Westbrook, he shuffled after Donna to Aboriginal Affairs. It felt different to walk in with the medicine woman than it had with Hector. He could tell that Doctor Donna expected to get her way, while Hector had been sure before setting foot inside that the AA Yapa were a useless mob. Jimmy liked the way she strode in with her high-heeled shoes, tight skirt, and collared shirt, and introduced herself, *Doctor Donna Cooper*, looking the people in the eye and joking about the weather.

She stepped aside and pushed Jimmy forward with slight pressure on his lower back, the way his mother would have. "I'd like you to meet my friend, Jimmy Jackboy. His uncle is in my care at the hospital, and though he is interning with me to learn about medicine, it would be prudent for us to enroll him in school. I was told you could arrange that."

He liked that she introduced him, didn't have him stand silently by her side. Liked the idea of "interning," though he didn't know that's what he'd been doing. But he'd been helping Doctor Donna with medicine and was more sure than ever he'd become a doc someday. He'd asked Doctor Donna what he needed to do, and she'd explained what exams he'd take, what courses in University he'd have, how to get internships, and then she'd waited patiently while he wrote it all down. He patted the list in his pocket.

Doctor Donna continued to speak to the AA woman. "The hospital does not have funds to pay Jimmy for his work, so I was wondering if you could arrange for Jimmy to receive a small stipend while he is stranded in Isa."

The Yapa at the desk, who hadn't offered them a seat yet, raised her eyebrows. "Sure, he can get on the dole."

Donna interrupted her. "He is working very hard for us, so he shouldn't feel that it's the dole."

The woman shrugged. "We'll get him a check. Fill in this form."

Jimmy knew Donna's comments were meant for him, not the woman. She probably thought Jimmy wouldn't take a bed in the hospital because he was afraid of charity. She and Esther had offered him a cot in Hector's room. Nan, the cute nurse with the wicked smile, had shown him a room that they used only if the other beds were completely full and said she wouldn't tell anyone if she found him in it.

It wasn't a fear of charity. He ate their food, didn't he? Jimmy simply preferred his swag in the billabong. Liked looking up at Yaraandoo through the dancing coolabah leaves at night. Liked taking tea with the old Yapa who camped there, telling Dreaming stories, talking about his initiation. He knew that initiation meant finding his new mother in mother earth. He needed to sleep with her at night. Besides, camping in the billabong kept him from getting too much mothering from the sisters. That was the thing about sisters—they loved to take care of people.

The AA woman passed the form and he filled it out. When he handed it back, she asked, "Weren't you in here before?"

"Needed help to get to me Land. You offered to file a native title claim." Jimmy hesitated, looking at Donna from the corner of his eye. "I may be interested in following up on that." Might as well if he was stuck in town anyway. Besides, he was willing to try anything, even if Hector had said not to bother.

The woman's smile brightened. "Let's get you signed up for

school, then we can spend more time. A new claim. Good onya."
Everyone had things they liked to do. Galahs flew, emus ran, and
apparently Aboriginal Affairs people filed native title claims.

On Thursday morning, Esther took Jimmy to the cashier at the
hospital to cash his first dole check, and when he showed Donna
the money, she told him to walk over to the Kmart and buy
some skivvies and pants for school. He paused outside the sliding
doors of the hospital. Mum had said the medicine man would
come at Rodeo. But wasn't there a good chance the white medicine would work first? Maybe Hector would wake up this weekend without the Kardachi man, and then Jimmy'd have wasted
all that good money in his pocket. He looked around at the car
park, and then his feet led his stomach to the tuck shop. The food
was good in hospital, but the puddings couldn't be compared to
a Violet Crumble.

The screen door slammed behind him. He was relieved to see
a strange new woman and not the frizzy-haired lady behind the
counter. He let his hand close on the purple wrapper, could almost taste the honeycomb through his palm. He listened to the
crinkle as he piled one, another, then the next on the counter.

The lady scanned each one. "Ten? Having a party?"

"May I have a brown bag?"

He sat behind the bushes next to the hospital eating one after the other, letting the honeycomb melt in his mouth, hardly
chewing. He'd let each bite exist for as long as it could on his
tongue, pass it all over his mouth before sending it to his stomach. After he'd eaten five, he stuck two more in his pocket and
walked upstairs to Hector's room, where he stashed the bag behind the window blinds. From the looks of the desert dust that
had collected on the sill, it didn't seem like the cleaners focused
on that area of the room often.

When Donna came to get him for afternoon rounds, she handed

him her stethoscope and he handed her a Violet Crumble.

She examined the purple wrapper, tracing the yellow writing with her finger. "For me?"

"Do you like them?"

"Violent Crumble. Never seen one before."

"*Violet*, Doctor. Try it." He watched her separate the end of the wrapper carefully, not quickly as he would.

Her red lips—sometimes she wore lipstick and sometimes she didn't and he liked them better without—closed around the chocolate. She closed her eyes, concentrating on the taste and then finished chewing the whole bite before she spoke. "It's so light. Like there's nothing there."

"So you like it?"

She wrapped up the end and stuck it in her lab coat. "Yes. Thank you, Jimmy. Did you go to Kmart?"

"Have all I need for school." Jimmy stuck her stethoscope in his ears. "Can we start with Hector?"

Two weeks after Doctor Donna had picked him up on the Boulia road, Jimmy made an early Sunday morning visit to Hector. He'd have to go to school the next day if Hector didn't awaken.

He went to the EKG machine and ripped off the roll of white paper mapping the mountains and valleys of Hector's heart. Peak, trough, peak, trough, for a whole night. Hector's vitals were the same. Every morning and afternoon, Jimmy had read them. This wasn't the right map for a Galah. Galahs had peaks, waterholes, saltsoaks, rockpiles, and then valleys. Jimmy felt his father's bone heavy in his pocket.

He tucked the paper roll into the back of his pants, hurried over to the sisters' station to borrow some markers, and ran down the empty stairwell of the hospital. Shielding his eyes from the sun, he went around the back where there was a small patio for patients who would come for a smoke.

It took him almost all Sunday without moving his bum from the hot concrete to draw his Dreaming, holding the roll of EKG paper with his foot so it wouldn't roll back onto itself. As the sun set over the bush, Jimmy went back upstairs, found some medical tape in the supply cabinet, and mounted the Dreaming on Hector's wall. Now maybe the Galah Land could pull Hector from his sleep just like the smells of damper in the morning woke Jimmy. Maybe his map could help the white medicine work—Dreaming and Yuti together.

The bright greens of town soothe the Galah now. They are the shades of easy water. In the wide world the waterholes of monsoon time are dry, berries have fallen to the ground and been buried by the sands to burst into life with the next Wet. But in town the water is brought up from deep in the earth by the humans, sprayed in arcs over the bright green patches to linger as round drops on petals and grass tips. Round drops seep into the ground, droplets split open the seeds, bursting into long stems of brown and green with flowers of every hue, rainbows like the rainbow arcs of water. It is always breeding time in town. There is water.

If she had a choice she would glide on updrafts to the edge of town, where the bright greens meet the brown, beyond where the boy frolics, where the red rolling hills begin. There the rock wallabies play among the boulders, peeking in and out with no fear. There she would pick a dying gum for their nest, hardly noticeable as it blends into the rocks.

But she must be near the boy. Her new mate has found a hollow high in the trunk of the mango tree from which they look onto the flatness of the human houses, surrounded by greens. Her mate has lined the nest with gum leaves and his feathers, nettles on the edge to keep out the feral cats of town.

A thin wisp of human smoke trails off at eye level and disappears into the spirit world. She calls the boy to the black cockatoo house to make a nest below her own.

M onday morning, Jimmy woke before dawn and listened
to the coolabah leaves dance above him. He rolled up his
swag and hurried on his half-hour walk to the hospital. Maybe
Hector was awake. Maybe Jimmy wouldn't have to go to school,
but would leave today for Galah land *without* permission, to
cross. He imagined the Dreaming on Hector's wall working its
magic.

He dashed up the hospital stairs, but as soon as he entered Hector's room he knew, even in the dark, that Jimmy was no closer
to his initiation. He gave Hector's toe a hard squeeze. "Hope
that hurts." He hadn't gone to the waterhole for a bath last night,
thinking it wouldn't be necessary, so now he climbed into Hector's hospital shower. Wouldn't do to go to the white people's
school without a bath.

Donna was examining the Galah Dreaming in Hector's room
when Jimmy came out of the bathroom. She looked at him and
her almond eyes narrowed. "What about those new shirts I told
you to buy?"

"Didn't."

"Thought not. Look."

She pointed to the orange chair. Piled on it was a blue backpack, three blue shirts, short pants, and a pair of blue athletic
shoes. He thought back to the day at hospital when she'd asked
him his favorite color, and he'd looked out the window at the
clear sky and chosen blue. He'd meant the color of the day sky—
Donna's gifts were dark blue, the color of the night sky. He took
a blue shirt from the top. It felt heavy and stiff, but he quickly
stripped off his own and put hers on. She picked up his dirty shirt

and held it away from her body, pinched between her thumb and forefinger. "I'll give it a wash, okay? School starts at eight-fifteen. Should I get you a Timex from the Kmart?"

Jimmy wondered if that would be blue, too. "I don't need one." He looked at her lips, flat like the horizon, no smile. "No worries. Gotta go."

"Let's look at your stitches first. Then I'll drive you."

He pulled up his short pants to show his thigh. "Already took them out with me flint knife."

She ran her finger over his scar, the same way she'd traced the words on the Violet Crumble. "By the way, I like your artwork." Her long black hair brushed his nose as she turned her head to look up at his Dreaming.

Sitting in the car seat next to the Doctor, he tossed his father's finger bone from hand to hand and thought of the shiver that had run between his shoulder blades down to his penis when Doctor Donna had touched his scar. Would that scar be forever linked to her, the way the scar on his foot was linked to Mum? Could a scar link you to a woman who wasn't kin? Or had he shivered because her hands were so smooth and pretty on his leg? Or that lovely smell in her hair. It was a flower he'd smelled only once before and now couldn't place. Anyway, why had she agreed to drive him? Because she feared he wouldn't show up at school or because she wanted to see him off? He wished he could talk to Hector about all these questions.

She drove slowly on the city streets. It was good to have a ride since it would take him an hour to walk to school from hospital. Mum had been right. Donna was a good person to stay close to. Donna and Esther, Esther and Donna. They were a funny-looking pair, greenish-white skinny woman next to the big Yapa. Esther was Galah, like Jimmy. Galahs and cockatoo cousins, always together.

They turned onto the street where Jimmy had found his dead Galah kin and Doctor Donna stopped the car in front of a green house. "Forgot my cell phone."

He watched her run up the concrete steps, her pony tail bobbing more like a willy wagtail than a cockatoo. His Galah kin must have wanted him to find Doctor Donna when he'd first arrived in Isa. No worries; she'd been found. Moments later, she ran down the steps and jumped in the car. They rounded a corner and then another, and Donna pointed ahead to a huge building with tall white doors. He sank lower in his seat and pocketed the finger bone. The building was twice, no, *three* times the size of his old school. What if he were a country boy, so far behind the city kids? Bloody Hector.

The car crunched in the gravel of the school lot as Donna parked. She started to open her car door and his arm shot out to stop her. He was surprised by the strength of her bicep. She looked so fragile, but there was meat on her bones. "I can go in meself."

She hesitated, her door cracked open.

"Mates me age don't have mums walk them to school. See ya later. Thanks for the ride." He'd mentioned Mum and immediately got a flutter in his gut. He wished he remembered the last time Mum had held him. Like death, the day Uncles seized him had come without warning; he hadn't known it would be his last day to be a boy. How he wished he could go back and have a last hug. And despite the excitement of staying in town and learning white medicine, he wished his initiation didn't include going to a new school. He watched the kids streaming into the school, took a deep breath, and swung his door open.

He didn't look back, didn't want Donna to feel the invitation to get out of the car. One of the school's heavy doors was propped open and kids dragged their feet in front of him, not ready for a new quarter. Jimmy thought about the doors to kuurlu in Yuendumu. The clan had painted the school doors with their Fire Ant Dreaming. The doors told the story of the Land, so that often the kids would pause to study them, not because they were hesitant to go into kuurlu. When he passed through these blank doors in Mount Isa, would he be heading even further away from his initiation? He took a deep breath, walked forward, and looked around for Room #15. A sign pinned to the wall to the right announced *Science Fete 26 August, Grand Prize: Two Tickets to Brisbane Courtesy of Ansett*. He liked science. A fete wouldn't be too bad and neither would a trip to Brisbane. He passed the sign and headed down a hall, Room #10, #9, #8. His old school had just four rooms. He wandered to the end, then made his way back past the Science Fete poster and the front door, down another long hall. Kids were calling out each other's names, chatting by lockers. At home, school and life were all the same. His kin sat in the chairs around him, chanting back at Mrs. Westbrook. Uncles and Aunties roamed through the halls.

The number fifteen loomed above the room to his right. He forced his feet to walk through the door. His eyes raced over the shelves of books, saw the charts on the walls from science experiments, saw the tins of scissors, the four shiny computers, the maps of continents. Mrs. Westbrook would be jealous of all these supplies. They didn't have nearly so much in their classroom in Yuendumu.

Two girls looked at him, then kept talking to each other. One or two boys looked up, but no one seemed to take notice. The desks were in rows. Should he take one? Were they already assigned? He put his back to the wall and stood there until the teacher walked in.

She didn't notice him at first, so Jimmy walked up to her desk. "Excuse me."

The teacher, Mrs. Brunswick, gave him tests in maths and reading to see what groups to put him in. He sat in the corner, half listening to the class doing fractions on the chalkboard and then discussing types of cumulus and cirrus clouds, half finishing his exams. When class was excused for Phys. Ed., Mrs. Brunswick had him wait. He was surprised to see her yellow-toothed smile as she checked his answers. She was halfway through and looked up at him. "You're a good student. Go ahead to the gymnasium."

At playlunch, he sat alone with his back against the school yard wall watching the other kids chatter over their tucker boxes—he'd forgotten to bring one and Doctor Donna hadn't thought of it either. He envied their vegemite sandwiches. He would have rather had tea than a new skivvy. Soon a bunch of mates began a cricket game while the sheilas bunched up in groups talking and playing tether ball. Was the same as in Yuendumu.

He was surprised when he felt the air cool above him and a shadow crossed the knees that were clasped to his chest. "Good game in Phys. Ed. Want to play? We're losing." A dark-haired boy with perfectly round freckles stood above him, holding a cricket bat. As Jimmy looked closer; he saw that the brown marks on his face were indeed freckles, but many of the others were red with a white puss ball in the middle. Auntie Tess would have put gum sap on those pimples and they would've healed right away. Jimmy had never seen anyone with so many—he wondered if maybe the boy had a disease. The boy handed him a sunhat. "If teacher sees you without, you have to stay in the shade. I keep an extra, case I forget. Me name's Tom."

Jimmy already knew his name. Mrs. Brunswick had sighed, *Come in for help after school, Tom* after Tom got every maths problem on the blackboard wrong. Tom had turned red all the way down to his lumpy Adam's apple. His throat reminded Jimmy of a snake that had just eaten a desert mole. Jimmy's eyes kept watching the mole bounce when the boy swallowed.

Tom's head stuck up higher than all the others as they'd sat in their chairs listening to Mrs. Brunswick, so Jimmy wasn't surprised Tom had been one of the first to be picked for teams in Phys. Ed. Jimmy, of course, had been the last. How surprised they'd been when it turned out he was good at bat. A bat felt right in his arm. How many hours had he spent with a cricket bat swinging through the air? Mum would go crazy. Tell him to go find a boomerang or something useful to do.

Jimmy stood up, put on the sunhat—missed the feel of the air in his hair—and followed Tom to the cricket pitch. Tom handed him the bat. When the bat connected with the ball, Jimmy wasn't surprised. It went exactly where he'd imagined it would go a moment before, giving him plenty of time to run past Tom, the other batter, and change ends. Tom smiled, showing his buck teeth.

Jimmy was so good that he was at bat the whole lunch hour. Before they walked back into class, Tom took his hat back. "No worries. You can use it again for the game tomorrow. Did you see League on Sunday?"

"I like AFL."

As they jostled with everyone else towards the classrooms, Tom asked, "Who's your team?"

Jimmy headed to the back of the rows of desks. "Essedon. You?"

Tom followed him even though his desk was in front. "Brisbane."

"Their best year was 2002. Good team."

Mrs. Brunswick cleared her throat. "Tom, can we have you in your seat?"

The end of the day arrived swiftly for Jimmy, and he streamed down the hall with the crowd. A bird in the flock, a fish in the stream. He heard the clicks and clomps of shoes on linoleum and thought how different it sounded from the slapping of bare feet in Yuendumu. He'd enjoyed the lessons on meteors and poetry. He left the cool of the school and re-entered the heat, the sun welcoming him and wrapping her arms around him like Mum had after school when he was a boy.

Jimmy followed the other kids down the front walk of the school, the sun as his company. He'd hoped maybe Tom would wait for him so he'd have someone to walk out with, but Tom had hurried out the door. He saw the sea of bright backpacks and wished he had a yellow one. Ahead of him, some kids turned left, some turned right. They turned without hesitation; they had a destination. Until then Jimmy had considered his Dreaming site his destination, the hospital, a detour. But now he was without a place to go.

He needed a branch to perch on, like the Galahs. A nest. Some parrots came back to the same tree year after year. But a nest was never meant to be permanent, was only used when there were eggs to hatch or babies to feed. And that's what he needed. A place to rest until baby down turned from pink fluff to pink and gray feathers and a Galah chick could launch himself into the air to be cast away on the currents.

His shoulders were weighed down with his school work in the backpack. For homework, he had to do four pages in the book Mrs. Brunswick had lent him—the other kids had to bring in dollars for theirs—but where would he go to do it? Back to the orange chair next to Hector. But it wasn't much of a place to concentrate, with the sisters' chattering. It would be a long walk, and he wanted to finish all his homework before the sun went down. He wanted to show the city teachers how much Mrs. Westbrook had taught him.

He was almost at the end of the walkway. Could feel the tide in front of him beginning to part so that he too would be faced with the decision. Left or right?. He could feel the mob of kids behind him. Would they roll right into him if he stopped there to breathe and let the wind tell him where to go?

Chi chi. He followed the call of the Galah and turned left, but where *to*?

He stopped and untied his shoes, tossing them into the backpack. Doctor Donna said he couldn't go to school in bare feet. Purple bougainvillea—Doctor Donna taught him the name— hung over a front gate, and he paused to breathe deeply, a flower he'd never seen before town. Too delicate for the desert. It didn't have prickles or fur on its stem; it climbed lazily around fences and over trees. He would like to bring some back for Mum.

His feet were relieved to feel the ground, not rubber soles. Jimmy wiggled his toes and followed his feet. They would take him somewhere. Maybe because he was thinking about Doctor Donna and the flowers and his backpack, his feet turned left at Gracie. And there he stood, outside the house Donna had walked into that morning. His feet took him into her yard, plopped him down on her front steps. He slid the pencil out of the small pocket on the front of the pack. His teacher had given him an extra in case he broke a tip. He held it up to his nose. Wished he could sharpen it again and again to smell the wood shavings.

He was finished with all his maths problems and closed his eyes. When Donna's car crunched up the gravel driveway, he realized he'd been Dreaming her to come home. He got up to meet her so she wouldn't be surprised. "Hey, Doc."

She smiled like the half moon. "Thought you'd come to the hospital after school. Report in to Hector."

"I have me homework. It's too far."

"That's true." She pointed at the backpack. "You've filled it up already."

"Keep all me stuff in it. The skivvies you bought me at the Kmart."

She jingled her house keys. "Join me for dinner?"

When Doctor Donna disappeared behind the screen door, Jimmy threw his shirt over his backpack and went through the chain fence to the backyard. The yard was square with patches of grass and dirt under the laundry pole, a rusty shed with a huge padlock at the far corner, and a bright little shed next to the house. He ran to the rusty shed and tested the lock. It didn't move. Disappointed, he tried to imagine the treasures within, the dark corners for hiding, the lizards he could surprise and catch, cold and sluggish from their time hidden away from the sun.

A mango tree shaded the center of the yard, its wide leaves interlaced above his head. He shook the rough trunk to see if there were any loose fruits. Nothing fell. He eyed a few green mangos on the top branches. It didn't look promising. He could climb it easily, but he knew not to. The sap would stick to his arms and legs and give him little red bumps that would itch all night. Anyway, from the shape of its leaves he could tell it was a male; its mangos wouldn't be very sweet.

Right over the fence were some beautiful oranges that bent the branches of the neighbors' tree into a boomerang. He went over and dug his toes into small holds in the chain fence—how he wished the fence around the Galah land had been this friendly—hoisting himself to the top and eyeing the fruits rotting on the ground. What a waste. When it was fully dark, he would relieve the tree of her burden, pick the heavy oranges and hide them behind the house. He could make wonderful meals of those oranges. Maybe he'd bring some in to Doctor Donna.

He turned his back to the neighbor's tree, balancing on his heels in the holes of the fence, his bum carrying most of his weight as he rested against the chains. He examined the back of the house. He didn't like how the smooth green lines of the siding were broken by the screen door and back steps. He could see the Doctor through one of the two windows, pouring wine. He guessed she knew how to drink it since she was a medicine woman. Hoped she wouldn't end up poisoned like Hector. She looked up and waved, and Jimmy jumped from the fence, worried he shouldn't be on it. He ran to the laundry pole. Similar to Mum's, it looked like a three-meter tall telly antennae with three wires strung between each two-meter branch, built to spin on the breeze when there was one. Only a pair of jeans and two towels hung from the wires. At home, so many clothes hung from each clothesline. He took hold of an antenna and pulled, feet slapping the dying grass, faster, faster, round and round until it twirled on its aluminum pole. He stood, legs spread, feet pushing into the prickly grass, arms held wide, face still, to feel the brush of the laundry as they whirled by, the jeans leg grazing his face. The breeze he created smelled of hospital soap, like Doctor Donna.

He watched the laundry pole slow until it wobbled just slightly. He spun the laundry pole again, then ran around with it faster and faster. Made him feel like the Galah flying through the sky. Wait until he became a pilot. Then he'd fly tricks with the parrots. He'd be a wilder flyer than a budgie. When he tired, he began to twirl himself in little circles, arms outstretched, the eagle. Jimmy twirled in the backyard, round and around, until the air felt heavy on his arms, until he could no longer keep them out wide. He pulled them back into his body, feeling their warmth, losing sense of the wind, of the weight of the air, feeling light, so light, as if he might float up into the blue sky, float all the way home to Yuendumu. He let himself fly, another Galah at his side, her wing almost touching his fingers, together looking down on the path he'd taken. Through scorched earth, the gums of the red Tanami. He could still see his footprints, double prints for each one of his and Hector's, and the dust swirling from the shuffling gait of his Ancestors walking beside them. He saw the places where they'd camped, rich brown earth under which they'd buried their wastes, tree roots where they'd found fat white ngarlkirdi hiding, ready to be fried crisp, cool water holes where they'd bathed. He flew south of Isa to Galah Land, past the onion field and bush banana gathering, and on to the rocks that grew from the starseeds that his Galah ancestor had dropped. From there he Beheld his Land. *I will see my sacred sites. I will become a man.*

The earth's force finally found him, pulled him, thrust him to the ground. He fell face down and smelled the hollow earth, zinc and the copper filling his nostrils, the musky smell of worms and bugs below him. At once his hands were covered with wet flecks of orange and brown. They smelled of vomit and his stomach hurt.

He wiped his hands in the dirt, rolled away from the stinky mess onto his back and pulled his knees to his chest. The leaves of the mango spun in the blue sky. He tried to sit up, then threw himself backwards. The house had gone crooked, its window moving from side to side. He splayed his arms wide to brace himself, then pushed down hard onto the flimsy layer of earth.

When the sky stopped spinning, he noticed a pair of Galahs on a branch of the mango tree. Jimmy smiled wide and whispered *G'day*. His relations were watching him. One of them had been with him as he'd flown over his Dreaming just now.

In the last light of day, a rainbow bee-eater buzzed by. Jimmy watched it dip suddenly and catch a wasp in mid-air, then fly to a perch below the Galahs to smash its prey, dislodge the stinger, swallow the wasp whole, and fly on. Jimmy lay still, still as the Galahs, and listened to the city sounds, a truck going up Gracie Street, someone hammering, a dog barking, the hum of the Telstra wires. He wanted to ask the Doctor for a Coke but didn't know if he should.

He flipped onto his belly and let his eyes travel across the lawn, over ants and pointy blades of half-dead grass. At once his body tightened. Bush tucker. Who would have thought you'd find such delicacies in the city? He dragged his body closer without taking his eyes off his prey, slowly drew his knees under his chest, then pushed his toes into the ground until he crouched, steady on his feet, balancing his weight on his soles. In one smooth motion he hopped, his arm making a full circle in the air, coming down over the grasshopper. It was as long as his hand and he had a hard time covering it. He felt it jump against his palm over and over, reacting to the sudden shade. One Galah in the tree started squawking and hopped along the branch to get a better view.

How was he going to cook it? Whitefellas didn't like to eat those things. When he had the grasshopper by its bum, he called up to the parrots. "Cousins, shhhh. Tea for you." He held the grasshopper out at arms length and the male climbed down the tree trunk, beak-toes, beak-toes, to the ground beside him. With a nod of thanks, it grabbed the grasshopper from his hand. Jimmy watched the bird bite the head off, the wiggling body falling to the ground.

Ancestor Galah had dropped starseeds that made waterholes. Near his home there were three huge leaf-shaped starseed holes that would fill with water in the Wet. They were surrounded by many small holes that ran in tracks as if many Galahs had fed together. Mrs. Westbrook said maybe starseeds fell from the Ancestors, but also a big meat-eating dinosaur made the leaf-shaped tracks as he was running after a herd of little dinosaurs.

Jimmy watched the male Galah spear the rest of its tea with a sharp beak. Both stories were true. Dinosaurs and Galahs together, the same energy, but two different Ancestors seeding the earth. He leaned into the knobby trunk of the mango tree in the company of his kin who shared the grasshopper body with his mate. Good company.

Jimmy was jiggling the rusted lock on the backyard shed when the Doctor came out to fetch him. "Dinner's ready."

He took one last tug on the lock. "Got a key for that?"

She shook her head as she waited for him to join her.

"Bugger. Could be full of treasure."

"Treasure?" Her shoulder next to his, they walked up the back steps. She opened the door for him. "Let's call a locksmith."

She poured another glass of wine at dinner. It smelled fruity and he liked the wine-smell of her breath as she talked. Jimmy pointed at the bottle. "Can I have a taste, Doctor?"

"You should stick with water, Jimmy."

He hated being treated like a child. If he'd been an initiated man, she wouldn't have said that. "I can handle it, you know." Jimmy looked at his plate of rice, beans, and barramundi. "Not going to let meself get pissed on grog like Hector."

She kept her lips in a straight line as she finished chewing. "My body can handle it, while Hector's can't. It's the matter of a simple enzyme that Aboriginal people are lacking. Your body will probably never process alcohol well either."

It was as if she were giving him bad news of a disease he had. He was trying to think of a retort when she broke into a smile and stood up to rummage in a cupboard. She brought down a gold box and opened it. Brown balls of chockie.

"Truffles." She handed him one, even though he still had half his fish on his plate. "Stick to chocolate. You can handle it much better than I can. Chocolate makes me break out in pimples."

The truffles tasted heavy like earth. "Gonna enter a Science Fete and win tickets to Brisbane. Won't Hector be surprised when he wakes and I tell him we're flying to the coast?" He spoke with his mouth full, something Mum would never stand for.

"What about that initiation?"

He didn't need the doctor to remind him. "No worries. We'll take care of that too."

An hour later a big man with a mermaid tattoo came and cut open the lock on the shed. It was dark so Jimmy held the flashlight as the man positioned the huge cutting jaws, like a Galah beak, against the metal. The lock snapped in two. Jimmy remembered Donna's wire cutter joke. Those jaws could get him through the fence that surrounded his Land. Maybe he could save his dole money and buy the jaws at the Kmart. Or maybe they could borrow them from the mermaid man when Hector woke.

The man stuck the jaws back into his tool belt. "Go fetch your mum."

Jimmy was about to answer that Mum was in Yuendumu. But he realized the man meant Doctor Donna. What a thought, a white medicine woman for a mum.

He ran through the dead grass and went up the back stairs to the kitchen, jumping over the bottom two steps. Then again, for a bunch of his uncles, white mums were not so unusual. Stolen from their own mums, given to white ladies. How awful that would be. One day off hunting a roo and then suddenly in a paddywagon, driven for days, never to see Mum again, never to see brothers, sisters, cousins, aunts, uncles, mothers-in-law, kin. Alone with strangers, an empty body without them. Kin were like air. Can't live without air.

"Are you okay, Jimmy?" She stood by the table, a dirty dish in hand. "Can I get you something?"

"The man. He wants you."

With a toss of her cockatoo hair, she went out the door.

A few minutes later, she came in jingling the car keys in her pocket. "Let's get you home. I'm not opening that shed in the dark. Why don't you come back after school tomorrow and see the treasure."

He studied the little purple flowers on the wallpaper. Not the bougainvillea, not a flower he'd seen in the desert. Maybe it was the flower that made her hair smell nice. He stood up and took a quick sniff at the wallpaper—of course it smelled like wall and not flowers. Then he followed her out the front door, down the steps, and grabbed his shirt and backpack. He swung the pack over his shoulder and almost swung himself into her as she stopped abruptly and turned to him. "Where should I drop you?"

"The billabong."

Doctor put her hand on his arm. "Jimmy, why don't you take a bath and sleep here? Good to get some sleep on a school night." The heat of her palm was startling in the cool night air. No mothering. No mother. He was on his way to being initiated. He loved his bed in the billabong under the coolabahs, though he didn't like the thought of the hour-and-a-half walk to school in the morning. Maybe he could bum a ride. He shook his head and started to pass her to get into the car. Her tiny body seemed suddenly huge and he could not get to the car door. She nodded, then went back into the house. He heard her keys as they landed on the coffee table.

He followed her in. She disappeared down the hall and after a moment he heard the water turn on in the bathroom. He was too old to have someone run his bath. Did she think he was a child? He should walk out the open door at his back, all the way to the billabong, but instead he paced the living room, his arms crossed tight over his chest.

When she came out of the bathroom, she pointed to the room on the other side of the living room. "The guest room. You can put your things in there." And without another word she went into the kitchen and began washing dishes. He stood at a distance, watching her. Her movements were slow, deliberate. The electric kettle screamed and she poured her tea. Didn't offer him any, just stood looking out the window at her reflection in the glass. What did she see? Pretty oval eyes. Her bones so tiny, despite her height, compared to his aunties. Compared to Esther. Was that what happened when you lived in America, away from the good sun and the Land? Finally she spoke. "Your bath."

At first he thought she was talking to herself in the window, but then her words registered. He meant to go out the front door with a slam, but his feet passed the dusty telly and entered the steamy bathroom. Then his hands had his clothes off before he could say fair dinkum. He pushed at the water with his big toe, to see water slide up the sides of the tub, then got in. With eyes closed, he floated just under the surface with his nose sticking out like a side-necked turtle, allowing the water to hold him up.

Perched on the branch outside their nest, the Galahs dance the centuries, he on top of her for a few flaps of wing and then it is done. The dance has been buried in their bodies since the beginning of time. She peels the bark from the tree below the hole. It is her message to the others of her flock. Do not come in, we are busy.

She can feel already, no bigger than a grain of sand, the four eggs that will grow. They will become round as the earth. She will grow them like the seeds of life that drop from the flowers, the kangaroo berries hanging in clumps by the river.

The boy lies below the nest, below where her partner sits on the branch. Like her, this boy does not belong in mango trees, but under wild gums in rocky deserts. He is like dropstone, smoothed by the ices long ago as ice traveled over the land, dropping rocks far from home. Round pebble among craggy granite is the boy. But here there is water. Here he will grow for a time. Here the Galah can watch over him and the black cockatoo woman.

Chi chi. Her mate breaks the stillness. His wings flutter and the air stirs around the nest. He uses his beak and his four toes to climb lower down the trunk as the boy reaches to the tree, a grasshopper offered from his hand.

\∩/

When the bathroom door slammed behind Jimmy, Donna released her breath. She dried her hands on the dish towel and went into the spare room. Under the desk, she found a twin sheet set for the daybed. The sheets billowed out over the mattress. Making beds was a task she usually hated. But now, she smoothed and patted the white Queensland Health sheets.

As she bent over the bed, she felt the familiar cramping that meant her period had come. She hurried to the toilet room, grateful the Aussies had had the sense to separate the dunny from the bath. Why had she let herself believe Esther and Peter? As she sat on the toilet, she remembered her hollow words to Nan. It was impossible to be immune from dashed hopes.

She wanted to linger in the loo, let all that promise empty out of her womb so she could be done with it. She put her palm to the thin wall. Jimmy was in the tub on the other side. If he hadn't been, she might have wept. Esther had said *baby* but had Peter said *baby* or *child*? Was she sure he said *her*? Jimmy, Jessie. Both J names. Childless women found many creative ways to have children in their lives. Maybe she was meant to mother him? Maybe that was what Peter and Esther had meant. When she saw him again, maybe she'd know, really know.

Donna sat at the kitchen table with a cup of tea and an empty cup for Jimmy when she heard the bathroom door open. She called, "Tea's ready if you like."

"No, ta." He stood in the doorway stark naked, as unaware of his nudity as the toddlers in the pediatric wards during her rotations. "Going to bed."

192

She wanted to focus on his long eyelashes, but instead watched water drip from his hair, onto his chest, over his belly, finally collecting into a river that ran to his groin. He was becoming a man, pubic hairs sprouting, penis having grown longer than one would expect for his body, testicles hanging—was that from the heat of the tub? She willed herself to look at his face again. "Sleep well. Let me know if you need anything." What would she have said if he'd sat down next to her, his naked body shimmering from the bath?

Donna blew on her tea. How could he be her child? Would a mother have been riveted to his penis, to the lines of his muscles ready to burst through his skin, seemingly growing faster than their encasing could keep up?

Or maybe a mother *would* look at her son that way. A mother who knew every inch of her son's naked body and who had wiped his behind for years would be curious about what changes were occurring. She'd seen Kate's four-year-old, Ryan, give Kate a full-body hug while stark naked, his penis like any other appendage. When would his budding sexuality drive him to hide his body from her? Would a mother acknowledge objectively that he was sexually attractive?

Embarrassed by her thoughts, she poured the rest of her tea down the drain and turned off the lights. She peeked out the window at the Southern Cross, which had just cleared the horizon, and thought of Andy. Since that night in Boulia two-and-a-half weeks ago, Peter, Nick, Andy, and Jimmy were connected, four men of different generations, all sparking something within her.

She went to bed but couldn't sleep. Her little house felt full, Jimmy's warm breath and hers mingling in the air. She heard Jimmy cough. She rose and went to her dresser, picking up the photo of her parents. Had they been aware of her breaths, sound asleep but detecting if she coughed, if she rolled over? She fingered her gray velvet bag and brought it back to bed with her. She'd never heard her baby's breath. He'd woken her with kicks only. She finally fell asleep holding the bag tight to her belly.

She woke at two; the house felt cool, empty. No breathing, no sense of another person keeping her company. She wished she could roll over, not to Greg, but to Andy, to press her body up close to his for the comfort of another person in the night. Yesterday, Andy was off to Townsville for a holiday. And while she'd spoken to him daily since Boulia to give medical advice, he never mentioned his plans, never made flirtatious comments, almost as if nothing had happened between them. Now, in the dark, the time in Boulia felt like one of her vivid dreams. How else to explain the prophecy, the out-of-body experiences, the blood, the boy appearing out of nowhere on the highway? Jimmy could be a dream, too.

After ten minutes, she couldn't bear the uncertainty. She pulled on her sweatsuit and padded down to Jimmy's room, telling herself that if Jimmy were real, then Boulia was real. The bed was empty, but there was a clear imprint of a body. She felt the rumpled sheet. Still warm. A breeze tickled her back and she crept through the kitchen to the screen door. In the dim light of the moon, she saw Jimmy naked under the mango tree, atop a white Queensland Health blanket.

He was real but unlike any child she'd ever met, more comfortable under the stars than between cozy walls. She'd believed that on some cellular level, all humans sought safety during the vulnerable night hours. Not Jimmy.

He was offering his body to the night sky. This land created such odd creatures—kangaroos, platypus, Jimmy Jackboys, as if nature operated under a foreign law. So dare she think it? Could Esther and Peter still be right?

Donna went back to her bed and fished the velvet bag from the covers. She twirled it in the moonlight and stared up at the shadows of the Honey Ant Dreaming hanging above. The bag felt heavier. She *should* empty it, as Esther had advised. Make way for a new Honey Ant baby. Bury the ashes in the dirt beneath the mango tree, see how they would grow in this land of magic, perhaps into scrubby wattle, or a cactus, or spinifex.

How had she thought she could mother Jimmy, such a different creature than any she'd ever known? For that matter, what if she *did* empty the bag? What kind of Honey Ant child would come to her in Australia, a land where pink parrots were as plentiful as pigeons, yet poisonous spiders and snakes lurked in every corner? How could she mother him *or* her, alien and wild, born of this land? She'd never adopted because she was afraid she might not be able to love a child who smelled differently than she did, whose hair texture and facial expressions might seem foreign. She shoved the bag under her pillow. Jimmy was under the mango for now. Her bag would remain with her.

When her alarm rang a few minutes before the morning blast, she hurried to the shower with thoughts of making Jimmy oatmeal for brekky. Twenty minutes later, she peered out the back door into the gray dawn to call him in.

He wasn't there. The angel boy had been a dream. She had an urge to get her velvet bag, to empty it in the spot under the mango where she'd dreamt that Jimmy was sleeping, to recreate the angel boy from ash and dirt and grass. She ran to her room and came back with the bag. But as she opened the back door, she saw the white blanket folded carefully on the top step, and she stuffed the bag into her pocket.

She ate her oatmeal alone, fighting the feeling of having had a one-night stand. Before meeting Greg, many men had left before any coffee or breakfast—the sign that she'd never see them again. Each time she'd wake up in an empty bed, her hopes that she might have found *the one* were dashed. And as for the one-night stands she'd had after Greg left, *she* had been the one to slip out at three in the morning, climbing into the taxi, grateful to return home to clean sheets. Andy had been the third one-night stand since the divorce. And now Jimmy, in a way, was the fourth.

She looked out at the mango tree. Jimmy was a child, not a

lover. And obviously, she felt jilted by Andy—and perhaps even by Nick, who had been e-mailing light-hearted quips but had never asked her out again—but not by Jimmy. She buried her hurt, then hurried to her car. It was time to get to work.

When the faintest light of the sun had barely touched the sky, he said g'day to the Galahs nesting above him in the mango tree, folded his blanket, and went to examine the shed's treasures. Jimmy swung open the squeaky door. The shed looked empty at first: dirt floor, lots of old spider webs. He should have Dreamt something up before opening the door. But as his eyes adjusted, he saw a glass jar of nails sitting on a shelf, a shovel, and rusty lawn mower, and a ratty tarp covering something. He pulled the tarp gingerly by its corner, revealing an old bicycle. He hadn't dared to Dream *that* up. Its tires were flat and the chain was off, but those things could be fixed. It was a man-sized bike—the seat was too high, but no matter. Back home, he and his cousins would pile on one of the two bicycles in town, taking each other on thrill rides, trying to go around curves so fast that the others would fall. He couldn't remember if he'd ever sat on a seat while pedaling.

He traced a circle in the center of the shed with his foot, then began to dig. The shovel's handle bowed slightly as he pressed down on the head, but the dirt gave way easily. As the earth shook below him, he stopped. What if he broke through the roof of the mine? He'd never thought of the earth being hollow before, had always trusted its ability to hold him up. He ignored his worry and dug down almost a half-meter, patting the extra dirt into the corners of the shed. The pit was deep enough that the neighbors wouldn't know when he built a fire for his billy. He didn't want Doctor Donna to have to explain why a Yapa was setting fires in the backyard instead of using the barbie.

When he was done with his firepit, he found a bucket in the

laundry shed and filled it with water from the spigot and a bit of detergent. He grabbed one of the blue skivvies and soaked it, then washed the bicycle from end to end, careful to avoid the greasy chains. He threaded the chain onto the gears, rinsed the skivvy in the dirty bucket, and mounted the bicycle.

The bike glowed red in the dawn light. It was hard to ride with flat tires, but as soon as he got them pumped, he'd be able to ride from the school to the hospital in no time. He'd go retrieve his swag from the billabong, collect enough dried scrub for his fires, and bring everything back to the shed on his bike. What a find! He rode around the block and back toward the yard, just in time to see Donna's car as she headed to the hospital. He waved, but she didn't slow. He was sorry she wasn't home to see the bicycle. Well, he'd wait for her that evening to show her.

He had a half hour before school, so he took the hose and sprayed the whole shed, cleaning off the dead spiders and webs from the walls. He hung his wet garment on a nail and took the other clothes Donna had bought him out of his backpack. He folded them neatly and placed them on the shelf. He left the door open so the wind could fill the shed with fresh air. He thought of the dole checks that were coming. He'd have to go to Woolies to buy some tucker he could keep in the shed and take to school for lunch. And he could use the rest of the money to fix up the bicycle. Forget saving for fence cutters. Those he'd have to borrow.

\∩/

At the end of afternoon rounds, Donna sat on Hector's bed and whispered, *Tell me what you're dreaming, Hector.* She thought that behind his closed lids might lie answers to her questions about the mysteries she'd experienced since coming to the Isa. *Maybe you are my angel.*

She massaged his arm and studied the Dreaming Jimmy had taped to the wall, so different than her Honey Ant Dreaming. Honey Ant was more earthy; Jimmy's seemed to be of water and air. Could Hector be tracing the map in his coma? It was the end of May, almost a month since Hector had been admitted to the hospital. Surely that was enough time to complete the dream journey drawn in blue, red, and black markers

The squiggles and dots danced, reminding her of the motions of the trailer in Doomadgee as Esther and Jocko had rocked them to sleep. One thing was clear—she needed to have sex again, to banish all the strange feelings. Sex with Andy had awakened the need, which before had been squelched by years of ovulation charts and pregnancy hopes. This insatiable need for sex often descended upon women in peri-menopause, just as their partners' libidos were taking a nose dive, which is why a twenty-six-year-old would be perfect. But a fifty-something would do. She stood up and called *Information* on Hector's bedside phone. She dialed Nick's number and the message machine picked up. Donna asked him to dinner.

She hung up the phone and moved to Hector's opposite side. She looked up at Jimmy's Galah Dreaming from her new vantage and thought of a book she'd read about American slaves and the Underground Railroad, how they'd make maps of the paths to freedom out of a quilt, using colored squiggles, circles, squares. The quilts would be kept in their houses to be studied and memorized, the slave owners none the wiser.

But from Jimmy's explanation, Donna understood that a Dreaming was more than a map. Maybe it was like the family tree she'd created in third grade, which hung on her mother's kitchen wall for years. Donna had ambitiously taped together eight sheets of paper, two wide and four high, with her parents, Patricia Massima and Ben Meyer connected mid-trunk. Between them she drew a picture of a Ferris wheel—they'd met when they were nineteen, in a long line for the Ferris wheel at Coney Island. Below the Ferris wheel was Donna Meyer's box—with a picture of a horse, her third-grade obsession. Above Patricia and Ben were all the empty boxes in the branches Donna had hoped to fill. Her father had joked it was the family blade of grass.

Now, Donna wanted more than a faint memory of cinnamon breath and a drink she later recognized as Brandy Alexander—how startled she'd been when she'd taken a sip in a bar—when she tried to conjure up her paternal grandfather. Wanted more than a faded photo of her paternal grandmother, who held a cigarette and wore a mink stole. Wanted a name for her maternal grandmother, who'd been right up there with Frankenstein and Hitler in Donna's imagination, given the way Patricia had spoken of her. Her parents had cast off their ancestries like the wrapper of a candy bar listing its ingredients. And as if, in analyzing her own family history, Donna could taste the chocolate and an obvious hint of vanilla, but everything else that had been mixed together to create her was a mystery.

"G'day, Doc. G'day, lazy man." Jimmy swung into the room. "Did you wait for me to do blood pressure?"

He tossed a pencil from hand to hand. Boys were strange creatures who grew up to be men. Always moving things through space—balls, bullets, loyalties. If only she could understand all their energy. Maybe it was his boyishness that was foreign, and not that he was from *this* land. "What does it mean if someone said Honey Ant is their kin?"

Jimmy scrunched his wide nose so that it buried itself further into his cheeks. "Honey Ant Dreaming."

"Ah."

"You don't get it, do you?"

"No."

Jimmy held out his hand for the stethoscope and she removed it from her neck and handed it to him. As he bent over Hector's chest, he spoke slowly. "The Ancestors created the world during the Jukurrpa. That means Dreaming. The ancestors' energies are still alive from the Dreaming. Everyone has a certain responsibility with those energies. Animals, plants, Yapa. Yapa each have a Dreaming. We Behold our Land, keep the seed power alive, tell our stories to the next generation, share our secrets with our Yapa and animal kin."

"So your Dreaming is Galah and you are related to galah birds."

"Heart sounds good. Can you hand me the cuff?"

She stood up and strapped the cuff on Hector's arm herself. "And if my Dreaming is Honey Ant, then my energies are Honey Ant."

He closed his eyes as he listened to the heartbeat. "One-twenty over ninety."

"I may be Honey Ant."

Jimmy returned the stethoscope with a smile. "Don't eat one if you are one. That's cannibalism. Can we visit Bernice? Heard she's back in hospital."

She followed him, listening to the click of her flats and the silence of his bare feet. "You don't think white people have Dreamings?"

"Not that I know of, but the whites don't let Yapa know everything." He snorted. "But if they did, I bet Barrington Downs would let a white man onto the Station to do his Dreaming." He opened the door to the stairs for her.

She held tightly to the rail. "Flying Docs go to the Downs sometimes. You can go when you become one."

"Too late."

As they walked into the ICU, she imagined his land as barren rock and scrub. She was sure Jimmy had heard stories that the land practically flowed with milk and honey, stories exaggerated by the longing of people who couldn't be there. She'd heard American farmers talk about how their land was in their blood, how they knew every inch of it, how it had driven many to drinking or suicide when they'd lost family farms to the banks. This is what Jimmy was talking about. Land that had been in his family for more generations than whites could count. Could love of a land you've never seen be passed to you in your genes, or maybe even in your mitochondria? Could the bacteria powering human cells produce more power in certain geographic locations? Could they be imprinted to ramp up capacity when they felt the gravitational pull at a certain tilt of the world? "What do you do on your land? You said your initiation."

"Men's secrets. Can't tell."

She thought of Andy's words, *Australia is all about secrets.* She waved to Bernice, who was trying to prop herself up at the sight of Jimmy. Donna turned to the boy and handed him back the stethoscope. "Key to the house is under the mat. Help yourself to the fridge."

He took an orange from the neighbor's tree before preparing to lie down under Mister Mango for the night. He peeled it slowly and offered half to his cousins in the tree, noticing how his fingernails smelled sweet and tangy. He bit into his last slice and let the juice shoot over his tongue.

He looked up at Yaraandoo, then fell asleep as he rubbed the scar on his foot, two purple-and-yellow streaks waving like tiny flags under his closed lids. The wind rustled the leaves on Mister Mango and Jimmy woke. Mum was above him, perched on the branch. She dangled her feet like Jimmy would do in the water-hole, swinging them free just to feel their weight pulling down on his legs. The moon was more than a half circle behind her, glowing like a halo.

He spoke to the soles of her feet. "Mum. You shouldn't be visiting. Me initiation."

"I'm talking to you as a man now. You have grown up I see, in these past few weeks. I'll just pass on information to you. Is that okay?"

"I guess so."

"Good." She surveyed the yard. "How was school this week?"

She smelled of yucca and he breathed it in deeply. "They had lammies today, but I sang the anthem wrong."

She giggled like a girl. "That was your rebellion, huh?"

Jimmy was proud of his joke. "I sang *Australians all are ostriches.* No one knows the words anyway."

She let out a full-on laugh as her feet swung back and forth. She sniffed the town air. "Does the smell of the mine bother you?"

He shifted onto his side and adjusted the blanket. "The smoke makes for beautiful sunsets." He couldn't hide a yawn. "The worst is when the ground rumbles like an empty belly in the morning, and I know no one's gonna feed it. I'm going under a week from Sunday."

"Yeah?"

He put his palm on the ground, imagining the caverns below the mango tree. "With me mate, Tom."

"The Kardachi man will be here at Rodeo. You'll visit your Land and be back home by the Wet."

"Why so long here?"

"Can't question a medicine man."

"Can I stay two weeks longer to enter the Science Fete? Twenty-sixth of August."

She nuzzled her white shoulder feathers. "Mmmmm. No worries."

He was drifting off, but was roused as she spoke again. "Donna has been good to Hector, good to you. Auntie Tess will help her when she comes."

That roused him a bit more. "Tess'll come too?"

Mum shifted a wing. "We have Dreamt the Doctor to be part of your path. We must take care of her."

Jimmy drifted back to sleep.

\\∩/

On Friday evening, Donna was carefully applying some dried-up mascara to her second eye when Jimmy came rushing into her bedroom. He stopped short. "What is that?"

Donna poked her eye. "It's mascara. You should knock before coming into a woman's bedroom."

Jimmy drew closer to examine her reflection in the tarnished mirror. "Makes your eyes look completely like cockatoo eyes."

"Is that a compliment?"

He took the tube from her hand, twirled it around, then put it atop the gray velvet bag. "Cockatoo eyes have a circle round them, like you've painted." Jimmy sat down on the edge of her bed. "Off to the billabong to get me stuff. May sleep there tonight under the coolabahs."

How convenient. "Don't want you to scare me. Tell me for sure whether you'll be back tonight." She walked him to the front door, conscious of the thong beneath her skirt. She might have to rethink her underwear—it was way too uncomfortable. She could always tell a female patient was under thirty-five if she wore a thong. Somehow, young women had conditioned them-selves to withstand a constant wedgie.

"I won't be back."

"See you in the morning then," she said casually, watching him mount his bicycle.

Jimmy was at the end of the driveway as Nick swung his car in. She caught her breath as they nearly collided, but Jimmy waved at Nick and was off. She stood on the steps as Nick climbed out of the car. He watched Jimmy's back getting smaller in the dis-tance. "Who's that?"

Nick was more handsome than she remembered, carried himself assuredly as he walked toward her front steps. "Jimmy Jackboy. Young man who's staying with me while his uncle is in the hospital."

Nick smiled. "Didn't know hospital offered such wonderful service. May have to get someone I know admitted." He stopped and kissed her square on the lips, starting where they'd left off in the squash club car park.

She took a moment to look at his dark eyes, tanned skin, wide shoulders. "Like to come in for a glass of wine?"

She noticed her hands as she poured the wine. She could still see the trace of a dent where her wedding ring had been. By the time they'd made it through half a bottle of Shiraz, those ringless fingers were intertwined with his on the sofa between them.

An hour later her bra and blouse were on the floor, his hand nestled under her thong she was aching to be relieved of, when Nick stopped kissing her. "Will that boy be back tonight?"

She shook her head. Nick took her hands, pulled her off the couch, and led her backwards into the bedroom, never once taking his eyes from her chest. The sex wasn't as passionate as it had been with Andy, though Nick clearly had his own tactics. For Nick, it was all about her pleasure, and though he didn't last long, she was completely satisfied.

Wrapped in her robe, she went to the kitchen to order what passed for Chinese food in the Isa. Then she found Nick in the living room, looking through a photo album. "Where's this?" He pointed to a photo of five boys—probably Jimmy's age—in front of a Laotian temple. They were miming for the camera, dancing in saffron robes under shaved heads.

"Laos. We'd wake every morning to thousands of bells calling the monks to the monasteries. We could lie in bed and see bare feet hurrying down the street outside our window. That morning, I got up to take pictures."

"Southeast Asia's all about bells."

"You think?"

Nick leaned back on the sofa. He'd put his jeans back on and his gut folded slightly over his belt. "Have you been to Chiang Rai? There's a temple where each prayer wheel has bells attached to help send the prayers to the heavens."

"Not so different than the churches of Europe, is it?" She flipped over a few pages to a photo of the spires of San Gimignano in Tuscany.

"All of us across the world looking for a way to speak to the gods," Nick smiled.

They spent the evening comparing travel stories, his marked by the presence of his deceased wife, Ruth, and hers with Greg. Neither of them had been to Indonesia, and it was Nick who suggested maybe they should escape the Wet. "Christmastime, fares are cheap. More fun to explore with someone else."

"How do you know you'll still like me then?"

"I don't. And we don't have to even be like this." With that, he untied the belt of her robe and opened it to expose her breasts. He brushed his hand down her body and she felt every tiny hair stand on end. "We could be travel companions. Hard to find someone who likes adventure travel."

She thought of Christmas last year, newly alone in the brownstone, taking long walks with the velvet bag on streets illuminated by tiny white lights. "I'll keep it in mind."

The next morning they kissed goodbye on the front porch. Nick was off to Brisbane. He unrolled his window before driving off. "Check your e-mail tonight." A Galah called *chi chi* from the yard.

That evening, Donna watched the boy eat as he sat across from her, savoring every bite. The sour cream made a tiny beard on his chin, and she heard her mother's constant cajoling to *eat, eat.* When Jimmy raised his hand in a small wave, she turned. How could she have missed the squeak of the front door or the foot-steps in the living room?

Andy held out his hand to Jimmy. "Doctor Andrew."

"Jimmy Jackboy."

Andy pulled out a chair and sat down between them at the head of the table. "It's good to see you again, Donna."

She thought of her bedsheets, unchanged after her night with Nick. Why hadn't Andy called first? "And you," she replied. She stared for a moment, then found her manners. "Can I make you a plate?" As she stood up, she noticed Andy's swag on the sofa in the living room.

She'd said she would keep him company, and should have known he was the kind to take a promise seriously. She thought back to that night in Boulia, how it could have been either Peter or Andy she'd slept with, how badly she'd wanted somebody, and now it could be either Nick or Andy. She'd never thought herself capable of jumping from one man to another. *Balance* was what Esther called it. *Horny* was what Kate would say. Nan had said *slut*. She placed a burrito in front of Andy.

She was quiet for the rest of dinner, listening to the boy and the man—whom she would almost call a boy himself—discuss sports. She was relieved she had nothing to contribute. It gave her time to sit back and study them, each becoming more animated discussing AFL and Rugby League.

When she got up to clear the table, she motioned them to stay put. She felt the dishwater roll over her hands, made soapy circles around the pots and plates, and was enveloped in the fullness of the air in her home as laughter bounced off the walls. The house felt different when filled with people. It'd been ages since she'd felt that way in her New York apartment.

During residency, the year before she was with Greg, Donna and Kate had thrown a party. She was so tired from thirty-six hours on call that she'd fallen asleep on her bed as friends sat around in her room chatting, drinking, smoking. It was an hour of bliss, being barely aware of the conversation yet surrounded by friends, covered by the sound of their voices. That was how she felt now.

It was nine by the time the dishes were cleaned. She wiped her hands on her jeans and stood behind Jimmy's chair. She spoke to Jimmy but looked at Andy. "Don't you think you should get some sleep?"

Andy pushed back his chair and answered for Jimmy. "Please excuse me. I'm still a mess from the drive."

Donna's heart sank when she thought he was leaving for the night, but instead, he headed down the hall to the bathroom. All these males in her bath—Jimmy, Nick, Andy. Then she heard the shower running.

She remained behind Jimmy's chair, thighs feeling full as she thought of Andy naked in the bathroom next to them. "I need to check e-mail," she practically whispered, then walked quickly to the guestroom.

Jimmy followed her and stood behind her in the doorway. She had converted it back into her office, since Jimmy had been sleeping under the mango tree all week. They looked at the screensaver, her scrolling personal photographs, as she debated whether to check her e-mail.

"What's that?"

She smiled at the photo she'd taken of West 84th Street on an October morning, gold and red leaves still clinging to the trees. She pointed to a brownstone in the foreground. "This is my window. My apartment in New York. I knew I'd miss it."

Jimmy came closer to the screen. "New York."

"I have more photos. I'll show you sometime." She couldn't stand it anymore; she had to check before Andy got out of the shower. "Will you excuse me for a second?"

He nodded and moments later she heard the back door close. The water shut off. She skipped over an e-mail from Kate and two from other New York friends and clicked on Nick's e-mail.

Attached, there was a photo of tiered rice paddies in Obud, Bali.

She took the ten steps back into the kitchen and went to the screen door. She called *Goodnight* and Jimmy waved as he unfurled the Queensland Health blanket under the tree.

As she stood watching Jimmy, she felt arms around her waist and warm kisses on the back of her neck. Andy was wet from the shower. Naked, he pressed against her. "If Jimmy weren't here, I would have thrown you down on the kitchen table and given you a proper g'day," he whispered, leading her to the bedroom. As he lifted her onto the bed, she thought of Nick there just hours before, could still smell him in the sheets. Whoever knew what one was capable of?

The eggs grow inside her as the moon grows each night in the sky. Now the moon is ripe and hanging low in the sky like her pregnant belly. The Galah sits as the boy sleeps in the moonlight below. The people must help him now. She must be Galah.

She summons water, wind, sun, and rock to make the eggs. She brings to life moons beneath her to match the round moon in the sky. Round moon is the time for birth and death.

She drops them, one by one by one by one, into the soft bed of leaves, like kangaroo berries dropping to the sand. By the next time the moon is pregnant, they will hatch into four fluffy chicks. Two moons later, they will already be on their own.

She waits in the nest, warming the eggs, still like a rock, but for the slight swelling of her chest as she takes the hot air in, the deflating of her rosy feathers as she exhales. Her breath flows down the trunk as the tree's sap flows up into the leaves. Every moment of her stillness is a choice.

She is waiting, like those below her she cannot see. The underworld of creatures who spend their days buried deep in sandy soil, waiting for the sky to turn the Galah. She hears the breathing of the grub inching its way through the red soil. She feels the desert scorpion, the barking spider, the goanna, unmoving in their day beds of red sand and stone, safe underground. As the sun sets, they will poke noses out to the surface for food and air. There, way below, is the honey-pot ant, force-feeding its drones, who will feed the hive in the barrenness of the Dry.

As the day ends, she feels the agony of the gecko as the deaf and blind *mole surfaces, swimming with its huge front legs through the dunes to attack from below. All the while the baby moles wait in the pouch on the mole's belly for milk to flow from mama mole's teats, protected from gecko's flailing claws, oblivious to the life ending in front of them to create their own.*

The Galah's chicks will have two lives, two deaths. One life begins now, the spirit life within the white walls of the egg. The egg is the chick's sky, the nest his earth, the warmth from the Galah is his sun. And then the egg chick will die his first death as he breaks through the walls of his world. His second life will begin as he emerges from his egg with down of his own. Each chick will be fed and guarded until he again becomes part of the Galah. Each of them members of the flock, non-separable beings, flying rainbows over the land until they go back to the spirit world.

A week later, Jimmy sat in the back seat of Tom's car, behind Mr. Patterson's bald head. It had been a long time since he'd seen the top of a man's head bare to the sun. Every man he knew, white or black, wore a hat. What kind of man didn't? Trying to go against the rules? Or, like Jimmy, did Mr. Patterson love the feel of the wind on his head, couldn't bear to have it covered? Mr. Patterson's head was particularly pink. All the hair he had left—a tiny ring that went round his ears—was gray-white. He was an engineer in the mine, would go eight days—a full shift—without a glimpse of sunlight. Maybe he'd forgotten the strength of the sun. Or maybe he had to absorb its energy while he was above ground in order to survive the eight days below.

Their other mate, Henry, was droning on about Brisbane. Thought they had a chance at finals this year. But Jimmy was sure Essedon would take them and Mr. Patterson agreed. Jimmy had spent part of his dole check on footy cards and for the past week after school, he'd met Tom and Henry and some other boys to trade. Tom and Henry had let their loyalty to Brisbane get in the way of their trades, so Jimmy had earned four star AFL players. Couldn't wait to show his mates in Yuendumu.

When they were trading on that first afternoon, Tom mentioned the mine. It came up that neither Jimmy nor Henry had ever been under, so Tom invited them down. He said Mr. Patterson loved nothing more than taking people into the mine. Couldn't wait for the day when Tom joined him underground. Tom had grunted that he'd probably be a digger, not an engineer, given his marks in maths.

Jimmy'd felt sorry for Tom the first few days of school. He was the guy who was always embarrassing himself, who'd walk out of the loo with toilet paper stuck to his shoe, who never got the teacher's questions right, who always mooched off other people's homework. But Jimmy also noticed the girls watching Tom. Yes, those pimples were crook but his body was already a man's, while everyone else's was catching up. And Tom had a mob of mates. He was friends with sports blokes, study blokes, chess players, and had even befriended Jimmy. Jimmy passed his hands over the soft leather seats of the sparkling new Land Rover. Next to Tom's, Doctor Donna's car looked shabby. Tom was good at sports and his family was chockablock with money. Was that what made him so confident even if he weren't so smart?

Suddenly, the smokestacks were right in front of their windscreen. Jimmy could see the red bricks piled one atop of the other, like enormous red termite mounds. Mr. Patterson pointed at the taller of the two. "Lead smelter. Other's copper smelter."

Jimmy craned his neck up to see the top. It was one thing to see the smokestacks at sunset, to watch the beautiful orange smoke. It was another to pass under their shadow.

Mr. Patterson stopped at the security shed and handed the guard his badge, then spelled out the names of each of the boys inside the car. "Welcome," he said as the immense gates of Mount Isa Mines opened. "John Campbell Miles camped by the river here in 1923 and noticed the rocks were highly metalized. Can you believe all this came from that tiny observation?" He took his hand off the wheel and waved it around. "That's a lesson for you boys. You, too, could be the first to discover something."

They drove past huge trucks moving piles of metal, past backhoes and loaders, forklifts, and huge bins of coal. Jimmy had to turn his eyes away from the big bowl of the copper smelter pouring bright orange honey that looked hotter than the sun.

As they stepped out of the car, Jimmy was hit by a strong wind. But Tom's and Henry's hair wasn't moving, so it couldn't be wind. Jimmy looked above them. The energy was flowing from the webs of wires, all with a hum like thousands of grasshoppers lived inside. Jimmy looked over at Henry to see if he felt it, but Henry looked bored, as if he'd seen it all before.

Jimmy followed Tom's long strides over to a building that turned out to be the tour center. Mr. Patterson greeted a woman with blonde hair, who looked to be Doctor Donna's age.

The woman looked each of the boys up and down, lingering longest on Jimmy. He was glad he was there with Mr. Patterson, not just some bloke on a tour, where the guide would never notice if some Yapa was left behind down in that earth. Then the lady smiled and held up orange day-glo jumpsuits. She handed one to Jimmy. "You're just between a child size and a man's size. How about a man's suit for you."

Mr. Patterson and the boys jammed into the tiny elevator— the big freight elevator was busy transporting equipment. How silly they all looked in their orange suits, borrowed wellies, and helmets. He stopped himself from grabbing Tom's arm as the elevator jerked down.

He counted to one twenty-eight before they jostled together as they touched bottom. Two minutes to go two kilometers into the earth, which meant the elevator traveled just over sixty kilometers an hour. Mrs. Westbrook would be proud he could do the math in his head. Mr. Patterson pressed on the elevator button, but the doors didn't open. As he pressed again, Henry coughed nervously. Jimmy clenched his hands to his sides.

Mr. Patterson pushed the alarm button. "Let me tell you about miners, boys. Brave people. ANZACs came from the great mining tradition. Fiercest warriors at Gallipoli. Learned to face death in the mines, not fear it. Can't show fear."

The elevator jerked down as if finally finding the floor and the door opened. As they stepped into a small cavern, Jimmy whispered to Henry, "You're no ANZAC, eh?"

"Two kilometers of earth on top of our heads."

Jimmy didn't care. Now that they were out of the steel elevator, he felt the earth energy around him. Could taste in the air the same minerals he would taste in the grasses above as they sucked up nourishment from the ground. He could see the energy pulsing, like his heartbeat, like Hector's heartbeat, as Mr. Patterson pointed out the veins of metals in the rough walls. Fluorescent lights allowed him to see the rock as well as if it were daylight. He touched the vein and felt the pulse, and the Rainbow Serpent uncurled before his eyes, a rippling rainbow of the different spectrums of vibration. Rainbow Serpent was a powerful vision, did not come often. It was a message that he needed Mum or Hector to help him interpret.

They walked down a short dirt path and crossed a paved road. Mr. Patterson was telling them the mine stretched all over the Isa and beyond. The underground city was bigger than the city itself. Jimmy saw men in orange jumpsuits, roads, trucks, just like above ground. Jimmy pointed at a dump truck. "Fair dinkum? I had no idea trucks could fit down here."

Mr. Patterson put his hand on Jimmy's shoulder. "Isn't it amazing what we've done? Steam rollers, all kinds of earth movers, most efficient mine in Australia." Jimmy watched the huge yellow trucks moving forward and back underneath, cutting away the earth from its insides, like he'd gut a kangaroo. As he watched the men busy with their jobs, Jimmy marveled how each knew what to do and how hard they all seemed to be concentrating. He imagined the men as an ant colony.

Mrs. Westbrook told the class that ants were the most sensitive and adaptive insect. They could pick up any change in humidity or magnetic activity before a rainfall, pass that information chemically through their community, and adapt their anthill. He knew from the Warlpiri stories that an ant sting could pass the chemical information to a person, help their cells regulate to living in new land. Ants could balance even the most imbalanced, so deep healing could occur.

These miner ants were powerful. They were able to harness

the energies of the earth and bring them to the surface to create all the wonderful inventions of the whites. These men were the beginning of the chain, at the heart of the white world.

Mr. Patterson led them through a tunnel to an enormous round cavern, where he stopped to talk to a group of miners. The boys hung back, watching miners go this way and that. It was as if they stood in a hub and roads were the spokes. He guessed which spoke led under Hector's hospital bed and which one led under the mango tree. Without the sun, it was hard to keep direction. If he could feel the wall of the cavern, would he know north by the magnet of the metals?

A miner sat on a bench, eating a sandwich. Jimmy inched closer, was fascinated by the man's white teeth and dirt-blackened face flashing under the fluorescent lights.

The man caught his eye and waved him over. "Gonna work the mine someday? Honest work for an Abo."

For an Abo. "Could. Maybe an engineer."

The teeth flashed whiter. "Good onya. Think big."

Jimmy tried to read the man's dirty face. Was he making fun? "Are you afraid of a cave-in?"

The man put his sandwich down on his tucker bag, brushed his hand over his orange coveralls, and waved Jimmy closer. "Show ya something."

Jimmy inched forward. The man turned out the collar of his jumpsuit. "See this pocket stitched in?"

Jimmy nodded and the miner picked up his sandwich again. "Cyanide. Say g'day to me wife every morning. Never know if I'll see her or the little ones again. Everybody's gonna die someday, but those of us who work underground are always prepared for it. Wouldn't be such a bad way to go." The man laughed. "Still think you'll be a miner?"

Working in the mine helped whites prepare themselves for the realm of the dead, just as initiation was supposed to prepare Jimmy. He'd be ready to move on to the spirit realm. "Mining engineer or a doc. I'm not afraid to die."

"Come on," Mr. Patterson called and Jimmy waved *g'day* to the miner. In Mr. Patterson's floppy white hands were a number of rocks. He pointed out the veins of the metals that were being mined. "Almost everything you use comes from these metals. Silver, lead, copper, zinc are the bedrocks of your life. Want one?"

Maybe not the bedrock of life in Yuendumu, but definitely in Isa. Donna's house, the electric teakettle—okay, his billy too, his bicycle, the shed, the cars, the machines at the hospital, Donna's pots and pans and the fridge that kept the cow's milk cold, all these things were made from the rocks the boys were passing around.

Henry kept the biggest one and Jimmy chose one that was chockers with zinc and silver.

Mr. Patterson elbowed Tom. "Want to try something that used to scare the pants off Tom?"

Tom smiled his goofy smile. "Let's do it."

Mr. Patterson led them through a narrow spoke that Jimmy hadn't noticed, down a metal ladder and into a small hollow. "Sometimes the miners experience blackouts. If you feel panicked, turn around and you will see the lights of the tunnel behind us."

Tom whispered, "Don't turn and don't talk," and then the lights went out."

Before them was black, a deeper black than Jimmy had ever experienced. His eyes were open, yet there was not even a sense of shape in front of him, no sense of where the air ended and Henry, Tom, or Mr. Patterson began. The mineral smell got stronger. He looked down at his hands, could not see them. He'd become the earth.

He was sorry when the lights went back on. "Can we do that again?" Jimmy asked Mr. Patterson.

"I'd get in trouble. Just once looks like an accident."

So Jimmy had been right. Mr. Patterson didn't wear a hat because he was a rebel.

As they walked four abreast back through the main tunnel, Mr. Patterson said, "I remember me first day under. Got me lunch pail summer of me fourteenth birthday. That's when me and me mates got to start work, apprenticing, learning where to dig, where to plant the explosives. Made three dollars an hour."

Henry and Tom were rolling their eyes at each other as Tom's da went on, and Jimmy quickly looked away. He watched his feet slap the hard rock below them in his wellies, half the size of Mr. Patterson's wellies beside him. Mr. Patterson let his fingers brush Tom's shoulder. "Imagine me father's surprise. Never stopped studying and got me engineering. Came back to the mine on salary. Bought me father a car."

Jimmy felt the two-dollar coin in his pocket, hitting against his rocks and his da's bone. Maybe the Rainbow Serpent had come to tell him he was meant to go underground? "I could use a job during the Wet."

Mr. Patterson had the same round freckles as his son, but not the pimples. "Good onya, Jimmy. Can't let joeys work anymore. But study hard. Some day you'll run the place." They stopped at the side of the road to wait for a dumptruck loaded with rock to pass.

"Cause I won't," chimed in Tom. "I'm going to the coast."

Mr. Patterson waved them to cross, his mouth turning down at the corners. "More opportunity in the bush. Where's your pioneering spirit?"

Tom kept his gaze forward. "In the dunny with me maths. Not going to come down here and be a digger. Jimmy's got maths."

As they stopped at the elevator, Jimmy rested his palm on the cool rock wall. "Doubt they'd ever let a Yapa run the place."

Tom cuffed Jimmy lightly. "Why head the mine, why not be Prime Minister?"

Jimmy felt his face grow hot, had not realized they were

kidding. But Mr. Patterson moved closer to Jimmy and put his hand on his shoulder. "Never be afraid to be the first. That's what this country's all about. First miners ever were the Kalkadoon. They made stone knives and blades, axes from greenstone. Knew what was under this earth thousands of years before John Miles. Fierce as the ANZACs. No fear, the Kalkadoon." They stepped into the elevator, but Mr. Patterson kept his hand on Jimmy's shoulder. "I remember in the sixties, the last full-blooded Kalkadoon died. We're all one Australia now."

They stood silently, Mr. Patterson's hand still heavy on Jimmy's shoulder, as the elevator lurched upward. Jimmy fingered the new rock in his pocket.

Henry fidgeted and looked around the elevator. "So you blokes entering the Science Fete? I'm going in with Lou Riverton."

Tom looked at his father. "Dunno. Jimmy?"

"Like to."

Mr. Patterson moved his other hand to his son's shoulder. "Looks like we've got another entry. Do it together. Two sons of miners."

Jimmy almost said, *I'm Warlpiri, not Kalkadoon*, but thought better of it. Would be good to have a mate to work with. "What'll we do?"

Mr. Patterson held the elevator door as they walked out. "When I was a boy I did a presentation about light and color. How 'bout that?"

Tom grumbled as he followed Jimmy out of the elevator, "Which is it, pioneer or following your footsteps?"

The elevator doors slammed shut behind them. "One does not preclude the other." Mr. Patterson said. Jimmy didn't know what he meant and wasn't completely sure why Tom didn't want to follow in his father's path.

When Mr. Patterson dropped Jimmy off at Donna's house, no one was home. So Jimmy went to the backyard, took off his shirt and hung it on a nail in the shed, then lay down on the cool dirt floor. He imagined the miners below him, a colony of ants moving earth here and there.

He rolled over on his belly to smell the earth and felt his da's bone poking into his thigh. One by one he pulled out his rock collection, his new rock from the mine, some Galah feathers, Da's bone. Silly to carry them around all day. He hopped up and arranged them on a shelf in the back of his shed with his new rock in front.

He opened the box of pencils and markers Mrs. Brunswick had given him and found a black permanent pen. On the shelf he wrote *Careful*. Then he found a clean part of the wall and wrote *Jimmy Jackboy* in his best letters.

He wandered back to the house, wondering where Donna was, then remembered it was time for afternoon rounds. If he hurried, he could still do a few blood pressures. Hurrah for the bicycle.

He found Esther, Donna, and Andy in Hector's room. They seemed to like to gather there, beneath his Dreaming that was still taped to the wall. As Jimmy examined Hector's EKG under Donna's hawk-like gaze, he told them about his trip into the mine. "I think the mine is like a white initiation. Face death and be reborn without fear. I could skip me walkabout and become a miner."

Esther practically threw her large body over Hector and covered Hector's ears. "Don't you dare let him hear you say that, Galah boy. Don't you want him to wake up?"

\n/

Monday morning, Donna navigated her way down the three splintery back steps to the laundry shed, her sheets piled in her arms, using her chin to anchor them. A week after Andy's arrival, she could no longer smell Nick in the sheets. She paused at the bottom of the stairs and could just make out the lump that must be Jimmy asleep under the mango tree. It was still dark—Andy had been called into the hospital at five and she hadn't been able to go back to sleep.

She dumped the dirty sheets on the ground beside the door, took a deep breath, and turned the handle to the laundry shed. She yanked the string on the naked bulb in the ceiling, closing her eyes tightly so as not to see the spiders and lizards scuttling away. If the critters remained at their posts, she would often give a little roar to let them know she was boss.

She opened the washer's lid and pulled out her jeans, which were twisted around her bras, panties, Jimmy's T-shirt, and Andy's jeans and socks. She untied them all and held one of Jimmy's shirts against one of Andy's white T-shirts. There was only an inch outline of white behind the navy. If you stood the two of them side by side, you would see the two on the ends of the spectrum between boy and man, Jimmy just to the right of childhood, and Andy just to the left of manhood.

She replaced the wet clothes with the sheets, measured laundry soap, and watched as the water matted everything down. Then she lifted her basket of wets and hurried out of the shed. The sun was beginning to lighten the sky to a hazy gray. Jimmy rolled over and hid his head under his blanket.

She walked to the laundry pole and haphazardly hung the

wash on the line, pausing to hold Jimmy's blue shirt and Andy's socks up to her cheek, absorbing their cool dampness as a shield against the heat of the coming day. Suddenly, the beekeepers and sparrows awakened from their nests. She listened to their concert as she finished hanging the clothes.

She went inside and turned on the computer. This e-mail was difficult to compose. She was thankful to be able to edit her words, afraid how those words would have been tangled in a phone conversation. She settled on:

> Dearest Nick—A house guest has shown up unexpectedly, complicating things for a while. Who would have thought an old friend would drop by the Isa? I am planning on Bali in December. I'll understand if you find another travel companion in the meantime. For now, let's keep in touch by e-mail and know that I'm thinking of you.

She hit *Send*. Well, she'd thrown her hat in the ring with Andy. In just over a week, it was clear that Andy had moved in. He'd unpacked his swag—a few shirts and pairs of pants—and, without asking, hung everything in her closet. He clearly had an apartment somewhere because other items had found their way into Donna's closet since that first morning.

She could have considered it presumptuous—his just showing up and moving in. After all, there was Nick, and Andy had no way of knowing there wasn't. But she attributed his actions to twenty-six-year-old arrogance, and she liked the Andy-Jimmy-Donna threesome. She was scrolling through e-mails from friends at home when Jimmy came into the office. She smelled the cool morning air on him. His blond hair stuck out every which way.

"Did I wake you with the laundry?"

"Will you show me New York?"

She located her hard disk folder of photos and activated the computer slideshow mode. Jimmy brought a chair from the kitchen and they sat side by side, his blond head almost the height of hers as they sat in front of the monitor.

Jimmy moved his face an inch from the screen, squinting as if to see into the windows of the skyscrapers. "I wonder if metals from our mine are in their skeletons."

"Our mine? Since your tour yesterday, it's become yours?"

A photo of the inside of her apartment came up, rotated upside down. As Jimmy smiled his cheeks seemed to reach toward the screen. "I like your painting."

Greg had asked to keep it, but she'd refused. Since *he* was leaving *her*, he hadn't been in the position to make demands. "It's a thanka from Nepal. A medicine Buddha. It has a blessing on the back from a monk."

Jimmy touched the computer screen and it bubbled behind his warm finger, making ripples in the blue background. He drew his finger and face back quickly as if burnt. "What's it painted on?"

She hit the arrow button to bring the photo back as it disappeared. "Silk."

"I'll come to New York. Feel the colors."

"You're always welcome." She stood up and put her hands on his waist to lift him from the chair. "Time for me to go to work. You need brekky." His lats were hard and lean. Would he ever have a flabby tire tummy? She put her hand on the small of his back. His pants hung low on his narrow hips. With the pressure of her palm, she steered him toward the kitchen as he craned his neck to see the next photo that would appear on her screen.

The following evening she sat on the front stoop with Andy, each of them nursing a cold Fourex, backs pressed against the siding, legs extended. She rubbed her toes against the soft hair on his ankles, acutely conscious of his hand on her thigh.

Andy examined his beer. "When Jimmy gets home, we'll run out for McDonald's."

Donna focused on the word *home*. "He's at the movies with Esther." She'd been jealous all afternoon after finding out. Almost had said to Jimmy, *Do you think you should on a school night?* Why hadn't they invited her as well?

Andy pointed to the Southern Cross. "Real or false?"

"Real." Donna studied his profile. Andy's nose was like her own, the tip heading toward the ground rather than the sky. His easy smile was consolation for Jimmy's absence. "How long are you staying?"

"Me rotation is over in August. Then me loans are paid off. I'll see Rodeo before going to Townsville." He didn't take his eyes off the stars. They were the same stars as in Boulia. Boulia had brought the three of them together. Rodeo would send Andy and Jimmy away. Another coincidence?

The shadow from his stockman's hat sliced Andy's smile lines. True cowboy, he wore his hat almost always when not in the hospital. Donna wondered how he could even think about living on the coast. He turned to look her in the eye and said, "You're my Matilda. I'm Waltzing Donna." When she didn't answer, he pressed his full lips against hers.

She hadn't expected at the age of forty-one to become someone's walkabout. Yet it was impossible to refuse as the blond hairs on his strong thigh flexed against hers. She would be ready for Nick only after she could no longer press her body up against Andy's youth. She hoped it wasn't too much to ask from fate to have both.

After kissing for a while, they sat in silence. At one point, Andy brought out two more bottles. Orion rose from the horizon. It was not a cold silence, just a comfortable quiet between two people. A few times Donna thought of her non-stop conversations with Nick—even the pillow talk had been stimulating—and wondered if she and Andy had nothing to say to each other. She became aware of the night sounds around her.

The Southern Cross rose above the neighbor's tree. The alcohol was fuzzing her mind. "What is an Aboriginal initiation? Why does Jimmy have to get to his Land to finish it? He won't tell me. 'Men's secrets.'"

Andy chugged the last of his beer, then tossed his empty into the air, spinning it under the stars before catching it in his open palm. "Circumcision ceremony. First initiation rite happens when boys are in early puberty."

A car passed and she followed its taillights till they disappeared around the bend, heading toward the bush. "He'll go out to his Land, say some prayers, and then slice his foreskin?" she asked.

"Yup."

"I was being facetious." She moved her toes away from his.

He pinned her foot with his sole. "Well, it's true."

"I've seen those surgeries. You need sterile conditions, anesthesia if it's not a baby."

He snuck his hand around her waist between her back and the siding. With his other he rolled his cold empty over the back of her neck so that her chest arched forward into him. "Not if you are an Aboriginal. And speaking of circumcision, that reminds me." Andy shifted so his broad chest pressed fully into hers. He smelled like only a boy could smell, with that peculiar mix of earth, dirt, and sweat mingling in his hair. Like Jimmy, he carried the scents of outside in his skin. Kate had said her son smelled like dog, her daughter like flowers, and now Donna knew what she meant. She inhaled Andy and inhaled the smell of the land.

He stood up, pulled her to follow, his arm circling her waist to lead her inside. As she headed for the bedroom, he stopped her and leaned her against the wall in the hall. "The child is away," he whispered into her neck. "We don't need a bedroom. The house is ours."

The Galah closes her eyes and sleeps deep in the nest. In her dreams she visits places she will only see in visions that visit her body at night, visions that were in her body when she cracked open the world of her first life.

She flies from the south sea, past the beginning of the earth where dolomite cliffs form grey rock forests like dead pines, tall and straight, reaching to the sky, clumped close together, no sky in between. She flies north past the mountains tipped in white, down past the snow-covered feathers of the pandami trees whose palm heads spread like ferns to catch the white flakes. Past the heath where creeping white starflower vines peppered by crimson nettya berries hold tight to the rocks, as they are blasted by the winds.

She flies up the coast where corellas roost on a tree by a near-empty billabong, looking like the fresh white blossoms of spring. She wings above the edge of the red cliffs that drop suddenly into the vast blue, bluer still than the sky, capped by small puffs of clouds. If she flies out further, over that blue, she can see the edge of the world like the jagged leaf of the acorn coneflower, sharp against the sky.

She hugs the coast as she travels to the top end, to visit the rain forests where mossy wet hair covers the tree trunks and leaves as big as kangaroos drip water onto the earth. There the leaves are so dense the Galah can go for days bathed in water drops without seeing the sun. And at the edge of the rain forest she sees the mangrove swamps, where roots like snakes rise from the water to lift the trees into the tropical air, as if they too wished to fly.

She flies along the top edge to where the water spreads into the land like branches against the sky, then empties back into the sea. She sees the crabs and tiny fish scurry into the sands ahead of the tides so as not to be swept away by the blue.

In her dreams she has seen the flight of the great pelicans, forming flocks as big as those of the Galah, when once in thousands of moons the rains are so strong as to flood the lake in the Center. Then the shining salts are covered in wet and the water birds come in numbers to darken the sky, called by the reflection of the waters on the clouds. They come to feast on the rock shrimp brought to life after being buried for years in wait for the waters. She has seen as the waters recede, the tiny mangrove sprouts, covered in white salt rocks, determined to seek the sky, sprouting between bodies of dead birds too fragile to fly back to the edges.

In her dreams she has seen what once was. The lush, palm-tipped forests covering the earth. The ices that came down over the trees, mountains of ice that moved boulders across the world. The seas that covered the land, filled with reef fish and coral. The stars that fell and left their scars. The fires that burned the brush from one edge to the other, deflected by the smooth white bark of the snappy gum. The windstorms that a Galah could never survive, whipping the rocks into sands.

Her dreams and the story of the boy and the dancing grasses course through her body and into her eggs. Her chicks will know, will wake knowing, the story of the earth, the story of the Galah. What was, what is and what will be.

One Saturday morning at the end of June, Jimmy flew down Lookout Hill on Mister Bicycle, the wind blowing his hair. He held out his hand to feel the resistance. Friction was the only way you could feel air. That and when the wind blew, or the fans were on. You had to feel it on purpose or you'd never notice it was there. He screeched to a stop at the bottom, scaring a tiny wallaroo that bounded across the path. He looked up to where Doctor Donna was pointing the roo out to Doctor Andy, both still at the top of the hill. He liked to meet them at the end of their morning runs, when the smoke was bright pink from the sunrise.

He started back up the hill again as the sky began to lose its pink behind the tower. Since the doctors were so slow, he was going to take another ride down. He gave Andy a high five as he passed them and caught a whiff of Doctor Donna's hair. Donna always smelled of lavender—he'd read the label of her purple shampoo—and soap from the hospital. It was pleasant, not her own scent of course, but interesting. Most of the women he knew smelled like themselves, just a mixture of the earth where they were from and sweat.

At the top of the hill he laid Mister Bicycle down, watching Donna and Andy below him. Her palm rested flat against Andy's back, the way Mum would walk with Jimmy—a mix between a push and love. Donna had walked with Jimmy that way too, and he'd thought it was the way a mum touched a son to show him his path. But no, there she was, not with her arm circled round Andy's waist, but her palm leaving a print in the sweaty T-shirt on his back. So what did it mean when she walked with Jimmy that way?

The doctors stopped to kiss and Jimmy turned and ran the few meters up the dirt path to the lookout tower. Andy said it had been built during the Great War so Aussies could spot Japanese warplanes. Jimmy doubted any Japanese in his right mind would have been flying this far into the Center. Later, the tower had housed a telescope. Now it was empty, only crumbling white plaster. He brushed his hand against it and white chips fell into his hand. This tower would be useful for a Dreaming dance. Easy to paint yourself with the white stuff instead of having to search for white ochre.

From the tower he liked to look north, toward the open bush, rather than south, toward his Land, which was hidden from view by the smokestacks and the city in the valley below. The land rolled gently, hill after hill, like the back of the Rainbow Serpent as it traveled the land. Circles of spinifex and gum dotted the land beyond, and every so often a high cloud would throw a circle of darkness over a clump of spots. He would focus on those dark patches, watching how quickly they could traverse the land. If only he were a cloud or a Galah.

His people had spent so much time walking the Land, talking of the Serpent. Why had they not invented bicycles or cars or flying machines so they could visit their sites? Why had they been so concerned with stories instead of science? He'd always taken the story literally, the Serpent creating the land. It made so much sense when you looked at the terrain. But why hadn't the Yapa asked more questions? Questions that would have led to discoveries and machines, tools and mines, great buildings? Why hadn't his people built pyramids? Temples like the Mayans? Why hadn't they measured the distance to the moon like the ancient Egyptians? What was wrong with the Yapa?

The white plaster crumbles fell from his hand. Jimmy spread his arms like eagle's wings and embraced the tower, letting his cheek rest on the rough plaster. Someday he would go to New York, visit Donna in her apartment, visit a skyscraper and be close to the stars.

He turned down the path and mounted his bicycle, taking a moment to adjust his eyes. *Be the eagle,* he repeated, until he spotted a wallaroo camouflaged against the rocks. A rock with ears. If he were an eagle, he'd swoop down upon it for tea.

Jimmy gave a whoop and with a running start, threw himself atop the high seat, resting his bare feet on the middle bar, and let the bicycle carry him down at full speed. Donna and Andy turned around at the whoop—they were almost to the bottom—and stepped out of the path so Jimmy could really fly. For a moment he stuck both of his arms out, the eagle, but as Donna's hand flew up to her mouth he settled a hand back onto the handle. Flying, air whooshing over wings, arms, hair, feathers.

He passed them with a wave. Andy shouted *Faster,* and Jimmy waved both hands in response. Donna called out, *Do that again and you'll be the one in the hospital.*

That night, the Galah woke him. She shifted on her branch and knocked off a flake of bark. Jimmy could feel a drop of sticky sap on his forehead. His swag and the blanket were covered in it after a moon under the tree. The moon was high overhead. Must have been after three. From his bed under Mister Mango he peered into the black windows of the house.

The light flipped on in the hallway. Jimmy couldn't actually see the hallway from where he was, but he knew the faint glimmer that reached the kitchen window when it was on. He took off the Queensland Health blanket and felt the cool night air, which gave him goose bumps. His penis felt awake, wide awake.

With his toes, Jimmy searched the bottom of his swag for his pants, then pulled them on. Jimmy knew how to be silent. He was a hunter, after all. He opened the back door. What was that faint sweet smell? At first he thought it was the flowers, as pink as Galah heads, which Andy had brought home for Donna. Looked like bush daisies but had heads three times the size. Their stems were strong and straight, but not hearty enough for the bush. He stuck his nose right into their pinkness. Disappointing. Their beauty was in their looks, not smell. He'd rather have a beautiful scent than a beautiful sight. Like when Mum said it was the inside of a person that mattered, not their skin.

He still wanted to identify that scent. He crept into the hall and concentrated. He smelled Donna, he smelled Andy. He looked at the pile of shirts on the floor. Sex. The familiar noises of two people enjoying each other must have lured him there. Just a peek then. Down the hall and outside the open bedroom door he knelt. He could see Donna's black hair spread out over the pillow, her nose buried in the crook of Andy's neck. Her legs were wrapped around Andy's back.

She was beautiful, the black cockatoo woman with her brown nipples and long, strong legs. How could he not have noticed those legs before? And there were her hands, pressing flat on Andy's bum. He knew the feel of those palms pressing right above Jimmy's own pants on the small of his back as they walked the hospital's hallways. He felt guilty, as though he'd had those thoughts about someone who was mother-in-law, a kin relation where sex would be strictly forbidden. But Donna was his teacher, a great medicine woman. She wasn't a relation, so he let himself enjoy his growing penis.

He sat back on his haunches for a better view and thought of the sounds of Yuendumu: crickets, dingoes, and shagging. Heaps of shagging. Jimmy had to shift his weight. He must have cast a shadow from the nightlight because Andy's eyes opened wide. Jimmy knew he was caught. He smiled and gave a little half wave.

He knew what the flick of Andy's neck meant. *Get out.* He'd been caught spying before. He and his cousins had made sport of it in Yuendumu. In Yuendumu he'd tease the grownups afterwards—they didn't care—how else were the kids going to learn? As he was about to make his silent exit, he saw Donna's whole body shudder and Andy pump more fiercely.

Jimmy crawled onto his swag, wrapping the Queensland Health blanket around him. He smiled into the growing grin of the moon, playing with his stiffie. Whether or not he became initiated, he was ready. Yes, it was time for him to be a man.

The next morning, Jimmy bumped along beside Andy in his Land Rover, Tom in back, testing them on League and AFL stats. Andy drove fast over the dirt roads, howling, *Whoowhee!* as he took a bump at sixty kilometers. "Essedon are at Gabba tomorrow," Andy said.

"We know." Tom's tall head popped up between the seats, almost at the height of Andy's. "Our two teams playing."

Andy rubbed his thumb against his fingers in the air. "How much you gonna bet?"

Jimmy held the strap dangling above the door as Andy sent them flying again. "No need to bet. Essedon's gonna route Brisbane. Make finals this year."

Tom rubbed his head, sore from hitting the car's ceiling on the last bump. "Me arse. Lions rule."

Andy looked in the rear mirror. "Tom, you'd better put on a seatbelt. And be careful what you say around Jimmy. I've never seen a more loyal Essedon fan."

They were silent for a while as the bumps became more ferocious, Tom and Jimmy gritting their teeth as Andy repeatedly yelled, *Whoowhee!* He turned to Jimmy with a wicked smile. "Either of you got a girl, yet? Jimmy knows why I'm asking."

Jimmy looked at Tom, whose face was turning red, making his freckles disappear. "Looks like you do."

Tom's lump of an Adam's apple moved up and down. "I'm sweet on Kim and she's sweet on me. How about you, Jimmy?"

Jimmy couldn't take his eye off Tom's throat, thinking for sure an animal must live inside. "Laura Adams has nice titties, but she's never said a word to me. Probably never go with a Yapa."

Andy smiled wide. "You're a chest man, huh? I'm a leg man, meself. Donna's got great ones."

Jimmy looked out his side window thinking of how Donna's legs wrapped around Andy the night before. Was it jealousy that made him want to avoid Andy's smile?

Tom leaned forward over the front seat. "Me da likes ankles. Not sure why ankles would be so important."

Jimmy thought of Donna's brown ankles in her pointy shoes with the heels that click-clacked on hospital floors. Maybe he could see why Tom's da liked ankles.

When they got to a rock outcropping, Andy stopped. They tumbled out of the car and Andy handed them small iron garden tools. "Good ochre deposits over there." He pointed to the other side of the rocks.

Tom looked around. "Hey, I know where we are. Good place for fossiking. Got something to show you when we've got our ochre." He started walking but Jimmy stood with his hand on his hips. "We should buy paints at the Kmart. Ochre doesn't mix well."

"Let's do it the natural way. This will be more impressive." Andy pulled down on the brim of his hat.

Andy's hat was so much finer than Hector's, with its hole in the front brim. Would Andy get a new one every few years, or would his hat look like Hector's one day, carrying the dust of all the paths he'd taken? Jimmy grumbled, "It's *me* Science Fete, not yours." Andy and Mr. Patterson were more excited about the fete than Jimmy and Tom. It was still a while away, but both men had pretty firm ideas about what the boys should do.

Maybe it was time for Jimmy to buy his own hat, so Andy'd treat him like a man. He wasn't so much younger than Andy. Had all that money from the dole checks. Jimmy held his hand over his bare head. Could he live without feeling the wind in his hair? He followed the doctor around termite mounds that were as tall as Tom. They were everywhere out bush, as much a part of the land as the trees. He rubbed his finger along one and followed the tracing of red dirt. He was still sorry for having kicked a mound over. He pointed at a dead branch in a neighboring gum. "Perfect didg log." It looked to be hollowed out by the termites, not too fat and not too thin.

Andy turned around. "Yeah? Let's get it down."

"For what?" Jimmy looked at Tom a few feet away, chipping at the rocks, hunting for ochre.

Andy patted his shoulders. "Stand on me and pull it down. I want to make a didg."

Jimmy should be out here with Hector, not Andy, collecting didg logs. He was sorry he'd pointed it out. But Hector was too busy Dreaming. Jimmy had hardly visited Hector over the last week, he'd been so busy with Tom and Henry and the others swapping footy cards and playing cricket, not to mention doing homework. But Donna had said there were no changes. Jimmy sighed and climbed onto Andy's crouching knees, taking Andy's hands. "Gonna do some Dreaming dances?"

As Jimmy stepped up onto his shoulders, Andy grunted, "If you'll teach me." He stood up steadily.

Jimmy grabbed hold of the branch. "No way. Yapa secrets are Yapa secrets. Anyway, I'm too busy on me science project and in the hospital." Jimmy pulled on the branch, hung on it, but it wouldn't snap.

"You haven't been in hospital for a week."

Jimmy dropped to the ground. "Can't get it."

"Hold on." Doctor Andy walked over to the car. "Have me tools in the boot. Ever use a hacksaw?"

Jimmy didn't want to gather ochre, didn't want to cut a didg log. He took a moment to wee on a gum, watching the bark of a white gum darken with his stain.

Andy came back with his tool box and unzipped next to Jimmy. "Power of suggestion."

Jimmy finished his wee and watched the long arc of wee

coming from Andy. He reached beside him and let his fingertip brush along the ridge of the head of Andy's penis.

"What you doing?" Andy jerked his penis to the side and sprayed a termite mound.

Jimmy pulled on his own penis and circled the foreskin. "This where they cut?" If he really wanted, he could have Andy do it at the hospital. Didn't need initiation for that.

Andy shook himself out and hid his penis back in his pants. "Yeah. That's the place. Don't touch me willie, okay?"

Andy handed the saw up to Jimmy as he crouched again on the doctor's shoulders. Through the soles of Jimmy's feet he felt Andy shift his weight. Andy grunted up at him, "Doctor Donna would have a fit if she saw us now." Andy's white teeth clenched, "You'll see, Jimmy. As you get older. There's a lot to keep from women. A lot of things they're better off not knowing."

Sure, there were men's secrets and women's secrets from the Dreaming, but Jimmy had a feeling Andy wasn't talking about those. "Like what?" Jimmy held on to the branch, leaning his weight on it as he sawed away. It snapped and he came crashing down with the branch and saw, falling flat onto Andy.

Tom came running up. "You okay?"

Jimmy rolled over and Andy was laughing, his right arm bleeding. Tom held two rocks of ochre, one yellow and one red. Jimmy hopped up and took the red one. "Ochre, fair dinkum. You'll see though, we'll end up at Kmart."

Tom held the yellow rock above his head. "Follow me, first."

Andy brushed himself off, wiping the blood with his hanky and they followed Tom around the rocks. Less than fifty paces later they stopped at a small mound marked by a shovel head. Two metal handles of shovels made a makeshift cross.

Andy bent down. "Miner's grave. Friends probably buried him where he fell. You can see his name etched into the metal."

Tom crouched next to Andy, shielding his eyes. "Me da showed me it when I was little. *Patrick McCoy 1907.* Da wants to be buried out bush just like this." Jimmy could understand Mr. Patterson's desire. Good thing to be dead out bush with his tools. Sure way to make it up to Yaraandoo without city lights blocking the view of his destination.

Jimmy held the hollow tube in his lap and Tom held the ochre as they bumped home in the Land Rover. It was a good log, smoothed inside to match the outside by the termites. The best didgeridoos were hollowed by termites, but the ones they made in Yuendumu to sell in the tourist shops in the Alice were hollowed out by a machine in a big shed behind the community center.

He looked over at Doctor Andy. Sure Andy could waste time making didgeridoos. He was already a real doc. Jimmy didn't want to think about Yapa things. He wanted to do his science project, talk footy.

They glided along the smooth bitumen. Jimmy hated sticky bitumen when he was walking, preferred the hot sand that didn't stick in patches to his feet, but driving was another thing. He rolled down his window the way Andy and Da did. This was a man thing, another way to feel air. Air felt heavy from a car window. You could grab it like a ball in your hand.

Andy looked at him, eyes shaded by his hat. "What's the date of the Science Fete?"

"Twenty-six August, two weeks after Rodeo."

"Good. That'll be my last day in Isa. Off to Townsville."

Jimmy thought of Donna's black hair on the pillow. "Will you be lonely without Donna?"

"Got another woman in Townsville. Getting married. But I'll always miss Donna."

Jimmy couldn't see Andy's eyes under the shade of his hat, but thought he heard the doctor's voice go lower, as if talking at night. Jimmy asked, "Does Donna know?"

"Maybe. She's got another man, you know."

Jimmy let the wind whip his palm back. "She hasn't seen him

since you came. How'd you know?"

Andy scratched his penis through his pants. "Sisters talk. Women can't keep secrets."

Jimmy imagined Andy's penis, long and lean, but with a bulb at the end from being circumcised. "Yapa women can."

"Aussie women can't if they want to get you into their own bed."

"Mum said the Kardachi man will be here by Rodeo." Jimmy caught some air and tried to throw it inside the car.

Andy squinted into the sun. "You talk to her much?"

"Too much for a Yapa in the middle of initiation." Jimmy tried to throw the air back out the window. "But seems like initiation isn't happening. Hard to think of initiation in the Isa."

"Sure?"

Jimmy looked into the back seat to see if Tom were listening, but he was asleep, a string of drool creeping down his chin. "Could go down into the mine and work instead." Anyway, he wanted to be a doctor. Why would he need to be initiated? Would it affect his sex? "You could cut me."

Andy swerved for some roadkill. "If that's what you want. But I think you should do it the traditional way."

They passed a flock of budgies, a dark cloud on a blue sky, probably heading to the waterhole for a late arvo drink. There must have been a thousand of them and their cries and the sound of their wings pushing on the cooling air filled the car as they passed. Jimmy saw a boomer, bouncing away from them, out into the Center. Town suddenly rose in front of them, from out of nothingness. They'd passed a hill and there it was.

The highway became a street, and houses replaced gums. They wound around streets, passing the school, pulling into Kathy Street to drop off Tom at his super-sized house.

"Let's get home." Andy chuckled as he restarted the car. "They used to say that home is where you hang your hat. Now I think home is where you lay your swag."

For Jimmy, home was home, or home was camp, wherever his kin were, anywhere under Yaraandoo.

Andy shifted into first. "You and me, Jimmy Jackboy. We're two guys that are Waltzing Matilda. But we're both Waltzing Donna right now. One, two, three. One, two, three. We're a damn fine threesome, as threesomes go."

Andy's voice rang out through the open windows. He sang, "Jimmy, come a Waltzing Donna with me." Andy hummed the rest of the tune, one so familiar to Jimmy, sung to him since he could remember right along with the Dreaming songs. Jimmy couldn't help but join in.

They rounded Gracie Street, practically yelling out the windows of the Land Rover, "Waltzing Matilda, Waltzing Matilda, who'll come a Waltzing Matilda with me." Jimmy could see himself from out of his body. One crazy whitefella and one crazy Yapa boy swinging their way into Doctor Donna's yard, a hollow tube of gum branch bouncing along in the back next to two rocks of ochre.

An hour later, Andy lifted his hat and scratched his head, scowling at the pasty mix. "You were right."

"You think a Yapa doesn't know about ochre?" Andy had expected the red and yellow paste to turn orange. But Jimmy knew they wouldn't be able to grind the rock fine enough for the colors to mix. "Let's go to Kmart."

Andy looked at his watch. "I'm making tea tonight. We'll sit down in an hour."

"I'll go on me bike. Be back before that."

When he got to the Kmart, Jimmy knew exactly where his feet were heading. He also knew that when he went back to Yuendumu, he'd miss being able to pop into the air conditioning to pick up supplies.

He looked at the wall of paints, so beautiful together. He put cyan—the blue-green of the waterhole—in his basket, together with the bright magenta of the Galah, and the yellow of the sulphur-crested cockatoo. These three colors could make every other color in the world. He picked out neon purple and neon orange—the color of the smoke from the smokestack at sunset— and neon green. He loved the colors and could imagine them covering the hollow log he'd placed in the shed when they'd returned. In the paper aisle, he added three paintbrushes, three pencils, and five rolls of cardboard, then added another piece of tag paper, just in case.

He walked by an aisle with men's hats, but didn't stop. If he got a hat, it wouldn't be at the Kmart. He'd get a BC Hat from Molony's stockman's shop. As he passed by a row of books, he saw a map of Mount Isa. He opened it, letting his finger trace Miles and Main and all the routes from school to hospital to Donna's and beyond. He knew most of the streets already, but there were a few he hadn't explored. He folded the map carefully and put it in his basket.

At the checkout, he couldn't decide between the Caramello Koala for Donna, which he knew she liked, and the Violet Crumble, which he wanted her to like. *What is honeycomb? I don't get it*, she'd shake her head every time she saw him with a Crumble. For a woman who'd once said she couldn't handle chockie, she sure ate a lot of it. He wanted her to love the Violet Crumble, to understand its beauty, so full of air and possibility, like smoke bridging the gap between Yuti world and the world of the Ancestor, like the music of the didg. The caramel of the Koala was sticky like hot bitumen. But in the end he respected her taste and bought the Koala. Surely chocolate was better than flowers with no smell?

He put his supplies into the bicycle's flowered basket, then flew down the hill from the Kmart to Main to Gracie, past the shops and houses, lights just coming on. The wind in his hair, the paints jiggling in the basket, Jimmy felt like he was about to take off. He'd miss the bike when he left town.

He waved to the docs who sat on the front stoop with their tinnies. Donna's head was in her hands, and she looked as if she were studying the concrete steps. Andy was massaging her neck. Jimmy rode around back to unpack his gear. He leaned the bike against the shed and turned on a lantern so he could lay out his supplies on a shelf. He unfolded the map of Isa and stuck it on the wall with some tape, beneath where he'd written his name.

As he looked around the shed, he was surprised at how full it was. His lantern shone white on a cricket ball, paper and pens and markers for homework, glue, scissors, some pants and skivvies, underwear, sweatshirts. He'd never have so much stuff in Yuendumu. Cousins would share it and it'd be all over town within minutes.

He ran into the house with the chocolate and left it on the kitchen counter in front of Andy's pink flowers. He got a piece of paper and pen from the shed and wrote *To Donna, From Jimmy Jackboy* in his best curvy writing and stuck it under the candy. He started to leave, but turned back to push the flowers back toward the wall, next to the tea kettle, way behind his chocolate. Then he went outside to keep company with the docs while tea finished cooking.

\\\(\cap\)/

Sunday morning, Donna met Esther at the hospital to do early rounds. Finished by eight, they decided to take a morning walk. As they meandered through the sparse vegetation in the bushland behind the hospital, Esther picked leaves, closing her eyes to smell them. They walked up a small hill and looked down over some houses that bordered the bush, manicured yards ending in fences. On the other side of the fences the earth was brown. *"The grass is always greener* doesn't work here."

"What?"

"The gra– Ouch." Donna grabbed her ankle. "That ant bit me. I went to brush him off and—wow—oh my God, does it burn." Here was the bite she was owed by that spider she'd killed. Why hadn't she worn long socks? "Must be poison."

"No poison ants." Esther dropped her leaves and crouched to the ground, her wide hands lightly skimming the grass and brush beside them.

Even if it wasn't poisonous, the pain would kill her. Donna whimpered, "Oh, Esther."

A moment later Esther stood up with a smile, pinching a half inch long dead ant between her wrinkled brown fingers. "Bull ant. Hold on." She walked a circle around Donna, examining the ground plants. Moments later, Esther held a yellowed leaf high. "Bracken fern." She broke off a stem and squeezed a drop of sap onto the bite. "Always grows where bull ants live. Cure grows near the toxin. Good balance."

Donna rolled her eyes, but felt immediate relief from the pain, relief better than any orgasm. "More."

Esther rubbed the sap into the bite with her big thumb. Donna bent over and watched the hairy knuckles massaging her ankle and calf. Five minutes later, Donna could put weight back on that leg. "Amazing."

"If you're game, I'll show you some other medicines."

Two hours later, Donna poured tea at her kitchen table as Esther pulled leaves from her dilly bag and laid them in front of her. Esther sniffed then handed them to Donna. "Mangumberre leaves, flowers, and seeds."

"Smell like acacia."

Esther's voice was rich as she spoke in Pintupi, then translated. "Cooks into a paste. Dab it on open sores." Donna scribbled the instructions on a piece of paper, then laid the leaf on it. She planned to go to the library and find a book to help her identify each plant.

She was all for herbal medicines. Digitalis was a perfect example. Came from foxglove and was a crucial drug for treating heart failure. When her patients told her they took herbs, she encouraged them to continue if they worked.

Esther handed her other leaves. "Mangol and woollybutt. Miracle for rashes."

Mangol had been Jimmy's recommendation for the eye issues associated with lupus. She'd need to research that. She took a sniff and kept it by her nose, soaking up the eucalypt scent of spa steam rooms. "Bengay," she whispered.

Esther closed her eyes. "I heard that."

"Sorry. Please continue."

"Best woollybutt bark grows low on the tree, where the roots reach into the earth. It's hairy there like us." She pointed at her crotch. "Why it helps with menstrual cramps."

Donna imagined Esther following the paths of her Ancestors, walking naked among the eucalyptus, breasts feeling the pull of gravity, pubic hair ruffled slightly by the wind, strong arms clearing away the branches, reaching down the trunk of a tree to pull away the bark. Donna smelled the woollybutt. "My irregular periods have regulated since I've been down here. I could use that."

Esther looked over Donna's notes. "It's the South Pole magnet that makes you ovulate."

Andy had spoken of magnetics in Boulia. "I think it's that I'm de-stressed and detoxified for the first time since childhood. The *no worries* Aussie attitude is good for me."

Esther smiled and her globed cheeks almost hid her eyes. "Ready for the crown jewel?" She pulled a large brown clump of mud from the dilly bag. "Get me a pot please."

Donna got up and found her soup pot. She put it in front of Esther who dumped the mud into the pot. "Gabo. Green ant. Bull ant bit you, means you must get in harmony with the land here. Eat a bit of gabo so you'll feel better."

"I feel fine."

Esther shook her head and put her hand on Donna's shoulder. "The boys are gone all day?"

Donna nodded. Andy had taken Jimmy and his friend Tom out bush to find ochre and said he'd be home right before tea.

"Today we'll make you some gabo. Want to get stoned?"

Donna had been craving another out-of-body experience, had looked at her Honey Ant Dreaming every morning, willing it to transport her. Wanted the clarity, the lightness that those moments had brought, even though she'd been left with the confusion afterward of their meaning. "I'd love to but I shouldn't. I may be pregnant."

Esther took the pot to the sink and turned on the faucet over the mud clump. "You won't get preggers 'til you've emptied that bag of baby."

"I meant to. Couldn't do it." Donna grabbed another leaf and studied its veins. They looked like the paths of her palm. She held her palm up next to the leaf.

Esther called instructions from the sink. "If you soak the nest in cold water, ants and eggs come pouring out. Then we smash them down and eat them."

"Esther, I don't know if I can eat ants."

"We'll do it together."

Donna wasn't an adventurous eater. She hadn't been the one to eat whole roasted pigeons in Vietnam; Greg had bitten off their charred heads in one bite, nor chicken feet in Nepal. She liked to experience other cultures through art, not exotic foods.

Esther brought the pot to the table. "I'll put it in some milk for you. You'll never taste it. Too bad it isn't November. That's when the new ants hatch. Strongest medicine around then. Too strong for children."

Donna watched as the ants floated up through the cold water, paddling their tiny legs, but soon drowning. The water was black with ants and Esther scooped them into another pot with her spoon. "What do you do if things are out of season?"

Esther smashed the ants down into the small pot. "Medicine man or woman's always got the songs, got the didg—man blows it up and down over the body—got other magic. Medicine woman especially has the magic, but I don't need to tell you that. You're a healer."

Donna thought of herself as a scientist, a diagnostician, not as a medicine woman in the traditional sense. But a healer? She liked the ring of that. Would like that on her card. Dr. Donna Cooper. *Healer* instead of *Board Certified in Internal Medicine.*

When Esther handed her the glass of milk and gabo, Donna gagged. Then she remembered the days of shrooming in college. Her trick had been to think about something else and absently eat the shrooms. So she imagined the night in Boulia with Andy as she drank the milk and gabo down. Esther drank hers like a shot of whiskey.

Ten minutes later, as she chopped the vegetables for lunch and looked up every so often to see Esther spreading her leaves to dry in the grass, the gabo began to work. First Donna felt the ants crawling around in her stomach. She shook her head and scolded her imagination. But then the zucchini was moving, and the pepper. The knife's edge was a blur in her hand. She dropped the vegetables and knife, then ran outside. Two Galahs seemed to be talking to her from the mango tree branch. Were they saying *Honey Ant*? She saw a map—like the one Jimmy had made for Hector's room—etched in the dirt, all of its squiggles and dots moving and marching. Honey Ant Dreaming. "Esther, you said stoned. This is tripping."

Esther laughed. "Sit down, sit down. Help you travel into your healing center." She pushed Donna down on the step.

It was like riding a bicycle; you never forgot the art of tripping once you'd mastered it. "The grass is breathing. Veggies were breathing. Everything is orange."

Esther put her arm over Donna's shoulders. "Of course they're breathing."

"Now everything is pink. The house is breathing. How about you?"

"I'm breathing." The women broke into a fit of giggles. Esther said, "House just vibrating as the earth exhales."

Donna put her head in her hands. "Did I kill the zucchini?"

"Mister Zucchini wants you to eat him. His energy is ready to merge with yours."

Holding Esther's hand, she timidly opened her eyes and beheld the backyard. A bee eater flew by and she could see his individual feathers, the turquoise and yellow stripes of his throat against his blue-green body, the bright orange of his underwings waving like the orange smoke from the smokestacks at sunset. Two thin tail feathers extended long past the rest of his tail, painting his path in the sky, a black line through the blue. Now the yard was day-glo green, the smoke was day-glo orange, the birds day-glo pink. And Jimmy's hair glowed white, like hot molten glass. He'd ridden into the yard and was bent over his bicycle. No, it wasn't

Jimmy, it was an angel. Sprouting from his back were two shimmering wings, the size of monarch wings, pulsing. "Do you see Jimmy's wings? My angel baby."

Esther cupped Donna's chin in her rabbit palm. "Jimmy's out bush with Andy and he's *not* your baby. Stop calling the baby back." Esther kissed her on the nose. "We can let the gabo work its wonders. Let the baby fly back to your heaven. We're going on a ride. I'll get us ready."

Donna looked into Esther's black eyes. "You can't drive. We're stoned."

Esther stood up. "No police in the bush to give me a DUI. Just pray I can get us onto the Barkly."

They walked through the house and Esther said, "Need to get something. I'll meet you in the car."

Donna did as she was told, the colors of Australia ever-changing as she walked out the front door.

Esther took the Barkly to a dirt road Donna had never noticed on her runs. They stopped in the middle of nowhere—not even twenty minutes outside Isa, with no marker or sign anywhere. They walked through dense wattle glowing fluorescent yellow. The air turned yellow and all she could see was yellow. Donna struggled up the rocky hillside behind Esther, who pointed to a favorite hiding place for witchetty grubs, honey-pot ants, and the tracks of what had probably been a coral snake. Yet in Donna's haze of gabo, even the mention of snakes didn't faze her.

Esther steadied Donna as she slipped on the scree. "Kalkadoon bones used to litter this hill from the slaughter in 1884, but now they've mostly been carted off. You can feel them in the land." She kicked at the dry earth that was blown up in small cyclones by gusts of wind.

They reached the top of the bluff. More and more rocks and bluffs, mirrors of the one where they stood, stretched beyond them. The hills glimmered, a thin layer of water tracing each one; whether a mirage or the gabo, Donna didn't know.

Esther pointed to the horizon. "Jimmy's Land."

"So close." Donna felt Esther's palm heavy on her shoulder.

Esther squeezed her shoulder. "Let go of the child now."

"He'll be going back to Yuendumu after Rodeo."

Esther whispered, "Jimmy Jackboy is becoming a man. I mean the child." Esther's hand slid down from her shoulder, and at first she thought Esther was going to cup her breast, but then saw the gray velvet bag dangling from Esther's fingers.

"I knew you had it. I felt it when we were walking up the hill."

Esther's smooth cheek pressed her own. "Of course you did. It's time."

Donna held out her palm and Esther dropped it. Donna saw it float down into the warm cup of her hand, felt its weight.

Esther turned Donna's head with the pressure of her own cheek. "Kalkadoon warriors. He will be with the People."

She clutched the bag, shaking her head. "Not so far from home." Maybe she'd spread the ashes when she went home to New York. Maybe over the Hudson. But here? She'd never be able to find this bluff again, which was identical to so many others on this unmarked stretch of road.

"That's the point. You don't need to visit. He'll visit you."

Donna's hand shook. She wasn't going to do it just because some wacky Yapa said she should. This kind of thing should be carefully planned, not done while tripping.

Esther wrapped her arms around Donna. Her breast pressed into Donna's back. She widened the opening of the bag at Donna's chest. "Listen to the baby. He's pleading with us to let him go, so he can start over. Don't say his name again. You need to stop calling him back."

Did Donna hear a faint wail? Maybe just wind bending the grass? Esther cupped Donna's palm in hers and turned their hands over, letting the ashes sprinkle toward the ground. Donna saw the ashes fall, the boy's fairy dust drifting down to the red earth. But as ash was about to hit the ground and mix with the dirt and sand, a wind came and carried it away. A Galah called, *Chi, chi.*

The ashes and the velvet bag were the color of the Galah's back feathers as it swooped down past Donna. And with wind and the beating of wings, those ashes mingled in Donna's nostrils and amongst the spinifex. An arm in her nose, one leg east, one leg west, his torso caught on the hide of a roo as it bounded through the desert, carried to the billabong to be washed down to the Center, past Uluru to the moon salt lake. There his dust would settle and become part of the earth.

She kneeled down to see if there were anything left to salvage. Scooped the red dirt into her cupped hands to let it trickle through. She couldn't find the ash. She scooped more dirt, and more, and more, turning north, south, east, west. He was gone. The names came from her lips, her father, her mother, her baby, Michael Robson, Jill, no last name, she called louder and louder.

Esther clamped her hand over Donna's mouth. "You heard me. Don't you ever." She grabbed Donna's head and brought it close to her own lips, whispering fiercely, "Never, ever again, say the names of the dead aloud. Let their spirits go, once and for all."

Donna wrenched her head from the woman's grip and stumbled away. She listed the names in her head but didn't defy Esther, whose eyes flashed. Donna sat down where she thought some of her son's ashes might have landed. Rubbed the dirt along her legs, her son or not her son, dead men all over the hillside. She lay her cheek on the ground, lay with him as she would have cuddled him at night when he was teething, bare belly sweaty against hers in the summertime. She stroked the earth as she would have stroked his face to wipe away his tears.

Esther walked Donna to the door. The hallucinations had ended when they left Kalkadoon Hill; everything had seemed normal for a long while. Donna held her door handle, letting its heat sear her hand, as it had the first day she'd arrived in Isa. Andy called from the kitchen, "Where've you been, luv?"

Galahs chattered from the front wires. "Bring a Fourex out to the porch?" Donna said through the screen.

"Come on out here, Andy," Esther ordered. "Sit her outside for a while. Sit on the front porch and love Australia with her. Hmmm?"

The eggs have been shifting like the sands of dunes. Beneath her they clink against each other, already competing for position. It is an active clutch, all male this time. She can feel the male energy beneath her, the need to move, to fly, to turn.

The first has pipped, taken its egg tooth and pierced the shell. Over the day it turns in its egg, slowly cutting its path, taking time to rest. She watches the crack grow like the cracks in the dry soil of the desert as the days pass further into the Dry. She warms the other eggs but gives this one room to move. By the time the sun rises and the sky turns the Galah, she will meet him if he has the energy. Often the chicks die before cutting the whole egg, and then her new mate will roll the egg out of the nest, watch it crash to the earth where a gecko will make it a meal.

She will not help pierce the hard shell, will not roll it over for him, to better angle himself to exit. Better the chick dies before she has fed him, kept him warm against her breast as his wet down dries to pink fluff, if it does not have the strength to make it in this hard world. She hopes one in this clutch will be flying with the flock next monsoon. She hopes one will live to fifty to be the messenger for another Galah boy.

The first chick emerges when the moon is disappearing from the sky, everything he needs for the first day in the egg with him. He will drink the blood of the egg while he dries.

On Wednesday evening, Jimmy biked to hospital after tea. Esther had come over to Donna's and yelled at him for not visiting Hector for so long—he hadn't been to hospital since the day before he went ochre hunting with Andy, almost a week-and-a-half ago—and he'd promised he'd come that day. He'd meant to go right after school, but Tom wanted to trade AFL cards. The evening cooled his shoulders, and Jimmy took a detour through the streets, putting off the moment he'd have to go inside. The town looked different, more familiar now that he'd seen its body underground. He tried to trace the underground tour on the streets above as he enjoyed the last light of day. *Ambient light*. Donna called the time of the Galah *ambient light*. When the sun was already down, but plants and trees emitted some of the light they'd absorbed during the day. *Ambient* was a good word. Rolled off the tongue.

He rode the empty streets, looking up at the trees. The trees got progressively bigger as he moved from Donna's toward hospital, from the newer parts of town to the older. Instead of street names, they should have given areas the names of the underground deposits that precipitated more building. Like, Donna's house could be called *51st house of 1982 lead* and Tom's called *Second house of 1960 nickel*. He laughed at his joke.

In the last week, he'd studied his map and found all the streets he'd never been on. He left no street unridden by his bicycle. Town no longer looked as big as when he and Hector had first arrived. Now he could see the map of the streets in his head as he biked.

When it was finally dark, he rested his bicycle against the wall and ran up the two flights of stairs to Hector's room. On the last step he had a thought. *What if he just woke? What if the white medicine finally worked?* Jimmy had seen it work on so many other Yapa patients. He crashed through Hector's door, heart pounding in excitement. Esther was sitting in a chair next to Hector's bed, holding Hector's hand and speaking in Pintupi. He and Hector spoke Warlpiri, but that didn't stop Esther from rambling on. Jimmy could understand only a little of what she said.

She dropped Hector's hand and smiled. "You're in an awful hurry tonight."

"How's Hector?" Jimmy came up close and squeezed the man's toe. There had been no change. Jimmy suddenly felt tired, like an old Yapa.

Esther lifted a gelatin from the table. "Saved it for you."

"Ta," but Jimmy didn't take it. Instead, he flopped down in the orange bucket chair and watched the clock tick, tapping his fingers to the rhythm of the pings of the machine that signaled Hector's heartbeat. They pinged like a cuckoo bird, regular in their irregular pattern. He'd recognize Hector's heartbeat anywhere now, knew how it differed from his own. He wondered if heartbeats were like footprints, everyone different so you could track someone by the beats of their heart? He remembered the pulses of the mine. Maybe the coursing of the blood through the heart had a vibration that could be seen in the energy of the Rainbow Serpent?

He closed his eyes and Esther mumbled in Pintupi again. Jimmy concentrated on what she was saying. Was Esther telling a Dreaming story or a real world story? It was often hard to tell when you entered midway through a conversation. "Dreaming or Yuti?"

"Dreaming."

"Yapa bugger." Jimmy closed his eyes again.

Esther ignored him and kept talking. Jimmy stood up and took Esther's stethoscope. He held its rubber band in his hand and tossed it around his neck as he'd seen the docs do so often.

"You tell him a story." Esther stood up and pulled the stethoscope from his shoulders. Her eyes looked dark under her long forehead.

Jimmy slunk into the chair that Esther had left warmed with her ample behind. What to talk to him about? He thought of his bicycle ride and began to describe the town. He listed the streets then stopped. There had to be a better way. "Don't go anywhere." He laughed at the joke as he ran down to his bicycle to retrieve the Isa map.

Jimmy returned to Hector's room. The front of the map said *Visit the Isa: Take a left at Townsville*. It had a photo of a miner in his orange jumpsuit pointing to a city sign. Jimmy showed the cover to Hector's closed eyes, then unfolded it and held the map in front of Hector, tracing his favorite routes around town. But there was only so long he could talk to a sleeping body. He let the map fall onto Hector's face, and it moved slightly each time Hector inhaled and exhaled.

He lifted the white sheet covering Hector's body and legs. Hector's muscles were still strong, but his penis lay limp, like a witchetty grub. One fried and crisp, not long and powerful like a didg. He took hold of the grub and examined the tip. Like Andy's, so why not let Andy do it? He'd probably never be initiated the right way, anyway. Sure the Kardachi man was coming in six weeks, but Jimmy had learned from the doctors that a man in coma this long couldn't be expected to walk him to his Land, much less cut him with a knife.

He put back the sheet and folded his map. On his way out, he looked up at the Dreaming he'd made for Hector. He ripped it from the wall. Then he crinkled it into a ball and threw it in the trash, atop some bloody gauze.

Back at his shed, Jimmy turned on the lantern and lit a small fire in the fire pit with charcoal from Kmart. He poured water from the hose into his billy and put it over the fire, and filled a paper cup with Cocoa Bombs. As he waited for the billy to boil, he popped Bombs into his mouth and opened his Mount Isa map. Under the light of the lantern, he took a black marker to the underside of the waxy map paper and traced the skeleton shadow of the mine under the streets.

\∩/

Donna hadn't been able to run out the Barkly over the last week-and-a-half. She'd start, then turn around, not wanting to follow the path she'd taken with Esther to let go of her baby. So she signed up for the Wednesday evening round-robin at the squash club instead. She had a faint hope that Nick might be there. He'd answered her e-mail about the house guest with a non-committal *Okay*. If she could see his face, she would know if there was a chance to have him again when Andy left.

She was matched with Beth, one of the best players in the *Over-40s*, and Beth annihilated her. As they left the court, Beth apologized. "Kept imagining the ball was the head of me son. Got lucky today."

Donna wiped the sweat from her forehead. She usually hated to get routed, but today she was just grateful for the workout. "Not happy with him?"

Beth pulled the court door shut behind them and threw the ball into the recycle bin. "I'll tell you about boys. For the first two years, they're babies. You have about eleven more to mother. Then you let go and they go feral."

"I don't know teens well."

Beth plopped down on the lobby sofa and brushed back her graying-brown hair. "He's twenty-two."

Donna sat in an overstuffed love seat. Beth's son was only four years younger than Andy. "Everyone says there is nothing like motherhood."

Beth lifted her sport bag onto her lap. "It's exhausting. You never stop being a mum."

"What's sticking out from your bag?" Donna sat forward to get a better look. A hoof? Some macabre lucky charm?

Beth wrapped her hand around it, opened the bag and pulled. "Me baby roo."

Donna fell back into the couch. Attached to the leg was a cinnamon-colored kangaroo, the size of a large rabbit. Beth set the roo on the ground and it hopped around the sofas. She showed Donna the lining of her gym bag. "Put sheep's wool to make it soft and comfy and she thinks it's her pouch. Jumps in head first like she would into her mum. Waits for me to get her out."

"She's your pet?"

The roo started down the hall and Beth got up to corral her back to the area where they were sitting. "They don't domesticate well. Call her Peanut for now. We'll let her go when she's mature. Hope she doesn't get flattened by a road train like her mum."

"Can I pet her?" Donna crouched down and stuck her hand out. The roo dove headfirst into her lap and Donna fell backward.

Beth scooped Peanut up and pulled Donna's hand. "They're always looking for a pocket to dive into. When me hubby comes home, she tries to dive into the pencil pocket of his shirt."

Donna returned to the couch and Beth plopped Peanut into Donna's lap. "Found her mum freshly killed out on the Barkly. Me hubby stuck her down his bike shirt before the kites got to her. Biked home and called the kangaroo rescue lady, but she was out of town. Looked up what to do in the library. Now I like having her around."

Donna stroked Peanut's soft head. "Beautiful."

"Want to feed her a bottle?" Beth rummaged in her bag and handed Donna a towel. "First make her wee and poo. Rub this over her privates, then hold it under. They do it on command so they don't soil Mum's pouch."

Donna cradled the roo and wiped its bottom. Ever the doctor, she examined its anatomy. "I only see one hole."

"Only got one for shagging, weeing, and pooping."

The towel turned yellow, then little turds popped out. Beth took the towel from her and Donna sat back on the couch, letting the sweat dry on her body as she fed Peanut. She watched the roo tugging at the bottle's nipple, felt the warmth of its body spread through her lap. The roo fidgeted in Donna's grasp and Beth leaned forward and stroked the roo's ears. "Don't know how to teach her to be a good mum and make her own joey stay close so no dingoes get it. She may have poor success in the wild. But we'll let her go where we found her. Maybe on her land she'll find the right mob—unlike me son."

"On her land." Donna echoed Beth's words while concentrating on the black nose and black paws curled up, the soft gray insides of its ears, and the black rings around its huge eyes.

The next morning Donna visited Hector. She stopped in the doorway. Something was different. As she stepped all the way in, she realized it was not Hector who'd changed, but the room. The walls were gray and empty. Jimmy's Dreaming had disappeared, in the same way her grade school family tree had. No explanation, just gone.

She went to Hector's side and brushed the hair from his forehead. It had grown long in two months. "Jimmy hasn't given up. Don't worry." She liked being alone in the room with him. Despite the coma, she found his presence comforting, like he was aware of her, but without the complaints that usually accompanied a patient visit. "Can you tell me about this Jessie thing? Am I going to have a baby? Or a kangaroo?" Donna squeezed his calf. Still that amazing muscle tone. She felt his ankle for his pulse. Strong as ever, as was his breathing. Was he up at night unplugging his machine and doing calisthenics to prevent the decay that usually accompanied coma? She pricked the sole of his foot with a paperclip, but not a muscle twitched.

She stood under the blue light of the monitor at the end of

the bed, her hand on his ankle as the machine beeped. She would have turned all the machines onto silent mode after all this time, but Jimmy had insisted that they all listen to Hector's heartbeat.

She wanted Jimmy to have his uncle back. Hector was so close to consciousness, she could feel it. Yet what could she do? She hadn't found anything in the numerous articles she searched, and no neurologist had been able to give her new ideas. Do you put someone on your list of the dead whose body lingers but whose spirit has flown away?

Should Esther give Hector some gabo? Or maybe he needed an ant bite. She'd exhausted the list of her own medicines. She thought of Andy and Jimmy still at her breakfast table as Hector was being fed from the IV.

She thought of Jimmy's chocolate eyes, his smooth skin the color of tea, whether deep down she wanted to cure Hector. Maybe she hadn't figured how to wake Hector because she didn't really *want* to, because she liked having this borrowed boy around. But someone would come to fetch him soon anyway, so it didn't do any good for Hector to remain in coma. Could the subconscious really be that powerful? If so, maybe she hadn't really wanted her baby, had been too afraid of how a baby would change her life after all those years. Maybe there was a God who knew those things.

From deep inside the blue of the sky, the Galah looks down upon her Land. Moonprints, full and crescent, cover every part of her country.

From the sky, the tips of the spinifex shine, tiny dots upon the land. From the sky she can see earth-rainbows, patches of yellow melting into sienna, bronze, then brown. She sees squiggle trails where the snake has brushed over the sand, the moons of salt washes baked into the land until the next rain will create new ones. She knows the bumps, barely visible from above, where the brown men have built windbreaks, the half-circles the men leave by sitting in the sand. She knows every fold of the dunes. She was born knowing every roost, where to find the round shining circles of water.

She travels light upon the wind, the wind that carries her from one circle to the next, following the line of dots and moons to look for berries. From above she can see dots of green and red. She dives.

She gorges on the berries hanging low on the kangaroo bushes. They fall to the ground, and she picks more. She is not greedy, like the human. Let them fall to seed the earth. Next year there will be another bush where the berries have fallen and her chicks will eat from that bush, even if she is no longer alive.

She understands the power of the seed: to at once fill her belly and then to fill the earth. Each seed will be a tree, a bush, or flower even if she eats it. Waste will fall to the earth to help another plant grow. That plant will have a seed, and that seed will have the life force of the first seed within it. The first seed, which was there from the beginning, *is the same seed she eats now, is the tree that she roosts in, is the dust that blows in the wind. It is all the same. Full from the berries she flies back to her nest where her partner and the chicks wait, wait for the seed power inside her.*

The docs had gone out bush and Jimmy waited for Tom to come over. He laid out supplies in the backyard, then paced under the mango tree, looking out at the street for Tom's bicycle. Impatiently, he unrolled a piece of cardboard and opened his paints. The smell of the acrylics reminded him of the art center in Yuendumu. Would Auntie Tess be there today, dabbing her dots to sell?

He dipped a brush into cyan and drew a line of color. Next to the first, he painted lines of green, sulfur, and magenta. With a narrower brush, Jimmy traced a black outline around the block of colored lines, finishing with a black dot for an eye. The Rainbow Serpent. It danced in front of Jimmy's eyes.

"What's that?" Tom stood over him.

Jimmy hadn't heard him come into the yard. Why hadn't his parrots called a warning? They always let him know if non-kin was around. "Doodling."

"Looks like a snake." Tom plopped himself down next to Jimmy letting his long legs splay over the painting. "Hey, it's wet."

"Now you have the Rainbow Serpent on your ankle."

"Yeah?"

"Color is one of its energies. A wavelength we can see."

"What?" Tom squinted under his hat. It looked like he had popped a pimple that morning because a dot on his square chin oozed blood.

Jimmy moved the smeared Rainbow Serpent to the side. He handed Tom a circle that Jimmy had cut from cardboard. "Use this to trace more of them."

Tom cut the circles and on each, Jimmy painted a slice of

waterhole, Galah crest, and sulphur cockatoo crest. When they dried, the boys punctured the centers with a pencil, to make spinning tops. When the tops twirled, the colors blended together so quickly that to the human eye, the reflection of the light looked white, as Jimmy had expected.

"Good onya, Jimmy." Tom put his hand up for a high five.

While Jimmy created their absence-of-light experiment, Tom started another on a new piece of cardboard. He was mixing the three base colors in different measures to show that mixing pigments was different from mixing colored lights. The blended pigments reflected light differently than their individual components. Tom held up his creation. "You were right. Worked a lot better than the ochre. Let me see that."

He pointed at the shoe box Donna had donated, in which Jimmy had cut a hole in one end, and then painted it black both inside and out. The hole wouldn't reflect any light, so it would look more black than the black paint itself.

Jimmy held the box up. "Isn't it like the mine when your da turned off the lights?"

Tom was labeling each dab of mixed paint—⅓ *Cyan,* ⅔ *Magenta* and so on—because he had better handwriting. "You like the mine so much. You should live in me house."

Jimmy stepped back and admired their work. "Now all we need are the mirrors and water."

Tom stood with his hands on his hips. "Hardest part is giving the speech. I'll give you me Michael Long card if you'll do it. I hate talking in front of me mates."

Jimmy didn't think that would be so scary. "How about you talk about mixing pigments and I'll talk about the things that show light rays. You'll have the shorter part."

Tom put his hand out. "Deal."

They took turns practicing their parts, the other making goofy faces, trying to make the speaker laugh. The Galah called from the tree while Jimmy was speaking and he turned to the bird.

"Quiet. Can't you see we're working here?" Couldn't she have called before, when Tom came into the yard? "Stupid bird."

Jimmy's scolding sent Tom into hysterics, and Jimmy bent down and threw some grass at him. Tom threw it back and soon they were rolling over each other in a dirt fight. When they finally called truce, Jimmy went inside to get snacks. It was nice having the run of the Doctor's house.

They sat under Mister Mango, tucking into bikkies and Coke. Tom dug in the dirt with a stick. "You should talk about the Rainbow Serpent in your speech."

Jimmy looked up at the sky through the thick leaves of the mango. "What?"

Tom kept flicking at the dirt. "How the Rainbow Serpent is made of different wavelengths."

Jimmy tipped the Coke back letting the bubbles tickle his throat. He could live on Coke and Violet Crumbles. "This is science, not story time. We want to win. Can you imagine the laughs if I told Yapa bugger?"

The chicks squawked in the nest above, and Jimmy yelled, "Get stuffed, birds," sending Tom into another hysterics fit.

Before tea, Jimmy sat in the kitchen watching Donna cook. "May I have some of the raspberries for the Galah?" He'd felt bad all afternoon about the way he'd spoken to his kin in front of Tom, something he never would have done in Yuendumu. He could only imagine what Mum would say if she visited that night.

Donna was cutting ugli fruit, Jimmy's favorite. "The berries were seven dollars."

"Okay. I'll share some of me ugli fruit." He jumped off the stool and took a few slices that she'd already cut.

As he reached the door, she said, "Wait," and held out a handful of raspberries.

"Ta. Come meet me birds. Have you seen the chicks?"

Donna wiped her hands on her jeans and Jimmy led her out to the backyard, his empty palm pressing against her back the way she'd pressed Andy's, and his. Yes, the warmth there felt good, the small curve like the hollow under a chin or maybe the rise of the bum. "I should have shown you when they had pink fuzz. They have their feathers now. Be ready to fly soon." Under the tree he arranged the raspberries and ugli fruit for the Galahs, then whistled. The mother came out of the nest, looked around, then hopped to the ground. Jimmy whispered, "May we see the chicks?" He motioned Donna over and she peered into the hole.

"Ohhh." The creases on Donna's forehead smoothed as she pulled her head from the nest hole. "They deserve raspberries."

\\∩/

She stood with Jimmy, looking at the chicks with their fresh pink-and gray-feathers. "So what happens to them when they can fly?"

Jimmy rose onto his tip-toes and peeked into the nest. The fuzz on his cheek rubbed hers. Donna could swear he'd grown half an inch since she met him. He stepped back and gestured to the mother Galah. "She'll leave the nest and rejoin the flock. The chicks will fly together for a while until they're old enough to mate. This clutch is all male. You can tell by their color."

The chicks would fly away. It was time for Jimmy to do the same, regardless of what happened to Hector. "Did you take down your Dreaming from Hector's room?"

His eyes turned from chocolate to black. "So what?"

So everything. She would not have him give up under her watch. It was the mother's job, wasn't it? Kick the chick from the nest, return the kangaroo to its land. "The Flying Docs go out to Barrington Downs. Remember?"

He stepped close to her and she felt almost as if he were Andy approaching for a kiss. She stumbled back into the tree and whispered. "I'll make a phone call."

She didn't wait for his reaction. Instead, she made a wide circle around Jimmy—was she truly afraid he would've kissed her, or was she feeling that she would kiss him? All she knew as she dialed the number for the Flying Docs was that she would ask Clive if she and Jimmy could visit the Station with him. Jimmy could walk his land so he could say he'd been there. Then they could have him circumcised in the hospital, if that were so important. He would go back to Yuendumu a circumcised man.

A week later, Jimmy woke to Donna shaking his shoulder. The moon was high in the sky behind her. She pulled off his swag cover. "Clive called. They're going to Barrington this morning. Andy'll call you in sick to school. We need to be at the airport in twenty minutes." Jimmy popped out of his swag and was ready in no time. Flying in an airplane! Wait until his mates from Yuendumu heard. He grabbed the box of Cocoa Bombs from his shed to munch in the car.

As the airplane took off, Jimmy felt gravity pulling him back, then releasing him. They flew into the darkness, Jimmy aware of the engines' loud hum and Donna's flashlight shining on her book. As the sun rose, Jimmy looked down upon his Land. Why would you need songs? Why would you need Dreaming when you could travel on the wings of an airplane? He was surprised at how light he felt after escaping gravity. The last time he'd been so close to his Land, he'd felt every cell being pulled. The plane lurched and he put his hand on his pocket. Empty. How long had he been without Da's bone? Weeks? A month? More. How could he have remembered the Cocoa Bombs and forgotten Da's bone? Bugger. He put the cereal down. He was a bad son.

Barrington Downs Station opened up below them. Jimmy could see the fence he'd tried to cross, a straight line and sharp edge among all those circles. Jimmy counted ten white-sided buildings. They buzzed the first building to let the people on the ground know they'd arrived, and someone ran out to help them land.

The engines quieted as they taxied along the pasture and Donna turned to him. "You're on your Galah Land. Now you can become an initiated man."

He stroked the leather seat. "Only if I come back with Hector." He patted his empty pocket and sighed.

Donna's smile fell, so he added quickly, "No worries, Doctor."

Donna unbuckled her seat belt and put her hands on his knees. "Go ahead and walk on your Land while Clive and I work. No one will notice you."

Jimmy felt the pressure of her palms on his knees, felt the handprint she'd seared into his back over Mum's. "I'm staying with you, Doc."

She pushed harder. "No. Finish your initiation. Walk on your Land."

She'd thought this trip would be enough? She didn't understand. He couldn't tell her. He went to stand up as the plane stopped and she put her hand on his pants, right above his penis. He looked down to see her hand resting there.

"So maybe it's not exactly as you planned." She pressed. "Andy can circumcise you in the hospital. Make the most of this day."

He put his palm over hers. "There's still the Kardachi man." She looked as if she were begging at his feet and he took her under her armpits and lifted her. "I'll ask them if I can come back here. Either with Hector or after Andy takes care of it," Jimmy said. He put his palm on the small of her back and pushed her toward the open hatch.

Clive carried a large white crate, which had a red cross painted on it, down the steps of the airplane, and Donna followed. The cross reminded Jimmy of Yaraandoo, except shorter and fatter.

Donna smoothed back her hair without a smile and motioned Jimmy to follow. Jimmy stood at the top of the stairs with her medical bag, watching a stationhand run over to take the box from Clive. What would it feel like to be inside the fence? When he touched his foot to the ground, would the pull of the earth feel stronger?

One, two, three, fourth step on land. Yes, the ground felt solid. Strong. Healthy. He followed the stationhand with the box and the doctors past three white barns, past tractors and earth movers lined up in a neat row, past a paddock with some cattle, small horns pointing to the sky, past two unsaddled horses tied to a post and then up the steps of a white house. A man hurried toward them, taking off his hat. "Gavin Childs, Stationmaster."

The bubblegum girl had called Gavin Childs to ask if Jimmy and Hector could get permission to go onto the station. Now here Jimmy was with two doctors, and the man was falling all over them. Mr. Childs gushed, "Thank you so much for coming."

Maybe Jimmy would get permission to come back with Hector and the bone after all. Maybe Hector would wake if Jimmy told him they had been given permission. A real initiation ceremony would be a lot easier than working in the mine and having Andy cut him, wouldn't it? Better to come back with a Galah man and spill his blood on the land, than go underground with the whites.

Donna gave a fake smile. "Who are we here to see?" They followed the stationmaster through the tin front door and into a hallway. The wallpaper was full of faded lemons, not exactly what Jimmy expected from the stationmaster's office.

"Pretty," said Donna.

Mr. Childs took off his hat. "Was the family house, originally. Never in the corporate budget to redecorate." Mr. Childs led them into a sitting room. Jimmy looked up at the tin ceiling pressed into hearts and flowers. That was the difference between whites and Yapa. Whites took so much time decorating the places they lived, as if they'd last forever, when Yapa knew it was only the Land that was eternal. Mr. Childs opened a door at the far end. "Come into me office."

Donna stopped at the doorway and whispered to Jimmy, "Let me ask. Trust me."

The box they'd delivered sat in front of a big tin desk, which held a computer and lots of papers. Behind the desk was a chair with a sagging seat. It took Jimmy a moment to notice another man, who was hiding under his stockman's hat and sitting on a folding chair in the corner. The room was dark with just a desk lamp, but Jimmy knew if they opened the shutters to let in the sun, dust would overtake the whole room.

"Hello," Donna said.

The man jumped. Jimmy could see his face contorted in a grimace as he removed his hat. He pointed at his foot. "Hey, docs. The pain."

Clive asked for the dunny while Donna crouched down to examine the drover. While she bent his leg back and forth and the patient clenched his teeth from pain, she spoke to the stationmaster. "I didn't introduce you to my friend, Jimmy Jackboy."

Jimmy nodded to the man and wondered if Donna weren't being rougher with the patient than need be. "Jimmy and his uncle promised to take me to see some sacred sites, and they happen to be on the Barrington Downs Station."

Mr. Childs nodded vigorously, but still he didn't look Jimmy in the eye.

She wiped her hands with one of the anti-germ cloths she carried in her purse. "Mr. Childs, do you think we could drive out here one day for a tour?" She stood up.

"No worries, no worries. If you fix Stuart he can show you around. Anytime you want."

Donna looked at Jimmy and he shook his head, hoping she understood what he needed. It wouldn't do any good to come out escorted by a white man.

"I think we'd like to do it without a guide." She tossed her germ-cloth into the dustbin.

Mr. Childs cocked his head so that Jimmy couldn't see his eyes under his hat. "Can't do that."

Donna turned back to the patient. "It's likely gout. Impossible to diagnose for certain without obtaining fluid. Since I'm taking the fluid, I'll pop it with some cortisone."

Would she ask again? His cockatoo doctor wouldn't roll over, would she? She motioned for her medical bag and Jimmy brought it to her. She spoke to Jimmy as she arrayed three needles and four syringes on a white wash cloth. "Remember we aspirated Mrs. Gordon's shoulder? Have to do the same to the ankle." She turned to the patient. "Want me to numb it first?"

He nodded and as she turned back to the bag to fish out another needle, Donna raised her eyebrows at Jimmy. He was proud he hadn't let her numb his leg when she'd stitched him up. He was more of a man than this whitefella.

On her knees, she bent over the man's leg and wiped it with an alcohol pad. The man winced when she injected the lidocaine. Jimmy had seen lots of lidocaine used in the hospital. He'd seen hundreds of half-used jars flung into the dustbin.

He watched the angle of the aspirating needle, saw how gently she replaced the first syringe with the next two. Donna could change syringes without the patient flinching, but Andy and most of the other residents couldn't. Jimmy thought it had to do with how lightly she clasped the full vial in her delicate fingers.

She handed Jimmy the first syringe. "Synovial fluid. Can you put this in the left inside pouch?"

Jimmy examined the cloudy liquid as he placed the vial in the medical bag. It held all the answers to the man's pain. Maybe the pathologist at hospital would let him look at it under the microscope. He remembered the beautiful crystals he'd seen in Mrs. Gordon's fluid, crystals that were causing her such pain.

She turned to Clive, who entered as Donna gathered up her used materials. "Need to get him on a steroid treatment." She wiped her hands again on another germ cloth. "Do we have any in your magic box?"

"Before you go through it, let me get me secretary." Mr. Childs hurried out of the room and a moment later he came back in followed by a middle-aged white woman. "Need more than one person to listen to this."

Jimmy was starting to worry that Donna would not ask again

for Jimmy to come to his Land without a guide. *Can't do that* still rang in his ears. But Jimmy forgot about his Land when Clive opened the box. Inside there were all sorts of vials, syringes, and medicines, everything with a big black number on it. The same number was on the side of the box. Jimmy stuck his nose right in the box, looking at the straight lines of meds, liquids that threw prisms in the lamp light. A treasure. Clive held up a vial. "Want you to see this. Number twelve, anti-venom. Probably the med you'd need to get to the fastest." He handed it to Jimmy while his fingers danced over other medicines. "Twenty-two. Epinephrine." Clive motioned to the stationmaster. "Come see how it's organized. We've changed some things."

Jimmy turned the vial back and forth in his hand to see the yellow liquid slosh against the sides. Liquid that could save a man's life. Donna stood beside the crouching men. "Mr. Childs, I would like to have your permission to come on my tour without a guide."

Jimmy sucked in his breath and Mr. Childs looked up, his fat cheeks jiggling as he shook his head. He waved her away like a distracting fly. "Owned by a big corporation now. Can't have that. Deep pockets attract lawsuits. Can't take on the liability." He shook his finger at the box. "Where is the morphine?"

Clive held it up with a smile and Donna continued. "Why don't you get me a waiver? I'll sign it."

Mr. Childs wouldn't look Donna in the eye. He was silent as he eyed the anti-venom in Jimmy's hand. "A doc, fine. But child can't sign. Needs a guardian."

Jimmy felt the anti-venom getting heavy. Would serve the stationmaster right if he dropped it. But how could he ruin the symmetry of that box? Donna walked over to Mr. Childs and put her hand on his elbow. "I am his legal guardian. It is important to me."

"Bugger." Mr. Childs looked at Clive.

Clive nodded. "Important to all of us docs."

They stood in silence for what to Jimmy seemed like minutes. Finally, Mr. Childs growled at his secretary. "Martha, get something together for them to sign. Give them the combination and the directions to the gate."

Jimmy breathed deep, felt blood rush to his penis as he looked at Donna. She stood tall, her dark hair shimmering, her eyes shining strong. Jimmy slid the anti-venom into slot twelve in the box and went to stand by her side.

Walking back to the plane, Jimmy turned to Donna with a smile. "You lied about the tour, though I guess they deserved it. You will not be with me if I go to my Land."

Mum had taught him the difference between secrets, lying, joking, and kidding when he was a young boy. Donna took his hand like Mum used to. "Why can't I be there?"

They stopped at the plane's stairs as Clive adjusted them, Jimmy slowly extricating his palm from hers. "It's for men only. You know that."

When they got back in their seats, she looked out the window and her voice was higher than usual. "Let me know if you want to talk about it."

\∩/

After stops at two more stations, they flew back toward the Isa. It was different to see the land from a small plane than from the jet when Donna had first arrived. She could see roos bounding away from the noisy plane, flocks of budgies, clumps of spinifex like the dots on her Honey Ant Dreaming. How could she ever have thought this was a barren land? It teemed with life.

She gave Clive a big hug as she got out of the plane and dug for her keys in her purse. The sun was glinting orange off the body of the airplane.

"Hey, Doc." A pilot came jogging over from another aircraft that had landed soon before they had. "Going by hospital?"

She nodded.

He fished around in his medical bag. "Can you deliver something to Doctor Andy? Gotta fly back to Townsville before dark."

"You better hurry." The sun was already close to the horizon. She put out her hand. "No worries."

He handed her a thick manila envelope. "Stephanie wants him to pick out his wedding tux. Sent all the pics. Made me promise to get on his case."

She looked at Clive, who watched the exchange with a frown from his cockpit. "Let's get home, Jimmy."

The Land Rover stalled out as she put it in gear. She hadn't done that since she'd first arrived. She took a deep breath. Clive had backed out of the cockpit and down the small stairs and caught her as she turned the car. "You know he cares for you."

She forced a smile. "I knew he was borrowed. Hospital's no

place for secrets," and she shifted gear and pulled away. She willed the tears not to flow. Time was passing and real life calling. She turned to Jimmy, the way her mother had turned to her when she'd picked Donna up from school. "Was it a good trip?"

Jimmy put his hand on her knee, the way Andy usually did. "Good onya, Doctor Donna. You've done everything for me."

Everything but wake Hector. She watched the wattle fly by the window. She thought she'd helped Jimmy by getting him to his Land, but it wasn't enough. Now he had permission to return, but even that wouldn't do any good if she couldn't wake Hector. He'd mentioned a Kardachi man. Gabo was one thing, but could Yapa magic reactivate a brain?

As she turned into town, the envelope seemed to glare at her. It all came down to medicine. She could cure neither coma nor infertility. What if she'd become pregnant with Andy's child? What would he have told the girl in Townsville? She hadn't figured out how Andy would work into that equation. Anyway, Jimmy and Andy would be leaving soon. Jimmy uninitiated, and her not pregnant. Why had she become so invested in all of this Yapa talk?

The sun had set by the time they pulled into the driveway. She turned to Jimmy. "Go ahead in. I have to finish the laundry." She needed a moment to collect herself before facing Andy. She stuck his fiancée's envelope in her purse and went around the back to the laundry shed. The wire clotheslines glowed from the kitchen light, not the early moon. Donna eyed the lines and longed for a machine dryer, but they didn't sell them at Kmart. She tried to remember how it felt to pull on jeans that weren't stiffly baked, needing a day to work in. Socks dried on a line kept their creases, and if the creases were where the shoe hit above the heel, she'd get blisters. No wonder Andy usually went freeball. Who wanted to put on stiff Jockeys?

The back door slammed. She knew without turning it was Andy. The kitchen light cast his shadow against the laundry poles.

She felt the splintery grains of the clothespin in her mouth, then hurriedly spat it out to hang a pair of underwear.

She kept her back to him, even as she heard his footsteps on the dirt that had never fully turned back into grass, so close to the sticky sap of the mango tree. Donna bent down to the laundry basket, chose Jimmy's shirt and slapped two clothes pins on it to secure it to the line. She reached up to put a clothespin on her sock and felt Andy.

"Would you like some help?" He didn't touch her.

"I can do laundry."

"Yeah?" He reached out and felt one of her running socks. "You have creases in your clothes."

She looked at the haphazard assortment of sheets and clothes. "I'm from New York, where we have machine dryers." She reached down for her panties.

Andy put his hand on hers as she went to pin the panties to the wire. He pulled them from her hand, threw them into the nearly empty basket, and methodically pulled down everything else, putting each piece into the basket. She stood back, digging the toe of her shoe into the dirt.

"Now watch," he said. He hung shirts from their shoulders, socks from their big toe. He hung pants from the legs, pulling the pockets out. Donna watched Andy carefully choose a piece of clothing, examine it briefly to see how it should be hung, and then secure it to the line with a flick of the wrist.

Andy had saved her panties for last. She saw them in the basket, abandoned. A piece of her amidst everything borrowed. Andy lifted them into the air, pulled them tight, then speared their elastic with clothespins. As they dangled, he fingered the inside of her underwear, rubbing the cotton crotch, and, like voodoo, she could feel his fingers doing the same to her body.

The moon rose yellow and round, hogging the sky, blotting out any chance of a glimpse of the Southern Cross. Andy stood there rubbing her panties and tingles ran up her spine. He stopped rubbing and stuck his nose right into them, taking a loud breath of air. He looked at the moon. "Clive called after you landed."

"The envelope's in my purse." She was surprised to hear her voice so steady. She watched his back, his fingers stroking her panties again.

He stopped and turned. "We didn't talk about it, but you knew."

She twirled a strand of loose hair. "Maybe."

"I couldn't get married without knowing what an older woman would be like. I'm me pop's son."

Older woman? She looked at the laundry hanging neatly behind him and snorted. "That's why you were with me? That's it?"

He walked toward her, his shadow from the moonlight reaching her before he did. "Me mum's a looker for her age. But now I know why Da left Ma for a black woman twice as old."

Donna's feet pushed hard against the ground; she felt strong and planted in her backyard. "Your mum's probably forty-one."

Andy looked Donna up and down. "Seven years on you."

She kicked dirt at him. "I know what it's like to be cheated on. I never wanted to be the other woman."

He caught her leg in mid-kick. "Of course you did. Now you're on the other side. Tell me you didn't want to know."

She wrenched her foot away and stalked toward her back stairs, but he grabbed her shoulders. He pulled her toward him and pried her lips open with his, holding her tight to his body until she gave in and kissed back.

He whispered, "Living in Isa is like being marooned on a desert island. The rules are different here. I love you."

She couldn't stop the tears, didn't care about pride. "Rodeo's come so soon. Both of you will go."

He took her by the shoulders and led her up the stairs to the house. "Now we're in Isa. You, me, and Jimmy on this Land here."

As they opened the kitchen door, she caught sight of Jimmy's back, darting into the living room, then heard the front door close slowly. She wondered what Jimmy thought was right in Isa, but she'd never ask.

She turned to Andy. "Show me what she looks like."

Part Three

THE CUP SPILLS OVER

The Galah brings berries for her chicks. As the day turns into night and the starseeds shine down upon them, the chicks open their beaks wide to capture the earth's essence that the Galah disgorges from her belly. They are all strong males, with the energy of the sun. They fight for the food, flexing their wings, ready to fly away.

Now she can be their egg, nourishing them, giving them food and water. But soon the earth will be their mother, providing them with kangaroo berries, mulla mulla seeds, crystal drops of dew in the mornings, water holes in the evenings. Little more than a half moon left to be mother, and then it will be time to fly the boy to his Land, to introduce him to Earth Mother.

In the meantime, she feeds her chicks seeds of wild grasses as the night grows dark. She feeds them, for they themselves are the seeds that will be spread by the wind, to seed the world anew.

\∩/

The town of Mount Isa had only Rodeo on its mind. Newly creased Wrangler jeans and pressed plaid shirts under wide-brimmed cowboy hats replaced day-glo jumpsuits. Cowboys, Aboriginals, and whites began pouring in from the stations like the New York subway at rush hour. From her office at the hospital, Donna could hear the constant screeching of bus brakes as the scheduled arrivals in Isa tripled.

Donna heard from Jimmy that the billabong was chock-a-block with Aboriginal people who had come from neighboring towns, many of which were two days away by car. People were camped with their swags everywhere along the outskirts of town, all the way to the Rodeo grounds near the airport.

On Mardi Gras morning—Mardi Gras was the parade that marked the beginning of Rodeo—Esther called Donna down from the ward to the ER, "Need a woman doc."

When Donna arrived, she saw Esther cleaning blood off the face of a patient. Lips and noses bled profusely, so long blonde hair caked with blood did not necessarily make it a serious injury. As she approached, Donna noticed the woman's shoes. Spiked heels, so unusual in the Outback. Donna was used to bare feet and boots.

"What's up?" she asked.

Esther shook her head. "Some bloke beat her up good. Tough line of work."

"What do you do?" Donna asked, then bit her lip. Of course. The prostitutes had come in for Rodeo to service a bunch of men off the stations who hadn't seen anything but cattle and roos for months. "Strike that. Could you identify the guy?"

"Skipped out. Didn't pay. Please don't call police."

Donna pulled the curtain and gave the woman a complete exam. The guy had taken care of his own business, of course, before beating her, but the girl was stoic. *All in a day's work.* Esther admitted the girl to the medical ward while Donna went to the canteen for coffee.

She looked up as Esther came in a few minutes later. Donna gestured to the open chair. "Hate treating the whores. Can't imagine how they feel."

Esther sat down without getting herself anything. "I feel like a whore with Jocko."

"Is that good?"

Esther smiled and her brown skin glowed. "Yep. Magic whore. Sacred whore. Feels bloody fine."

"Come to think of it, I'm a whore with Andy. Can you imagine what would have happened with his fiancée if I got pregnant?" She and Andy had been having sex constantly since the night she came home with the envelope. As Rodeo loomed, they clung to each other tighter and the sex was more desperate, as if they were trying so hard to stay marooned on their island.

Esther ticked off on her fingers, "Whore with Jocko, a mother with me patients, a wife to me docs, making sure you all are taken care. Hmmm, now when am I a hag?"

"Hag? Meaning total bitch?" Donna opened the Arnott's that she'd bought to go with her coffee and handed one to Esther, who was holding her three fingers aloft and staring into space. Donna popped a cookie into her mouth. "You were a hag when you made me empty my ashes."

Esther stared at the ceiling, nibbling on the cookie. Finally she looked at Donna. "You're right, Doctor. I am a hag when I teach you the old ways. When I share my wisdom, my healing, I am the old woman."

Donna chewed. "I'm going to be alone soon. And I didn't get preggers like you said. What does your Yapa wisdom say about that?"

"To be a full woman, got to be all four. Mother, wife, whore, and old woman."

Donna grabbed Esther's hand, jerking her by the fingers. "Did you hear me? I didn't get pregnant. So I'm not a mother. I'm not a wife. I'm only a whore and a bitch." Donna held up her own two fingers.

"Patience." Esther pried her fingers loose. "You are a hag when you are a healer. You've already been a wife." She looked at her watch and stood up to leave. "One more hour, then I'm on to Jocko."

Jocko had come in from Doomadgee and Esther managed to get most of the three days of Rodeo off from work, clearly using her position as a senior sister to take full advantage of the party. Donna had heard much grumbling from the young sisters, especially Nan, who had to work Mardi Gras.

"Esther."

The large woman turned at the door. "Donna, have faith."

"In what? In your Dreams?" She spilled her coffee as she knocked the table with her knee.

"Yes." Esther pulled out her bun and let her curly hair fall wildly around her shoulders. "Yes."

Donna prepared an elaborate schedule for who would be the doc on duty at the Rodeo grounds and who would man the ER for the weekend. At Andy's insistence and following Esther's example, Donna made sure Andy and she were both free the for the Mardi Gras parade.

That evening, Andy and Jimmy stood on either side of Donna in their prime spot at the corner of West and Miles, which Andy had secured with a sign that read *Reserved for Medics* early that morning. Donna had thought he was crazy—he and Jimmy had been sitting there off and on, guarding their area all day—but now they had a perfect view of the marching bands and floats.

A baton twirled high and Donna looked into the black sky to follow it as they waited for the first float to approach. Moths were dancing in the street lamps. Strings of colored lights had been looped from telephone pole to telephone pole. She half-closed her eyes and the lights became a blur. She couldn't resist letting her hand come down on Jimmy's head for a moment. His hair felt silky like yellow wattle petals now that he was using Donna's shampoo. She would miss his head in fourteen days.

She drank her beer, leaning into Andy, trying not to feel as if the parade was the beginning of the end. She kept drinking so as not to think. The first floats were homemade by students at Mount Isa High School, pulled by beat-up cars and trucks. But the business floats became increasingly intricate. Not quite Macy's Thanksgiving Day parade-elaborate, but they were well-planned designs of chickenwire covered in crepe paper. A float of drag queens, *Priscilla Queen of the Desert*, drove by. The drag queens were followed by the Rodeo Queen contestants, waving from shiny convertibles, legs propped up provocatively on the front seats. A number of the contestants were overweight, a refreshing departure from American beauty queen contests. Donna cheered hard.

She and Andy passed a Fourex back and forth, and soon he reached into the ice-filled plastic bag beside him for a new one. "Two more left. Can't let them go to waste." He handed Jimmy a Coke.

The beer tasted of autumn football games, afternoon après ski at the Mangy Moose in Jackson Hole. Tasted of trekking in Nepal, when beer was all she would drink for days, so afraid was she of falling ill from poorly boiled water. Beer was a drink that could quench thirst. Tonight, she was thirsty.

Country music from the bars competed with music from the floats. People cheered and laughed. She could hear Andy's voice above the crowd, Jimmy's voice beside her. For a moment she thought she heard Peter's voice in the crowd, a voice she'd heard only that once in Boulia. But then no more.

A New Orleans-style float was in front of her. Bare-breasted women and practically naked men were whipping up the crowd. Girls on either side of her were lifting their shirts for beads. Some wore bras, and some, like Donna, didn't. Andy elbowed her. "Come on, babe. Get us some beads. Your tits are beautiful. Get us some beads."

Without thinking, she held her shirt up above her breasts, smiling wide at the float. The wind felt good, and she thought of the waterhole where she'd swum with Andy, remembered the feel of the water droplets on her nipples. The beads showered around them and she pulled down her shirt, but not before she saw Jimmy smiling straight at her. She felt her cheeks blush, but Andy was pulling her in, kissing her hard on the lips as the beads rained upon them, and Jimmy was yelling *More, more.* Andy stopped kissing her and she said, "I'm too drunk."

Andy shook his head. "Never drunk enough for Mardi Gras."

When the last float passed, the Mayor began his speech. After recounting past Rodeo heroes, he complimented himself for increasing garbage pickup to twice weekly. Andy leaned over and his lips brushed Donna's ear as he spoke, "He's an arse. Let's go have a dance." She squeezed Jimmy's shoulder as a signal to follow and took Andy's hand. They kicked away piles of confetti and plastic cups as they walked, drunkenly knocking into each other. Streamers hanging from telephone lines brushed their shoulders. Many from the crowd were walking the same direction, and she let herself be carried by it. The crowd determined the speed of her gait, and she, Andy, and Jimmy swayed with it, what a bird must feel when it flies with its flock.

They found themselves by the Isa Hotel, where the pokies were clanking away ferociously, not taking their usual breaths. The hotel was an old-fashioned homestead building, much like the office on Barrington Downs Station, with big wooden shutters that were almost always kept locked to keep out the dust and sun, and had no glass on the windows. But that night, the clapboard shutters had been thrown open. Fluorescent lights threw eerie shadows on the cowboys, beers in hand, who spilled out onto the porch and the street so you couldn't tell where the bar began and the sidewalk ended.

Andy motioned her and Jimmy to break away from the crowd and follow. She had a moment of misgiving—where might she end up if she'd just followed the current? As they helped each other up the steps, Donna could see a country music band set up in a far corner of the bar.

Kids ran around throwing sawdust up off the floor, which cast a brown haze over the crowd. Andy bought a pint of dark ale and offered her a sip. She shook her head. He took a long swallow, draining half the glass, then handed it to Jimmy. "Hold this for me, mate. Don't take even a whiff."

Jimmy reached out his hand obediently as Andy took Donna's hand and spun her around to the music. In a wild swing, she thought she saw Peter getting a pint, Peter, her first dance partner in Australia, Peter, who had the answer to the question of Jessie. She extricated herself from Andy's sweaty palms and tried to find him. Andy said, "You okay, Donna?"

"Fresh air." She ran down the steps and vomited in the alley by the side of the hotel. Jimmy and Andy followed her.

"I'm fine." She waved them away. Jimmy put Andy's pint down near her feet and ran back in. He came out with a wet paper towel. He handed it to Donna and pointed inside. "This place has the best fish 'n chips. Spent a night in this alley with Hector once."

Andy held her long hair back away from her face. "Don't talk of food when someone is upchucking."

Donna stood, feeling better. She wiped her mouth and followed Jimmy's gaze inside. He smiled. "I love watching white people dancing."

Andy put his arms around Donna. "Need to go home?"

She shook her head and fished in her pocket for some gum. Oh God. Jimmy and who knows who else had witnessed Donna, the Mount Isa Base Hospital Medical Chief, waving her tits around, then vomiting all over. Wasn't regret supposed to hold off until you were sober?

Jimmy elbowed Andy in the ribs and pointed to the white dancers. "Are they dancing a camel? Have you ever danced a feral camel? Ugly animal." He chuckled. "Me favorite dance is the Galah. Then the emu."

Donna had a faint recollection of being in a childhood dance class, pretending she was a cat, then a dog, then an airplane, walking and running to the beat of the teacher's drum. Andy walked her gently back up the stairs to finish their dance. They danced slowly, slower than the beat of the music, between stumbling cowboys, a few other couples draped over each other in an attempt to waltz without passing out, and poles holding up the old ceiling. There was no way Peter was there. It must have been a flashback to Boulia. When the song stopped, Andy led her to where Jimmy stood frowning by the wall, again holding beer, now stretched at arm's length. Andy downed his beer in one swallow and led both of them back outside.

Andy pulled them around the masses of people, stopping to buy Jimmy a bright blue cone of fairy floss. Jimmy asked them to stop at another stand, and his face glowed under the twinkling white lights that lined the booth. "Lollie gobble bliss bombs, me favorite. Can I buy you some, Doctor Donna?"

Her stomach felt better. Needed some food. She liked this young man giving her sweets. He'd seen her breasts; she deserved to be bought treats. "With a name like that, who wouldn't want some?" Donna looked over into the white bags of caramel corn lined up in a row. The three of them gorged in silence, licking fingers sticky from caramel.

Then Andy pointed towards the Ferris wheel sparkling in the gravel lot behind the ANZ Bank. "Tickets are on me." He ambled over to the ticket booth and Donna and Jimmy got in line for the Ferris wheel, the ride that had been missing from the Boulia fete.

Her mother had told the story so often. She'd met Donna's father as they watched the lights spin in front of them. He'd asked her to see the world with him, to share his seat. Patricia Massima had stepped onto the Ferris wheel and Patricia Meyer stepped off. Donna had ridden Ferris wheels with Greg in Gorky Park, Vietnam, London, Santa Monica, and Coney Island.

A bright yellow door opened up to a splintered seat. Gingerly Donna slid in, then Jimmy, then Andy. The carnie slammed the door behind them, bolted it shut, and then slowly the car climbed its way to the top, stopping when the carnie loaded new riders. Donna saw Isa sprawled out before them, an abrupt line in the darkness where the twinkling lights stopped and the desert began, the line she'd seen with Esther when the bull ant had bitten her.

As they hovered above the carnival, it seemed like they were in both bush and town at the same time, existing on both sides of that line in the desert. Donna understood what it must be like to stand on the Brooklyn Bridge ready to jump, to be alive and dead at the same time, just because you saw the possibility that you might leap.

She looked over at Jimmy, who peered seriously out into the darkness, awaiting the moment they would plummet towards earth. Alive and dead at the same moment. Massima and Meyer. What the Aboriginals could see so clearly at all times, what she could not. They were always on top of the Ferris wheel, could see the border between Dream and reality, could choose when to cross from one to the other.

She thought of quantum physics lectures at Princeton, remembered how she'd tried to get her arms around the concept but could never really see it: the cat in the box was alive and dead at the same time because there was always the possibility he was dead. Now she was in two worlds. One where Andy and Jimmy were beside her, and one where they were already gone. Was she in a world where she was not-pregnant and pregnant?

The Ferris wheel lights twinkled, the stars twinkled. Tears fell freely from her eyes. Jimmy pointed to the sky and lay his hand on her knee. "The Cross."

Reflexively, she grabbed the bar in front of her, and Andy put his arm around Jimmy's shoulders and squeezed hers. She was conscious not of the Ferris wheel spinning, but of the hand of one boy on her knee, the hand of the other on her shoulder.

Ten minutes later they stumbled off, all three arm-in-arm. Andy flashed some orange tickets at Jimmy. "Got a surprise for you. Three tickets to the next show."

Donna recognized them. The twinkling lights dimmed in her narrowing eyes. "Brophy's? I'm too drunk." She didn't want to see the sweat, smell the sawdust and the blood. Yet the temptation was great, to see if she could be there without panic, to see if she could fly again.

Andy pulled her close. "You'll be fine. This time it's with me. Jimmy should see it."

She turned to Jimmy. "You know the Yapa will not win. It is not a place that is good to your people."

Jimmy pulled a ticket from Andy's hand. "Let's go."

Whether it was that Isa had become home, or that Andy's and Jimmy's shoulders were protecting her from the crush of the crowd—as though they understood how she'd felt that first time under the tent, raw from Peter's kiss and prediction of a baby—the show this time was just a show. Like seeing a movie for the second time, she could enjoy the action, anticipate the outcome.

Blood, blood, the crowd demanded, and they weren't disappointed. Donna watched the blood pool onto the sawdust that had been strewn directly onto the dirt of the field where the carnival had been set up. She didn't watch the punches thrown, but watched instead the blood seep into the ground. Blood that would mingle with the blood of the whore, washed away through the hospital drains, and mingle with the ashes that had once been the blood of her baby now cast to the wind of the hillside. The baby, the fighters, the whore, their blood, their beings, all were part of this land forever. She let the crowd carry her out, Jimmy's and Andy's shoulders pushing her forward when it was over.

She and Andy made love that night, he in his drunken need, and she—for the first time with Andy—out of habit. She'd been here before, remembered a morning in Southampton at the end of a relationship, knowing as they were having sex that it would be the last. If there were no future, no possibility for a lover to become a life partner, if a relationship's only asset was passion, then predictable sex was a relationship's death knell. She closed her eyes to fight off that knowledge. There was a moment when she imagined Jimmy was in the room with them, watching. She got up after they'd finished to shower. She needed to wash the night from her skin. Her vomit, the sawdust, Queensland.

She woke up close to morning and padded out to the cold linoleum of the kitchen, peering into the starlight with her nose pressed the screen door. Jimmy was under Mister Mango, as he called it. Not for much longer would he call her home *home*.

Jimmy lay under the tree, rubbing his scar. It had been burning the whole time he was at Brophy's with Doctor Donna and Andy. Mum had wanted to come to him, but how could she, in that tent? He'd loved every second of Brophy's. Maybe he'd be a showman someday. Showman, doctor, mining engineer. So many possibilities. *We're all one Australia*. Yapa could do anything now. Hector had always said, *Just get initiated. Then everything else will be yours to choose*. Before he'd come to Isa, he hadn't known the extent of all the choices.

He saw a flicker of feathers above him and the Galah stirred. And there was Mum sitting on her branch, arms crossed. "Brophy doesn't treat the blackfellas right. Makes a spectacle of them, you know."

Jimmy rolled his eyes, the way he'd seen Donna do sometimes when she joked with Esther. The Galah moved further down the branch. "You'll leave, day after your Science Fete."

"Mum," Jimmy tried to interrupt.

She waved with her wing to him. "Look for the Kardachi man tomorrow by the lemonade. Doctor Donna's going to be upset she can't help wake Hector. You must tell her many times how she has cured him."

Donna hadn't cured Uncle. "That's a lie."

Mum's voice was stern. "Not a lie. She kept him alive until we could send someone. Anyway, we have Dreamt her up. We must take care of her."

When the kookaburra called the morning, Jimmy padded quietly into Donna's house. The shower was running.

The door to Donna's room was open so he peeked in. She was

on her side, looking at him. "I'll be up in a second, Jimmy Jack-boy." He came in anyway and sat at the foot of her bed. "Coming to calf-roping with me today, Doctor?"

She shook her head, dark hair spread over the pillow like a mess of snakes, hair that had been looped through Andy's fingers when they were shagging. Jimmy had come in to peek again, this time making sure Andy didn't catch him. She propped herself up on a pillow. "I have to be at the hospital today. I think Andy's going to be doc at the Rodeo. You could go over with him."

"I think I'll find Esther and Jocko." He looked at the thin straps of black silk that held her nightie over her shoulders. "You have pretty…" he almost said *titties* but caught himself. That was not the word a doctor would use. "Breasts. Much smaller than me aunties' and Mum's."

"Oh." She caught her breath funny. Had he embarrassed her? But he wanted to her to know. He'd seen a lot of breasts and hers were different than all the others.

"Thank you." She played with a string on the Queensland Health blanket, pulling the blanket up higher over her chest.

Too bad. He'd wanted to catch a glimpse of their outline again.

Rodeo was bigger than anything he'd ever seen. The camp-grounds were green, not with grass but with swags, row upon row. The cowboys were handsome in their spurs and chaps. Women in stalls sold trinkets they'd made on the stations.

He sat in the bleachers with Esther and Jocko, transfixed by the team calf-roping.

The horn sounded, the gate opened, and the two cowboys raced out on their horses. One cowboy roped the calf's tiny bud-ding horns and the other cowboy, the feet; then they tied it up together and dangled it in the air. He didn't think the calf was too happy, but it must be part of being a calf. Sometimes one of the cowboys would miss and they'd ride off with sad eyes, coiling their lassos.

The next event was mutton-busting. Kids strapped themselves atop huge ewes and tried to stay on for as long as possible. The announcer said it was the only legal form of child abuse, and while the crowd chuckled, Jimmy didn't get it. He'd heard that whites would strike their kids, and he didn't think that was funny. No Yapa he knew would do that, unless they had the grog on.

The announcer was going on about the Australian farming tradition and how Rodeo was a celebration that the kids were going to follow in their parents' footsteps and work the Land.

Esther snorted. "Celebrate the Land. How about Yapa footsteps?"

Jocko shushed her, but Jimmy leaned over into her warm musty smell. "Good onya, Esther. Did I tell you I was filing a native title claim? Started one for me at Aboriginal Affairs."

Esther looked at him, her nose disappearing into her cheeks. "What?"

"We're all one Australia."

They decided to get tea, so they walked around the grounds, looking at the food stalls, weighing their options. Jimmy kept an eye out for the Kardachi man, but Mum hadn't told him what to look for. He assumed the man had seen Jimmy in his Dreams and would find him, so Jimmy didn't look too hard.

He was standing by a fence drinking a lemonade when he saw Auntie Tess's footprint in the mud in front of the lemonade stall. "Auntie's in Isa," he announced. He should have been happy, but felt ill instead. He liked living here, doing medicine with Doctor Donna. Liked hanging out with Tom, trading footy cards. Liked the computers, the books, the markers, the maps in Mrs. Brunswick's school room. What would happen when they brought him back to Yuendumu? Would he be back to learning Yapa bugger? Would he ever become a doc? Or would he end up without a good education and become a drover? A stockman? Pumping gas at the servo like Da did? Push papers in an office like the bubblegum girl? That would be the worst. Away from the Land and from Yapa.

He walked to the back of the stand, hidden for a moment, looking out at the bush. Why hadn't he thought of this before? Did he want to go home? He didn't miss Mum so much. Initiated boys stayed away from their mums anyway. Maybe he could stay and live with Doctor Donna?

Esther came around to him. "She's brought the medicine man?"

"I saw her footprint." Jimmy leaned toward Esther, let her great body hold him up.

Esther waved Jocko over and said something in Pintupi that Jimmy didn't understand. Jocko put his hands on his hips. "Well if you're such a good tracker, let's see what you can do."

As Jimmy turned, he spilled his lemonade. He mourned the drops that sank into the dry earth. Jocko elbowed him. "Let's find Auntie."

Jimmy could not change what would be. The energies were already in motion. "She's probably over by the pokies." He led Esther and Jocko around to where the outdoor slots were jingling away. No Auntie Tess. Jimmy shrugged. "Maybe I better follow the footprints."

Jocko snorted. He was a big man and could snort out his long straight nose like a feral pig. "Brilliant. Thought you were doing that already."

Jimmy went back to the footprint by the lemonade stand but couldn't find another leading off in any direction. *Hmmm.* He stared around him at the crowds. Could he be mistaken? Maybe it wasn't Auntie Tess after all. He bent down and smelled the print, detecting yucca and the tin house in Yuendumu.

He looked up and Esther said, "Let's go have a lie under that tree. Then we'll go track Auntie."

Esther led him over to a gum behind the booths, whose sickly branches threw off smatterings of shade. They sat, their backs against the smooth bark. Jocko talked to some blackfellas in the shade of a neighboring tree. A tree was a good thing when you needed a little grounding. His mother was right. He could feel its strength holding him up and he let his spine press into its skin. And then there she was, standing in front of him, looking at him and Esther under the extra-wide brim of her hat.

He popped up like a goanna scared out of its hole by a wombat. Tess's hug was deep, hard, like it came from *all* his relations at once, like the Ancestors were crowding in around them.

It was good to have her there, good to feel Yuendumu. Yet, he'd been so used to his kin going on walkabouts—getting up one day, leaving without saying a thing and coming back weeks later—that he hadn't thought about her and Mum and his kin so much lately. Maybe he would stay in Isa. "Where's the Kardachi man?"

"You've grown." Tess stood back and looked him over. "Wise man needed to watch the buckaroos. That's why we didn't come until now. He said if he were coming to Isa, he wanted to see the events."

Jimmy knew that you didn't question or push a wise man. You let him make the decisions. Didn't want him to curse you while he was lifting the curse on Hector.

Esther stood up and Jimmy introduced the two women. Esther offered her hand. "So much better to meet you in person. Telephone doesn't do a voice justice."

Tess took Esther's hand and wrapped it around Tess's back. "Thank you for taking such good care of our Jimmy."

Esther smoothed her hair back from where it grew low down on her forehead. "It was Doctor Donna."

"It was all of you." The women embraced, and their feet seemed to grow roots in the ground, so they stood solid as the tree beside him, and their arms danced for joy in the breeze, giving off shade to anyone who needed it. Jimmy moved out of their shade. He'd taken care of himself. His auntie was forgetting he was no longer a boy. He moved next to Jocko and they stood shoulder-to-shoulder, their feet together making their own roots in the ground, waiting for the Kardachi man to come wake Hector.

The Kardachi man joined them when the day's events were over. "So Jimmy, I hear you've had a nice initiation so far."

Jimmy would never have recognized this man as a wise man. He wasn't much older than Jocko, with only a bit of gray in his beard, and he wore Wranglers and a striped shirt like the rest of the crowd. Tied to the Kardachi man's belt was a billy pot and some plastic bags. He had a small bedroll like the other cowboys, which he handed to Jimmy to carry.

The wise man took a drag on his cigarette. "Learning medicine, I hear?"

"Going to be a doc." Jimmy had expected to be more frightened of the wise man. But he had a jolly smile and winked every time he said something to Jimmy.

"Watch me carefully tonight. Learn some Yapa medicine too." Wink.

When the sun set, the Kardachi man announced it was time to leave. The five of them—the middle-aged and old woman, and Jimmy and Jocko each with an arm around the Kardachi man—made their way to the car park. As they passed the medical tent, Esther said to Jimmy, "Go in and tell Doctor Andy."

Doctor Andy was busy wrapping a bandage around a cowboy's wrist. Jimmy stood behind the patient and looked over his shoulder at Andy's work. Doctor smelled of grog. "Now I want you to head over to the hospital for some x-rays."

The cowboy didn't look to be too much older than Jimmy. "Aw, Doc."

Andy set the pins to hold the bandage. "Don't ride on that wrist again."

"But I've got the finals. Just need something for the pain."

Andy looked at Jimmy. "This young bloke isn't going to listen. Might as well be talking to the tent. But I'm not in the pain pill business."

Jimmy waved g'day. "Kardachi man's here. We're going to hospital to wake Hector."

"I gotta see this." Andy let go of the cowboy's wrist, stood up abruptly, and zipped his medical bag. "Rodeo's over for the day. Let them come to the hospital." He threw his stethoscope around his shoulders the way Jimmy hoped to someday, the way he'd practiced in the mirror. Jimmy led the way out to the little party they'd become, feeling the abandoned cowboy's eyes on his back.

Esther's car jerked back and forth as they drove from the Rodeo grounds to Esther's so Jocko could pick up his didgeridoo. Andy sat quietly in the front seat with Esther. Jimmy was pressed between Tess, Jocko, and the Kardachi man in the back seat and it felt like the car walls were closing in. It seemed long ago that he and ten of his cousins had piled into the back seat of the pickup in Yuendumu. Now he preferred catching the breezes from the front seats of Andy's and Donna's Land Rovers.

As Esther drove to the hospital, the Kardachi man reached over Jimmy's lap and pinched a strand of Esther's hair out of her messy bun. She jerked her head away. "Jocko, did he get one? You get it back or I'll never sleep again."

Jimmy felt Jocko's laughing belly pressing into his back. "His hands are empty, Esther."

The Kardachi man reached over to Jimmy, "Give me a few of these too," and he yanked out a bunch of Jimmy's hairs. "Hector needs them."

Jimmy's *Ouch* was stifled by the pressure of Auntie Tess's warm hand on his leg. The Wirrun had his hair, which meant he could do magic against him. Jimmy had better not make him angry. Now he understood why Esther was driving so poorly.

At the hospital, Jimmy clambered out of the car to follow Andy and Esther, but the Kardachi man took him by the shoulder. "We men'll be up in a few."

Andy stopped, but the Wirrun shook his huge head. "Yapa."

It seemed to Jimmy that the Kardachi man, who had seemed so regular at the Rodeo, was now a giant, eyes larger than ugli fruits, arms like ghost gum branches, legs as powerful as a red boomer. Jimmy ached to follow Andy up the familiar staircase, to sit at the end of Hector's bed. When Jimmy had first come to Isa, Jimmy had sat on that bed watching the doctors work, pleading with Hector to finish his Dreaming. But lately Jimmy had come to think of Hector more like a campfire, something to gather round for a good chat.

Reluctantly, Jimmy followed the Kardachi man and Jocko to the bushes on the side of the hospital. The giant man knelt on the ground, opening his plastic bags. Jimmy bent over to have a look. Red and white ochre, and Galah feathers.

Jimmy remembered the first night of his initiation, when the men had captured and spirited him away. How long ago that was, when all Jimmy wanted was to be initiated. He didn't desire it now in the same way. Now he had other goals—win a prize at the Science Fete, get into medical school, visit Donna in New York. But the rituals were familiar. The preparation of the ochre. Laying out the feathers. Drawing the circles in the dirt.

It seemed odd to be doing these things while hidden behind a shrub at hospital. Sacred time was always spent out bush. He was nervous someone would see him, maybe Nan, or a friend from school—how Tom would laugh—or even Doctor Donna. What would she think?

Jimmy peered through the branches, keeping his eye on the dark world beyond the shrub. He shifted so he could see who was entering and leaving the hospital. Wouldn't someone be curious if he heard noises coming from the shrubbery? The Kardachi man sang a song Jimmy recognized from the night his uncles seized him, and Jimmy wanted to say *Hush, don't call attention to us.* The song grew louder, yet no one glanced their way as they hurried through the hospital's automatic doors. Jimmy didn't want to listen, but the song drew him in. No matter how he resisted, he had to open his ears, his heart, his body to the words. As he became full of the song, the worry about the whitefellas emptied out of him.

The Wirrun sang as both Jocko and he each slit the skin on his own thigh to draw blood. Then Jocko helped guide the knife over Jimmy's thigh, and with a flick of his wrist, made the incision. Jimmy mirrored Jocko and the Wirrun, painting himself exactly the way the men did. In the familiar motions of the circles for waterholes, the inverted u's, the dots traced over his chest, Jimmy's fingers painted without a thought. Every so often, Jocko would reach over to help Jimmy, the way Uncles and Da had done when he was little.

Without a break in the song, the Kardachi man took out pink and gray feathers and stuck them to the blood and ochre. Jimmy felt his body pulsing with the ochre, with the blood, with the Galah. He was Galah, would always be, whether he were a doc or engineer. His body ached for the sky, not the underground of the mine.

On a sign from the Wirrun, Jimmy felt every muscle in his body move. What it took to stand. How the weight moved from his toes to his sole to his heel and through his calves up through his back. Heel-toe, heel-toe. He felt the power of his arms as he pushed himself up, the power of wings. The Kardachi man had begun a Galah dance. Jimmy chanted his body vibrations and Jocko played the didgeridoo. Together they flew over the Galah lines, traced the energies of the Galah Dreaming over the Land.

When the song was over, covered in blood, ochre, and feathers, concentrating on his feet, Jimmy led the men to the side stairs. Doctor Donna was in the hallway as he swung open the door to the second floor. She gasped.

"It's only me, Doctor Donna." He knew how frightening they must look. When he was a boy, he'd been terrified to see men painted in feathers, beings from another world.

She held the wall and nodded. "Jimmy. You look..."

"Grown up," finished the Kardachi man as he stepped forward.

"Peter." The pen in Donna's hand shook.

Jimmy remembered his manners. "This is a great medicine man who will wake up Hector." He gestured to the Kardachi man. "This is a great medicine woman who has helped Hector while he was Dreaming." He gestured to Donna, who gave a tiny smile with wide oval eyes.

The Kardachi man's teeth shone as the white lines painted on his face curved into a smile. "Thank you for your medicine, Doctor."

Doctor Donna was holding the wall, pushing her palm hard against it. "Peter. I had no idea."

She'd said *Peter* again. At first Jimmy had thought it was an American expression, like *bugger*, or something you said when you were surprised. But was she calling the Wirrun *Peter*? How could Donna know the Kardachi man? He was about to ask when Jocko stepped hard on his toe.

The Wirrun put his hand on Donna's shoulder. "Where is Hector?"

Donna turned to lead them to the room, and Jimmy noticed she walked more slowly than usual; she was usually in such a hurry. But tonight she walked heel-toe, heel-toe. When they got to Hector's door, she stopped. Her voice shook as she turned to the Wirrun, "Why were you expecting me? Who is Jessie?"

The Kardachi man brushed her cheek with the back of his hand and whispered something in her ear. As she listened, she closed her eyes tight. When the Wirrun stood back, white ochre dust clung to her black hair. Jimmy stepped forward to brush it out, but she stepped aside and swung the door open for them. Esther, Tess, and Andy were already inside.

"Oh, a party." Donna said and Jimmy saw her cheeks go pink under her green skin, her hand shaking on the knob as they filed into the room and she closed the door behind them.

Jimmy's old auntie stood up. "I am Tess."

Jimmy knew Donna and Tess had spoken many times over the phone. But he felt badly for not warning Donna that Tess would be coming in person. Donna smiled and put out her hand.

Tess grasped it with both hands. "I feel as if I have known you a very long time. Can we spend time tomorrow? Tonight we must wake Hector."

Donna looked over at Jimmy not at Tess. "Wake him? You think so?"

The Wirrun spoke and his voice vibrated so that even the instruments on the bedside tray shook. "Doctor Donna, Andy, you must leave. We cannot share this medicine with Kardiya."

Jimmy stood with his back to the door and didn't move. Could he defy the wise man? He tried to make his voice boom, imagined the air blowing through his windpipe like a didg. "Why can't they help?"

"It is for Yapa." The words hung in the air.

Jimmy shook. "But they've shared their medicine with me."

Andy pushed him aside. "We'll go. It's okay. Good luck."

Donna let Andy lead her out of the room. Jimmy had wanted Donna to see the blackfella magic—it was only fair. Donna's cockatoo hair glimmered in the light of the hallway and then the door swung shut.

They stood there in the dim light of the hospital room— it could never be entirely dark because of all the lights on the instruments. Little orange, yellow, blue, and green lights glowed, casting off a rainbow of colors, the lights on the instruments like the Jewel Box of Yaraandoo. The flimsy blinds couldn't hold out the twinkling lights of the town, either. He was afraid to look over at the Wirrun after questioning him, but the giant man came over and rested his palm on Jimmy's shoulder. "You are a loyal friend, Jimmy Jackboy."

Esther and Tess pulled chairs to the bedside. Esther rolled back the white sheet and took hold of Hector's gigantic foot. Jimmy watched her trace the lines of his feet, saw in those feet the path they'd taken to the Isa, and Tess did the same for the other foot. The Kardachi man nodded to Jocko, motioning Jimmy to his side, by Hector's head. Without a word between them, the Wirrun sang and Jocko played his didg, humming like the bees, rushing like the water of monsoon, the wind, the air. The tip of the didg almost touched Hector's skin. He watched Jocko pour the vibrations onto Hector from his head down to his toes, stopping for deep pulses at times over his temples, his elbow, his hips, and his knees, then moving back up to his heart. Jocko blew until Jimmy thought he saw Hector's chest vibrating along with the didg.

Jimmy felt the music rise through his own feet over his bum into his penis, giving him a stiffie, then into his chest. At some point he realized he was understanding the words of the song. Jimmy closed his eyes and listened closely to the voice of the instrument, and was able to understand its language, too. The Kardachi man sang the Galah sites. As the voice described them, air currents carried Jimmy and he was again soaring over the Land. He knew the way, from the songs, from his flight in the airplane with Donna, from his Dreams.

But this time he felt there was someone else on his wingtip. It was the Galah who accompanied him, and then a second Galah on his other wing. Was that Hector? Yes. Then another in front. Da! *Oh, Da!* Jimmy was with his flock as they flew, undulating with the winds over the spinifex. Their flight was a melody playing over the harmony of the Land. Together, they came to Hector's Dreaming site, saw Jimmy's da's seedpile, and then they turned, as one, flying in circles, circles, circles, to Behold the Land. Jimmy knew every tree, knew the pull from the earth, felt the energies planted by the Ancestors that fed each blade of grass, each stone, each goanna tucked under the soil, each tree as it reached to the sky. The energies shot from the rocks and the tree branches, up, up, up to him and the flock. The flock landed, made camp on the Land; they sang the legends and ate from the earth the nourishment that the Ancestors had provided.

Jimmy was home. This was home.

The town's lights twinkled brighter when the Kardachi man brought him back into Hector's room. The didgeridoo was propped by the corner of the bed. When Jimmy saw what the Kardachi man's hand held, he trembled. Should he run? He'd heard of bone pointing, but never seen it. He began to edge away, but the Wirrun pulled him back, and put a hand over his. Jimmy's hand became glued to the bed. Tears ran down his cheeks and he willed his legs to hold him.

The Kardachi man held a gum twig, and at the end was tied a Galah leg bone, now pointed at Hector. Was it tied with Jimmy's gold hair? A big lump of gray clay was stuck to the end the Wirrun held. The man made a small cut on Hector's ankle and with his index finger smeared blood over the bone. Jimmy felt the bone pulling at his own belly. He moved toward it, felt Jocko's strong hands on his shoulders pulling him back.

The Kardachi man pointed his bone stick at Hector's head while he chanted. Then he reached beneath Hector's head and from behind it, where Hector's Galah crest would have started, he pulled a piece of bloody skull. He heard Esther and Tess murmur, "Ah."

Jimmy sank back into Jocko. Then he heard the Wirrun speak inside his head, "You are a man. It is only death. Why do you cringe like a dingo?" The Wirrun held out the piece of bloody bone to Jimmy.

No one called Jimmy a cowardly dingo! He found muscles in his feet pushing up to his legs, through his body, to his arm, and reached out for the bone. The Wirrun pointed at the sink. Jimmy concentrated on his steps, heel-toe, heel-toe. He turned on the water and looked up at the medicine man. There were deep lines in his forehead, deepening by the second, black dark lines over his eyebrows like snakes in the sand.

Jimmy followed the instructions the Wirrun spoke in Jimmy's mind: he washed the skull bone that had come from Hector's head. The water and the bloody silt became one under his fingers as he scrubbed. The last words of the Wirrun echoed. "We have Dreamt your mate. Jimmy and Jessie. You are camping with your mother-in-law."

Donna. Mother-in-law. He thought of her brown breasts, of her black hair on the pillow, of the moans she made during sex, of her warm palm on his back. These were not the proper thoughts of a mother-in-law, which was one of the most distant Aboriginal kin relations. No joking, practically no speaking to each other. Panic rose in his throat, but the Wirrun in his head calmed him. "No worries for the past, Jimmy Jackboy. Today I set you back on your path."

Jimmy lifted the bone for everyone to see, hoping they could not see those images of Donna in his imagination. The bone in his hand felt lighter. He held it out to the Wirrun, but the Wirrun shook his head. "It will be buried on Galah Land, with your father's finger." As he stuffed the bone into his pocket, Jimmy knew when he got back to his shed that night, he would take Da's bone off its spot on the shelf and carry it with him. He'd been wrong to have left it.

The ochre lines on the Wirrun's face crinkled and a feather floated to the floor. "Tea?"

Esther bent to pick up the feather and laid it on Hector's chest. "You'll come over to me house. Hector, don't take too long to get there. All the tucker'll be gone with Jocko around." She kissed Hector's forehead.

They waved to the sleeping Hector as they filed out, down the stairs, and into Esther's car, as if they weren't covered in blood and ochre, and as if nothing had happened in the hospital room.

The Galah follows the Dreaming men along the lines of their Land. These are paths she has flown over and over, in her lifetime or in her cell-memory, she does not know which, for they feel the same, Yuti and Dreaming. The pull of the lines are as natural to her as the call to move, the messages in her head that tell the flock as one to fly, toward the west or east, north or south, to go, to stay.

The dead man, the father, rides on her wing. He is tired from his time in-between, his time avoiding the call of Yaraandoo. She had thought it would be only the boy who she would take to the seedpile, but his father, whose seed power had created the boy, also needed to fly. The father is light, though he had been too heavy a burden for the boy to carry.

Did the father know as she did that they would be buried together, in the earth beside the tree where she had emerged from her egg, into her second life, the life before the life of the dead?

The boy is a man. He will dig the hole and lay them in their earth, pour sands upon their wings. She looks up at the moon above, its belly growing. They will be buried when the moon is round as berries, to give them time to fly to the dark side before the moon disappears for its days behind the sky.

\∩/

Donna and Andy stood awkwardly in the hall as Hector's door swung shut behind them. Andy pulled her head close to his, giving her a quick peck on the forehead. "You okay?" She nodded and he whispered, "I'm taking call tonight, so I'd better get downstairs."

Donna felt tears welling in her eyes, so she turned in the opposite direction. Could she find a sleeping patient's room where she could pretend to busy herself without anyone noticing she was crying? Peter was the medicine man. She tried to remember back to that sun-drenched day in Boulia. Had she chosen her place at the fence beside him, or had he chosen his place beside her? Who'd been there first?

In science, one had to look for correlation, then explore causation. In her first statistics class, the students had been astounded by the correlation between rainfall in India and the performance of the stock market. But, Professor Gandhi instructed, there was no causation.

Was there causation here in Isa, or just correlation? Was she seeking out these people, or were they seeking her? And what Peter had said. Could it be true? If so, why her? Were they using her or was she lucky? Or unlucky?

Her shift was over, but she couldn't leave the hospital while Peter was in Hector's room. She sat in her office, which overlooked the car park, keeping an eye on Esther's car, halfheartedly reviewing charts. She logged onto the hospital schedule. There it was in black and white. Andy's last day was not even two weeks away, the day before the Science Fete. Time had passed quickly with good company.

It was close to midnight when her heart skipped. The gang who'd been holed up in Hector's room was filing out and climbing into Esther's car. Donna let her chair slam back into the door as she rushed up to the second floor. Then she burst through Hector's door.

He lay still, as he always had. What had she expected, that he'd be sitting up in bed with a smile, asking for something to eat? His forehead was unlined, free from worry in his dream state. Monitors lit up in the same patterns as they had for months. She sat down by his bed and let her head tilt back. He should be sent to Rockhampton to the large hospital. Isa couldn't continue to use a bed for him.

She'd wanted to help Hector so badly because Jimmy had counted on her. Her medicine had failed, and even the trip to Barrington Downs wasn't enough. Jimmy would go home to Yuendumu circumcised by Andy, a sterile, yet soulless initiation compared to what she imagined would have happened on his Land. She'd miss him, would miss their little family, but she had a vague anticipation about seeing Nick. Sex with Andy the night before had sealed it. She was ready to move on to a partner where there might be a future. Where there would be a father if she had her Jessie. She was done being the whore for now, the other woman.

"Ay, Doctor Gorgeous."

She'd imagined that Hector had spoken.

"How bout you and me?"

Donna sat upright. Hector's eyes were closed but was that an erection making a tent of his sheet? She buzzed the sisters' station, approached the bed, and stroked the side of the man's face. Nothing. She opened an eyelid and peered down into the depths of his retinas with a penlight.

"What do you say, Doctor Gorgeous?"

Donna jumped back. People did not wake from comas and start talking. They needed months of therapy to learn to speak again. "Hector," she whispered.

"Me." He was groggy but he moved his head side-to-side. Donna buzzed the nurses again, urgently pushing the button. She leaned over him and gave him a hug, avoiding the huge penis. Clung to his shoulders for Jimmy. "Jimmy has missed you. He will be so happy." She felt a tear fall and she stood up. "Do you know where you are, Hector? You are in the hospital."

He closed his eyes again, and his lips barely parted as he spoke. "Aye. In hospital. You look like black cockatoo. Pretty shiny feathers." His words were formed perfectly, with not even a slur. "Beautiful bird, Doctor Gorgeous. Number one doctor."

Shaking, she called Esther's house to tell them the news. "Is Peter there?"

Esther's voice was calm. "Left right after tea. Went out for a smoke and never came back. Typical Yapa, out on walkabout."

"How could he be that sure his medicine would work?" Medicine was a matter of weighing probabilities, never certainties. How could Peter not want to know Hector's fate?

Esther laughed, "He lifted a curse. Didn't matter what happened after."

"But I need to talk to him." Didn't he owe that to her? A doctor-to-doctor explanation of how to wake a man from a coma?

It was the middle of the night and Hector's room was crowded: Andy, Esther, Jocko, Tess, Jimmy, and some curious nurses and doctors mingled as Donna slipped out into the hallway. Had she imagined it, or was Jimmy avoiding her?

She opened the door to the stairwell and took one step. Her foot didn't want to move any further. She sank down, and didn't hear the door open above her, so deep was she involved in disbelief—hallucinogens were one thing, eucalyptus leaves, gabo, but a bloody bone pulled from his head? The CT scan had shown nothing. She felt Andy's arms pulling her to her feet, walking her down the stairs to the next landing. She balked. "No. I don't want to talk to the sisters yet."

Andy held her tightly to him. "No worries."

He opened the door, looked to the right and left, then scooped her up and darted with her into the broom closet. In the black darkness, he pressed his lips hard against hers. She felt his teeth press her teeth.

Andy had her skirt up before she knew it. The sex was silent and fast. He groped her breasts; she held his shoulders, each of them looking for grounding.

She wouldn't come. How could she, that image of the tented sheet burning in the back of her eyes. A man wakes up from months in a coma with an erection, just like a man waking from a good night's sleep. She opened her eyes to look through the darkness, but all she saw was the darker void of space beyond Andy's shoulders. She felt disconnected, as if she were perched high atop a pile of clean white sheets, looking down at her own back against the long line of a broom, wondering if it were uncomfortable. She felt a shudder and Andy whispered, "Accept it." It was a statement. Doctor's orders.

"I thought I was beginning to understand Yapa ways. The ESP But this? I'm a doctor." One who has sex in a broom closet, shows her tits, and gets stoned on gabo.

She flattened her skirt and heard him pull up his jeans, the unmistakable scratch of the denim on skin. She was glad he hadn't simply unzipped his fly, would not have relished the roughness of the zipper and his jeans rubbing against her.

He touched her hair. "Our medicine and Yapa medicine. They're good together." His voice reminded her of the bed talk of her childhood, when she and her best friend were able to divulge their secrets only because it was dark, with no reactions to be registered on each other's faces. Disembodied voices. How often she'd swapped dreams in the dark with men, talking away reality. With Andy, she'd talked dreams in the daytime. Not her dreams or his dreams, but Dreams. His voice floated as a ghost, echoing in the tiny closet.

Donna wanted a cigarette. Hadn't craved one in years, but it was what she wanted. "If you believe in fairies, clap your hands."

"What?"

Donna sighed. "A bloody bone? A bloody bone? I must've missed bloody bone day in med school. Do they teach that one in Australia?"

Andy was silent, so she said, "Hector can take Jimmy on his initiation." She thought about circumcision in the desert. "The binding of Isaac," She could imagine Jimmy's penis dripping with blood, pooling in the red sands.

Andy leaned up against her, pinning her to the wall. "After that," Andy said, "he will never fear death the way you and I fear it." His lips brushed the tip of her nose, and he found her hand and put it on his groin. He pushed her hand down and she felt him grow hard again. Oh, to be a twenty-six-year-old man. He kissed her neck. "I'll see you at home in the morning."

The crack of light was startling as he opened the door. She grabbed his arm as he moved, half his body in darkness, the other half white as a dead man under the fluorescent light. "Come home with me now."

He shook his head, whole body in the hall, whole body deathly white, "I'm on call." She let the door swing closed. First they were doctors; next, they were people.

She waited until she was sure that Andy had disappeared before exposing herself to the bright lights. Then she grasped the brass knob of the door and swung it so wide, it hit the wall. She bounded down the hall and out into the car park, where she gulped in fresh air. The Southern Cross was disappearing from the sky.

Her hands gripped the steering wheel. She turned the key. Combustion, two sparks drove pistons to turn the four wheels, lights shined beams on the dark road. Bugs and moths flew between the light beacons, in and out like a strobe. This was science, not magic. The car moved forward. Otherwise, would it not have flown like a Galah, screeching into the ebony sky? Or explode, a falling comet in its quest to kiss the earth, to make a lake out of the flatness? But no. It drove. Below her white straight lines glowed on black bitumen.

Should she be on the left of the line, or the right? She couldn't remember. Did she ever check which way the water swirled in the toilet bowl? A traffic light turned red. Why stop? Why obey the rules? Red was an artificial construct. She pushed on the gas pedal. *Officer, the light was green. No doctor, it was clearly red. But how could we be sure? What you saw and I saw can never be the same.* The story you tell is different than the story that I will tell. But only one thing happened. True.

The steps to the pea-green house shifted under her. They were floating on the thin crust without an anchor or oar. The earth was hollow.

She threw her clothes into a heap on the floor. Naked, in mid-motion, she was about to crawl under the sheet, but instead sank to her knees. What a world. What a beautiful world when a man can wake from coma, an Uncle to a boy whom she loved. Yes, loved.

She was a girl again, praying with her mother, face brushing against cool silk, the smell of mothballs and freshly-shined shoes filling her nose. She let her forehead rest against the mattress. *Hector has woken. I think I have seen a burning bush. The Lord is my shepherd I shall not want. He makes me lie down in green pastures. He leads me beside still waters. He restores my soul. Yea, though I walk through the valley of the shadow of death, I fear no evil. For you are with me, Your rod and Your staff, they comfort me.*

The Kardachi man, Peter, smiled behind her eyelids as she said the Psalm again and again, the worn carpet burning her knees. Finally, she crawled under the cotton blanket and smooth cool sheet, the Honey Ant Dreaming glowing above her. She stared blankly into the dark, waiting for a voice to tell her something. Would Jessie be a miracle too? She pulled the blanket to her chin. A loose thread. Starting at the edge of the blanket and then reaching over to Andy's side, the same side of the bed where Greg used to sleep, she began to unravel it. A long thread dangled in the glow of the nightlight, the lines from the road she had brought into the home.

Round moon rises gold and brown, covering the Northern sky, dark blue with wisps of white clouds that will grow in time to bring monsoon. The Galah feels the moon pull hard on her wings, pulling the growing chicks from their hollow tree nest of yellow wattle to begin to fly. One by one she nudges them out of the nest. Fly away chicks, live the lives determined ages ago by the breath and movement of the Ancestors in the sky and earth.

She watches the last tail feathers as they fly far from the mango tree. The chicks will group with other young ones, knowing their land until it is time to mate. Then again they will join the flock.

Soon the monsoon will come. Then the mulla mulla will peek through the grasses, its purple cone flowers bursting with seeds. Yellow stars of everlastings will spring up overnight, turning dry sandy brown meadows into a feast of seeds. Red desert peas will sprout in clumps under the gums, black berry centers tempting bird and insect. The chicks will fly far and gorge.

She imagines her chicks gliding on the wind to the last drops of a pool, which will soon be no more than an indentation in the claypan rocks. They will watch it teeming with life in the moonglow. They will open their beaks. They will gobble shield shrimp as the shrimp struggle to bury their eggs in the sand, each egg no bigger than the grains that surround it. The chicks will swallow two at a time, feeling them squiggle in the belly.

Then again it will not be long until the Dry, when the flowers wither away and the spinifex will be left golden-tipped, each blade lit by the *moon, waving in the dry heat. Then their wing tips will stir one blade, who will whisper to his neighbor to bend, BEND! And the whispers will go on and on until the ripple is complete and turns back on itself, another wing setting it off in the opposite direction. The Galahs will glide over the grass tips, skimming golden tops, looking deep into the green stalks for beetles and grasshoppers. They will fly.*

Jimmy walked with Hector up and down the hospital halls, patting the two bones in his pocket. Hector couldn't stop moving, refused to be in his bed. Guess that's what happened when a bloke slept too much. He looked over at Jimmy. "You grew."

"Not much."

"Don't care what docs say. I'm leaving hospital today. Can't stop me from walking out that door. Got two good feet." He smiled down at Jimmy. "Got to say g'day to Doctor Gorgeous first. I'd like to get inside that girl. Nice bum."

Jimmy clenched his fist. "That's me mother-in-law." It wasn't right for Hector to talk about her like that. "Respect a medicine woman."

"You sweet on her, eh? Time to be initiated. Sure you want to wait for this bloody Science Fete?" Hector ambled so fast that he almost knocked into Nan, who'd come around the corner.

"Hey, Jimmy. Hey, Hector," Nan waved as she popped into another room.

Hector looked after her, long red hair trailing. "I'd take that one too. Them both together."

"Wake up and all you can think of is sex?" Jimmy looked out the window at the end of the hall. He had schoolwork. Had better head home. "I'm off."

"See you at the billabong."

Jimmy stopped. "Not at the billabong anymore."

"Naw?" Hector kept walking, feet slapping on the linoleum, couldn't stop for anything.

Jimmy caught back up to him. "Camping under Doctor Donna's tree. Want me to go get your swag?"

"I'm gonna go back to the billabong until we leave," Hector said. "With the blackfellas." His right eye didn't open as far as the left.

Jimmy felt disapproval in Hector's voice, but he wasn't going to let it bother him. "Science Fete's on Friday at the high school. Want you to be there."

"Hector seems a bit different to me," Jimmy confided to Jocko as they sat in the hospital tuck shop over tea. What if Hector weren't all there anymore? *Bloody Science Fete.* What if he didn't understand that Jimmy was going to be a real doctor or engineer?

Jocko stirred his tea. "Didn't know him before."

"Wears his hat crooked. And he couldn't remember Mum's name."

Jocko took a bite of bikkie. "Yapa names change all the time. What is her name?"

"Gloreen."

"Nice name."

They sat there in silence, Jimmy's frustration growing with the rotations of the fan. "I mean it, Jocko. Something's not right." His voice carried to the counter and the frizzy-haired lady looked up.

"That'll happen to a bloke's been Dreaming."

Jimmy pushed around crumbs from the Tam Tams with his finger. "Think he remembers me Galah story?"

Jocko nodded like a kookaburra. "He remembers."

Jimmy could hear the bikkies crunching in his own mouth. Was a lot louder hearing from the inside than out. "What if..."

"You study birds in school? They have a magnet in their heads that gets them halfway across the world. Once they are told the way to go, they never forget it. Albatross will fly round the world without landing, then go back and meet his mate to make chicks. That's like Hector, like you, like our People. You can lose a foot, lose an arm, but every cell in your body has a magnet for your

Dreaming places. For your Land. You won't ever forget it. Hector won't either." Jocko pushed back his chair. "I'm gonna go with you blokes. Men deal with the men's secrets. Tess, Esther, and Donna deal with the women's."

"They're gonna let Donna come?"

"They're going out there *for* her. Spirit child waiting for her womb. Spirit child that's gonna be your wife someday."

Jimmy choked on his biscuit and Jocko had to give him a pat on the back. "Everybody knows Donna's going to be me mother-in-law?"

Jocko nodded.

"Does she know?"

"You could ask her, but I wouldn't."

Jimmy closed his eyes. "Doesn't feel like she's mother-in-law. Can't stop being with her."

Jocko laughed, his straight nose blowing like his didg. "She's a white woman. Rules are different. "

"Wirrun said I'm going to be a medicine man and win our Galah Land. Already filed my native title claim. Hector'll never believe that."

Jocko stared at him. "Fair dinkum?" At Jimmy's silence he added, "You're the one to do it."

The afternoon before the Science Fete, Jimmy sat with his back against the shed, painting the didg log for Andy. Andy stood above, holding it steady. Jimmy painted Galah Dreaming—it was the only thing he knew to paint—though technically he should be initiated first. But initiation was only days away. As he painted, he changed the location of a dry-salt soak and a bush tucker site from where they were supposed to be in order to keep his Dreaming sacred. He stopped painting a waterhole and rested his eyes on Andy's fly. "Do women like it better when you're cut?"

"Cut?"

"Circumcised." Jimmy had learned that word first in Isa, and still hated to use it.

Andy twisted the log for him. "Do you care?"

"Show me again where you're supposed to cut. Want Hector to do it right." He would never have questioned Hector before this time in Isa. But surprisingly, Jimmy had gotten used to the idea of being circumcised in hospital. Hector had been in coma for a long time, and Jimmy didn't want him to take off too much.

Andy examined the edge of the didgeridoo. "You've already looked at me willie once. I'll show you on yours." Andy took the didg and propped it against the shed. "Inside. Can't have the neighbors talking."

He followed Andy into the shed and dropped his pants. Andy took the end of Jimmy's paint brush. "This is where the foreskin attaches to the penis. Cut along the dotted line."

Jimmy bent his head down and cranked his willie around to see. Sure enough, it was almost as if there were a line. Would be hard for Hector to mess it up.

"What are you two doing?"

Jimmy looked at Donna's body, framed by the sun behind her. Mother-in-law. What would she think, his pants at his ankles? Andy crouched. Jimmy pulled up his pants.

Andy was stammering, "Showing Jimmy circumcision. Case came up at hospital that he didn't understand."

Donna's face came into focus and she laughed. "I expect this from five-year-olds, but not you two." She could barely get the words out, she was laughing so hard. "Case in hospital. Right."

Hours later, Jimmy picked up the didgeridoo branch. He could still trace a tiny ridge, despite his careful sanding. The wood needed a spine, like a man needed one. The naked gum glowed beneath the paint, the exact color of honey ant nectar. He brought the wood to his nose to smell the tree from where it had come, covering the end with his lips and making a few pulsing vibrations. After he varnished it, he'd cover the rim with beeswax to make it smooth for Andy.

Jimmy went into the shed for the varnish and noticed a black square hanging in the corner. He pulled it down from the hook. A black skivvy with a red sash on the left shoulder, an Essedon Footy skivvy, Michael Long's team. How did she know? He thought she never listened when he and Andy went over the AFL scores in the morning paper. He smelled the newness of it, smelled how all their days together were absorbed into its blackness, for him to take home.

But he'd forgotten a present for Donna. Violet Crumbles and Caramello Koalas weren't enough. How could he have forgotten? He looked at the paints and the one last piece of cardboard he and Tom hadn't used. It was the only thing he could do: Galah map. He didn't alter the drawing as he had for Andy. She would get the real thing because someday she would be kin. He thought of the medicine Buddha hanging in her New York apartment, awaiting her return. He would tell her to hang the Galah map between the Buddha and the Honey Ant Dreaming. He would see it again when he visited.

He painted carefully: the waterholes, the Galah, the Rainbow Serpent, the seed piles, the salt wash. He painted all he remembered from his flight over his Land, in the airplane and with the Kardachi man. How similar those flights had been. He'd seen the same Land. Both ways had been good.

He'd heard so many stories of initiations and walkabouts, but no one had had airplanes, mines, white women, Kmarts, hospitals, or doctors in theirs. On a whim, Jimmy added smokestacks to Donna's Dreaming. He reached under his shorts and touched the tip of his penis. Then he touched the paint. It had dried moments after he withdrew his brush.

Andy came out to the yard and stood over him with a smile. "I like your skivvy."

"It's Essedon."

He crouched down and examined Jimmy's work. "I know."

"For Donna." Jimmy picked up the painting and put it in the shed. Then he took out the didg and turned it slowly so Andy could see. "Michael Long's da was born in Ti Tree. Near Yuendumu."

"So you told me." Jimmy held the didg out to Andy, who carefully examined it from top to bottom, spinning it as he went. Jimmy nodded in approval. Andy knew how to read the story.

Andy blew on the didg. Had a pretty good seal around the mouth for a whitefella. But the sounds he could make were baby sounds compared to Hector's. Jimmy sat back on the grass and watched the white man struggle. "When you stopped hugging your mum, who'd ya start hugging?"

Andy puffed a few more times and let the didg rest at his side. He looked up at the clouds. Jimmy followed his gaze to the smoke trail from the smokestack. "Guess that was when I became ready for women."

"I'll miss being a boy. But I guess women are worth it, huh?"

Andy spoke to the sky. "Try to find one that's a friend."

"Is Donna a good one?"

"She's a good one. Too bad she isn't ten years younger."

"That doesn't matter in Yuendumu."

Andy handed him back the didg. "The older wife doesn't have the babies, does she?"

How could the girl in Townsville be so much better than Donna? Why choose her? "You and your girl want babies?"

"Want a boy just like you." He laughed. "Especially one who can play the didgeridoo."

"Make the sound a part of your breath and it will play better." Jimmy closed his eyes. "You sure you're making the right choice?"

"You'll understand when you're older."

"I've been told already who I'll marry. She's going to be born within the year. Spirit child like me." Jimmy blew on the didg. It gave a rich, full sound. "Name's Jessie."

Andy looked surprised. Jimmy waited to be asked about his future wife, but Andy was silent. They applied the varnish. The didg turned a rich coffee brown, darker than Jimmy had expected. The dry wood drank the varnish, absorbed each coat quickly, like a straggler in the desert being offered water.

Jimmy followed Andy inside the house to where Donna, Esther, and Tess were making tea. In the living room they rolled the didg up in Andy's swag. Then Jimmy went back outside to sit under Mister Mango for a last go at his Science Fete speech.

\\∩/

Donna walked up Lookout Hill tightly holding Andy's hand. It would be their last walk together, and tonight they'd have their last dinner, the last time sitting on the stoop to watch the moon, the last kiss, the last time they'd hold each other in bed. She felt like a woman seeing her man off to war, but without the pretense that he'd survive.

She watched the rock wallabies hopping. It was hard to believe that the first time she had come to Lookout Hill, she hadn't seen any. Her eyes hadn't known how to see a small kangaroo, camouflaged against rocks. Now she saw them in every crevice.

A wallaby stood next to the path, stock still, and she stopped. He was the same color as the rescued joey Peanut, but with a rounder nose—sign of a wallaby instead of a roo. She turned to Andy. "I never told you. The Kardachi man who woke Hector was the same man who kissed me in Boulia."

"Fair dinkum?" He pulled on her hand.

They were almost at the top and wanted to make it for sunset, which happened so quickly in the bush. You could see the sun sinking, actually watch it move down the horizon. "He said it's time."

"For Jessie?"

"Yes," said Donna. They reached the watchtower and she ran her palm over the rough plaster. When she turned her palm over, it was white.

Andy pulled her close. The smoke from the lead smelter was bright orange. They watched the sun ball drop, first its tip resting on the horizon. When it was gone, he put his palm over her belly. "Do you want her?"

"Yes."

He stripped off his T-shirt and spread it out on the ground. Then he rubbed his hands with the red dirt, and took a rock and scraped his knee until he brought out blood. "I want what you want." He gently pulled her down on top of the shirt, then pulled up her shirt and painted her belly—seven concentric circles—with his blood. They looked in each other's eyes as the light dimmed around them.

They were finishing as they'd started—wetting the hard dry Australian dirt, a tunnel spider centered on its web not a foot from her head. After, they stared up at the dark sky. She whispered in his ear. "Do you want to know her?"

"When she's older. After I've been married for a long time." He kissed her neck. "Just promise me one thing."

"Anything." Either Andy's tears or sweat dampened her cheek; she couldn't tell which.

"I want her born in Isa."

After tea, the gang loaded the cars for the next day's departures. Jimmy noticed Donna was missing and went to look for her. She was in the kitchen, her hands still, deep in the dish water. Her head craned to look through the window.

She jumped when he said, "I have a surprise for you. Out back."

She turned and smiled, wiping her hands on her jeans. "Need a better view of the stars anyway." She went to the fridge and handed him a Coke and took a stubbie for herself. He studied the Coke and put it back on the counter. "Can I have a Fourex instead?"

She went to reach for one and then drew back her hand quickly from the fridge. "I can't."

Jimmy took the Coke and followed her out to the back steps. They sat there and watched the Cross rising in the sky. Jimmy's shoulder brushed hers and he felt his penis harden. So he leaned into the siding instead. "What happens when whitefellas die?" The Warambool looked like the Coke in the sky.

Donna peeled the corner of the label from her stubbie. "I suppose we go to heaven." Donna took a long sip of beer. "I never forget anyone I've known who's died. I keep lists in my head of all the people—my mom and dad, patients." She paused, "None of them have come back to tell me, so I can't be certain what happens."

He squinted up at the place where he would go when he died. "Remember when you asked me what I'd do at my initiation?"

Donna nodded, following his gaze to the sky. "I've taught you sterile conditions, right? Use bacitracin three times a day. I'll give you some to take. And some pain killers if you want them."

"Hector'll teach me to do it without pain." She was silent and he added, "But I'll take the bacitracin."

"Are you nervous?"

Jimmy leaned further into the house so as not to touch her smooth skin. "About me speech tomorrow. Not me initiation." Her breath smelled like the beer. He liked the smell of the grains, could imagine them waving in the wind. One sip couldn't be poison, could it? He held out his hand and tried again. "One taste. May I?"

She hesitated and then handed it to him. "You're a man now."

He inhaled the air from the bottle before he took a sip. It was cold on his tongue. He swirled it in his mouth. Pleasant. But not good enough—nothing like a Violet Crumble—to risk getting poisoned. He handed the bottle back. "Ancestors send messages with the birds. Maybe your dead are sending you messages all the time, but you just haven't learned how to listen."

She held out the beer to him. He refused, and she smiled. Donna took a sip and turned the last drops out onto the lawn. "We call those messengers angels. My mother used to see them. I thought I saw one when I first came here."

"Did you?"

"Yes." Donna hesitated. "Can I ask you something?"

Jimmy shrugged and took the empty stubbie. He'd watched Donna picking at the label and began to do so himself. He was surprised at the satisfying feeling as it slowly came away from the brown glass.

"How did the Kardachi man pull out the bloody bone?"

"I don't know his magic." He knew he hadn't given a satisfying answer. "Hector woke himself. The songs we sang linked him to the energy of his Dreaming places. Also, the Kardachi man removed a curse. Hector got in a fight with a bloke in town."

"Ta." Donna squeezed his knee.

He jumped up. "Don't you want the surprise?" He could hear

Jocko's and Esther's laughs inside. He ran to the shed and brought back his painting.

She sucked in her breath. "It's beautiful."

He pointed at the bottom left corner. "I am going to tell you the Galah Dreaming. I want you to remember it. We are kin now."

\n/

In her bed that night, Donna realized it was harder than she'd expected to relinquish Andy to his fiancée. After hours of talking in each other's arms, they fell into an exhausted sleep. She dreamt of Andy and his blonde wife walking down the beach with two young boys about Jimmy's age. The boys were darting back and forth in the surf, carrying boogie boards that hid their faces. Donna was walking toward them, her feet cooled by the water. Next to her walked a beautiful young woman, maybe sixteen or seventeen, with dark hair and olive skin. The girl shielded her eyes with her hand. "Those the mates we're meeting, Mum?"

Tom stumbled on his words only a few times in his speech, and then Jimmy found himself up at the microphone. Mrs. Brunswick, the doctors, Tess, Esther, Jocko, and Nan were in front. He scanned the audience for Hector. Couldn't find the big man in the torn hat amid any of the smiling faces.

He showed the audience enlarged photos of the black box with the hole cut in the end, demonstrating how much darker the absence of light was than mere black paint. Then he adjusted the mirror in the tray of water. The audience clapped when he refracted the rainbow onto the white tag board behind him. He waved a magnifying glass between the mirror and the board, and the rainbow disappeared. "This shows how white light is made up of all the different colors of the spectrum. Each color travels at different speeds—in other words, has different wavelengths or vibrations." He was about to end the presentation, had memorized his conclusion from note cards from which he'd practiced with the doctors. Then he saw Hector in the back of the gym. Hector's face seemed to be part of the wall; only his eyes and bright teeth glowed between the white lines he'd painted on his face. His face was painted Galah.

The Kardachi man's song echoed in Jimmy's mind. He remembered the Rainbow Serpent dancing in front of his eyes when he'd first gone down into the mine and rested his palm against the wall of rock. Science was Yuti and it was Dreaming. Dreaming had stirred Hector from his coma, not science. Jimmy spoke clearly. "I am Warlpiri. My moiety is Galah. We believe that these energies, these colors that you see on the screen behind me," he turned to point at his rainbow and saw Tom give him a thumbs up, "represent the Rainbow Serpent. During the Dreaming, the Rainbow Serpent traveled through the land, and the waves of her body brought up rocks, mountains, rivers, people, plants, and animals. Her movements created the seeds, the energies, from which everything grows and moves today. These energies link the world that we can touch with the invisible world." Here he made the rainbow disappear with the magnifying glass. "The colors are still there, yet we can't see them. The Rainbow Serpent is everywhere."

He saw the men in orange jumpsuits who'd taken time off work to see their sons and daughters. And they were listening, not laughing. "The miners know it best. Energies of light are down underground, even without the sun. This Land below us and beside us is all of ours."

He walked off the stage and heard applause behind him. Tomorrow he'd finish his initiation. Next time he came to Isa, he'd be a man.

S pinifex waved, tipped by starlight. The Galah perched on the highest branch of the dead ghost gum and watched the stars rise in the vast sky, drops of shiny dew on the net that circled, catching the minnows and riverbugs of the great waters above. If she watched from the moments the white points cut through the dark until her flock started to stir and the jays called morning, she could see circles, circles, the wake of the net dragged through the sky waters, like rings of a dead gum. She should have been sleeping like the rest, head tucked under wing. But the stars pulled at her, made her watch, made her memorize their migration, so when she became one of them, she would know the way, just as she had known the way across the great Land that had been her home for this life.

The flock was traveling far, away from town, to their Center, where the Galah first hatched from the rockeggs, the starseeds sent to earth. There the flock would fly amongst the rockeggs, wings brushing on shale, cheeks rubbing against earth when the boy danced and sang, and when storm clouds emptied above them, lightning feeding the earth with its heat.

101

Donna kissed Andy goodbye in the high school car park after Jimmy had finished his speech. Andy needed to get on the road; Townsville was a ten-hour drive. The end had come, and there was no point in prolonging it.

She waved at his car long after the dust had settled around her ankles, then went back into the school where tables had been set up for the kids to exhibit their experiments.

Donna knew that people quickly adjusted to changes in their lives, even horrific ones. She'd seen it many times as patients accepted cancer diagnoses, ALS, infertility, and then resumed the daily routine of living with and treating their diseases. They'd trade book club for chemo appointments, golf for chess, whatever it took to survive.

She knew how rapidly *she'd* adapted to the notion of being childless. One day she'd been pregnant, reveling in her round belly, and the next, the baby was dead. She'd cried deep sobs, and months later, could hardly remember the hope that had come along with impending motherhood. Soon after, she accepted that Greg would divorce her. Likewise, she'd adapted to Hector's miraculous recovery. And so, too, would she adapt to the absence of Andy and Jimmy.

The night before, she and Andy had returned from their walk to Lookout Hill. Andy began to pack—Donna hadn't noticed how much he'd spread out over the house. As Jimmy, Andy, Esther, Jocko, and Tess loaded his Land Rover, Donna was alone in the house, her hands in the dishwater, listening to the silence. It didn't feel as empty as when she'd first arrived, as if some of their laughter as they sat for burrito night, barramundi, and steaks, had seeped into the aluminum walls. Though Nick had slept over but once, his deep laugh was part of it, as well.

For a moment, she thought she saw a Galah on the neighbor's fence looking at her through the window. She craned her head to watch as it flew up toward the moon. The galahs would keep her company on the wires outside. The neighbor's dog would wag its tail at her. She wouldn't be alone.

Now, she walked into the high school gym and saw Tess waving at her in front of Jimmy's table. Esther, Nan, and three other sisters stood laughing in a circle. Before, she'd been used to a tiny family, had been content to rely on Greg as her only companion. She'd never thought of bringing anyone other than Kate deep into their lives. What a mistake. With Esther and the sisters, Andy and Jimmy, she had more of a family than she'd ever had before. There was nothing to do but be together, support these people. They were all marooned in the Center, together. In New York there was little physical space, so you gave even your closest friends privacy. In Isa, space was all there was, so you drew the people you cared about close in, allowed your love to be their shelter.

Jimmy walked over to her. "Was I good, Doctor?"

She remembered the shining faces of her own parents at her graduation from college. They were proud, but had expected her success. They'd already anticipated graduation from med school, four years ahead of them. But Donna hadn't foreseen her father's empty chair at med school graduation, her mother sitting stiffly. Why hadn't she arranged for Kate to meet her beforehand so Mom wouldn't have had to sit alone? She looked at Jimmy's expectant face and tried to let all her pride radiate through her smile. "Brilliant. I have never been more proud of anyone." She wanted to pet his blond hair, clutch him to her, but refrained. He hadn't let her touch him since Hector had awoken. "Jimmy Jackboy, someday I hope you will teach me to put Dreaming into my medicine."

Surprisingly, he gave her a hug. She could feel and see the man he would become, right there pushing on his outsides.

The fence on Barrington Downs Station was waist high, not much of a barrier. Donna wanted to chuckle. This was what had kept them out? Jimmy had said it was high as the sky. A strong red boomer could clear it without a problem, might hardly notice it as the red rust of the chains blended into the flat scrub beyond. There was no perceptible difference to the land inside the fence or outside. An arbitrary boundary, which made the space contained within it so much more valuable. Depending on whether a person was being fenced in or out, the barrier could make a person feel protected, jailed, or excluded. So much power in an arbitrary line.

Red rust flicked off her fingers as she reached for the corroding links. The directions were to walk east from the road, less than a kilometer, to a cattle gate. From there, they could walk to Jimmy's sites. Gavin Childs had laughed as she had described the sites. "You want to visit that pile of rocks? Ain't nothing there to see. But you Yankees have wild ideas."

She fingered the scrap of paper with the numbers scribbled for the lock. Jimmy had given it to her for safekeeping. She was tempted to lift Jimmy over the fence and let him run, let him know that he hadn't needed any of them to finish his Dreaming. She could hobble over it, but there was no way that Hector or Tess could. Wouldn't bet that Esther and Jocko could, either. She trotted forward and handed the paper to Jimmy, who'd been avoiding her since they got out of the cars. He'd been glued to Hector's side, walking a bit ahead of the others. "This belongs to you."

She fell back, waiting for Esther. A swag, borrowed from Nan, hung across Donna's shoulders. Esther had insisted that though the blackfellas could sleep without a swag, Donna should take one into the bush. She took a sip from the water bottle hanging from her belt. The others had said they'd find water as they walked. They kept their right shoulders to the fence.

Esther touched her hand. "Is it hard to walk in those boots?"

Donna noticed for the first time that the rest of them were barefoot. "Don't think so." She'd been so proud of how she'd learned to dress for the bush, like she were planning a date with the Crocodile Hunter himself.

Esther held her hand like her girlfriends used to in elementary school. "Can you feel the ground?"

Donna looked sideways under her wide-brimmed hat. "I'd burn my feet if I took them off."

Esther was serene as the Buddha walking beside her. "Don't you want to feel Jimmy's Land?"

"What does it feel like?"

"Like a Violet Crumble."

Donna squeezed her friend's hand and watched tumbleweed crashing into the fence ahead of them. "You and Jimmy and your Violet Crumbles. I've come to like them now. Full of space, like Queensland."

"You need to walk heel-toe, Donna."

"I do." How else did anyone walk?

Esther let go of her hand. "No. Watch."

Donna mimicked Esther, though it was hard in her ankle boots. She felt her heel hit the ground, and then her toe. Heel, then toe. She looked at Hector's and Jimmy's feet as they walked ahead. Yes, they too were exaggerating the movement of heel, then toe. Heel then toe. Hector's feet were huge, as were Esther's. Jimmy's were puppy feet, still too big for his body. Heel-toe. The dust swirled around their legs as they walked. Red dust, like the smoke from the priests' incense at her mother's funeral. The same priest had performed last rites, taking his wrinkled thumb to her mother's forehead, heart, each shoulder, so Patricia could profess her love for Jesus with all her mind and heart and strength and body.

Jimmy ran to the gate when it came into view. Donna saw him stoop over the lock, then walk through alone. This would be how she'd remember him, smiling with the sun low on his face, turning his hair into golden ribbons. The lock was in the dirt, and no one moved to pick it up as they followed Jimmy to the other side.

As they crossed the gate, there were no goodbyes. The three men just walked straight for the horizon and Esther and Tess simply didn't follow. They stood by the fence and watched the men disappear.

They made camp just to the west of the gate. And though Donna had been sorry at first not to go with the men, as the sun went down and a dingo howled nearby, she was happy for the fence on her one side and the firepit on the other, which gave her a sense of walls in the vast open bush—false comfort—but comfort nonetheless.

When the night was almost black, Tess took out two beautiful colored sticks from her dilly bag and began to beat them together. She sang and Esther clapped along. Donna didn't understand the words, but she felt the music move through her, felt the story of the land as she assumed it was. The moon was high when she excused herself to climb into her swag. Tess's chanting filled her dreams through the night, and when she woke every so often, Tess was still singing. The sun was rising and the kookaburra laughing when Tess put her sticks back into the dilly bag.

Donna put her head back on the jacket and watched the sun pop up from behind a mesa, watched its slow arc in the sky, watched the sky turn from pink to orange to blue, and marveled at where she was. So far from New York. What a thing, to be able to watch a sunrise over an open sky. It was hard to believe she'd ever compared Isa to an airport. In Australia, there could be no such thing as a non-place. Every centimeter of land was loved by someone, appreciated by some tribe for its unique properties, was a home. Isa's most essential quality was place; it was nontransportable. Of a specific latitude and longitude.

Donna was surprised when Tess and Esther rolled up her swag and hustled her forward. She'd assumed they'd wait at the gate until the men returned. Tess looked around and sniffed the air. Then she turned at a forty-five degree angle to the gate and stepped forward into the barren land, aiming for some point on the horizon.

Donna took a deep breath and followed them. First she'd left the car, now the fence. Her finger didn't seem to want to let go of the fence, her last tie to civilization. Her body stepped forward and finally pulled her finger away. She heard a twang, the fence letting go, saying goodbye. She was on Jimmy's Land.

His Land had hardly a tree, and was full of scrubby wattle, yellow flowers on prickly stems. Round clumps of spinifex stood amid patches of red dirt. She hurried to catch up with Tess, who walked carefully, one foot in front of the other.

"Monsoon will reach us soon," Esther said as she tasted the air with her tongue.

Donna looked at her friend in surprise. "But it's not even September."

"Unusually early this year."

With those words, Donna noticed how the day *did* feel different from the day before, the air more humid. She followed Tess's footsteps for over an hour, concentrating on heel-toe, to while away the time.

Esther finally pointed to some coolabahs in the distance, so surprising after the scarcity of trees. "That's where we're going."

"A waterhole?" Would she dare to take a quick dip, watching out for freshies?

"Good girl. You remember your bush lessons."

They got to the waterhole and Tess pointed to the ground under the tallest of the coolabahs. Its roots reached high up to its branches, making a little shelter. "There."

Donna walked over, surveying the ground, and then felt Tess

pushing her shoulder down. Donna sat. Esther took the swag off Donna's back and practically lifted her under the arms, pushing her back against the tree. Donna protested, "What?"

Tess took Donna's right ankle and Esther took the left and they spread her legs wide.

"Ouch, what…"

The women looked down at her and Tess shook her finger. "You sit like this against this coolabahs. Do not move, do you hear?"

Donna looked from one woman to the other. "Jesus, Esther. You people are crazy."

"Too right," laughed Esther.

Donna tried to pull her feet closer together and Esther kicked them apart. She watched Tess feeling the tree. She began to struggle up and Esther pushed her down. "Donna, trust me."

Tess was patting the tree, talking to it. "You strong Minggah for the little girl. Right here on Barrington Downs. Good Minggah."

"What the hell are you saying?" Donna struggled to get up. Tess continued whispering to the tree, and Esther put her hands on her hips. "Peter told you. I know he did. We Dreamt you. Do I have to tie you down? You want a baby or no?"

"I have to do this?"

"Don't question Yapa magic."

They'd been pushing her toward this moment ever since she'd arrived in Isa. She thought of her gray velvet bag, hanging empty from Esther's hand. "Do you like me? Am I your friend? Or am I just some vessel you're using for your Dreaming?" She thought of the first time she'd spoken on the phone to Gloreen. Her intuition had said that Jimmy had chosen her, rather than the other way around. Pearl, Peter, nothing was random. As if they were acting out their parts in a drama only they could know.

The heat was already overwhelming. Esther's face was shadowed by the sun behind her. It wasn't fair that the Yapa had the secret to waking people from comas, or curing infertility. *She* was a doctor. *She* had studied for years. Donna pulled her legs together. "I don't want you to do Yapa magic. I want to understand it first."

Esther pulled her legs apart. "You want a baby girl or no?" Esther touched her toe to Donna's boot. "Last time I'm going to ask. You want a baby?"

The answer came. Direct from her womb? Certainly not from her head. She wanted a baby more than she wanted to be a good doctor. More than she wanted a husband. "Yes."

Eyes flashing, Esther crouched down beside her. Donna had seen her look that way at patients who were out in the courtyard smoking, oxygen tanks propped up by the wall beside them. "Sit there and watch those spirit children hanging from those branches and playing in the water." She pointed at the hot air shimmering over the waterhole. You sit there and tell them how wonderful your big womb is, how comfortable it is. What a good mama you are. Tell them about tasting honey ants someday."

"Out loud?"

"How else do you think those spirit children are gonna hear? Think they can read your mind?"

Donna gritted her teeth. "How the hell do I know how spirit children hear? The rest of you Yapa seem to have ESP. They should too."

Esther's hand was hot on Donna's thigh. "We're adults. Takes practice."

"Sorry. I had no idea." Donna tone was sarcastic.

At this, Esther stood up, her shoulders rocking with laughter. "Right. We'll be back tomorrow."

Donna tried to stand up too. "You're kidding." She thought of the endless wattle between her and the fence. Nothing but one clump of spinifex after another.

Esther gently helped her back down. "Don't you move. You'll get lost and we'll never find you again."

Donna shook her head. "I can't stay overnight. I'll freeze."

Esther patted the swag next to Donna. "Don't close up your legs until Yaraandoo is high above you." Esther pointed straight above in the sky. "You know Yaraandoo?"

"The Southern Cross?"

Esther smiled like a proud school teacher. "You got it. I'll come back when the sky is still pink in the morning. Your jumper's next to you if you get chilled." Esther motioned to Tess and they turned to leave the waterhole.

Donna called, "What if I get a spider bite or a bull ant bite? You know I have bad luck with bush animals."

Tess laughed. "Nothing's gonna hurt you."

Donna's voice rose a pitch. "What about snakes?"

Tess pointed up into the coolabahs above Donna. "She'll protect you." Donna looked up into the tree and there sat one of the most beautiful birds she had ever seen. Twice the size of a Galah, with a black crest, black feathers, glossy in the sunlight.

"Missus Cockatoo will stay with you." Esther nodded her head to the bird.

Donna had forgotten that Esther talked to parrots, but this was ridiculous. A wild bird couldn't protect her. She'd been in Australia long enough to have respect for the dangers and wilds of the Outback. "What if she flies away?"

Tess came back over to her. She patted Donna's head with her gnarled hand. "Donna, we have Dreamt you. We have been talking about you up and down this line for a number of years. Nothing's going to happen to you."

Donna pointed at Esther. "You were using me."

Esther pulled Tess away and wagged a finger back at Donna. "Shut up, luv. We're using each other. Now start talking about the virtues of your womb. Better make it seem nicer than the Queen's palace." And with that, the pair turned and disappeared, blending into the wattle. Donna was going to follow—her head told her to follow—but before she could close her legs, Esther and Tess were gone. The cockatoo called *chioo, chioo*, nodding her black head. And Donna heard, *Open your legs, daughter. Listen to the women. I will be with you.*

The sounds Donna heard next scared her. Wailing, baby cries. No, her own cries. She was crying as she had when she learned about her baby. Crying as she had that night, clutching the gray bag and looking at the empty spot in the bed. She looked up at the black bird, which was framed by the intense sun, and squeezed her eyes shut. Instead of the black silhouette of the bird, she saw her mother's face. "Mama," Donna sobbed.

The cockatoo called again in time to her sobs until they finally subsided. The coolabahs arched gracefully over the water. A slight breeze spun their leaves. And then *chioo, chioo*, the cockatoo called again. *Hail Mary, full of grace the Lord is with you.* The words of the angel Gabriel, words which Mary had believed, echoed in her head as the bird called. *Hail Mary, full of grace, the Lord is with you.*

Mary had embraced the miracle. A spirit child. She called out the next lines herself and they echoed over the water. "Blessed are you among women and blessed is the fruit of your womb." The cockatoo's head bobbed along with her prayers. Donna reached for her pearl necklace, but just the smooth skin of her throat met her fingers. Her hand sifted through the sand beside her and she found a rock. She let her fingers run over it like a rosary bead. She could polish it smooth over night, singing her prayers over and over across the water.

It was three in the afternoon according to her watch when she had finished her one-hundred-and-fifty Hail Marys and could bear the spread-legged position no longer. She massaged her hips and began to pull her legs in, but the cockatoo screeched, *Chioo, chioo.* "Okay, okay," she said to the bird. She shifted her weight to a more bearable position and leaned her head back. Resuming her Hail Marys, her breath was timed with the words. Yes, the sunlight threw beautiful diamonds off the water. Yes, a rock wallaby had come for a bit of a drink. Yes, the leaves of the coola-bahs danced in the wind. *Hail Mary...*

Her voice trailed off. A gentle wind blew leaves into the water-hole, and soon a leaf regatta was underway. *He who makes winds his messengers.* She shivered and was startled by a splash out of the corner of her eye—a jumping fish.

Louder she called, "Full of grace, the Lord is with you." She'd witnessed the waking of Hector, a miracle at the hands of Peter. She'd come to Australia as Mary had gone to Jerusalem. The desert. Land where life could spring from nothing.

This is why she had come to Australia. To hear a message. To have faith in something. Anything. Couldn't the splash be not a fish but a spirit child swinging from a branch and plunging into the water? "Spirit child, come to me, choose me." Her voice was timid. Everything was still and she could practically see the sound waves pass over the lake, rippling its surface as they trav-eled. "Yoo-hoo, spirit children."

She imagined the spirit children dangling from the trees like the von Trapp children in the *The Sound of Music*, so she sang the entire score. Her voice grew louder. After exhausting her repertoire of Broadway hits, she moved on to Springsteen. Then her throat grew sore and she sobered. "Okay, kids. For real. I'd be a good mom." Why would she be a good mom? She had no husband. She was almost forty-two. She'd be sixty when the kid went to college.

She couldn't tell the child about honey ants. But she could talk about New York. Donna spoke aloud to the cockatoo, to the branches of the tree, to the ripples in the water, told them all about New York City, about the street vendors, and the rumble of the subway underfoot. About the cherry blossoms along the reservoir, about the leaves crunching under her boots as she watched the Marathon. About the life she'd lived there and would soon live again. This had been a lovely detour, Australia, but she would leave after the baby was born. Sell the apartment on the Upper West Side and find a small apartment in the Village, a neighborhood she'd always loved but Greg had hated.

She was hungry as the sun was setting, so she told the cockatoo and the spirit children about Harry's Burritos, about Ray's Pizza at two in the morning, about Sunday mornings at Zabar's. She watched the moon and the cross rise in the sky.

A cloud obscured the moon for a moment and she began to panic that the coolabahs' roots were snakes. She shut her eyes tightly and spoke to the spirit children about the reptiles at the Central Park Zoo. By midnight she'd described every part of the city, from the Upper West Side to the Lower East. Donna was surprised at how much of the city she knew, how the subway map had been etched into her brain, how she could see the red, blue, and yellow lines running under her feet as she imagined walking the streets. Subway lines were her version of songlines.

Gradually, she pulled her legs together. She could hardly move them, could barely crawl into her swag. Esther and Tess would have to carry her back to the car the next day. She looked up and saw the blackness of the cockatoo, the way its head rested underneath its wing, how its blackness was like the black hole under the cross. Tess and Esther had been right. The cockatoo hadn't moved from the branch. Donna pulled the swag's tarp over her head. Without Andy, without the sounds of the song sticks clapping beside her, she couldn't open her eyes to the vast sky above for fear of getting lost in the stars. The cockatoo was company, but not enough to brave the world any longer on this night.

She woke to Esther's singing and poked her head out of the swag. She'd been dreaming of Jimmy, who was filled with light, like a firefly. He was with Patricia, her mother, and they were leading Donna to a well. *Every desert hides a well.*

In front of her, the waterhole was pink, and there were Galahs and budgies taking baths along its side. Monsoon clouds hung in the distance, where the day before had been only blue. She looked above into the tree and the black cockatoo cocked its head and flitted toward the water. "Thank you," Donna whispered.

Chioo, chioo. Her name's Jessie, echoed in her head.

Pregnant moon hangs over the bluff. She has said goodbye to her last clutch of chicks. She has seen more than her share of monsoons, the pink underbelly of the clouds, like her own, flying across the evening sky before breaking open to pelt the ground with water. She has watched saplings brought to town become large firs upon which to rest. She has seen the belly of the earth emerge at the surface in great piles. She has seen brave new gums grow tall, after bush fires burned forests of wattle to black embers.

She spreads her stiffening wings down to the tiniest feather tip, out against the sky, exploring the dark night, space. The night massages her tired wings, settles in among her downy feathers. She wraps her wings around her belly, gathering the night and the stars. Their warm light pricks holes in the heavy air trapped between wings and belly. A kite screeches. She hugs herself closer and searches the sky.

The boy's fire burns below her. Now she can fly high, fly into the twinkling stars, drink from their dewdrops. She will stop when she can no longer taste the yucca in the air, and she will pull her wings tight and dive into the earth, her beak boring a hole through the ground until she reaches its center. She will dive like the lightning over Kata Tjuta, her heart bursting into flames to turn the night sky the colors of her rosy belly-feathers. She will burn into a ruby dewdrop that will hang near the South Star, where the dew glitters red and gold. When her flock flies south, guided by the Star, they will see her shining for them.

When the boy calls it in his song, she jumps into the sky, pumping higher and higher. She pulls up, crested head to the sky, wings arched *and flexing, and then plummets toward the brown earth, spinning, hurling, streaking ruby fire behind her like a comet, until she sees the mounds of dry dirt, barely raised, shadowing the grubs beneath, sees the ant's legs propelling it forward through its tunnels below the thorny tuft of creeper grass, sees the fire, sees no more.*

The boy and the two men pluck the feathers from her dead body as they chant. The boy holds them to his ear. Listen, boy. Listen to the song. From the changing rhythms know that the Galah soared first over trees, then mountains, then rocks, then rivers; there, where she paused, there's the river's bend, where she trilled there were rapids, churning and bubbling. See the animals and insects as they crossed the land, as the koala baby clutched onto its mother's back, as the spider wove its way across the gums. Listen. Heartbeats. The beating of the earth, as the life force wells up from the mud and the dust.

The boy is cut, he does not cry out, but buries his pain deep within her feathers. To him passes the Law. He will bless this Land, our only earth.

His body was fire, fire like the sun, fire like the sands from the center of the earth. He glowed red as an ember as the knife seared into his flesh. He burned the knife as it cut him, cut away the flesh of his penis, round in a circle like the earth, like the raindrops, like the eye of the Galah who'd died at his feet, whom he'd buried with the bone of his father and Hector's skull bone at the seedpile.

The Warambool covered his eyes. He could see each star clearly, separated, no longer a blur, but like grains of sand. He grew feathers, and he flew above the fire where the men stood chanting, where his penis gave blood back to the earth. The air was cool along his wings, currents pushed him up and further up, so it required no effort to fly. He stopped at Yaraandoo and stretched out his arms along her branches. He would come again to rest here when he left the realm of the living and dying for good, when his body would no longer be needed.

Yaraandoo was cool to his feet. Death was a good place. He could see the Galahs who'd come before him, resting next to him on Yaraandoo's branch, and those who would come after him, their seed power still buried in the veins of the Land. From his perch of death he could see the events of his life, days of regrets and days where he added to the powers of the Land. Those days outnumbered the bad and he was satisfied.

He could see himself a tall man, stethoscope around his neck, could see himself arguing in front of the whites for his Land. Next to him was the woman. Green skin. Jessie. She would fly across the ocean and be with him.

An Ancestor flew to the branch of Yaraandoo, and with his

wing pushed him to leave. Jimmy wanted to stay, to see the Dreaming of all time. But it was not yet his turn. His penis pulled him down, back to the earth. On his way, he Beheld his Land. He Beheld every rock, each blade of spinifex, each seed planted deep in the sands, and he willed them to grow. He Beheld every mole, goanna, grub and ant, his blood coursing with theirs.

He saw the veins under the earth, full of magnets of their own; these were the body of the Galah Land. Saw how the blood coursed through the Land, how it lived and breathed like his body. Saw the Rainbow Serpent as it retreated under the Land, leaving it to the Galah for safe-keeping.

He came down to earth to dance his feet in orange sands, heel-toe, heel-toe, Hector and Jocko kicking up crystals of dust beside him. Their chanting grew louder and he realized he was surrounded by his flock. The Ancestors had come to the Land to greet him. *Welcome, Jimmy Jackboy, welcome back to the beginning, back to your Land.*

Glossary of Aboriginal and Australian Terms

Behold: Behold one's Land refers to seeing the Dreaming stories from a certain place, often in a defined position or stance.

Billabong: Waterhole.

Didgeridoo or didg: Musical instrument made from a hollowed-out log.

Dreaming: Creation, and the basis for spirituality. Events during the Dreaming left vibrations in the place where they occurred, thus the physical features of the earth are manifestations of past conflicts and relationships between the Ancestors during the Dreaming. The Dreaming may also refer to codes of behavior established during the creation (the Law), and Dreaming stories can relate to an Ancestor, an animal totem, a place, or natural forces. These stories are the truths of the subconscious.

Gabo: Green ant.

Jukurrpa: The Dreaming.

Kardachi man: Medicine man, Aboriginal man of very high initiation.

Kardiya: Non-Aboriginal person (Warlpiri).

Kata Tjuta: Mount Olga; the Olgas.

Kuurlu: School (Warlpiri).

Mabo: Refers to the Mabo decision by the Australian High Court in 1992. Before Mabo, colonization had been justified by the claim of *terra nullis* (Australia had been unoccupied before the Europeans arrived because it hadn't been farmed). In Mabo, the Court rejected the claim of *terra nullis*, establishing a path for indigenous people to pursue native title claims.

Mangumberre: Acacia tree.

Mangol: Cocky apple.

Meamei: The Pleiades star cluster.

Minggah: Tree beneath which someone is born. That person is always linked to that tree spiritually.

Moiety: A division of the community into two opposed halves, helping to define relationship and regulate social behavior (e.g., sun moiety and moon moiety).

Mooyi: Two stars that point to the Southern Cross.

Ngarlkirdi: Witchetty grubs (Warlpiri).

Warlpiri: Aboriginal language spoken in a large region of the Northern Territory and western Australia.

Warambool: The Milky Way.

Wijipirtili: Hospital (Warlpiri)

Wirrun: Kardachi man, shaman, medicine man, Aboriginal man of very high initiation.

Uluru: Ayers Rock.

Yaraandoo: The Southern Cross.

Yapa: Aboriginal person (Walpiri).

Yowie: Spirit of Death.

Yuti: Reality. The truth of the conscious.

 A symbol used by Aboriginal artists to represent a woman. The inverted *u* shape is the mark left behind after a person has been sitting in the sand. The lines are digging sticks, used for gathering food, and as clapping sticks in sacred ceremonies.

 A symbol used by Aboriginal artists to represent a nest or gathering site.

A symbol used by Aboriginal artists to represent spears.

Author's Note

The Aboriginal people of Australia have traditions dating back about sixty thousand years, to the First Day, the beginning of time in the Dreaming. During those six hundred centuries, they spent much of their human capital on mystical knowledge such as dream travel and natural healing, rather than on scientific pursuits. They developed a sophisticated oral tradition to pass on skills, laws, and values using dance, song, stories, and art. They elevated the importance of knowledge that came from myth over that of logic, as opposed to Western society, which focused on farming and building.

The indigenous Australians survived the decimation of their population caused by European colonization in the late 1700s, only to have their losses further compounded in the first half of the twentieth century by a government policy that forcibly removed Aboriginal children from their homes and institutionalized them to "help them integrate into modern society." These children are now known as the Stolen Generations.

According to the definition under the 1948 United Nations Convention on the Prevention and Punishment of the Crime of Genocide, the policy of separating the Aboriginal children from their communities can be considered a form of genocide, though the appropriateness of this definition is contested. In 2008, the Australian government made a formal apology for this policy.

Aboriginal Australians are an incredibly diverse group, coming from many clans, with distinct languages and belief systems, ceremonies, and traditions. I have borrowed names and language from two groups in particular, the Pintupi and Warlpiri.

In order to write this novel, I researched Aboriginal rites and traditions. Having said that, this *is* a work of fiction, and what is presented in this novel is an interpretation barely skimming the surface of the complexity and richness of Aboriginal traditions. Sacred Aboriginal rites are secret, and as such, I have used my imagination liberally to fill in details. Likewise, the Mount Isa in my novel is meant to embody the essence of Mount Isa, and I have adapted its geography to suit the needs of the story.

What sparked my interest in this land? In 1997 I left my Wall Street career and moved with my husband to Mount Isa, Queensland, Australia so he could be a doctor at the Mount Isa Base Hospital. After more than one of his patients experienced seemingly miraculous recoveries, I decided to investigate.

Dreaming stories explain that the vibrations of the Ancestor-beings are manifest in the Australian topography, and to this day, every site resonates with the energy of creation. This energy can be harnessed for many things, including healing and, as I have discovered, growing a novel.

Waltzing Jimmy Jackboy was born of images of brightly-colored Galahs swooping across a tiny road through the desert, of an Aboriginal boy examining himself in a waterhole, of a red kangaroo bounding across yellow wattle. This book was born out of a landscape so wide and open that infinite stories have germinated there for sixty thousand years.

With the utmost respect to the indigenous peoples of Australia, I thank them for allowing me to tell my story of their Land. I would also like to thank William Haywood Henderson, Lighthouse Writers Workshop, Pamela Johnson of Lush Literary Management, Sonya Unrein, David Korman, Marci Alboher, Samantha Ravich, Andra Davidson, Cheryl Patrick, Brett Miller, Lindsay Casamassima, Alison Dinn, Susan Dinn, Irwin Dinn,

Naomi Usher, Emily Sinclair, Marcelina Rivera, Kathy Neustadt Hankin, the late Richard Brickner, Rachel Greenwald, Carolyn Lane, Rachel Brown, Megan Bendis, Daniel Semler, Shana Kelly, the Rocky Mountain Fiction Writers for its 2003 Colorado Gold Prize in Fiction, and all the friends and family who have been so gracious over these years. The biggest thank you is reserved for the temporary and permanent residents of Mount Isa, who helped me redefine the word *home*.

Made in the USA
San Bernardino, CA
06 December 2016